London Pride
Or When the World Was Younger

M. E. Braddon

Contents

LONDON PRIDE
OR WHEN THE WORLD WAS
YOUNGER

BY

M. E. Braddon

CHAPTER I.
A HARBOUR FROM THE STORM.

The wind howled across the level fields, and flying showers of sleet rattled against the old leathern coach as it drove through the thickening dusk. A bitter winter, this year of the Royal tragedy. A rainy summer, and a mild rainy autumn had been followed by the hardest frost this generation had ever known. The Thames was frozen over, and tempestuous winds had shaken the ships in the Pool, and the steep gable ends and tall chimney-stacks on London Bridge. A never-to-be-forgotten winter, which had witnessed the martyrdom of England's King, and the exile of her chief nobility, while a rabble Parliament rode roughshod over a cowed people. Gloom and sour visages prevailed, the maypoles were down, the play-houses were closed, the bear-gardens were empty, the cock-pits were desolate; and a saddened population, impoverished and depressed by the sacrifices that had been exacted and the tyranny that had been exercised in the name of Liberty, were ground under the iron heel of Cromwell's red-coats.

The pitiless journey from London to Louvain, a journey of many days and nights, prolonged by accident and difficulty, had been spun out to uttermost tedium for those two in the heavily moving old leathern coach. Who and what were they, these wearied travellers, journeying together silently towards a destination which promised but little of pleasure or luxury by way of welcome--a destination which meant severance for those two?

One was Sir John Kirkland, of the Manor Moat, Bucks, a notorious Malignant, a grey-bearded cavalier, aged by trouble and hard fighting; a soldier and servant who had sacrificed himself and his fortune for the King, and must needs begin the world anew now that his master was murdered, his own goods confiscated, the old family mansion, the house in which his parents died and his children were born, emptied of all its valuables, and left to the care of servants, and his master's son a wanderer in a foreign land, with little hope of ever winning back crown and sceptre.

Sadness was the dominant expression of Sir John's stern, strongly marked countenance, as he sat staring out at the level landscape through the unglazed coach window, staring blankly across those wind-swept Flemish fields where the cattle were clustering in sheltered corners, a monotonous expanse, crossed by ice-bound dykes that looked black as ink, save where the last rays of the setting sun touched their iron hue with blood-red splashes. Pollard willows indicated the edge of one field, gaunt poplars marked the boundary of another, alike leafless and unbeautiful, standing darkly out against the dim grey sky. Night was hastening towards the travellers, narrowing and blotting out that level landscape, field, dyke, and leafless wood.

Sir John put his head out of the coach window, and looked anxiously along the straight road, peering through the shades of evening in the hope of seeing the crocketed spires and fair cupolas of Louvain in the distance. But he could see nothing save a waste of level pastures and the gathering darkness. Not a light anywhere, not a sign of human habitation.

Useless to gaze any longer into the impenetrable night. The traveller leant back into a corner of the carriage with folded arms, and, with a deep sigh, composed himself for slumber. He had slept but little for the last week. The passage from Harwich to Ostend in a fishing-smack had been a perilous transit, prolonged by adverse winds. Sleep had been impossible on board that wretched craft; and the land journey had been fraught with vexation and delays of all kinds--stupidity of postillions, dearth of horseflesh, badness of the roads--all things that can vex and hinder.

Sir John's travelling companion, a small child in a cloak and hood, crept closer to him in the darkness, nestled up against his elbow, and pushed her little cold hand into his leathern glove.

"You are crying again, father," she said, full of pity. "You were crying last night. Do you always cry when it grows dark?"

"It does not become a man to shed tears in the daylight, little maid," her father answered gently.

"Is it for the poor King you are crying--the King those wicked men murdered?"

"Ay, Angela, for the King; and for the Queen and her fatherless children still more than for the King, for he has crowned himself with a crown of glory, the diadem of martyrs, and is resting from labour and sorrow, to rise victorious at the great day, when his enemies and his murderers shall stand ashamed before him. I weep for that once so lovely lady--widowed, discrowned, needy, desolate--a beggar in the land where her father was a great king. A hard fate, Angela, father and husband both murdered."

"Was the Queen's father murdered too?" asked the silver-sweet voice out of darkness, a pretty piping note like the song of a bird.

"Yes, love."

"Did Bradshaw murder him?"

"No, dearest, 'twas in France he was slain--in Paris; stabbed to death by a madman."

"And was the Queen sorry?"

"Ay, sweetheart, she has drained the cup of sorrow. She was but a child when her father died. She can but dimly remember that dreadful day. And now she sits, banished and widowed, to hear of her husband's martyrdom; her elder sons wanderers, her young daughter a prisoner."

"Poor Queen!" piped the small sweet voice, "I am so sorry for her."

Little had she ever known but sorrow, this child of the Great Rebellion, born in the old Buckinghamshire manor house, while her father was at Falmouth with the Prince--born in the midst of civil war, a stormy petrel, bringing no message of peace from those unknown skies whence she came, a harbinger of woe. Infant eyes love bright colours. This baby's eyes looked upon a house hung with black. Her mother died before the child was a fortnight old. They had christened her Angela. "Angel of Death," said the father, when the news of his loss reached him, after the lapse of many days. His fair young wife's coffin was in the family vault under the parish church of St. Nicholas in the Vale, before he knew that he had lost her.

There was an elder daughter, Hyacinth, seven years the senior, who had been sent across the Channel in the care of an old servant at the beginning of the troubles between King and Parliament.

She had been placed in the charge of her maternal grandmother, the Marquise de Montrond, who had taken ship for Calais when the Court left London, leaving her royal mistress to weather the storm. A lady who had wealth and prestige in her own country, who had been a famous beauty when Richelieu was in power, and who had been admired by that serious and sober monarch, Louis the Thirteenth, could scarcely be expected to put up with the shifts and shortcomings of an Oxford lodging-house, with the ever-present fear of finding herself in a town besieged by Lord Essex and the rebel army.

With Madame de Montrond, Hyacinth had been reared, partly in a mediaeval mansion, with a portcullis and four squat towers, near the Chateau d'Arques, and partly in Paris, where the lady had a fine house in the Marais. The sisters had never looked upon each other's faces, Angela having entered upon the troubled scene after Hyacinth had been carried across the Channel to her grandmother. And now the father was racked with anxiety lest evil should befall that elder daughter in the war between Mazarin and the Parliament, which was reported to rage with increasing fury.

Angela's awakening reason became conscious of a world where all was fear and sadness. The stories she heard in her childhood were stories of that fierce war which was reaching its disastrous close while she was in her cradle. She was told of the happy peaceful England of old, before darkness and confusion gathered over the land; before the hearts of the people were set against their King by a wicked and rebellious Parliament.

She heard of battles lost by the King and his partisans; cities besieged and taken; a flash of victory followed by humiliating reverses; the King's party always at a disadvantage; and hence the falling away of the feeble and the false, the treachery of those who had seemed friends, the impotence of the faithful.

Angela heard so often and so much of these things--from old Lady Kirkland, her grandmother, and from the grey-haired servants at the manor--that she grew to understand them with a comprehension seemingly far beyond her tender years. But a child so reared is inevitably older than her years. This little one had never known childish pleasures or play, childish companions or childish fancies.

She roamed about the spacious gardens, full of saddest thoughts, burdened with all the cares that weighed down that kingly head yonder; or she stood before the pictured face of the monarch with clasped hands and tearful eyes, looking up at him with the adoring compassion of a child prone to hero-worship--thinking of him already as saint and martyr--whose martyrdom was not yet consummated in blood.

King Charles had presented his faithful servant, Sir John Kirkland, with a half-length replica of one of his Vandyke portraits, a beautiful head, with a strange inward look--that look of isolation and aloofness which we who know his story take for a prophecy of doom--which the sculptor Bernini had remarked, when he modelled the royal head for marble. The picture hung in the place of honour in the long narrow gallery at the Manor Moat, with trophies of Flodden and Zutphen arranged against the blackened oak panelling above it. The Kirklands had been a race of soldiers since the days of Edward III. The house was full of war-like decorations--tattered colours, old armour, memorials of fighting Kirklands who had long been dust.

There came an evil day when the rabble rout of Cromwell's crop-haired soldiery burst into the manor house to pillage and destroy, carrying off curios and relics that were the gradual accumulation of a century and a half of peaceful occupation.

The old Dowager's grey hairs had barely saved her from outrage on that bitter day. It was only her utter helplessness and afflicted condition that prevailed upon the Parliamentary captain, and prevented him from carrying out his design, which was to haul her off to one of those London prisons at that time so gorged with Royalist captives that the devilish ingenuity of the Parliament had devised floating gaols on the Thames, where persons of quality and character were herded together below decks, to the loss of health, and even of life.

Happily for old Lady Kirkland, she was too lame to walk, and her enemies had no horse or carriage in which to convey her; so she was left at peace in her son's plundered mansion, whence all that was valuable and easily portable was carried away by the Roundheads. Silver plate and family plate had been sacrificed to the King's necessities.

The pictures, not being either portable or readily convertible into cash, had remained on the old panelled walls.

Angela used to go from the King's picture to her father's. Sir John's was a more rugged face than the Stuart's, with a harder expression; but the child's heart went out to the image of the father she had never seen since the dawn of consciousness. He had made a hurried journey to that quiet Buckinghamshire valley soon after her birth--had looked at the baby in her cradle, and then had gone down into the vault where his young wife was lying, and had stayed for more than an hour in cold and darkness alone with his dead. That lovely French wife had been his junior by more than twenty years, and he had loved her passionately--had loved her and left her for duty's sake. No Kirkland had ever faltered in his fidelity to crown and king. This John Kirkland had sacrificed all things, and, alone with his beloved dead in the darkness of that narrow charnel house, it seemed to him that there was nothing left for him except to cleave to those fallen fortunes and patiently await the issue.

He had fought in many battles and had escaped with a few scars; and he was carrying his daughter to Louvain, intending to place her in the charge of her great-aunt, Madame de Montrond's half sister, who was head of a convent in that city, a safe and pious shelter, where the child might be reared in her mother's faith.

Lady Kirkland, the only daughter of the Marquise de Montrond, one of Queen Henrietta Maria's ladies-in-waiting, had been a papist, and, although Sir John had adhered steadfastly to the principles of the Reformed Church, he had promised his bride, and the Marquise, her mother, that if their nuptials were blessed with off-spring, their children should be educated in the Roman faith--a promise difficult of performance in a land where a stormy tide ran high against Rome, and where Popery was a scarlet spectre that alarmed the ignorant and maddened the bigoted. And now, duly provided with a safe conduct from the regicide, Bradshaw, he was journeying to the city where he was to part with his daughter for an indefinite pe-riod. He had seen but little of her, and yet it seemed as hard to part thus as if she had prattled at his knees and nestled in his arms every day of her young life.

At last across the distance, against the wind-driven clouds of that stormy win-ter sky, John Kirkland saw the lights of the city--not many lights or brilliant of their kind, but a glimmer here and there--and behind the glimmer the dark bulk of masonry, roofs, steeples, watch-towers, bridges.

The carriage stopped at one of the gates of the city, and there were questions asked and answered, and papers shown, but there was no obstacle to the entrance of the travellers. The name of the Ursuline Convent acted like a charm, for Louvain was papist to the core in these days of Spanish dominion. It had been a city of refuge nearly a hundred years ago for all that was truest and bravest and noblest among English Roman Catholics, in the cruel days of Queen Elizabeth, and Englishmen had become the leading spirits of the University there, and had attracted the youth of Romanist England to the sober old Flemish town, before the establishment of Dr. Allan's rival seminary at Douai, Sir John could have found no safer haven for his little ewe lamb.

The tired horses blundered heavily along the stony streets, and crossed more than one bridge. The town seemed pervaded by water, a deep narrow stream like a canal, on which the houses looked, as if in feeble mockery of Venice--houses with steep crow-step gables, some of them richly decorated; narrow windows for the most part dark, but with here and there the yellow light of lamp or candle.

The convent faced a broad open square, and had a large walled garden in its rear. The coach stopped in front of a handsome doorway, and after the travellers had been scrutinised and interrogated by the portress through an opening in the door, they were admitted into a spacious hall, paved with black and white marble, and adorned with a statue of the Virgin Mother, and thence to a parlour dimly lighted by a small oil lamp, where they waited for about ten minutes, the little girl shivering with cold, before the Superior appeared.

She was a tall woman, advanced in years, with a handsome, but melancholy countenance. She greeted the cavalier as a familiar friend.

"Welcome to Flanders!" she said. "You have fled from that accursed country where our Church is despised and persecuted----"

"Nay, reverend kinswoman, I have fled but to go back again as fast as horses and sails can carry me. While the fortunes of my King are at stake, my place is in England, or it may be in Scotland, where there are still those who are ready to fight to the death in the royal cause. But I have brought this little one for shelter and safe keeping, and tender usage, trusting in you who are of kin to her as I could trust no one else--and, furthermore, that she may be reared in the faith of her dead mother."

"Sweet soul!" murmured the nun. "It was well for her to be taken from your troubled England to the kingdom of the saints and martyrs."

"True, reverend mother; yet those blasphemous levellers who call us 'Malignants' have dubbed themselves 'Saints.'"

"Then affairs go no better with you in England, I fear, Sir John?"

"Nay, madam, they go so ill that they have reached the lowest depth of infamy. Hell itself hath seen no spectacle more awful, no murder more barbarous, no horrider triumph of wickedness, than the crime which was perpetrated this day se'nnight at Whitehall."

The nun looked at him wistfully, with clasped hands, as one who half apprehended his meaning.

"The King!" she faltered, "still a prisoner?"

"Ay, reverend lady, but a prisoner in Paradise, where angels are his guards, and saints and martyrs his companions. He has regained his crown; but it is the crown of martyrdom, the aureole of slaughtered saints. England, our little England that was once so great under the strong rule of that virgin-queen who made herself the arbiter of Christendom, and the wonder of the world----"

The pious lady shivered and crossed herself at this praise of the heretic queen--praise that could only come from a heretic.

"Our blessed and peaceful England has become a den of thieves, given over to the ravening wolves of rebellion and dissent, the penniless soldiery who would bring down all men's fortunes to their own level, seize all, eat and drink all, and trample crown and peerage in the mire. They have slain him, reverend mother, this impious herd--they gave him the mockery of a trial--just as his Master, Christ, was mocked. They spurned and spat upon him, even as our Redeemer was spurned; and then, on the Sabbath day, they cried aloud in their conventicles, 'Lord, hast Thou not smelt a sweet savour of blood?' Ay, these murderers gloried in their crime, bragged of their gory hands, lifted them up towards heaven as a token of righteousness!"

The cavalier was pacing to and fro in the dimness of the convent parlour, with quick, agitated steps, his nostrils quivering, grizzled brows bent over angry eyes, his hand trembling with rage as it clutched his sword-hilt.

The reverend mother drew Angela to her side, took off the little black silk hood, and laid her hand caressingly on the soft brown hair.

"Was it Cromwell's work?" she asked.

"Nay, reverend mother, I doubt whether of his own accord Cromwell would have done this thing. He is a villain, a damnable villain--but he is a glorious villain. The Parliament had made their covenant with the King at Newport--a bargain which gave them all, and left him nothing--save only his broken health, grey hairs, and the bare name of King. He would have been but a phantom of authority, powerless as the royal spectres Aeneas met in the under-world. They had got all from him--all save the betrayal of his friends. There he budged not, but was firm as rock."

"'Twas likely he remembered Strafford, and that he prospered no better for having flung a faithful dog to the wolves," said the nun.

"Remembered Strafford? Ay, that memory has been a pillow of thorns through many a sleepless night. No, it was not Cromwell who sought the King's blood--it has been shed with his sanction. The Parliament had got all, and would have been content; but the faction they had created was too strong for them. The levellers sent their spokesman--one Pride, an ex-drayman, now colonel of horse--to the door of the House of Commons, who arrested the more faithful and moderate members, imposed himself and his rebel crew upon the House, and hurried on that violation of constitutional law, that travesty of justice, which compelled an anointed King to stand before the lowest of his subjects--the jacks-in-office of a mutinous common-alty--to answer for having fought in defence of his own inviolable rights."

"Did they dare condemn their King?"

"Ah, madam, they found him guilty of high treason, in that he had taken arms against the Parliament. They sentenced their royal master to death--and seven days ago London saw the spectacle of judicial murder--a blameless King slain by the minion of an armed rabble!"

"But did the people--the English people--suffer this in silence? The wisest and best of them could surely be assembled in your great city. Did the citizens of London stand placidly by to see this deed accomplished?"

"They were like sheep before the shearer. They were dumb. Great God! can I ever forget that sea of white faces under the grey winter sky, or the universal groan that went up to heaven when the stroke of the axe sounded on the block, and men knew that the murder of their King was consummated; and when that anointed head with its grey hairs, whitened with sorrow, mark you, not with age, was lifted up, bloody, terrible, and proclaimed the head of a traitor? Ah, reverend mother, ten such moments will age a man by ten years. Was it not the most portentous tragedy which the earth has ever seen since He who was both God and Man died upon Calvary? Other judicial sacrifices have been, but never of a victim as guiltless and as noble. Had you but seen the calm beauty of his countenance as he turned it towards the people! Oh, my King, my master, my beloved friend, when shall I see that face in Paradise, with the blood washed from that royal brow, with the smile of the redeemed upon those lips!"

He flung himself into a chair, covered his face with those weather-stained hands, which had broadened by much grasping of sword and pistol, pike and gun, and sobbed aloud, with a fierce passion that convulsed the strong muscular frame. Of all the King's servants this one had been the most steadfast, was marked in the black book of the Parliament as a notorious Malignant. From the raising of the standard on the castle-hill at Nottingham--in the sad evening of a tempestuous day, with but scanty attendance, and only evil presages--to the treaty at Newport, and the prison on the low Hampshire coast, this man had been his master's constant companion and friend; fighting in every battle, cleaving to King and Prince in spite of every opposing influence, carrying letters between father and son in the teeth of the enemy, humbling himself as a servant, and performing menial labours, in those latter days of bitterness and outrage, when all courtly surroundings were denied the fallen monarch.

And now he mourned his martyred King more bitterly than he would have mourned his own brother.

The little girl slipped from the reverend mother's lap, and ran across the room to her father.

"Don't cry, father!" she murmured, with her own eyes streaming. "It hurts me to see you."

"Nay, Angela," he answered, clasping her to his breast. "Forgive me that I think more of my dead King than of my living daughter. Poor child, thou hast seen nothing but sorrow since thou wert born; a land racked by civil war; Englishmen changed into devils; a home ravaged and made desolate; threatenings and curses; thy good grandmother's days shortened by sorrow and rough usage. Thou wert born into a house of mourning, and hast seen nothing but black since thou hadst eyes to notice the things around thee. Those tender ears should have heard only loving words. But it is over, dearest; and thou hast found a haven within these walls. You will take care of her, will you not, madam, for the sake of the niece you loved?"

"She shall be the apple of my eye. No evil shall come near her that my care and my prayers can avert. God has been very gracious to our order--in all troublous times we have been protected. We have many pupils from the best families of Flanders--and some even from Paris, whence parents are glad to remove their children from the confusion of the time. You need fear nothing while this sweet child is with us; and if in years to come she should desire to enter our order----"

"The Lord forbid!" cried the cavalier. "I want her to be a good and pious papist, madam, like her sweet mother; but never a nun. I look to her as the staff and comfort of my declining years. Thou wilt not abandon thy father, wilt thou, little one, when thou shalt be tall and strong as a bulrush, and he shall be bent and gnarled with age, like the old medlar on the lawn at the Manor? Thou wilt be his rod and staff, wilt thou not, sweetheart?"

The child flung her arms round his neck and kissed him. It was her only answer, but that mute reply was a vow.

"Thou wilt stay here till England's troubles are over, Angela, and that base herd yonder have been trampled down. Thou wilt be happy here, and wilt mind thy book, and be obedient to those good ladies who will teach thee; and some day, when our country is at peace, I will come back to fetch thee."

"Soon," murmured the child, "soon, father?"

"God grant it may be soon, my beloved! It is hard for father and children to be scattered, as we are scattered; thy sister Hyacinth in Paris, and thou in Flanders, and I in England. Yet it must needs be so for a while!"

"Why should not Hyacinth come to us and be reared with Angela?" asked the reverend mother.

"Nay, madam, Hyacinth is well cared for with your sister, Madame de Montrond. She is as dear to her maternal grandmother as this little one here was to my good mother, whose death last year left us a house of mourning. Hyacinth will doubtless inherit a considerable portion of Madame de Montrond's wealth, which is not insignificant. She is being brought up in the precincts of the Court."

"A worldly and a dangerous school for one so young," said the nun, with a sigh. "I have heard my father talk of what life was like at the Louvre when the Bearnais reigned there in the flower of his manhood, newly master of Paris, flushed with hard-won victory, and but lately reconciled to the Church."

"Methinks that great captain's court must have been laxer than that of Queen

Anne and the Cardinal. I have been told that the child-king is being reared, as it were, in a cloister, so strict are mother and guardian. My only fear for Hyacinth is the troubled state of the city, given over to civil warfare only less virulent than that which has desolated England. I hear that the Fronde is no war of epigrams and pamphlets, but that men are as earnest and bloodthirsty as they were in the League. I shall go from here to Paris to see my first-born before I make my way back to London."

"I question if you will find her at Paris," said the reverend mother. "I had news from a priest in the diocese of the Coadjutor. The Queen-mother left the city secretly with her chosen favourites in the dead of the night on the sixth of this month, after having kept the festival of Twelfth Night in a merry humour with her Court. Even her waiting-women knew nothing of her plans. They went to St. Germain, where they found the chateau unfurnished, and where all the Court had to sleep upon was a few loads of straw. Hatred of the Cardinal is growing fiercer every day, and Paris is in a state of siege. The Princes are siding with Mathieu Mole and his Parliament, and the Provincial Parliaments are taking up the quarrel. God grant that it may not be in France as it has been with you in your unhappy England; but I fear the Spanish Queen and her Italian minister scarce know the temper of the French people."

"Alas, good friend, we have fallen upon evil days, and the spirit of revolt is everywhere; but if there is trouble at the French Court, there is all the more need that I should make my way thither, be it at St. Germain or at Paris, and so assure myself of my pretty Hyacinth's safety. She was so sweet an infant when my good and faithful steward carried her across the sea to Dieppe. Never shall I forget that sad moment of parting; when the baby arms were wreathed round my sweet saint's neck; she so soon to become again a mother, so brave and patient in her sorrow at parting with her first-born. Ah, sister, there are moments in this life that a man must needs remember, even amidst the wreck of his country." He dashed away a tear or two, and then turned to his kinswoman with outstretched hands and said, "Good night, dear and reverend mother; good night and good-bye. I shall sleep at the nearest inn, and shall be on the road again at daybreak. Good-bye, my soul's delight"

He clasped his daughter in his arms, with something of despair in the fervour of his embrace, telling himself, as the soft cheek was pressed against his own, how many years might pass ere he would again so clasp that tender form and feel those innocent kisses on his bearded lips. She and the elder girl were all that were left to him of love and comfort, and the elder sister had been taken from him while she was a little child. He would not have known her had he met her unawares; nor had he ever felt for her such a pathetic love as for this guiltless death-angel, this baby whose coming had ruined his life, whose love was nevertheless the only drop of sweetness in his cup.

He plucked himself from that gentle embrace, and walked quickly to the door.

"You will apply to me for whatever money is needed for the child's maintenance and education," he said, and in the next moment was gone.

CHAPTER II.
WITHIN CONVENT WALLS.

More than ten years had come and gone since that bleak February evening when Sir John Kirkland carried his little daughter to a place of safety, in the old city of Louvain, and in all those years the child had grown like a flower in a sheltered garden, where cold winds never come. The bud had matured into the blossom in that mild atmosphere of piety and peace; and now, in this fair springtide of 1660, a girlish face watched from the convent casement for the coming of the father whom Angela Kirkland had not looked upon since she was a child, and the sister she had never seen.

They were to arrive to-day, father and sister, on a brief visit to the quiet Flemish city. Yonder in England there had been curious changes since the stern Protector turned his rugged face to the wall, and laid down that golden sceptre with which he had ruled as with a rod of iron. Kingly title would he none; yet where kings had chastised with whips, he had chastised with scorpions. Ireland could tell how the little finger of Cromwell had been heavier than the arm of the Stuarts. She had trembled and had obeyed, and had prospered under that scorpion rule, and England's armaments had been the terror of every sea while Cromwell stood at the helm; but now that strong brain and bold heart were in the dust, and it had taken

England little more than a year to discover that Puritanism and the Rump were a mistake, and that to the core of her heart she was loyal to her hereditary King.

She asked not what manner of man this hereditary ruler might be; asked not whether he were wise or foolish, faithful or treacherous. She forgot all of tyranny and of double-dealing she had suffered from his forbears. She forgot even her terror of the scarlet spectre, the grim wolf of Rome, in her disgust at Puritan fervour which had torn down altar-rails, usurped church pulpits, destroyed the beauty of ancient cathedrals. Like a woman or a child, she held out her arms to the unknown, in a natural recoil from that iron rule which had extinguished her gaiety, silenced her noble liturgy, made innocent pleasures and elegant arts things forbidden. She wanted her churches, and her theatres, her cock-pits and taverns, and bear-gardens and maypoles back again. She wanted to be ruled by the law, and not by the sword; and she longed with a romantic longing for that young wanderer who had fled from her shores in a fishing-boat, with his life in his hand, to return in a glad procession of great ships dancing over summer seas, eating, drinking, gaming, in a coat worth scarce thirty shillings, and with empty pockets for his loyal subjects to make haste and fill.

Angela had the convent parlour all to herself this fair spring morning. She was the favourite pupil of the nuns, had taken no vows, pledged herself to no noviciate, ever mindful of her promise to her father. She had lived as happily and as merrily in that abode of piety as she could have lived in the finest palace in Europe. There were other maidens, daughters of the French and Flemish nobility, who were taught and reared within those sombre precincts, and with them she had played and worked and laboured at such studies as became a young lady of quality. Like that fair daughter of affliction, Henrietta of England, she had gained in education by the troubles which had made her girlhood a time of seclusion. She had been first the plaything of those elder girls who were finishing their education in the convent, her childishness appealing to their love and pity; and then, after being the plaything of the nuns and the elder pupils, she became the favourite of her contemporaries, and in a manner their queen. She was more thoughtful than her class-fellows, in advance of her years in piety and intelligence; and they, knowing her sad story--how she was severed from her country and kindred, her father a wanderer with his King, her sister bred up at a foreign Court--had first compassionated and then admired her. From her twelfth year upwards her intellectual superiority had been recognised in the convent, alike by the nuns and their pupils. Her aptitude at all learning, and her simple but profound piety, had impressed everybody. At fourteen years of age they had christened her "the little wonder;" but later, seeing that their praises embarrassed and even distressed her, they had desisted from such loving flatteries, and were content to worship her with a silent adulation.

Her father's visits to the Flemish city had been few and far apart, fondly though he loved his motherless girl. He had been a wanderer for the most part during those years, tossed upon troubled seas, fighting with Conde against Mazarin and Anne of Austria, and reconciled with the Court later, when peace was made, and his friends the Princes were forgiven; an exile from France of his own free will when Louis banished his first cousin, the King of England, in order to truckle to the triumphant usurper. He had led an adventurous life, and had cared very little what became of him in a topsy-turvy world. But now all things were changed. Richard Cromwell's brief and irresolute rule had shattered the Commonwealth, and made Englishmen eager for a king. The country was already tired of him whose succession had been admitted with blank acquiescence; and Monk and the army were soon to become masters of the situation. There was hope that the General was rightly affected, and that the King would have his own again; and that such of his followers as had not compounded with the Parliamentary Commission would get back their confiscated estates; and that all who had suffered in person or pocket for loyalty's sake would be recompensed for their sacrifices.

It was five years since Sir John's last appearance at the convent, and Angela's heart beat fast at the thought that he was so near. She was to see him this very day; nay, perhaps this very hour. His coach might have passed the gate of the town already. He was bringing his elder daughter with him, that sister whose face she had never seen, save in a miniature, and who was now a great lady, the wife of Baron Fareham, of Chilton Abbey, Oxon, Fareham Park, in the County of Hants, and Fareham House, London, a nobleman whose estates had come through the ordeal of the Parliamentary Commission with a reasonable fine, and to whom extra favour had been shown by the Commissioners, because he was known to be at heart a Republican. In the mean time, Lady Fareham had a liberal income allowed her by the Marquise, her grandmother, and she and her husband had been among the most splendid foreigners at the French Court, where the lady's beauty and wit had placed her conspicuously in that galaxy of brilliant women who shone and sparkled about the sun of the European firmament--Le roi soleil, or "the King," par excellence, who took the blazing sun for his crest. The Fronde had been a time of pleasurable excitement to the high-spirited girl, whose mixed blood ran like quicksilver, and who delighted in danger and party strife, stratagem and intrigue. The story of her courage and gaiety of heart in the siege of Paris, she being then little more than a child, had reached the Flemish convent long after the acts recorded had been forgotten at Paris and St. Germain.

Angela's heart beat fast at the thought of being restored to these dear ones, were it only for a short span. They were not going to carry her away from the convent; and, indeed, seeing that she so loved her aunt, the good reverend mother, and that her heart cleaved to those walls and to the holy exercises which filled so great a part of her life, her father, in replying to a letter in which she had besought him to release her from her promise and allow her to dedicate herself to God, had told her that, although he could not surrender his daughter, to whom he looked for the comfort of his closing years, he would not urge her to leave the Ursulines until he should feel himself old and feeble, and in need of her tender care. Meanwhile she might be a nun in all but the vows, and a dutiful niece to her kind aunt, Mother Anastasia, whose advanced years and failing health needed all consideration.

But now, before he went back to England, whither he hoped to accompany the King and the Princes ere the year was much older, Sir John Kirkland was coming to visit his younger daughter, bringing Lady Fareham, whose husband was now in attendance upon His Majesty in Holland, where there were serious negotiations on hand--negotiations which would have been full of peril to the English messengers two years ago, when that excellent preacher and holy man, Dr. Hewer, of St. Gregory, was beheaded for having intelligence with the King, through the Marquess of Ormond.

The parlour window jutted into the square over against the town hall, and Angela could see the whole length of the narrow street along which her father's carriage must come.

The tall, slim figure and the fair, girlish face stood out in full relief against the grey stone mullion, bathed in sunlight. The graceful form was undisguised by courtly apparel. The soft brown hair fell in loose ringlets, which were drawn back from the brow by a band of black ribbon. The girl's gown was of soft grey woollen stuff, relieved by a cambric collar covering the shoulders, and by cambric elbow-sleeves. A coral and silver rosary was her only ornament; but face and form needed no aid from satins or velvets, Venetian lace or Indian filagree.

The sweet, serious face was chiefly notable for eyes of darkest grey, under brows that were firmly arched and almost black. The hair was a dark brown, the complexion somewhat too pale for beauty. Indeed, that low-toned colouring made some people blind to the fine and regular modelling of the high-bred face; while there were others who saw no charm in a countenance which seemed too thoughtful for early youth, and therefore lacking in one of youth's chief attractions--gladness.

The face lighted suddenly at this moment, as four great grey Flanders horses came clattering along the narrow street and into the square, dragging a heavy painted wooden coach after them. The girl opened the casement and craned out her neck to look at the arrival The coach stopped at the convent door, and a footman alighted and rang the convent bell, to the interested curiosity of two or three loungers upon the steps of the town hall over the way.

Yes, it was her father, greyer but less sad of visage than at his last visit. His doublet and cloak were handsomer than the clothes he had worn then, though they were still of the same fashion, that English mode which he had affected before the beginning of the troubles, and which he had never changed.

Immediately after him there alighted a vision of beauty, the loveliest of ladies, in sky-blue velvet and pale grey fur, and with a long white feather encircling a sky-blue hat, and a collar of Venetian lace veiling a bosom that scintillated with jewels.

"Hyacinth!" cried Angela, in a flutter of delight.

The portress peered at the visitors through her spy-hole, and being satisfied that they were the expected guests, speedily opened the iron-clamped door.

There was no one to interfere between father and daughter, sister and sister, in the convent parlour. Angela had her dear people all to herself, the Mother Superior respecting the confidences and outpourings of love, which neither father nor children would wish to be witnessed even by a kinswoman. Thus, by a rare breach of conventual discipline, Angela was allowed to receive her guests alone.

The lay-sister opened the parlour door and ushered in the visitors, and Angela ran to meet her father, and fell sobbing upon his breast, her face hidden against his velvet doublet, her arms clasping his neck.

"What, mistress, hast thou so watery a welcome, now that the clouds have passed away, and every loyal English heart is joyful?" cried Sir John, in a voice that was somewhat husky, but with a great show of gaiety.

"Oh, sir, I have waited so long, so long for this day. Sometimes I thought it would never come, that I should never see my dear father again."

"Poor child! it would have been only my desert hadst thou forgotten me altogether. I might have come to you sooner, pretty one; indeed, I would have come, only things went ill with me. I was down-hearted and hopeless of any good fortune in a world that seemed given over to psalm-singing scoundrels; and till the tide turned I had no heart to come nigh you. But now fortunes are mended, the King's and mine, and you have a father once again, and shall have a home by-and-by, the house where you were born, and where your angel-mother made my life blessed. You are like her, Angela!" holding back the pale face in his strong hands, and gazing upon it earnestly. "Yes, you favour your mother; but your face is over sad for your years. Look at your sister here! Would you not say a sunbeam had taken woman's shape and come dancing into the room?"

Angela looked round and greeted the lady, who had stood aside while father and daughter met. Yes, such a face suggested sunlight and summer, birds, butterflies, all things buoyant and gladsome. A complexion of dazzling fairness, pearly, transparent, with ever-varying carnations; eyes of heavenliest blue, liquid, laughing, brimming with espieglerie; a slim little nose with an upward tilt, which expressed a contemptuous gaiety, an inquiring curiosity; a dimpled chin sloping a little towards the full round throat; the bust and shoulders of a Venus, the waist of a sylph, set off by the close-fitting velvet bodice, with its diamond and turquoise buttons; hair of palest gold, fluffed out into curls that were traps for sunbeams; hands and arms of a milky whiteness emerging from the large loose elbow-sleeves--a radiant apparition which took Angela by surprise. She had seen Flemish vraus in the richest attire, and among them there had been women as handsome as Helena Forment; but this vision of a fine lady from the court of the "roi soleil" was a revelation. Until this moment, the girl had hardly known what grace and beauty meant.

"Come and let me hug you, my dearest Puritan," cried Hyacinth, holding out her arms. "Why do you suffer your custodians to clothe you in that odious grey, which puts me in mind of lank-haired psalm-singing scum, and all their hateful works? I would have you sparkling in white satin and silver, or blushing in brocade powdered with forget-me-nots and rosebuds. What would Fareham say if I told him I had a Puritan in grey woollen stuff for my sister? He sends you his love, dear, and bids me tell you there shall be always an honoured place in our home for you, be it in England or France, in town or country. And why should you not fill that place at once, sister? Your education is finished, and to be sure you must be tired of these stone walls and this sleepy town."

"No, Hyacinth, I love the convent and the friends who have made it my home. You and Lord Fareham are very kind, but I could not leave our reverend mother; she is not so well or so strong as she used to be, and I think she likes to have me with her, because though she loves us all, down to the humblest of the lay-sisters, I am of her kin, and seem nearest to her. I don't want to forsake her; and if it was not against my father's wish I should like to end my days in this house, and to give my thoughts to God."

"That is because thou knowest nought of the world outside, sweetheart," protested Hyacinth. "I admire the readiness with which folks will renounce a banquet they have never tasted. A single day at the Louvre or the Palais Royal would change your inclinations at once and for ever."

"She is too young for a court life, or a town life either," said Sir John. "And I have no mind to remove her from this safe shelter till the King shall be firm upon his throne, and our poor country shall have settled into a stable and peaceful condition. But there must be no vows, Angela, no renunciation of kindred and home. I look to thee for the comfort of my old age!"

"Dear father, I will never disobey you. I shall remember always that my first duty is to you; and when you want me, you have but to summon me; and whether you are at home or abroad, in wealth and honour, or in exile and poverty, I will go to you, and be glad and happy to be your daughter and your servant."

"I knew thou wouldst, dearest. I have never forgotten how the soft little arms clung about my neck, and how the baby lips kissed me, in this same parlour, when my heart was weighed down by a load of iron, and there seemed no ray of hope for England or me. You were my comforter then, and you will be my comforter in the days to come. Hyacinth here is of the butterfly breed. She is fair to look upon, and tender and loving; but she is ever on the wing. And she has her husband and her children to cherish, and cannot be burdened with the care of a broken-down greybeard."

"Broken-down! Why, you are as brave a gallant as the youngest cavalier in the King's service," cried Hyacinth. "I would pit my father against Montagu or Buckingham, Buckhurst or Roscommon--against the gayest, the boldest of them all, on land or sea. Broken-down, forsooth! We will hear no such words from you, sir, for a score of years. And now you will want all your wits to take your proper place at Court as sage counsellor and friend of the new King. Sure he will need his father's friends about him to teach him state-craft--he who has led such a gay, good-for-nothing life as a penniless rover, with scarce a sound coat to his back."

"Nay, Hyacinth, the King will have no need of us old Malignants. We have had our day. He has shrewd Ned Hyde for counsellor, and in that one long head there is craft enough to govern a kingdom. The new Court will be a young Court, and the fashion of it will be new. We old fellows, who were gallant and gay enough in the forties, when we fought against Essex and his tawny scarves, would be but laughable figures at the Court of a young man bred half in Paris, and steeped in French fashions and French follies. No, Hyacinth, it is for you and your husband the new day dawns. If I get back to my old meads and woods and the house where I was born, I will sit quietly down in the chimney corner, and take to cattle-breeding, and a pack of harriers, for the diversion of my declining years. And when my Angela can make up her mind to leave her good aunt she shall keep house for me."

"I should love to be your housekeeper, dearest father. If it please Heaven to restore my aunt to health and strength, I will go to you with a heart full of joy," said the girl, hanging caressingly upon the old cavalier's shoulder.

Hyacinth flitted about the room with a swift, birdlike motion, looking at the sacred images and prints, the *tableau* over the mantelpiece, which told, with much flourish of penmanship, the progress of the convent pupils in learning and domestic virtues.

"What a humdrum, dismal room!" she cried. "You should see our convent parlours in Paris. At the Carmelites, in the Rue Saint Jacques, *par exemple*, the

Queen-mother's favourite convent, and at Chaillot, the house founded by Queen Henrietta--such pictures, and ornaments, and embroidered hangings, and tapestries worked by devotees. This room of yours, sister, stinks of poverty, as your Flemish streets stink of garlic and cabbage. Faugh! I know not which is worse!"

Having thus delivered herself of her disgust, she darted upon her younger sister, laid her hands upon the girl's shoulders, and contemplated her with mock seriousness.

"What a precocious young saint thou art, with no more interest in the world outside this naked parlour than if thou wert yonder image of the Holy Mother. Not a question of my husband, or my children, or of the last fashion in hood and mantle, or of the new laced gloves, or the French King's latest divinity."

"I should dearly like to see your children, Hyacinth," answered her sister.

"Ah! they are the most enchanting creatures, the girl a perpetual sunbeam, ethereal, elfish, a being of life and movement, and with a loquacity that never tires; the boy a lump of honey, fat, sleek, lazily beautiful. I am never tired of admiring them, when I have time to see them. Papillon--an old friend of mine has surnamed her Papillon because she is never still--was five years old on March 19. We were at St. Germain on her birthday. You should have seen the toys and trinkets and sweetmeats which the Court showered upon her--the King and Queen, Monsieur, Mademoiselle, the Princess Henrietta, her godmother--everybody had a gift for the daughter of *La folle Baronne Fareham*. Yes, they are lovely creatures, Angela; and I am miserable to think that it may be half a year before I see their sweet faces again."

"Why so long, sister?"

"Because they are at the Chateau de Montrond, grandmother's place near Dieppe, and because Fareham and I are going hence to Breda to meet the King, our own King Charles, and help lead him home in triumph. In London the mob are shouting, roaring, singing, for their King; and Montagu's fleet lies in the Downs, waiting but the signal from Parliament to cross to Holland. He who left his country in a scurvy fishing-boat will go back to England in a mighty man-of-war, the *Naseby*--mark you, the *Naseby*--christened by that Usurper, in insolent remembrance of a rebel victory; but Charles will doubtless change that hated name. He must not be put in mind of a fight where rebels had the better of loyal gentlemen. He will sail home over those dancing seas, with a fleet of great white-winged ships circling round him like a flight of silvery doves. Oh, what a turn of fortune's wheel! I am wild with rapture at the thought of it!"

"You love England better than France, though you must be almost a stranger there," said Angela, wonderingly, looking at a miniature which her sister wore in a bracelet.

"Nay, love, 'tis in Paris I am an insignificant alien, though they are ever so kind and flattering to me. At St Germain I was only Madame de Montrond's grand-daughter--the wife of a somewhat morose gentleman who was cleverer at winning battles than at gaining hearts. At Whitehall I shall be Lady Fareham, and shall enjoy my full consequence as the wife of an English nobleman of ancient lineage and fine estate, for, I am happy to tell you, his lordship's property suffered less than most people's in the rebellion, and anything his father lost when he fought for the good cause will be given back to the son now the good cause is triumphant, with additions, perhaps--an earl's coronet instead of a baron's beggarly pearls. I should like Papillon to be Lady Henrietta."

"And you will send for your children, doubtless, when you are sure all is safe in England?" said Angela, still contemplating the portrait in the bracelet, which her sister had unclasped while she talked. "This is Papillon, I know. What a sweet, kind, mischievous face!"

"Mischievous as a Barbary ape--kind, and sweet as the west wind," said Sir John.

"And your boy?" asked Angela, reclasping the bracelet on the fair, round arm, having looked her fill at the mutinous eyes, the brown, crisply curling hair, dainty, pointed chin, and dimpled cheeks. "Have you his picture, too?"

"Not his; but I wear his father's likeness somewhere betwixt buckram and Flanders lace," answered Hyacinth, gaily, pulling a locket from amidst the splendours of her corsage. "I call it next my heart; but there is a stout fortification of whalebone between heart and picture. You have gloated enough on the daughter's impertinent visage. Look now at the father, whom she resembles in little, as a kitten resembles a tiger."

She handed her sister an oval locket, bordered with diamonds, and held by a slender Indian chain; and Angela saw the face of the brother in law whose kind ness and hospitality had been so freely promised to her.

She explored the countenance long and earnestly.

"Well, do you think I chose him for his beauty?" asked Hyacinth. "You have devoured every lineament with that serious gaze of yours, as if you were trying to read the spirit behind that mask of flesh. Do you think him handsome?"

Angela faltered: but was unskilled in flattery, and could not reply with a compliment.

"No, sister; surely none have ever called this countenance handsome; but it is a face to set one thinking."

"Ay, child, and he who owns the face is a man to set one thinking. He has made me think many a time when I would have travelled a day's journey to escape the thoughts he forced upon me. He was not made to bask in the sunshine of life. He is a stormy petrel. It was for his ugliness I chose him. Those dark stern features, that imperious mouth, and a brow like the Olympian Jove. He scared me into loving him. I sheltered myself upon his breast from the thunder of his brow, the lightning of his eye."

"He has a look of his cousin Wentworth," said Sir John. "I never see him but I think of that murdered man--my father's friend and mine--whom I have never ceased to mourn."

"Yet their kin is of the most distant," said Hyacinth. "It is strange that there should be any likeness."

"Faces appear and reappear in families," answered her father. "You may observe that curiously recurring likeness in any picture-gallery, if the family portraits cover a century or two. Louis has little in common with his grandfather; but two hundred years hence there may be a prince of the royal house whose every feature shall recall Henry the Great"

The portrait was returned to its hiding-place, under perfumed lace and cobweb lawn, and the reverend mother entered the parlour, ready for conversation, and eager to hear the history of the last six weeks, of the collapse of that military despotism which had convulsed England and dominated Europe, and was now melting into thin air as ghosts dissolve at cock-crow, of the secret negotiations between Monk and Grenville, now known to everybody; of the King's gracious amnesty and promise of universal pardon, save for some score or so of conspicuous villains, whose hands were dyed with the Royal Martyr's blood.

She was full of questioning: and, above all, eager to know whether it was true that King Charles was at heart as staunch a papist as his brother the Duke of York was believed to be, though even the Duke lacked the courage to bear witness to the true faith.

Two lay-sisters brought in a repast of cakes and syrups and light wines, such delicate and dainty food as the pious ladies of the convent were especially skilled in preparing, and which they deemed all-sufficient for the entertainment of company; even when one of their guests was a rugged soldier like Sir John Kirkland. When the light collation had been tasted and praised, the coach came to the door again, and swallowed up the beautiful lady and the old cavalier, who vanished from Angela's sight in a cloud of dust, waving hands from the coach window.

CHAPTER III.
LETTERS FROM HOME.

The quiet days went by, and grew into years, and time was only marked by the gradual failure of the reverend mother's health; so gradual, so gentle a decay, that it was only when looking back on St. Sylvester's Eve that her great-niece became aware how much of strength and activity had been lost since the Superior knelt in her place near the altar, listening to the solemn music of the midnight Mass that sanctified the passing of the year. This year the reverend mother was led to her seat between two nuns, who sustained her feeble limbs. This year the meek knees, which had worn the marble floor in long hours of prayer during eighty pious years, could no longer bend. The meek head was bowed, the bloodless hands were lifted up in supplication, but the fingers were wasted and stiffened, and there was pain in every movement of the joints.

There was no actual malady, only the slow death in life called old age. All the patient needed was rest and tender nursing. This last her great-niece supplied, together with the gentlest companionship. No highly trained nurse, the product of modern science, could have been more efficient than the instinct of affection had made Angela. And then the patient's temper was so amiable, her mind, undimmed after eighty-three years of life, was a mirror of God. She thought of her fellow-creatures with a Divine charity; she worshipped her Creator with an implicit faith. For her in many a waking vision the heavens opened and the spirits of departed saints descended from their abode in bliss to hold converse with her. Eighty years of her life had been given to religious exercises and charitable deeds. Motherless before she could speak, she had entered the convent as a pupil at three years of age, and had taken the veil at seventeen. Her father had married a great heiress, whose only child, a daughter, was allowed to absorb all the small stock of parental affection; and there was no one to dispute Anastasia's desire for the cloister. All she knew of the world outside those walls was from hearsay. A rare visit from her lovely half-sister, the Marquise de Montrond, had astonished her with the sight of a distinguished Parisienne, and left her wondering. She had never read a secular book. She knew not the meaning of the word pleasure, save in the mild amusements permitted to the convent children--till they left the convent as young women--on the evening of a saint's day; a stately dance of curtsyings and waving arms; a little childish play, dramatising some incident in the lives of the saints. So she lived her eighty years of obedience and quiet usefulness, learning and teaching, serving and governing. She had lived through the Thirty Years' War, through the devastations of Wallenstein, the cruelties of Bavarian Tilly, the judicial murder of Egmont and Horn. She had heard of villages burnt, populations put to the sword, women and children killed by thousands. She had conversed with those who remembered the League; she had seen the nuns weeping for Edward Campion's cruel fate; she had heard Masses sung for the soul of murdered Mary Stuart. She had heard of Raleigh's visions of conquest and of gold, setting his prison-blanched face towards the West, in the afternoon of life, to encounter bereavement, treachery, sickening failure, and go back to his native England to expiate the dreams of genius with the blood of a martyr. And through all the changes and chances of that eventful century she had lived apart, full of pity and wonder, in a charmed circle of piety and love.

Her room, in these peaceful stages of the closing scene, was a haven of rest. Angela loved the seclusion of the panelled chamber, with its heavily mullioned casement facing the south-west, and the polished oak floor, on which the red and gold of the sunset were mirrored, as on the dark stillness of a moorland tarn. For her every object in the room had its interest or its charm. The associations of childhood hallowed them all. The large ivory crucifix, yellow with age, dim with the kisses of adoring lips; the delf statuettes of Mary and Joseph, flaming with gaudy colour; the figure of the Saviour and St. John the Baptist, delicately carved out of boxwood, in a group representing the baptism in the river Jordan, the holy dove trembling on a wire over the Divine head; the books, the pictures, the rosaries: all these she had gazed at reverently when all things were new, and the convent passages places of shuddering, and the service of the Mass an unintelligible mystery. She had grown up within those solemn walls; and now, seeing her kinswoman's life gently ebbing away, she could but wonder what she would have to do in this world when another took the Superior's place, and the tie that bound her to Louvain would be broken.

The lady who would in all probability succeed Mother Anastasia as Superior was a clever, domineering woman, whom Angela loved least of all the nuns--a widow of good birth and fortune, and a thorough Fleming; stolid, bigoted, prejudiced, and taking much credit to herself for the wealth she had brought to the convent, apt to talk of the class-room and the chapel her money had helped to build and restore as "my class-room," or "my chapel."

No; Angela had no desire to remain in the convent when her dear kinswoman should have vanished from the scene her presence sanctified. The house would be haunted with sorrowful memories. It would be time for her to claim that home which her father had talked of sharing with her in his old age. She could just faintly remember the house in which she was born--the moat, the fish-pond, the thick walls of yew, the peacocks and lions cut in box, of which the gardener who clipped them was so proud. Faintly, faintly, the picture of the old house came back to her; built of grey stone, and stained with moss, grave and substantial, occupying three sides of a quadrangle, a house of many windows, few of which were intended to open, a house of dark passages, like these in the convent, and flights of shallow steps, and curious turns and twistings here and there. There were living birds that sunned their spreading tails and stalked in slow stateliness on the turf terraces, as well as those peacocks clipped out of yew. The house lay in a Buckinghamshire valley, shut round and sheltered by hills and coppices, where there was an abundance of game. Angela had seen the low, cavern-like larder hung with pheasants and hares.

Her heart yearned towards the old house, so distinctly pictured by memory, though perchance with some differences from the actual scene. The mansion would seem smaller to her, doubtless, beholding it with the eyes of womanhood, than childish memory made it. But to live there with her father, to wait upon him and tend him, to have Hyacinth's children there, playing in the gardens as she had played, would be as happy a life as her fancy could compass.

All that she knew of the march of events during those tranquil years in the convent came to her in letters from her sister, who was a vivacious letter-writer, and prided herself upon her epistolary talent--as indeed upon her general superiority, from a literary standpoint, to the women of her day.

It was a pleasure to Lady Fareham in some rare interval of solitude--when the weather was too severe for her to venture outside the hall door, even in her comfortable coach, and when by some curious concatenation she happened to be without visitors--to open her portfolio and prattle with her pen to her sister, as she would have prattled with her tongue to the visitors whom snow or tempest kept away. Her letters written from London were apt to be rare and brief, Angela noted; but from his lordship's mansion near Oxford, or at the Grange between Fareham and Winchester--once the property of the brothers of St. Cross--she always sent a budget. Few of these lengthy epistles contained anything bearing upon Angela's own existence--except the oft-repeated entreaty that she would make haste and join them--or even the flippant suggestion that Mother Anastasia should make haste and die. They were of the nature of news-letters; but the news was tinctured by the feminine medium through which it came, and there was a flavour of egotism in almost every page. Lady Fareham wrote as only a pretty woman, courted, flattered, and indulged by everybody about her, ever since she could remember, could be forgiven for writing. People had petted her and worshipped her with such uniform subservience that she had grown to thirty years of age without knowing that she was selfish, accepting homage and submission as a law of the universe, as kings and princes do.

Only in one of those letters was there that which might be called a momentous fact, but which Angela took as easily as if it had been a mere detail, to be dismissed from her thoughts when the letter had been laid aside.

It was a letter with a black seal, announcing the death of the Marquise de Montrond, who had expired of an apoplexy at her house in the Marais, after a supper party at which Mademoiselle, Madame de Longueville, Madame de Montausier, the Duchesse de Bouillon, Lauzun, St. Evremond, cheery little Godeau, Bishop of Vence, and half a dozen other famous wits had been present, a supper bristling with royal personages. Death had come with appalling suddenness while the lamps of the festival were burning, and the cards were still upon the tables, and the last carriage had but just rolled under the *porte cochere*.

"It is the manner of death she would have chosen," wrote Hyacinth. "She never missed confession on the first Sunday of the month; and she was so generous to the Church and to the poor that her director declared she would have been too saintly for earth, but for the human weakness of liking fine company. And now, dearest, I have to tell you how she has disposed of her fortune; and I hope, if you should think she has not used you generously, you will do me the justice to believe that I have neither courted her for her wealth nor influenced her to my dear sister's disadvantage. You will consider, *tres chere*, that I was with her from my eighth year until the other day when Fareham brought me to England. She loved me passionately in my childhood, and has often told me since that she never felt towards me as a grandmother, but as if she had been actually my mother, being indeed still a young woman when she adopted me, and by strangers always mistaken for my mother. She was handsome to the last, and young in mind and in habits long after youth had left her. I was said to be the image of what she was when she rivalled Madame de Hautefort in the affections of the late King. You must consider, sweetheart, that he was the most moral of men, and that with him love meant a passion as free from sensual taint as the preferences of a sylph. I think my good grandmother loved me all the better for this fancied resemblance. She would arrange her jewels about my hair and bosom, as she had worn them when Buckingham came wooing for his master; and then she would bid her page hold a mirror before me and tell me to look at the face of which Queen Anne had been jealous, and for which Cinq Mars had run mad. And then she would shed a tear or two over the years and the charms that were gone, till I brought the cards and cheered her spirits with her favourite game of primero.

"She had her fits of temper and little tantrums sometimes, Ange, and it needed some patience to restrain one's tongue from insolence; but I am happy to remember that I ever bore her in profound respect, and that I never made her seriously angry but once--which was when I, being then almost a child, went out into the streets of Paris with Henri de Malfort and a wild party, masked, to hear Beaufort address the populace in the market-place, and when I was so unlucky as to lose the emerald cross given her by the great Cardinal, for whom, I believe, she had a sneaking kindness. Why else should she have so hated his Eminence's very much favoured niece, Madame de Combalet?

"But to return to that which concerns my dear sister. Regarding me as her own daughter, the Marquise has lavished her bounties upon me almost to the exclusion of my own sweet Angela. In a word, dearest, she leaves you a modest income of four hundred louis--or about three hundred pounds sterling--the rental of two farms in Normandy; and all the rest of her fortune she bequeaths to me, and Papillon after me, including her house in the Marais--sadly out of fashion now that everybody of consequence is moving to the Place Royale--and her chateau near Dieppe; besides all her jewels, many of which I have had in my possession ever since my marriage. My sweet sister shall take her choice of a carcanet among those old-fashioned trinkets. And now, dearest, if you are left with a pittance that will but serve to pay for your gloves and fans at the Middle Exchange, and perhaps to buy you an Indian night-gown in the course of the year--for your Court petticoats and mantuas will cost three times as much--you have but to remember that my purse is to be yours, and my home yours, and that Fareham and I do but wait to welcome you either to Fareham House, in the Strand, or to Chiltern Abbey, near Oxford. The Grange near Fareham I never intend to re-enter if I can help it. The place is a warren of rats, which the servants take for ghosts. If you love water you will love our houses, for the river runs near them both; indeed, when in London, we almost think ourselves in Venice, save that we have a spacious garden, which I am told few of the Venetians can command, their city being built upon an assemblage of minuscule islets, linked together by innumerable bridges."

Angela smiled as she looked down at her black gown--the week-day uniform of the convent school, exchanged for a somewhat superior grey stuff on Sundays and holidays--smiled at the notion of spending the rent of two farms upon her toilet. And how much more ridiculous seemed the assertion that to appear at King Charles's Court she must spend thrice as much! Yet she could but remember that Hyacinth had described trains and petticoats so loaded with jewelled embroidery that it was a penance to wear them--lace worth hundreds of pounds--plumed hats that cost as much as a year's maintenance in the convent.

Mother Anastasia expressed considerable displeasure at Madame de Montrond's disposal of her wealth.

"This is what it is to live in a Court, and to care only for earthly things!" she said. "All sense of justice is lost in that world of vanity and self-love. You are as near akin to the Marquise as your sister; and yet, because she was familiar with the one and not with the other--and because her vain, foolish soul took pleasure in a beauty that recalled her own perishable charms, she leaves one sister a great fortune and the other a pittance!"

"Dear aunt, I am more than content----"

"But I am not content for you, Angela. Had the estate been divided equally you might have taken the veil, and succeeded to my place in this beloved house, which needs the accession of wealth to maintain it in usefulness and dignity."

Angela would not wound her aunt's feelings by one word of disparagement of the house in which she had been reared; but, looking along the dim avenue of the future, she yearned for some wider horizon than the sky, barred with tall poplars which rose high above the garden wall that formed the limit of her daily walks. Her rambles, her recreations, had all been confined within that space of seven or eight acres, and she thought sometimes with a sudden longing of those hills and valleys of fertile Buckinghamshire, which lay so far back in the dawn of her mind, and were yet so distinctly pictured in her memory.

And London--that wonderful city of which her sister wrote in such glowing words! the long range of palaces beside the swift-flowing river, wider than the Seine where it reflects the gloomy bulk of the Louvre and the Temple! Were it only once in her life, she would like to see London--the King, the two Queens, Whitehall, and Somerset House. She would like to see all the splendour of Court and city; and then to taste the placid retirement of the house in the valley, and to be her father's housekeeper and companion.

Another letter from Hyacinth announced the death of Mazarin.

"The Cardinal is no more. He died in the day of success, having got the better of all his enemies. A violent access of gout was followed by an affection of the chest which proved fatal. His sick-room was crowded with courtiers and sycophants, and he was selling sinecures up to the day of his death. Fareham says his death bed was like a money-changer's counter. He was passionately fond of hocca, the Italian game which he brought into fashion, and which ruined half the young men about the Court. The counterpane was scattered with money and playing cards, which were only brushed aside to make room for the last Sacraments. My Lord Clarendon declares that his spirits never recovered from the shock of his Majesty's restoration, which falsified all his calculations. He might have made his favourite niece Queen of England; but his Italian caution restrained him, and the beautiful Hortense has to put up with a new-made duke--a title bought with her uncle's money--to whom the Cardinal affianced her on his death-bed. He was a remarkable man, and so profound a dissembler that his pretended opposition to King Louis' marriage with his niece Olympe Mancini would have deceived the shrewdest observer, had we not all known that he ardently desired the union, and that it was only his fear of Queen Anne's anger which prevented it. Her Spanish pride was in arms at the notion, and she would not have stopped short at revolution to prevent or to revenge such an alliance.

"This was perhaps the only occasion upon which she ever seriously opposed Mazarin. With him expires all her political power. She is now as much a cypher as in the time of the late King, when France had only one master, the great Cardinal. He who is just dead, Fareham says, was but a little Richelieu; and he recalls how when the great Cardinal died people scarce dared tell one another of his death, so profound was the awe in which he was held. He left the King a nullity, and the Queen all powerful. She was young and beautiful then, you see; her husband was marked for death, her son was an infant. All France was hers--a kingdom of courtiers and flatterers. And now she is old and ailing; and Mazarin being gone, the young King will submit to no minister who claims to be anything better than a clerk or a secretary. Colbert he must tolerate--for Colbert means prosperity--but Colbert will have to obey. My friend, the Duchesse de Longueville, who is now living in strict retirement, writes me the most exquisite letters; and from her I hear all that happens in that country which I sometimes fancy is more my own than the duller climate where my lot is now cast. Fifteen years at the French Court have made me in heart and mind almost a Frenchwoman; nor can I fail to be influenced by my maternal ancestry. I find it difficult sometimes to remember my English, when conversing with the clod-hoppers of Oxfordshire, who have no French, yet insist, for finery's sake, upon larding their rustic English with French words.

"All that is most agreeable in our court is imitated from the Palais Royal and the Louvre.

"'Whitehall is but the shadow of a shadow,' says Fareham, in one of his philosophy fits, preaching upon the changes he has seen in Paris and London. And, indeed, it is strange to have lived through two revolutions, one so awful in its final catastrophe that it dwarfs the other, yet both terrible; for I, who was a witness of the sufferings of Princes and Princesses during the two wars of the Fronde, am not inclined to think lightly of a civil war which cost France some of the flower of her nobility, and made her greatest hero a prisoner and an exile for seven years of his life.

"But oh, my dear, it was a romantic time! and I look back and am proud to have lived in it. I was but twelve years old at the siege of Paris; but I was in Madame de Longueville's room, at the Hotel de Ville, while the fighting was going on, and the officers, in their steel cuirasses, coming in from the thick of the strife. Such a confusion of fine ladies and armed men--breast-plates and blue scarves--fiddles squeaking in the salon, trumpets sounding in the square below!"

*   *   *   *   *

In a letter of later date Lady Fareham expatiated upon the folly of her sister's spiritual guides.

"I am desolated, **ma mie**, by the absurd restriction which forbids you to profit by my New Year's gift. I thought, when I sent you all the volumes of la Scudery's enchanting romance, I had laid up for you a year of enjoyment, and that, touched by the baguette of that exquisite fancy, your convent walls would fall, like those of Jericho at the sound of Jewish trumpets, and you would be transported in imagination to the finest society in the world--the company of Cyrus and Mandane--under which Oriental disguise you are shown every feature of mind and person in Conde and his heroic sister, my esteemed friend, the Duchesse de Longueville. As I was one of the first to appreciate Mademoiselle Scudery's genius, and to detect behind the name of the brother the tender sentiments and delicate refinement of the sister's chaster pen, so I believe I was the first to call the Duchesse 'Mandane,' a sobriquet which soon became general among her intimates.

"You are not to read 'Le Grand Cyrus," your aunt tells you, because it is a romance! That is to say, you are forbidden to peruse the most faithful history of your own time, and to familiarise yourself with the persons and minds of great people whom you may never be so fortunate as to meet in the flesh. I myself, dearest Ange, have had the felicity to live among these princely persons, to revel in the conversations of the Hotel de Rambouillet--not, perhaps, as our grandmother would have told you, in its most glorious period--but at least while it was still the focus of all that is choicest in letters and in art. Did we not hear M. Poquelin read his first comedy before it was represented by Monsieur's company in the beautiful theatre at the Palais Royal, built by Richelieu, when it was the Palais Cardinal? Not read 'Le Grand Cyrus,' and on the score of morality! Why, this most delightful book was written by one of the most moral women in Paris--one of the chastest--against whose reputation no word of slander has ever been breathed! It must, indeed, be confessed that Sapho is of an ugliness which would protect her even were she not guarded by the aegis of genius. She is one of those fortunate unfortunates who can walk through the furnace of a Court unscathed, and leave a reputation for modesty in an age that scarce credits virtue in woman.

"I fear, dear child, that these narrow-minded restrictions of your convent will leave you of a surpassing ignorance, which may cover you with confusion when you find yourself in fine company. There are accomplishments without which youth is no more admired than age and grey hairs; and to sparkle with wit or astonish with learning is a necessity for a woman of quality. It is only by the advantages of education that we can show ourselves superior to such a hussy as Albemarle's gutter-bred duchess, who was the faithless wife of a sailor or barber--I forget which--and who hangs like a millstone upon the General's neck now that he has climbed to the zenith. To have perfect Italian and some Spanish is as needful as to have fine eyes and complexion nowadays. And to dance admirably is a gift indispensable to a lady. Alas! I fear that those little feet of yours--I hope they *are* small--have never been taught to move in a coranto or a contre-danse, and that you will have to learn the alphabet of dancing at an age when most women are finished performers. The great Conde, while winning sieges and battles that surpassed the feats of Greeks and Romans, contrived to make himself the finest dancer of his day, and won more admiration in high-bred circles by his graceful movements, which every one could understand and admire, than by prodigies of valour at Dunkirk or Nordlingen."

The above was one of Lady Fareham's most serious letters. Her pen was exercised, for the most part, in a lighter vein. She wrote of the Court beauties, the Court jests--practical jokes some of them, which our finer minds of to-day would consider in execrable taste--such jests as we read of in Grammont's memoirs, which generally aimed at making an ugly woman ridiculous, or an injured husband the sport and victim of wicked lover and heartless wife. No sense of the fitness of things constrained her ladyship from communicating these Court scandals to her guileless sister. Did they not comprise the only news worth anybody's attention, and relate to the only class of people who had any tangible existence for Lady Fareham? There were millions of human beings, no doubt, living and acting and suffering on the surface of the earth, outside the stellary circles of which Louis and Charles were the suns; but there was no interstellar medium of sympathy to convey the idea of those exterior populations to Hyacinth's mind. She knew of the populace, French or English, as of something which was occasionally given to become dangerous and revolutionary, which sometimes starved and sometimes died of the plague, and was always unpleasing to the educated eye.

Masquerades, plays, races at Newmarket, dances, duels, losses at cards--Lady Fareham touched every subject, and expatiated on all; but she had usually more to tell of the country she had left than of that in which she was living.

"Here everything is on such a small scale, *si mesquin!*" she wrote. "Whitehall covers a large area, but it is only a fine banqueting hall and a labyrinth of lodgings, without suite or stateliness. The pictures in the late King's cabinet are said to be the finest in the world, but they are a kind of pieces for which I care very little--Flemish and Dutch chiefly--with a series of cartoons by Raphael, which connoisseurs affect to admire, but which, did they belong to me, I would gladly exchange for a set of Mortlake tapestries.

"His Majesty here builds ships, while the King of France builds palaces. I am told Louis is spending millions on the new palace at Versailles, an ungrateful site--no water, no noble prospect as at St. Germain, no population. The King likes the spot all the better, Madame tells me, because he has to create his own landscape, to conjure lakes and cataracts out of dry ground. The buildings have been but two years in progress, and it must be long before these colossal foundations are crowned with the edifice which Louis and his architect, Mansart, have planned. Colbert is furious at this squandering of vast sums on a provincial palace, while the Louvre, the birthplace and home of dynasties, remains unfinished.

"The King's reason for disliking St. Germain--a chateau his mother has always loved--has in it something childish and fantastic, if, as my dear duchess declares, he hates the place only because he can see the towers of St. Denis from the terrace, and is thus hourly reminded of death and the grave. I can hardly believe that a being of such superior intelligence could be governed by any such horror of man's inevitable end. I would far sooner attribute the vast expenditure of Versailles to the common love of monarchs and great men for building houses too large for their necessities. Indeed, it was but yesterday that Fareham took me to see the palace--for I can call it by no meaner name--that Lord Clarendon is building for himself in the open country at the top of St. James's Street. It promises to be the finest house in town, and, although not covering so much ground as Whitehall, is judged far superior to that inchoate mass in its fine proportions and the perfect symmetry of its saloons and galleries. There is a garden a-making, projected by Mr. Evelyn, a great authority on trees and gardens. A crowd of fine company had assembled to see the newly finished hall and dining parlour, among them a fussy person, who came in attendance upon my Lord Sandwich, and who was more voluble than became his quality as a clerk in the Navy Office. He was periwigged and dressed as fine as his master, and, on my being civil to him, talked much of himself and of divers taverns in the city where the dinners were either vastly good or vastly ill. I told him that as I never dined at a tavern the subject was altogether beyond the scope of my intelligence, at which Sandwich and Fareham laughed, and my pertinacious gentleman blushed as red as the heels of his shoes. I am told the creature has a pretty taste in music, and is the son of a tailor, but professes a genteel ancestry, and occasionally pushes into the best company.

"Shall I describe to you one of my latest conquests, sweetheart? 'Tis a boy--an actual beardless boy of eighteen summers; but such a boy! So beautiful, so insolent, with an impudence that can confront Lord Clarendon himself, the gravest of noblemen, who, with the sole exception of my Lord Southampton, is the one man who has never crossed Mrs. Palmer's threshold, or bowed his neck under that splendid fury's yoke. My admirer thinks no more of smoking these grave nobles, men of a former generation, who learnt their manners at the court of a serious and august King, than I do of teasing my falcon. He laughs at them, jokes with them in Greek or in Latin, has a ready answer and a witty quip for every turn of the discourse; will even interrupt his Majesty in one of those anecdotes of his Scottish martyrdom which he tells so well and tells so often. Lucifer himself could not be more arrogant or more audacious than this bewitching boy-lover of mine, who writes verses in English or Latin as easy as I can toss a shuttlecock. I doubt the greater number of his verses are scarce proper reading for you or me, Angela; for I see the men gather round him in corners as he murmurs his latest madrigal to a chosen half-dozen or so; and I guess by their subdued tittering that the lines are not over modest; while by the sidelong glances the listeners cast round, now at my Lady Castlemaine, and anon at some other goddess in the royal pantheon, I have a shrewd notion as to what alabaster breast my witty lover's shafts are aimed at.

"This youthful devotee of mine is the son of a certain Lord Wilmot, who fought on the late King's side in the troubles. This creature went to the university of Oxford at twelve years old--as it were, straight from his go-cart to college, and was master of arts at fourteen. He has made the grand tour, and pretends to have seen so much of this life that he has found out the worthlessness of it. Even while he woes me with a most romantic ardour, he affects to have outgrown the capacity to love.

"Think not, dearest, that I outstep the bounds of matronly modesty by this airy philandering with my young Lord Rochester, or that my serious Fareham is ever offended at our pretty trifling. He laughs at the lad as heartily as I do, invites him to our table, and is amused by his monkeyish tricks. A woman of quality must have followers; and a pert, fantastical boy is the safest of lovers. Slander itself could scarce accuse Lady Fareham, who has had soldier-princes and statesmen at her feet, of an unworthy tenderness for a jackanapes of seventeen; for, indeed, I believe his eighteenth birthday is still in the womb of time. I would with all my heart thou wert here to share our innocent diversions; and I know not which of all my playthings thou wouldst esteem highest, the falcon, my darling spaniels, made up of soft silken curls and intelligent brown eyes, or Rochester. Nay, let me not forget the children, Papillon and Cupid, who are truly very pretty creatures, though consummate plagues. The girl, Papillon, has a tongue which Wilmot says is the nearest approach to perpetual motion that he has yet discovered; and the boy, who was but seven last birthday, is full of mischief, in which my admirer counsels and abets him.

"Oh, this London, sweetheart, and this Court! How wide those violet eyes would open couldst thou but look suddenly in upon us after supper at Basset, or in the park, or at the play-house, when the orange girls are smoking the pretty fellows in the pit, and my Lady Castlemaine is leaning half out of her box to talk to the King in his! I thought I had seen enough of festivals and dances, stage-plays and courtly diversions beyond sea; but the Court entertainments at Paris or St. Germain differed as much from the festivities of Whitehall as a cathedral service from a dance in a booth at Bartholomew Fair. His Majesty of France never forgets that he is a king. His Majesty of England only remembers his kingship when he wants a new subsidy, or to get a Bill hurried through the Houses. Louis at four-and-twenty was serious enough for fifty. Charles at thirty-four has the careless humour of a schoolboy. He is royal in nothing except his extravagance, which has squandered more millions than I dare mention since he landed at Dover.

"I am growing almost as sober as my solemn spouse, who will ever be railing at the King and the Duke, and even more bitterly at the favourite, his Grace of Buckingham, who is assuredly one of the most agreeable men in London. I asked Fareham only yesterday why he went to Court, if his Majesty's company is thus distasteful to him. 'It is not to his company I object, but to his principles,' he answered, in that earnest fashion of his which takes the lightest questions *au grand serieux*. 'I see in him a man who, with natural parts far above the average, makes himself the jest of meaner intellects, and the dupe of greedy courtesans; a man who, trained in the stern school of adversity, overshadowed by the great horror of his father's tragical doom, accepts life as one long jest, and being, by a concatenation of circumstances bordering on the miraculous, restored to the privileges of hereditary monarchy, takes all possible pains to prove the uselessness of kings. I see a man who, borne back to power by the irresistible current of the people's affections, has broken every pledge he gave that people in the flush and triumph of his return. I see one who, in his own person, cares neither for Paul nor Peter, and yet can tamely witness the persecution of his people because they do not conform to a State religion--can allow good and pious men to be driven out of the pulpits where they have preached the Gospel of Christ, and suffer wives and children to starve because the head of the household has a conscience. I see a king careless of the welfare of his people, and the honour and glory of his reign; affecting to be a patriot, and a man of business, on the strength of an extravagant fancy for shipbuilding; careless of everything save the empty pleasure of an idle hour. A king who lavishes thousands upon wantons and profligates, and who ever gives not to the most worthy, but to the most importunate.'

"I laughed at this tirade, and told him, what indeed I believe, that he is at heart a Puritan, and would better consort with Baxter and Bunyan, and that frousy crew, than with Buckhurst and Sedley, or his brilliant kinsman, Roscommon."

From her father directly, Angela heard nothing, and her sister's allusions to him were of the briefest, anxiously as she had questioned that lively letter-writer. Yes, her father was well, Hyacinth told her; but he stayed mostly at the Manor Moat. He did not care for the Court gaieties.

"I believe he thinks we have all parted company with our wits," she wrote. "He seldom sees me but to lecture me, in a sidelong way, upon my folly; for his railing at the company I keep hits me by implication. I believe these old courtiers of the late King are Puritans at heart; and that if Archbishop Laud were alive he would be as bitter against the sins of the town as any of the cushion-thumping Anabaptists that preach to the elect in back rooms and blind alleys. My father talks and thinks as if he had spent all his years of exile in the cave of the Seven Sleepers. And yet he fought shoulder to shoulder with some of the finest gentlemen in France--Conde, Turenne, Gramont, St. Evremond, Bussy, and the rest of them. But all the world is young, and full of wit and mirth, since his Majesty came to his own; and elderly limbs are too stiff to trip in our new dances. I doubt my father's mind is as old-fashioned, and of as rigid a shape as his Court suit, at sight of which my best friends can scarce refrain from laughing."

This light mention of a parent whom she reverenced wounded Angela to the quick; and that wound was deepened a year later, when she was surprised by a visit from her father, of which no letter had forewarned her. She was walking in the convent garden, in her hour of recreation, tasting the sunny air, and the beauty of the many-coloured tulips in the long narrow borders, between two espalier rows trained with an exquisite neatness, and reputed to bear the finest golden pippins and Bergamot pears within fifty miles of the city. The trees were in blossom, and a wall of pink and white bloom rose up on either hand above the scarlet and amber tulips.

Turning at the end of the long alley, where it met a wall that in August was flushed with the crimson velvet of peaches and nectarines, Angela saw a man advancing from the further end of the walk, attended by a lay sister. The high-crowned hat and pointed beard, the tall figure in a grey doublet crossed with a black sword-belt, the walk, the bearing, were unmistakable. It might have been a figure that had stepped out of Vandyke's canvas. It had nothing of the fuss and flutter, the feathers and ruffles, the loose flow of brocade and velvet, that marked the costume of the young French Court.

Angela ran to receive her father, and could scarce speak to him, she was so startled, and yet so glad.

"Oh, sir, when I prayed for you at Mass this morning, how little I hoped for so much happiness! I had a letter from Hyacinth only a week ago, and she wrote nothing of your intentions. I knew not that you had crossed the sea."

"Why, sweetheart, Hyacinth sees me too rarely, and is too full of her own affairs, ever to be beforehand with my intentions; and, although I have been long heartily sick of England, I only made up my mind to come to Flanders less than a week ago. No sooner thought of than done. I came by our old road, in a merchant craft from Harwich to Ostend, and the rest of the way in the saddle. Not quite so fast as they used to ride that carried his Majesty's post from London to York, in the beginning of the troubles, when the loyal gentlemen along the north road would galop faster with despatches and treaties than ever they rode after a stag. Ah, child, how hopeful we were in those days; and how we all told each other it was but a passing storm at Westminster, which could all be lulled by a little civil concession here and there on the King's part! And so it might, perhaps, if he would but have conceded the right thing at the right time--yielded but just the inch they asked for when they first asked--instead of shilly-shallying till they got angry, and wanted ells instead of inches. 'Tis the stitch in time, Angela, that saves trouble, in politics as well as in thy petticoat."

He had flung his arm round his daughter's neck as they paced slowly side by side.

"Have you come to stay at Louvain, sir?" she asked, timidly.

"Nay, love, the place is too quiet for me. I could not stay in a town that is given over to learning and piety. The sound of their everlasting carillon would tease my ear with the thought, 'Lo, another quarter of an hour gone of my poor remnant of days, and nothing to do but to doze in the sunshine or fondle my spaniel, fill my pipe, or ride a lazy horse on a level road, such as I have ever hated.'"

"But why did you tire of England, sir? I thought the King would have wanted you always near him. You, his father's close friend, who suffered so much for Royal friendship. Surely he loves and cherishes you! He must be a base, ungrateful man if he do not."

"Oh, the King is grateful, Angela, grateful enough and to spare. He never sees me at Court but he has some gracious speech about his father's regard for me. It grows irksome at last, by sheer repetition. The turn of the sentence varies, for his Majesty has a fine standing army of words, but the gist of the phrase is always the same, and it means, 'Here is a tiresome old Put to whom I must say something civil for the sake of his ancient vicissitudes.' And then his phalanx of foppery stares at me as if I were a Topinambou; and since I have seen them mimic Ned Hyde's stately speech and manners, I doubt not before I have crossed the ante-room I have served to make sport for the crew, since their wit has but two phases--ordure and mimickry. Look not so glum, daughter. I am glad to be out of a Court which is most like--such places as I dare not name to thee."

"But to have you disrespected, sir; you, so brave, so noble! You who gave the best years of your life to your royal master!"

"What I gave I gave, child. I gave him youth--that never comes back--and fortune, that is not worth grieving for. And now that I have begun to lose the reckoning of my years since fifty, I feel I had best take myself back to that roving life in which I have no time to brood upon losses and sorrows."

"Dear father, I am sure you must mistake the King's feelings towards you. It is not possible that he can think lightly of such devotion as yours."

"Nay, sweetheart, who said he thinks lightly? He never thinks of me at all, or of anything serious under God's sky. So long as he has spending money, and can live in a circle of bright eyes, and hear only flippant tongues that offer him a curious incense of flattery spiced with impertinence, Charles Stuart has all of this life that he values. And for the next--a man who is shrewdly suspected of being a papist, while he is attached by gravest vows to the Church of England, must needs hold heaven's rewards and hell's torments lightly."

"But Queen Catherine, sir--does not she favour you? My aunt says she is a good woman."

"Yes, a good woman, and the nearest approach to a cypher to be found at Hampton Court or Whitehall. Young Lord Rochester has written a poem upon 'Nothing.' He might have taken Queen Catherine's name as a synonym. She is nothing; she counts for nothing. Her love can benefit nobody; her hatred, were the poor soul capable of hating persistently, can do no one harm."

"And the King--is he so unkind to her?"

"Unkind! No. He allows her to live. Nay, when for a few days--the brief felicity of her poor life--she seemed on the point of dying, he was stricken with remorse for all that he had not been to her, and was kind, and begged her to live for his sake. The polite gentleman meant it for a compliment--one of those pious falsehoods that men murmur in dying ears--but she took him at his word and recovered; and she is there still, a little dark lady in a fine gown, of whom nobody takes any notice, beyond the emptiest formality of bent knees and backward steps. There are long evenings at Hampton Court in which she is scarce spoken to, save when she fawns upon the fortunate lady whom she began by hating. Oh, child, I should not talk to you of these things; but some of the disgust that has made my life bitter bubbles over in spite of me. I am a wanderer and an exile again, dear heart. I would sooner trail a pike abroad than suffer neglect at home. I will fight under any flag so long as it flies not for my country's foe. I am going back to my old friends at the Louvre, to those few who are old enough to care for me; and if there come a war with Spain, why my sword may be of some small use to young Louis, whose mother was always gracious to me in the old days at St. Germain, when she knew not in the morning whether she would go safe to bed at night. A golden age of peace has followed that wild time; but the Spanish king's death is like to light the torch and set the war-dogs barking. Louis will thrust his sword through the treaty of the Pyrenees if he see the way to a throne t'other side of the mountains."

"But could a good man violate a treaty?"

"Ambition knows no laws, sweet, nor ever has since Hannibal."

"Then King Louis is no better a man than King Charles?"

"I cannot answer for that, Angela; but I'll warrant him a better king from the kingly point of view. Scarce had death freed him from the Cardinal's leading-strings than he snatched the reins of power, showed his ministers that he meant to drive the coach. He has a head as fit for business as if he had been the son of a woollen-draper. Mazarin took pains to keep him ignorant of everything that a king ought to know; but that shrewd judgment of his taught him that he must know as much as his servants, unless he wanted them to be his masters. He has the pride of Lucifer, with a strength of will and power of application as great as Richelieu's. You will live to see that no second Richelieu, no new Mazarin, will arise in his reign. His ministers will serve him, and go down before him, like Nicolas Fouquet, to whom he has been implacable."

"Poor gentleman! My aunt told me that when his judges sentenced him to banishment from France, the King changed the sentence to imprisonment for life."

"I doubt if the King ever forgave those fetes at Vaux, which were designed to dazzle Mademoiselle la Valliere, whom this man had the presumption to love. One may pity so terrible a fall, yet it is but the ruin of a bold sensualist, who played with millions as other men play with tennis balls, and who would have drained the exchequer by his briberies and extravagances if he had not been brought to a dead stop. The world has been growing wickeder, dearest, while this fair head has risen from my knee to my shoulder; but what have you to do with its wickedness? Here you are happy and at peace----"

"Not happy, father, if you are to hazard your life in battles and sieges. Oh, sir, that life is too dear to us, your children, to be risked so lightly. You have done your share of soldiering. Everybody that ever heard your name in England or in France knows it is the name of a brave captain--a leader of men. For our sakes, take your rest now, dear sir. I should not sleep in peace if I knew you were with Conde's army. I should dream of you wounded and dying. I cannot bear to think of leaving my aunt now that she is old and feeble; but my first duty is to you, and if you want me I will go with you wherever you may please to make your home. I am not afraid of strange countries."

"Spoken like my sweet daughter, whose baby arms clasped my neck in the day of despair. But you must stay with the reverend mother, sweetheart. These bones of mine must be something stiffer before they will consent to rest in the chimney corner, or sit in the shade of a yew hedge while other men throw the bowls. When I have knocked about the world a few years longer, and when Mother Anastasia is at rest, thou shalt come to me at the Manor, and I will find thee a noble husband, and will end my days with my children and grandchildren. The world has so changed since the forties, that I shall think I have lived centuries instead of decades, when the farewell hour strikes. In the mean time I am pleased that you should be here. The Court is no place for a pure maiden, though some sweet saints there be who can walk unsmirched in the midst of corruption."

"And Hyacinth? She can walk scatheless through that Court furnace. She writes of Whitehall as if it were Paradise."

"Hyacinth has a husband to take care of her; a man with a brave headpiece of his own, who lets her spark it with the fairest company in the town, but would make short work of any fop who dared attempt the insolence of a suitor. Hyacinth has seen the worst and the best of two Courts, and has an experience of the Palais Royal and St. Germain which should keep her safe at Whitehall."

Sir John and his daughter spent half a day together in the garden and the parlour, where the traveller was entertained with a collation and a bottle of excellent Beaujolais before his horse was brought to the door. Angela saw him mount, and ride slowly away in the melancholy afternoon light, and she felt as if he were riding out of her life for ever. She went back to her aunt's room with an aching heart. Had not that kind lady, her mother in all the essentials of maternal love, been so near the end of her days, and so dependent on her niece's affection, the girl would have clung about her father's neck, and implored him to go no more a-soldiering, and to make himself a home with her in England.

CHAPTER IV.
THE VALLEY OF THE SHADOW.

The reverend mother lingered till the beginning of summer, and it was on a lovely June evening, while the nightingales were singing in the convent garden, that the holy life slipped away into the Great Unknown. She died as a child falls asleep, the saintly grey head lying peacefully on Angela's supporting arm, the last look of the dying eyes resting on that tender nurse with infinite love.

She was gone, and Angela felt strangely alone. Her contemporaries, the chosen friend who had been to her almost as a sister, the girls by whose side she had sat in class, had all left the convent. At twenty-one years of age, she seemed to belong to a former generation; most of the pupils had finished their education at seventeen or eighteen, and had returned to their homes in Flanders, France, or England. There had been several English pupils, for Louvain and Douai had for a century been the seminaries for English Romanists.

The pupils of to-day were Angela's juniors, with whom she had nothing in common, except to teach English to a class of small Flemings, who were almost unteachable.

She had heard no more from her father, and knew not where or with whom he might have cast in his lot. She wrote to him under cover to her sister; but of late Hyacinth's letters had been rare and brief, only long enough, indeed, to apologise for their brevity. Lady Fareham had been in London or at Hampton Court from the beginning of the previous winter. There was talk of the plague having come to London from Amsterdam, that the Privy Council was sitting at Sion House, instead of in London, that the judges had removed to Windsor, and that the Court might speedily remove to Salisbury or Oxford. "And if the Court goes to Oxford, we shall go to Chilton," wrote Hyacinth; and that was the last of her communications.

July passed without news from father or sister; and Angela grew daily more uneasy about both. The great horror of the plague was in the air. It had been raging in Amsterdam in the previous summer and autumn, and a nun had brought the disease to Louvain, where she might have died in the convent infirmary but for Angela's devoted attention. She had assisted the over-worked infirmarian at a time of unusual sickness--for there was a good deal of illness among the nuns and pupils that summer--mostly engendered of the fear lest the pestilence in Holland should reach Flanders. Doctor and infirmarian had alike praised the girl's quiet courage, and her instinct for doing the right thing.

Remembering all the nun had told of the horrors of Amsterdam, Angela awaited with fear and trembling for news from London; and as the summer wore on, every news-letter that reached the Ursulines brought tidings of increasing sickness in the great prosperous city, which was being gradually deserted by all who could afford to travel. The Court had moved first to Hampton Court, in June, and later to Salisbury, where again the French Ambassador's people reported strange horrors--corpses found lying in the street hard by their lodgings--the King's servants sickening. The air of the cathedral city was tainted--though deaths had been few as compared with London, which was becoming one vast lazar-house--and it was thought the Court and Ambassadors would remove themselves to Oxford, where Parliament was to assemble in the autumn, instead of at Westminster.

Most alarming of all was the news that the Queen-mother had fled with all her people, and most of her treasures, from her palace at Somerset House--for Henrietta Maria was not a woman to fly before a phantom fear. She had seen too much of the stern realities of life to be scared by shadows; and she had neither establishment nor power in France equal to those she left in England. In Paris the daughter of the great Henry was a dependent. In London she was second only to the King; and her Court was more esteemed than Whitehall.

"If she has fled, there must be reason for it," said the newly elected Superior, who boasted of correspondents at Paris, notably a cousin in that famous convent, the Visitandines de Chaillot, founded by Queen Henrietta, and which had ever been a centre of political and religious intrigue, the most fashionable, patrician, exalted, and altogether worldly establishment.

Alarmed at this dismal news, Angela wrote urgently to her sister, but with no effect; and the passage of every day, with occasional rumours of an increasing death-rate in London, strengthened her fears, until terror nerved her to a desperate resolve. She would go to London to see her sister; to nurse her if she were sick; to mourn for her if she were dead.

The Superior did all she could to oppose this decision, and even asserted authority over the pupil who, since her eighteenth year had been released from discipline, subject but to the lightest laws of the convent. As the great-niece and beloved child of the late Superior she had enjoyed all possible privileges; while the liberal sum annually remitted for her maintenance gave her a certain importance in the house.

And now on being told she must not go, her spirit rose against the Superior's authority.

"I recognise no earthly power that can keep me from those I love in their time of peril!" she said.

"You do not know that they are in sickness or danger. My last letters from Paris stated that it was only the low people whom the contagion in London was attacking."

"If it was only the low people, why did the Queen-mother leave? If it was safe for my sister to be in London it would have been safe for the Queen."

"Lady Fareham is doubtless in Oxfordshire."

"I have written to Chilton Abbey as well as to Fareham House, and I can get no answer. Indeed, reverend mother, it is time for me to go to those to whom I belong. I never meant to stay in this house after my aunt's death. I have only been waiting my father's orders. If all be well with my sister I shall go to the Manor Moat, and wait his commands quietly there. I am home-sick for England."

"You have chosen an ill time for home-sickness, when a pestilence is raging."

Argument could not touch the girl, whose mind was braced for battle. The reverend mother ceded with as good a grace as she could assume, on the top of a very arbitrary temper. An English priest was heard of who was about to travel to London on his return to a noble friend and patron in the north of England, in whose house he had lived before the troubles; and in this good man's charge Angela was permitted to depart, on a long and weary journey by way of Antwerp and the Scheldt. They were five days at sea, the voyage lengthened by the almost unprecedented calm which had prevailed all that fatal summer--a weary voyage in a small trading vessel, on board which Angela had to suffer every hardship that a delicate woman can be subjected to on board ship: a wretched berth in a floating cellar called a cabin, want of fresh water, of female attendance, and of any food but the coarsest. These deprivations she bore without a murmur. It was only the slowness of the passage that troubled her.

The great city came in view at last, the long roof of St. Paul's dominating the thickly clustered gables and chimneys, and the vessel dropped anchor opposite the dark walls of the Tower, whose form had been made familiar to Angela by a print in a History of London, which she had hung over many an evening in Mother Anastasia's parlour. A row-boat conveyed her and her fellow-traveller to the Tower stairs, where they landed, the priest being duly provided with an efficient voucher that they came from a city free of the plague. Yes, this was London. Her foot touched her native soil for the first time after fifteen years of absence. The good-natured priest would not leave her till he had seen her in charge of an elderly and most reputable waterman, recommended by the custodian of the stairs. Then he bade her an affectionate adieu, and fared on his way to a house in the city, where one of his kinsfolk, a devout Catholic, dwelt quietly hidden from the public eye, and where he would rest for the night before setting out on his journey to the north.

After the impetuous passage through the deep, dark arch of the bridge, the boat moved slowly up the river in the peaceful eventide, and Angela's eyes opened wide with wonder as she looked on the splendours of that silent highway, this evening verily silent, for the traffic of business and pleasure had stopped in the terror of the pestilence, like a clock that had run down. It was said by one who had seen the fairest cities of Europe that "the most glorious sight in the world, take land and water together, was to come upon a high tide from Gravesend, and shoot the bridge to Westminster;" and to the convent-bred maiden how much more astonishing was that prospect!

The boat passed in front of Lord Arundel's sumptuous mansion, with its spacious garden, where marble statues showed white in the midst of quincunxes, and prim hedges of cypress and yew; past the Palace of the Savoy, with its massive towers, battlemented roof, and double line of mullioned windows fronting the river; past Worcester House, where Lord Chancellor Hyde had been living in a sober splendour, while his princely mansion was building yonder on the Hounslow Road, or that portion thereof lately known as Piccadilly. That was the ambitious pile of which Hyacinth had written, a house of clouded memories and briefest tenure; foredoomed to vanish like a palace seen in a dream; a transient magnificence, indescribable; known for a little while opprobriously as Dunkirk House, the supposed result of the Chancellor's too facile assistance in the surrender of that last rag of French territory. The boat passed before Rutland House and Cecil House, some portion of which had lately been converted into the Middle Exchange, the haunt of fine ladies and Golconda of gentlewomen milliners, favourite scene for assignations and intrigues; and so by Durham House, where in the Protector Seymour's time the Royal Mint had been established; a house whose stately rooms were haunted by tragic associations, shadows of Northumberland's niece and victim, hapless Jane Grey, and of fated Raleigh. Here, too, commerce shouldered aristocracy, and the

New Exchange of King James's time competed with the Middle Exchange of later date, providing more milliners, perfumers, glovers, barbers, and toymen, and more opportunity for illicit loves and secret meetings.

Before Angela's eyes those splendid mansions passed like phantom pictures. The westering sunlight showed golden above the dark Abbey, while she sat silent, with awe-stricken gaze, looking out upon this widespread city that lay chastened and afflicted under the hand of an angry God. The beautiful, gay, proud, and splendid London of the West, the new London of Covent Garden, St. James's Street, and Piccadilly, whose glories her sister's pen had depicted with such fond enthusiasm, was now deserted by the rabble of quality who had peopled its palaces, while the old London of the East, the historic city, was sitting in sackcloth and ashes, a place of lamentations, a city where men and women rose up in the morning hale and healthy, and at night-fall were carried away in the dead-cart, to be flung into the pit where the dead lay shroudless and unhonoured.

How still and sweet the summer air seemed in that sunset hour; how placid the light ripple of the incoming tide; how soothing even the silence of the city! And yet it all meant death. It was but a few months since the fatal infection had been brought from Holland in a bundle of merchandise: and, behold, through city and suburbs, the pestilence had crept with slow and stealthy foot, now on this side of a street, now on another. The history of the plague was like a game at draughts, where man after man vanishes off the board, and the game can only end by exhaustion.

"See, mistress, yonder is Somerset House," said the boatman, pointing to one of the most commanding facades in that highway of palaces. "That is the palace which the Queen-mother has raised from the ashes of the ruins her folly made, for the husband who loved her too well. She came back to us no wiser for years of exile--came back with her priests and her Italian singing-boys, her incense-bearers and golden candlesticks and gaudy rags of Rome. She fled from England with the roar of cannon in her ears, and the fear of death in her heart. She came back in pride and vain-glory, and boasted that had she known the English people better, she would never have gone away; and she has squandered thousands in yonder palace, upon floors of coloured woods, and Italian marbles--the people's money, mark you, money that should have built ships and fed sailors; and she meant to end her days among us. But a worse enemy than Cromwell has driven her out of the house that she made beautiful for herself; and who knows if she will ever see London again?"

"Then those were right who told me that it was for fear of the plague her Majesty left London?" said Angela.

"For what else should she flee? She was loth enough to leave, you may be sure, for she had seated herself in her pride yonder, and her Court was as splendid, and more looked up to than Queen Catherine's. The Queen-mother is the prouder woman, and held her head higher than her son's wife has ever dared to hold hers; yet there are those who say King Charles's widow has fallen so low as to marry Lord St. Albans, a son of Belial, who would hazard his immortal soul on a cast of the dice, and lose it as freely as he has squandered his royal mistress's money. She paid for Jermyn's feasting and wine-bibbing in Paris, 'tis said, when her son and his friends were on short commons."

"You do wrong to slander that royal lady," remonstrated Angela. "She is of all widows the saddest and most desolate--ever the mark of evil fortune. Even in the glorious year of her son's restoration sorrow pursued her, and she had to mourn a daughter and a son. She is a most unhappy lady."

"You would scarcely say as much, young madam, had you seen her in her pomp and power yonder. And as for Lord St. Albans, if he is not her husband--! Well, thou art a young innocent thing--so I had best hold my peace. Both palaces are empty and forsaken, both Whitehall and Somerset House. The rats and the spiders can take their own pleasure in the rooms that were full of music and dancing, card-playing and feasting, two or three months ago. Why, there was no better sight in London, after the dead-cart, than to watch the train of carriages and horsemen, carts and wagons, upon any of the great high-roads, carrying the people of London away to the country, as if the whole city had been moving in one mass like a routed army."

"But in palaces and noblemen's houses surely there would be little danger?" said Angela. "Plagues and fevers are the outcome of hunger and uncleanliness, and all such evils as the poor have to suffer."

"Nay, but the pestilence that walketh in darkness is no respecter of persons," answered the grim boatman. "I grant you that death has dealt hardest with the poor who dwell in crowded lanes and alleys. But now the very air reeks with poison. It may be carried in the folds of a woman's gown, or among the feathers of a courtier's hat. They are wise to go who can go. It is only such as I, who have to work for my grandchildren's bread, that must needs stay."

"You speak like one who has seen better days," said Angela.

"I was a sergeant in Hampden's regiment, madam, and went all through the war. When the King came back I had friends who stood by me, and bought me this boat. I was used to handle an oar in my boyhood, when I lived on a little bit of a farm that belonged to my father, between Reading and Henley. I was oftener on the water than on the land in those days. There are some who have treated me roughly because I fought against the late King; but folks are beginning to find out that the Brewer's disbanded red-coats can be honest and serviceable in time of peace."

After passing the Queen-mother's desolate palace the boat crept along near the Middlesex shore, till it stopped at the bottom of a flight of stone steps, against which the tide washed with a pleasant rippling sound, and above which there rose the walls of a stately building facing south-west; small as compared with Somerset and Northumberland houses, midway between which it stood, yet a spacious and noble mansion, with a richly decorated river-front, lofty windows with sculptured pediments, floriated cornice, and two side towers topped with leaded cupolas, the whole edifice gilded by the low sun, and very beautiful to look upon, the windows gleaming as if there were a thousand candles burning within, a light that gave a false idea of life and festivity, since that brilliant illumination was only a reflected glory.

"This, madam, is Fareham House," said the boatman, holding out his hand for his fee.

He charged treble the sum he would have asked half a year ago. In this time of evil those intrepid spirits who still plied their trades in the tainted city demanded a heavy fee for their labour; and it would have been hard to dispute their claim, since each man knew that he risked his life, and that the limbs which toiled to-day might be lifeless clay to-night. There was an awfulness about the time, a taste and odour of death mixed with all the common things of daily life, a morbid dwelling upon thoughts of corruption, a feverish expectancy of the end of all things, which no man can rightly conceive who has not passed through the Valley of the Shadow of Death.

Angela paid the man his price without question. She stepped lightly from the boat, while he deposited her two small leather-covered trunks on the stone landing-place in front of the Italian terrace which occupied the whole length of the facade. She went up a flight of marble steps, to a door facing the river. Here she rang a bell which pealed long and loud over the quiet water, a bell that must have been heard upon the Surrey shore. Yet no one opened the great oak door; and Angela had a sudden sinking at the heart as the slow minutes passed and brought no sound of footsteps within, no scrooping of a bolt to betoken the opening of the door.

"Belike the house is deserted, madam," said the boatman, who had moored his wherry to the landing-stage, and had carried the two trunks to the doorstep. "You had best try if the door be fastened or no. Stay!" he cried suddenly, pointing upwards, "Go not in, madam, for your life! Look at the red cross on the door, the sign of a plague-stricken house."

Angela looked up with awe and horror. A great cross was smeared upon the door with red paint, and above it some one had scrawled the words, "Lord, have mercy upon us!"

And the sister she loved, and the children whose faces she had never seen, were within that house, sick and in peril of death, perhaps dying--or dead! She did not hesitate for an instant, but took hold of the heavy iron ring which served as a handle for the door and tried to open it.

"I have no fear for myself," she said to the boatman; "I have nursed the sick and the fever-stricken, and am not afraid of contagion--and there are those within whom I love. Good night, friend."

The handle of the door turned somewhat stiffly in her hand, but it did turn, and the door opened, and she stood upon the threshold looking into a vast hall that was wrapped in shadow, save for a shaft of golden light that streamed from an oval window on the staircase. Other windows there were on each side of the door, shuttered and barred.

Seeing her enter the house, the old Cromwellian shrugged his shoulders, shook his head despondently, shoved the two trunks hastily over the threshold, ran back to his boat, and pushed off.

"God guard thy young life, mistress!" he cried, and the wherry shot out into the stream.

There had been silence on the river, the silence of a deserted city at eventide; but that had seemed as nothing to the stillness of this marble-paved hall, where the sunset was reflected on the dark oak panelling in one lurid splash like blood.

Not a mortal to be seen. Not a sound of voice or footstep. A crowd of gods and goddesses in draperies of azure and crimson, purple and orange, looked down from the ceiling. Curtains of tawny velvet hung beside the shuttered windows. A great brazen candelabrum, filled with half-consumed candles, stood tall and splendid at the foot of a wide oak staircase, the banister-rail whereof was cushioned with tawny velvet. Splendour of fabric, wood and marble, colour and gilding, showed on every side; but of humanity there was no sign.

Angela shuddered at the sight of all that splendour, as if death were playing hide and seek in those voluminous curtains, or were lurking in the deep shadow which the massive staircase cast across the hall. She looked about her, full of fear, then seeing a silver bell upon the table, she took it up and rang it loudly. Upon the same carved ebony table there lay a plumed hat, a cane with an amber handle, and a velvet cloak neatly folded, as if placed ready for the master of the house, when he went abroad; but looking at these things closely, even in that dim light, she saw that cloak and hat were white with dust, and, more even than the silence, that spectacle of the thick dust on the dark velvet impressed her with the idea of a deserted house.

She had no lack of courage, this pupil of the Flemish nuns, and her footstep did not falter as she went quickly up the broad staircase until she found herself in a spacious gallery, and amidst a flood of light, for the windows on this upper or noble floor were all unshuttered, and the sunset streamed in through the lofty Italian casements. Fareham House was built upon the plan of the Hotel de Rambouillet, of which the illustrious Catherine de Vivonne was herself at once owner and architect. The staircase, instead of being a central feature, was at the western end of the house, allowing space for an unbroken suite of rooms communicating one with the other, and terminating in an apartment with a fine oriel window looking east.

The folding doors of a spacious saloon stood wide open, and Angela entered a room whose splendour was a surprise to her who had been accustomed to the sober simplicity of a convent parlour and the cold grey walls of the refectory, where the only picture was a pinched and angular Virgin by Memling, and the only ornament a crucifix of ebony and brass.

Here for the first time she beheld a saloon for whose decoration palaces had been ransacked and churches desecrated--the stolen treasures of many an ancestral mansion, spoil of rough soldiery or city rabble, things that had been slyly stowed away by their possessors during the stern simplicity of the Commonwealth, and had been brought out of their hiding-places and sold to the highest bidder. Gold and silver had been melted down in the Great Rebellion; but art treasures would not serve to pay soldiers or to buy ammunition; so these had escaped the melting-pot. At home and abroad the storehouses of curiosity merchants had been explored to beautify Lady Fareham's reception-rooms; and in the fading light Angela gazed upon hangings that were worthy of a royal palace, upon Italian crystals and Indian carvings, upon ivory and amber and jade and jasper, upon tables of Florentine mosaic, and ebony cabinets incrusted with rare agates, and upon pictures in frames of massive and elaborate carving, Venetian mirrors which gave back the dying light from a thousand facets, curtains and portieres of sumptuous brocade, gold-embroidered, gorgeous with the silken semblance of peacock plumage, done with the needle, from the royal manufactory of the Crown Furniture at the Gobelins.

She passed into an ante-room, with tapestried walls, and a divan covered with raised velvet, a music desk of gilded wood, and a spinet, on which was painted the story of Orpheus and Eurydice. Beyond this there was the dining-room, more soberly though no less richly furnished than the saloon. Here the hangings were of Cordovan leather, stamped and gilded with *fleur-de-lys*, suggesting a French origin, and indeed these very hangings had been bought by a Dutch Jew dealer in the time of the Fronde, had belonged to the hated minister Mazarin, and had been sold among other of his effects when he fled from Paris: to vanish for a brief season behind the clouds of public animosity, and to blaze out again, an elderly phoenix, in a new palace, adorned with new treasures of art and industry that made royal princes envious.

Angela gazed on all this splendour as one bewildered. In front of that gilded wall, quivering in mid-air, as if it had been painted upon the shaft of light that streamed in from the tall window, her fancy pictured the blood-red cross and the piteous legend, "Lord, have mercy on us!" written in the same blood colour. For herself she had neither horror of the pestilence nor fear of death. Religion had familiarised her mind with the image of the destroyer. From her childhood she had been acquainted with the grave, and with visions of a world beyond the grave. It was not for herself she trembled, but for her sister, and her sister's children; for

Lord Fareham, whose likeness she recalled even at this moment, the grave dark face which Hyacinth had shown her on the locket she wore upon her neck, the face which Sir John said reminded him of Strafford.

"He has just that fatal look," her father had told her afterwards when they talked of Fareham, "the look that men saw in Wentworth's face when he came from Ireland, and in his Majesty's countenance, after Wentworth's murder."

While she stood in the dying light, wavering for a moment, doubtful which way to turn--since the room had no less than three tall oak doors, two of them ajar--there came a pattering upon the polished floor, a scampering of feet that were lighter and quicker than those of the smallest child, and the first living creature Angela saw in that silent house came running towards her. It was only a little black-and-tan spaniel, with long silky hair and drooping ears, and great brown eyes, fond and gentle, a very toy and trifle in the canine kingdom; yet the sight of that living thing thrilled her awe-stricken heart, and her tears came thick and fast as she knelt and took the little dog in her arms and pressed him against her bosom, and kissed the cold muzzle, and looked, half laughing, half crying, into the pathetic brown eyes.

"At least there is life near. This dog would not be left in a deserted house," she thought, as the creature trembled against her bosom and licked the hand that held him.

The pattering was repeated in the adjoining room, and another spaniel, which might have been twin brother of the one she held, came through the half open door, and ran to her, and set up a jealous barking which reverberated in the lofty room, and from within that unseen chamber on the other side of the door there came a groan, a deep and hollow sound, as of mortal agony.

She set down the dog in an instant, and was on her feet again, trembling but alert. She pushed the door a little wider and went into the next apartment, a bed-room more splendid than any bed-chamber her fancy had ever depicted when she read of royal palaces.

The walls were hung with Mortlake tapestries, representing in four great panels the story of Perseus and Andromeda, and the Rape of Proserpine. To her who knew not the old Greek fables those figures looked strangely diabolical. Naked maiden and fiery dragon, flying horse and Greek hero, Demeter and Persephone, hell-god and chariot, seemed alike demonaic and unholy, seen in the dim light of expiring day. The high chimney-piece, with its Oriental jars, blood-red and amber, faced her as she entered the room, and opposite the three tall windows stood the state bed, of carved ebony, the posts adorned with massive bouquets of chased silver flowers, the curtains of wine coloured velvet, heavy with bullion fringes. One curtain had been looped back, showing the amber satin lining, and on this bed of state lay a man, writhing in agony, with one bloodless hand plucking at the cambric upon his bosom, while with the other he grasped the ebony bed-post in a paroxysm of pain.

Angela knew that dark and powerful face at the first glance, though the features were distorted by suffering. This sick man, the sole occupant of a deserted mansion, was her brother-in-law, Lord Fareham. A large high-backed armchair stood beside the bed, and on this Angela seated herself. She recollected the Superior's injunction just in time to put one of the anti-pestilential lozenges into her mouth before she bent over the sufferer, and took his clammy hand in hers, and endured the acrimony of his poisonous breath. That anxious gaze, the dark yellow complexion, and those great beads of sweat that poured down the pinched countenance too plainly indicated the disease which had desolated London. The Moslem's invisible plague-angel had entered this palace, and had touched the master with his deadly lance. That terrible Presence, which for the most part had been found among the dwellings of the poor, was here amidst purple and fine linen, here on this bed of state, enthroned in ebony and silver, hung round with velvet and bullion. She needed not to discover the pestilential spots beneath that semi-diaphanous cambric which hung loose upon the muscular frame, to be convinced of the cruel fact. Here, abandoned and alone, lay the master of the house, with nothing better than a pair of spaniels for his companions, and neither nurse nor watcher, wife nor friend, to help him towards recovery, or to comfort his passing soul.

One of the little dogs leapt on the bed, and licked his master's face again and again, whining piteously between whiles.

The sick man looked at Angela with awful, unseeing eyes, and then burst into a wild laugh--

"See them run, the crop-headed clod-hoppers!" he cried. "Ride after them-- mow them down--scatter the rebel clot-pols! The day is ours!" And then, passing from English to French, from visions of Lindsey and Rupert and the pursuit at Edgehill to memories of Conde and Turenne, he shouted with the voice that was like the sound of a trumpet, "*Boutte-selle! boutte-selle! Monte a cheval! monte a cheval! a l'arme, a l'arme!*"

He was in the field of battle again. His wandering wits had carried him back to his first fight, when he was a lad in his father's company of horse, following the King's fortunes, breathing gunpowder, and splashed with human blood for the first time--when it was not so long since he had been blooded at the death of his first fox. He was a young man again, with the Prince, that Bourbon prince and hero whom he loved and honoured far above any of his own countrymen.

"*O, la folle entreprise du Prince de Conde,*" he sang, waving his hand above his head, while the spaniels barked loud and shrill, adding their clamour to his. He raved of battles and sieges. He was lying in the trenches, in cold and rain and wind--in the tempestuous darkness. He was mounting the breach at Dunkirk against the Spaniard; at Charenton in a hand-to-hand fight with Frondeurs. He raved of Chatillon and Chanleu, and the slaughter of that fatal day when Conde mourned a friend and each side lost a leader. Fever gave force to gesture and voice; but in the midst of his ravings he fell back, half fainting, upon the pillow, his heart beating in a tumult which fluttered the lace upon the bosom of his shirt, while the acrid drops upon his brow gathered thicker than poisonous dew. Angela remembered how last year in Holland these death-like sweats had not always pointed to a fatal result, but in some cases had afforded an outlet to the pestilential influences, though in too many instances they had served only to enfeeble the patient, the fire of disease still burning, while the damps of approaching dissolution oozed from the fevered body--flame within and ice without.

CHAPTER V.
A MINISTERING ANGEL.

Angela flung off hood and mantle, and looked anxiously round the room. There were some empty phials and ointment boxes, some soiled linen rags and wet sponges, upon a table near the bed, and the chamber reeked with the odour of drugs, hartshorn and elder vinegar, cantharides, and aloes; enough to show that a doctor had been there, and that there had been some attempt at nursing the patient. But she had heard how in Holland the nurses had sometimes robbed and abandoned their charges, taking advantage of the confusions and uncertainties of that period of despair, quick and skilful to profit by sudden death, and the fears and agonies of relatives and friends, whose grief made plunder easy. She deemed it likely that one of those devilish women had first pretended to succour, and had then abandoned Lord Fareham to his fate, after robbing his house. Indeed, the open doors of a stately inlaid wardrobe between two windows over against the bed, and the confused appearance of the clothes and linen on the shelves, indicated that it had been ransacked by hasty hands; while, doubtless, there had been many valuables lying loose about a house where there was every indication of a careless profusion.

"Alas! poor gentleman, to be left by some mercenary wretch--left to die like the camel in the desert!"

She bent over him, and laid her hand with gentle firmness upon his death-cold forehead.

"What! are there saints and angels in hell as well as felons and devils?" he cried, clutching her by the wrist, and looking up at her with distended eyes, in which the natural colour of the eye-ball was tarnished almost to blackness with injected blood.

For long and lonely hours, that seemed an eternity, he had been tossing in a burning fever upon that disordered bed, until he verily believed himself in a place of everlasting torment. He had that strange, double sense which goes with delirium--the consciousness of his real surroundings, the tapestry and furniture of his own chamber, and yet the conviction that this was hell, and had always been hell, and that he had descended to this terrible under-world through infinite abysses of darkness. The glow of sunset had been to him the fierce light of everlasting flames; the burning of fever was the fire that is never quenched; the pain that racked his limbs was the worm that dieth not. And now in his torment there came the vision of a seraphic face bending over him in gentle solicitude; a face that brought comfort with it, even in the midst of his agony. After that one wild question he sank slowly back upon the pillows, and lay faint and weak, his breathing scarce audible. Angela laid her fingers on his wrist. The pulse was fluttering and intermittent.

She remembered every detail of her aunt's treatment of the plague-patient in the convent infirmary, and how the turning-point of the malady and beginning of cure had seemed to be brought about by a draught of strong wine which the reverend mother had made her give the poor fainting creature at a crisis of extreme weakness. She looked about the room for any flask which might contain wine; but there was nothing there except the apothecary's phials and medicaments.

It was dusk already, and she was alone in a strange house. It would seem no easy task to find what she wanted, but the case was desperate, and she knew enough of this mysterious disease to know that if the patient could not rally speedily from his prostrate condition the end must be near. With steady brain she set herself to face the difficulty--first to administer something which should sustain the sick man's strength, and then, without loss of time, to seek a physician, and bring him to that deserted bed. Wine was the one thing she could trust to in this crisis; for of the doses and lotions on yonder table she knew nothing, nor had her experience made her a believer in the happy influence of drugs.

Her first search must be for light with which to explore the lower part of the house, where in pantry or stillroom, or, if not above ground, in the cellars, she must find what she wanted. Surely somewhere in that spacious bed-chamber there would be tinder-box and matches. There were a pair of silver candlesticks on the dressing-table, with thick wax candles burnt nearly to the sockets.

A careful search at last discovered a tinder-box and matches in a dark angle of the fireless hearth, hidden behind the heavy iron dog. She struck a light, kindled her match, and lighted a candle, the sick man's eyes following all her movements, but his lips mute. As she went out of the door he called after her--

"Leave me not, thou holy visitant--leave not my soul in hell!"

"I will return!" she cried. "Have no fear, sir; I go to fetch some wine."

Her errand was not done quickly. Amidst all the magnificence she had noted on her journey through the long suite of reception-rooms--the littered treasures of amber and gold, and ivory and porcelain and silver--she had seen only an empty wine-flask; so with quick footfall she ran down the wide, shallow stairs to the lower floor, and here she found herself in a labyrinth of passages opening into small rooms and servants' offices. Here there were darkness and gloom rather than splendour; though in many of those smaller rooms there was a sober and substantial luxury which became the inferior apartments of a palace. She came at last to a room which she took to be the butler's office, where there were dressers with a great array of costly Venetian glass, and a great many pieces of silver--cups, tankards, salvers, and other ornamental plate--in presses behind glazed doors. One of the glass panels had been broken, and the shelves in that press were empty.

Wine there was none to be found in any part of the room; but a small army of empty bottles in a corner of the floor, and a confusion of greasy plates, knives, chicken bones, and other scraps, indicated that there had been carousing here at no remote time.

The cellars were doubtless below these offices; but the wine-cellars would assuredly be locked, and she had to search for the keys. She opened drawer after drawer in the lower part of the presses, and at last, in an inner and secret drawer, found a multitude of keys, some of which were provided with parchment labels, and among these happily were two labelled "Ye great wine cellar, S." and "Ye smaller wine cellar, W."

This was a point gained; but the search had occupied a considerable time. She had yet enough candle to last for about half an hour, and her next business was to find one of those cellars which those keys opened. She was intensely anxious to return to her patient, having heard how in some cases unhappy wretches had leapt from the bed of death and rushed out-of-doors, delirious, half naked, to anticipate their end by a fatal chill.

On her way to the butler's office she had seen a stone archway at the head of a flight of stairs leading down into darkness. By this staircase she hoped to find the wine-cellars, and presently descended, her candlestick in one hand, and the two great keys in the other. As she went down into the stone basement, which was built with the solidity of a dungeon, she heard the plash of the tide, and felt that she was now on a level with the river. Here she found herself again in a labyrinth of passages, with many doors standing ajar. At the end of one passage she came to a locked door, and on trying her keys, found one of them to fit the lock; it was "Ye great wine cellar, S.," and she understood by the initial "S." that the cellar looked south and faced the river.

She turned the heavy key with an effort that strained the slender fingers which held it; but she was unconscious of the pain, and wondered afterwards to see her hand dented and bruised where the iron had wrung it. The clumsy door revolved on massive hinges, and she entered a cellar so large that the light of her candle did not reach the furthermost corners and recesses.

This cellar was built in a series of arches, fitted with stone bins, and in the upper part of one southward-fronting arch there was a narrow grating, through which came the cool breath of evening air and the sound of water lapping against stone. A patch of faint light showed pale against the iron bars, and as Angela looked that way, a great grey rat leapt through the grating, and ran along the topmost bin, making the bottles shiver as he scuttled across them. Then came a thud on the sawdust-covered stones, and she knew that the loathsome thing was on the floor upon which she was standing. She lowered her light shudderingly, and, for the first time since she entered that house of dread, the young brave heart sank with the sickness of fear.

The cellar might swarm with such creatures; the darkness of the fast-coming night might be alive with them! And if yonder dungeon-like door were to swing to and shut with a spring lock, she might perish there in the darkness. She might die the most hideous of deaths, and her fate remain for ever unknown.

In a sudden panic she rushed back to the door, and pushed it wider--pushed it to its extremest opening. It seemed too heavy to be likely to swing back upon its hinges; yet the mere idea of such a contingency appalled her. Remembering her labour in unlocking the door from the outside, she doubted if she could open it from within were it once to close upon that awful vault. And all this time the lapping of the tide against the stone sounded louder, and she saw little spirts of spray flashing against the bars in the lessening light.

She collected herself with an effort, and began her search for the wine. Sack was the wine she had given to the sick nun, and it was that wine for which she looked. Of Burgundy, and claret, labelled "Clary Wine," she found several full bins, and more that were nearly empty. Tokay and other rarer wines were denoted by the parchment labels which hung above each bin; but it was some minutes before she came to a bin labelled "Sherris," which she knew was another name for sack. The bottles had evidently been undisturbed for a long time, for the bin was full of cobweb, and the thick coating of dust upon the glass betokened a respectable age in the wine. She carried off two bottles, one under each arm, and then, with even quicker steps than had brought her to that darksome place, she hastened back to the upper floor, leaving the key in the cellar door, and the door unlocked. There would be time enough to look after Lord Fareham's wine when she had cared for Lord Fareham himself.

His eyes were fixed upon the doorway as she entered. They shone upon her in the dusk with an awful glassiness, as if life's last look had become fixed in death. He did not speak as she drew near the bed, and set the wine bottles down upon the table among the drugs and cataplasms.

She had found a silver-handled corkscrew in the butler's room among the relics of the feast, and with this she opened one of the bottles, Fareham watching her all the time.

"Is that some new alexipharmic?" he asked with a sudden rational air, which was almost as startling as if a dead man had spoken. "I will have no more of their loathsome drugs. They have made an apothecary's shop of my body. I would rather they let me rot by the plague than that they should poison me with their antidotes, or dissolve me to death with their sudorifics."

"This is not a medicine, Lord Fareham, but your own wine; and I want you to drink a long draught of it, and then, who knows but you may sleep off your malady?"

"Ay, sleep in the grave, sweet friend! I have seen the tokens on my breast that mean death. There is but one inevitable end for all who are so marked. 'Tis like the forester's notch upon the tree. It means doom. He was king of the forest once, perhaps; but no matter. His time has come. Oh, Lord, thou hast tormented me with hot burning coals!" he cried, in a sudden access of pain; and in the next minute he was raving.

Angela filled a beaker with the bright golden wine, and offered it to the sick man's lips. It was not without infinite pains and coaxing that she induced him to drink; but, when once his parched lips had tasted the cold liquor, he drank eagerly, as if that strong wine had been a draught of water. He gave a deep sigh of solace when the beaker was empty, for he had been enduring an agony of thirst through all the glare and heat of the afternoon, and there was unspeakable comfort in that first long drink. He would have drunk foul water with almost as keen a relish.

He talked fast and furiously, in the disjointed sentences of delirium, for some little time; and then, little by little, he grew more tranquil; and Angela, sitting beside the bed, with her fingers laid gently on his wrist, marked the quieter beat of the pulse, which no longer fluttered like the wing of a frightened bird. Then with deep thankfulness she saw the eyelids droop over the bloodshot eyeballs, while the breathing grew slower and heavier as sleep clouded the wearied brain. The spaniels crept nearer him, and nestled close to his pillow, so that the man's dark locks were mixed with the silken curls of the dogs.

Would he die in that sleep? she wondered.

It was only now for the first time since she entered this unpeopled house that she had leisure to speculate on the circumstances which had brought about such loneliness and neglect, here where rank and state, and wealth almost without limit should have secured the patient every care and comfort that devoted service could lavish upon a sufferer. How was it that she found her sister's husband abandoned to the care of hirelings, left to the chances of paid service?

To the cloister-reared maiden the idea of wifely duty was elevated almost to a religion. To father or to husband she would have given a boundless devotion, in sickness most of all devoted. To leave husband or father in a plague-stricken city would have seemed to her a crime as abominable as Tullia's, a treachery base as Goneril's or Regan's. Could it be that her sister, that bright and lovely creature, whose face she remembered as a sunbeam incarnate, could she have been swept away by the pestilence which spared neither youth nor beauty, neither the strong man nor the weakling child? Her heart grew heavy as lead at the thought that this stranger, by whose pillow she was watching, might be the sole survivor in that forsaken palace, and that in a few more hours he, too, would be numbered with the dead, in that dreadful city where Death reigned omnipotent, and where the living seemed but a vanishing minority, pale shadows of living creatures passing silently along one inevitable pathway to the pest-house or pit.

That calm sleep of the plague-stricken might mean recovery, or it might mean death. Angela examined the potions and unguents on the table near the bed, and read the instructions on jars and phials. One was an alexipharmic draught, to be taken the last thing at night, another a sudorific, to be administered once in every hour.

"I would not wake him to give him the finest medicine that ever physician prescribed," Angela said to herself. "I remember what a happy change one hour of quiet slumber made in Sister Monica, when she was all but dead of a quartan fever. Sleep is God's physic."

She knelt upon a Prie-Dieu chair remote from the bed, knowing that contagion lurked amid those voluminous hangings, beneath that stately canopy with its lustrous satin lining, on which the light of the wax candles was reflected in shining patches as upon a lake of golden water. She had no fear of the pestilence; but an instinctive prudence made her hold herself aloof, now that there was nothing more to be done for the sufferer.

She remained long in prayer, repeating one of those litanies which she had learnt in her infancy, and which of late had seemed to her to have somewhat too set and mechanical a rhythm. The earnestness and fervour seemed to have gone out of them in somewise since she had come to womanhood. The names of the saints her lips invoked were dull and cold, and evolved no image of human or superhuman love and power. What need of intercessors whose personality was vague and dim, whose earthly histories were made up of truth so interwoven with fable that she scarce dared believe even that which might be true? In the One Crucified was help for all sinners, gospel and creed, the rule of life here, the promise of immortality hereafter.

The litanies to Virgin and Saints were said as a duty--a part of implicit obedience which was the groundwork of her religion; and then all the aspirations of her heart, her prayers for the sick man yonder, her fears for her absent sister, for her father in his foreign wanderings, went up in one stream of invocation to Christ the Redeemer. To Him, and Him alone, the strong flame of faith and love rose, like the incense upon an altar--the altar of a girl's trusting heart.

She was so lost in meditation that she was unconscious of an approaching footstep in the stillness of the deserted house, till it drew near to the threshold of the sick-room. The night was close and sultry, so she had left the door open, and that slow tread had crossed the threshold by the time she rose from her knees. Her heart beat fast, startled by the first human presence which she had known in that melancholy place, save the presence of the pest-stricken sufferer.

She found herself face to face with a middle-aged gentleman of medium stature, clad in the sober colouring that suggested one of the learned professions. He appeared even more startled than Angela at the unexpected vision which met his gaze, faintly seen in the dim light.

There was silence for a few moments, and then the stranger saluted the lady with a formal reverence, as he laid down his gold-handled cane.

"Surely, madam, this mansion of my Lord Fareham's must be enchanted," he said. "I left a crowd of attendants, and the stir of life below and above stairs, only this forenoon last past. I find silence and vacancy. That is scarce strange in this dejected and unhappy time; for it is but too common a trick of hireling nurses to abandon their patients, and for servants to plunder and then desert a sick house. But to find an angel where I left a hag! That is the miracle! And an angel who has brought healing, if I mistake not," he added, in a lower voice, bending over the speaker.

"I am no angel, sir, but a weak, erring mortal," answered the girl, gravely. "For pity's sake, kind doctor--since I doubt not you are my lord's physician--tell me where are my dearest sister, Lady Fareham, and her children. Tell me the worst, I entreat you!"

"Sweet lady, there is no ill news to tell. Her ladyship and the little ones are safe at my lord's house in Oxfordshire, and it is only his lordship yonder who has fallen a victim to the contagion. Lady Fareham and her girl and boy have not been in London since the plague began to rage. My lord had business in the city, and came hither alone. He and the young Lord Rochester, who is the most audacious infidel this town can show, have been bidding defiance to the pestilence, deeming their nobility safe from a sickness which has for the most part chosen its victims among the vulgar."

"His lordship is very ill, I fear, sir?" said Angela interrogatively.

"I left him at eleven o'clock this morning with but scanty hope of finding him alive after sundown. The woman I left to nurse him was his house-steward's wife, and far above the common kind of plague-nurse. I did not think she would turn traitor."

"Her husband has proved a false steward. The house has been robbed of plate and valuables, as I believe, from signs I saw below stairs; and I suppose husband and wife went off together."

"Alack! madam, this pestilence has brought into play some of the worst attributes of human nature. The tokens and loathly boils which break out upon the flesh of the plague-stricken are less revolting to humanity than the cruelty of those who minister to the sick, and whose only desire is to profit by the miseries that surround them; wretches so vile that they have been known wilfully to convey the seeds of death from house to house, in order to infect the sound, and so enlarge their area of gains. It was an artful device of those plunderers to paint the red cross on the door, and thus scare away any visitor who might have discovered their depredations. But you, madam, a being so young and fragile, have you no fear of the contagion?"

"Nay, sir, I know that I am in God's hand. Yonder poor gentleman is not the first plague-patient I have nursed. There was a nun came from Holland to our convent at Louvain last year, and had scarce been one night in the house before tokens of the pestilence were discovered upon her. I helped the infirmarian to nurse her, and with God's help we brought her round. My aunt, the reverend mother, bade me give her the best wine there was in the house--strong Spanish wine that a rich merchant had given to the convent for the use of the sick--and it was as though that good wine drove the poison from her blood. She recovered by the grace of God after only a few days' careful nursing. Finding his lordship stricken with such great weakness, I ventured to give him a draught of the best sack I could find in his cellar."

"Dear lady, thou art a miracle of good sense and compassionate bounty. I doubt thou hast saved thy sister from widow's weeds," said Dr. Hodgkin, seated by the bed, with his fingers on the patient's wrist, and his massive gold watch in the other hand. "This sound sleep promises well, and the pulse beats somewhat slower and steadier than it did this morning. Then the case seemed hopeless, and I feared to give wine--though a free use of generous wine is my particular treatment--lest it should fly to his brain, and disturb his intellectuals at a time when he should need all his senses for the final disposition of his affairs. Great estates sometimes hang upon the breath of a dying man."

"Oh, sir, but your patient! To save his life, that would sure be your first and chiefest thought?"

"Ay, ay, my pretty miss; but I had other measures. Apollo twangs not ever on the same bowstring. Did my sudorific work well, think you?"

"He was bathed in perspiration when first I found him; but the sweat-drops seemed cold and deadly, as if life itself were being dissolved out of him."

"Ay, there are cases in which that copious sweat is the forerunner of dissolution; but in others it augurs cure. The pent-up poison which is corrupting the patient's blood finds a sudden vent, its virulence is diluted, and if the end prove fatal, it is that the patient lacks power to rally after the ravages of the disease, rather than that the poison kills. Was it instantly after that profuse sweat you gave him the wine, I wonder?"

"It was as speedily as I could procure it from the cellar below."

"And that strong wine, given in the nick of time, reassembled Nature's scattered forces, and rekindled the flame of life. Upon my soul, sweet young lady, I believe thou hast saved him! All the drugs in Bucklersbury could do no more. And now tell me what symptoms you have noted since you have watched by his bed; and tell me further if you have strength to continue his nurse, with such precautions as I shall dictate, and such help as I can send you in the shape of a stout, honest, serving-wench of mine, and a man to guard the lower part of your house, and fetch and carry for you?"

"I will do everything you bid me, with all my heart, and with such skill as I can command."

"Those delicate fingers were formed to minister to the sick. And you will not shrink from loathsome offices--from the application of cataplasms, from cleansing foul sores? Those blains and boils upon that poor body will need care for many days to come."

"I will shrink from nothing that may be needful for his benefit. I should love to go on nursing him, were it only for my sister's sake. How sorry she would feel to be so far from him, could she but know of his sickness!"

"Yes, I believe Lady Fareham would be sorry," answered the physician, with a dry little laugh; "though there are not many married ladies about Rowley's court of whom I would diagnose as much. Not Lady Denham, for instance, that handsome, unprincipled houri, married to a septuagenarian poet, who would rather lock her up in a garret than see her shine at Whitehall; or Lady Castlemaine, whose husband has been uncivil enough to show discontent at a peerage that was not of his own earning; or a dozen others I could name, were not such scandals as these Hebrew to thine innocent ear."

"Nay, sir, my sister has written of Court scandals in many of her letters, and it has grieved me to think her lot should be cast among people of whose reckless doings she tells me with a lively wit that makes sin seem something less than sin."

"There is no such word as 'sin' in Charles Stuart's Court, my dear young lady. It is harder to achieve bad repute nowadays than it was once to be thought a saint. Existence in this town is a succession of bagatelles. Men's lives and women's reputations drift down to the bottomless pit upon a rivulet of epigrams and chansons. You have heard of that Dance of Death, which was one of the nervous diseases of the fifteenth century--a malady which, after beginning with one lively caperer, would infect a whole townspeople, and send an entire population curvetting and prancing, until death stopped them. I sometimes think, when I watch the follies at Whitehall, that those graceful dancers, sliding upon pointed toe through a coranto, amid a blaze of candles and star-shine of diamonds, are capering along the same fatal road by which St. Vitus lured his votaries to the grave. And then I look at Rowley's licentious eye and cynical lip, and think to myself, 'This man's father perished on the scaffold; this man's lovely ancestress paid the penalty of her manifold treacheries after sixteen years' imprisonment; this man has passed through the jaws of death, has left his country a fugitive and a pauper, has returned as if by a miracle, carried back to a throne upon the hearts of his people; and behold him now--saunterer, sybarite, sensualist--strolling through life without one noble aim or one virtuous instinct; a King who traffics in the pride and honour of his country, and would sell her most precious possessions, level her strongest defences, if his cousin and patron t'other side the Channel would but bid high enough.' But a plague on my tongue, dear lady, that it must always be wagging. Not one word more, save for instructions."

Dr. Hodgkin loved talking even better than he loved a fee, and he allowed himself a physician's licence to be prosy; but he now proceeded to give minute directions for the treatment of the patient--the poultices and stoups and lotions which were to reduce the external indications of the contagion, the medicines which were to be given at intervals during the night. Medicine in those days left very little to Nature, and if patients perished it was seldom for want of drugs and medicaments.

"The servant I send you will bring meat and all needful herbs for making a strong broth, with which you will feed the patient once an hour. There are many who hold with the boiling of gold in such a broth, but I will not enter upon the merits of aurum potabile as a fortifiant. I take it that in this case you will find beef and mutton serve your turn. I shall send you from my own larder as much beef as will suffice for to-night's use; and to-morrow your servant must go to the place where the country people sell their goods, butchers' meat, poultry, and garden-stuff; for the butchers' shops of London are nearly all closed, and people scent contagion in any intercourse with their fellow-citizens. You will have, therefore, to look to the country people for your supplies; but of all this my own man will give you information. So now, good night, sweet young lady. It is on the stroke of nine. Before eleven you shall have those who will help and protect you. Meanwhile you had best go downstairs with me, and lock and bolt the great door leading into the garden, which I found ajar."

"There is the door facing the river, too, by which I entered."

"Ay, that should be barred also. Keep a good heart, madam. Before eleven you shall have a sturdy watchman on the premises."

Angela took a lighted candle and followed the physician through the great empty rooms, and down the echoing staircase; under the ceiling where Jove, with upraised goblet, drank to his queen, while all the galaxy of the Greek pantheon circled his imperial throne. Upon how many a festal procession had those Olympians looked down since that famous house-warming, when the colours were fresh from the painter's brush, and when the third Lord Fareham's friend and gossip, King James, deigned to witness the representation of Jonson's "Time Vindicated," enacted by ladies and gentlemen of quality, in the great saloon, a performance which--with the banquet and confectionery brought from Paris, and "the sweet waters which came down the room like a shower from heaven," as one wrote who was present at that splendid entertainment, and the *feux d'artifice* on the river--cost his lordship a year's income, but stamped him at once a fine gentleman. Had he been a trifle handsomer, and somewhat softer of speech, that masque and banquet might have placed Richard Revel, Baron Fareham, in the front rank of royal favourites; but the Revels were always a black-visaged race, with more force than comeliness in their countenances, and more gall than honey upon their tongues.

It was past eleven before the expected succour arrived, and in the interval Lord Fareham had awakened once, and had swallowed a composing draught, having apparently but little consciousness of the hand that administered it. At twenty minutes past eleven Angela heard the bell ring, and ran blithely down the now familiar staircase to open the garden door, outside which she found a middle-aged woman and a tall, sturdy young man, each carrying a bundle. These were the nurse and the watchman sent by Dr. Hodgkin. The woman gave Angela a slip of paper from the doctor, by way of introduction.

"You will find Bridget Basset a worthy woman, and able to turn her hand to anything; and Thomas Stokes is an honest, serviceable youth, whom you may trust upon the premises, till some of his lordship's servants can be sent from Chilton Abbey, where I take it there is a large staff."

It was with an unspeakable relief that Angela welcomed these humble friends. The silence of the great empty house had been weighing upon her spirits, until the sense of solitude and helplessness had grown almost unbearable. Again and again she had watched Lord Fareham turn his feverish head upon his pillow, while the parched lips moved in inarticulate mutterings; and she had thought of what she should do if a stronger delirium were to possess him, and he were to try and do himself some mischief. If he were to start up from his bed and rush through the empty rooms, or burst open one of yonder lofty casements and fling himself headlong to the terrace below! She had been told of the terrible things that plague-patients had done to themselves in their agony; how they had run naked into the streets to perish on the stones of the highway; how they had gashed themselves with knives; or set fire to their bed-clothes, seeking any escape from the torments of that foul disease. She knew that those burning plague-spots, which her hands had dressed, must cause a continual anguish that might wear out the patience of a saint; and as the dark face turned on the tumbled pillow, she saw by the clenched teeth and writhing lips, and the convulsive frown of the strongly marked brows, that even in delirium the sufferer was struggling to restrain all unmanly expressions of his agony. But now, at least, there would be this strong, capable woman to share in the long night watch; and if the patient grew desperate there would be three pair of hands to protect him from his own fury.

She made her arrangements promptly and decisively. Mrs. Basset was to stay all night with her in the patient's chamber, with such needful intervals of rest as each might take without leaving the sick-room; and Stokes was first to see to the fastening of the various basement doors, and to assure himself that there was no one hidden either in the cellars or on the ground floor; also to examine all upper chambers, and lock all doors; and was then to make himself a bed in a dressing closet adjoining

Lord Fareham's chamber, and was to lie there in his clothes, ready to help at any hour of the night, should help be wanted.

CHAPTER VI.
BETWEEN LONDON AND OXFORD.

Three nights and days had gone since Angela first set her foot upon the threshold of Fareham House, and in all that time she had not once gone out into the great city, where dismal silence reigned by day and night, save for the hideous cries of the men with the dead-carts, calling to the inhabitants of the infected houses to bring out their dead, and roaring their awful summons with as automatic a monotony as if they had been hawking some common necessary of life--a dismal cry that was but occasionally varied by the hollow tones of a Puritan fanatic, stalking, gaunt and half clad, along the Strand, and shouting some sentence of fatal bodement from the Hebrew prophets; just as before the siege of Titus there walked through the streets of Jerusalem one who cried, "Woe to the wicked city!" and whose voice could not be stopped but by death.

In those three days and nights the worst symptoms of the contagion were subjugated. But the ravages of the disease had left the patient in a state of weakness which bordered on death; and his nurses were full of apprehension lest the shattered forces of his constitution should fail even in the hour of recovery. The violence of the fever was abated, and the delirium had become intermittent, while there were hours in which the sufferer was conscious and reasonable, in which calmer intervals he would fain have talked with Angela more than her anxiety would allow.

He was full of wonder at her presence in that house; and when he had been told who she was, he wanted to know how and why she had come there. By what happy accident, by what interposition of Providence, had she been sent to save him from a hideous death?

"I should have died but for you," he said. "I should have lain here till the cart fetched my putrid carcase. I should be rotting in one of their plague-pits yonder, behind the old Abbey."

"Nay, indeed, my lord, your good doctor would have discovered your desolate condition, and would have brought Mrs. Basset to nurse you."

"He would have been too late. I was drifting out to the dark sea of death. I felt as if the river were bearing me so much nearer to that unknown sea with every ripple of the hurrying tide. 'Twas your draught of strong wine snatched me back from the cruel river, drew me on to *terra firma* again, renewed my consciousness of manhood, and that I was not a weed to be washed away. Oh, that wine! Ye gods! what elixir to this parched, burning throat! Did ever drunkard in all Alsatia snatch such fierce joy from a brimmer?"

Angela put her finger on her lip, and with the other hand drew the silken coverlet over the sick man's shoulders.

"You are not to talk," she said, "you are to sleep. Slumber is to be your diet and medicine after that good soup at which you make such a wry face."

"I would swallow the stuff were it Locusta's hell-broth, for your sake."

"You will take it for wisdom's sake, that you may mend speedily, and go home to my sister," said Angela.

"Home, yes! It will be bliss ineffable to see flowery pastures and wooded hills after this pest-haunted town; but oh, Angela, mine angel, why dost thou linger in this poisonous chamber where every breath of mine exhales infection? Why do you not fly while you are still unstricken? Truly the plague-fiend cometh as a thief in the night. To-day you are safe. To-night you may be doomed."

"I have no fear, sir. You are not the first plague-patient I have nursed."

"And thou fanciest thyself pestilence-proof! Sweet girl, it may be that the divine lymph which fills those azure veins has no affinity with poisons that slay rude mortals like myself."

"Will you ever be talking?" she said with grave reproach, and left him to the care of Mrs. Basset, whose comfortable and stolid personality did not stimulate his imagination.

She had a strong desire to explore that city of which she had yet seen so little, and her patient being now arrived at a state of his disorder when it was best for him to be tempted to prolonged slumbers by silence and solitude, she put on her hood and gloves and went out alone to see the horrors of the deserted streets, of which nurse Basset had given her so appalling a picture.

It was four o'clock, and the afternoon was at its hottest; the blue of a cloudless sky was reflected in the blue of the silent river, where, instead of the flotilla of gaily painted wherries, the procession of gilded barges, the music and song, the ceaseless traffic of Court and City, there was only the faint ripple of the stream, or here and there a solitary barge creeping slowly down the tide with ineffectual sail napping in the sultry atmosphere.

That unusual calm which had marked this never-to-be-forgotten year, from the beginning of spring, was yet unbroken, and the silent city lay like a great ship becalmed on a tropical ocean; the same dead silence; the same cruel, smiling sky above; the same hopeless submission to fate in every soul on board that death-ship. How would those poor dying creatures, panting out their latest breath in sultry, air-less chambers, have welcomed the rush of rain, the cool freshness of a strong wind blowing along those sun-baked streets, sweeping away the polluted dust, dispersing noxious odours, bringing the pure scents of far-off woodlands, of hillside heather and autumn gorse, the sweetness of the country across the corruption of the town. But at this dreadful season, when storm and rain would have been welcomed with passionate thanksgiving, the skies were brass, and the ground was arid and fiery as the sands of the Arabian desert, while even the grass that grew in the streets, where last year multitudinous feet had trodden, sickened as it grew, and faded speedily from green to yellow.

Pausing on the garden terrace to survey the prospect before she descended to the street, Angela thought of that river as her imagination had depicted it, after reading a letter of Hyacinth's, written so late as last May; the gay processions, the gaudy liveries of watermen and servants, the gilded barges, the sound of viol and guitar, the harmony of voices in part songs, "Go, lovely rose," or "Why so pale and wan, fond lover?" the beauty and the splendour; fair faces under vast plumed hats, those picturesque hats which the maids of honour snatched from each other's heads with giddy laughter, exchanging head-gear here on the royal barge, as they did sometimes walking about the great rooms at Whitehall; the King with his boon companions clustered round him on the richly carpeted dais in the stern, his court-iers and his favoured mistresses; haughty Castlemaine, empres, regnant over the royal heart, false, dissolute, impudent, glorious as Cleopatra when her purple sails bore her down the swift-flowing Cydnus; the wit and folly and gladness. All had vanished like the visions of a dreamer; and there remained but this mourning city, with its closed windows and doors, its watchmen guarding the marked houses, lest disease and death should hold communion with that poor remnant of health and life left in the infected town. Would that fantastic vision of careless, pleasure-loving monarch and butterfly Court ever be realised again? Angela thought not. It seemed to her serious mind that the glory of those wild years since his Majesty's restoration was a delusive and pernicious brightness which could never shine again. That extravagant splendour, that reckless gaiety had borne beneath their glittering surface the seeds of ruin and death. An angry God had stretched out His hand against the wicked city where sin and profaneness sat in the high places. If Charles Stuart and his courtiers ever came back to London they would return sobered and chastened, taught wisdom by adversity. The Puritan spirit would reign once more in the land, and an age of penitence and Lenten self-abasement would succeed the orgies of the Restoration; while the light loves of Whitehall, the noble ladies, the impudent actresses, would vanish into obscurity. Angela's loyal young heart was full of faith in the King. She was ready to believe that his sins were the sins of a man whose head had been turned by the sudden change from exile to a throne, from poverty to wealth, from dependence upon his Bourbon cousin and his friends in Holland to the lavish subsidies of a too-indulgent Commons.

No words could paint the desolation which reigned between the Strand and the City in that fatal summer, now drawing to its melancholy close. More than once in her brief pilgrimage Angela drew back, shuddering, from the embrasure of a door, or the inlet to some narrow alley, at sight of death lying on the threshold, stiff, stark, unheeded; more than once in her progress from the New Exchange to St Paul's she heard the shrill wail of women lamenting for a soul just departed. Death was about and around her. The great bell of the cathedral tolled with an inexorable stroke in the summer stillness, as it had tolled every day through those long months of heat, and drought, and ever-growing fear, and ever-thickening graves.

Eastward there rose the red glare of a great fire, and she feared that some of those old wooden houses in the narrower streets were blazing, but on inquiry of a solitary foot passenger, she learnt that this fire was one of many which had been burning for three days, at street corners and in open spaces, at a great expense of sea-coal, with the hope of purifying the atmosphere and dispersing poisonous gases--but that so far no amelioration had followed upon this outlay and labour.

She came presently to a junction of roads near the Fleet ditch, and saw the huge coal-fire flaming with a sickly glare in the sunshine, tended by a spectral figure, half-clad and hungry-looking, to whom she gave an alms; and at this juncture of ways a great peril awaited her, for there sprang, as it were, out of the very ground, so quickly did they assemble from neighbouring courts and alleys, a throng of mendicants, who clustered round her, with filthy hands outstretched, and shrill voices imploring charity. So wasted were their half-naked limbs, so ghastly and livid their countenances, that they might have all been plague-patients, and Angela recoiled from them in horror.

"Keep your distance, for pity's sake, good friends, and I will give you all the money I carry," she exclaimed, and there was something of command in her voice and aspect, as she stood before them, straight and tall, with pale, earnest face.

They fell off a little way, and waited till she scattered the contents of her purse--small Flemish coin--upon the ground in front of her, where they scrambled for it, snarling and scuffling with each other like dogs fighting for a bone.

Hastening her footsteps after the horror of that encounter, she went by Ludgate Hill to the great cathedral, keeping carefully to the middle of the street, and glancing at the walls and shuttered casements on either side of her, recalling that appalling story which the Italian choir-mistress at the Ursulines had told her of the great plague in Milan--how one morning the walls and doors of many houses in the city had been found smeared with some foul substance, in broad streaks of white and yellow, which was believed to be a poisonous compost carrying contagion to every creature who touched or went within the influence of its mephitic odour; how this thing had happened not once, but many times; until the Milanese believed that Satan himself was the prime mover in this horror, and that there were a company of wretches who had sold themselves to the devil, and were his servants and agents, spreading disease and death through the city. Strange tales were told of those who had seen the foul fiend face to face, and had refused his proffered gold. Innocent men were denounced, and but narrowly escaped being torn limb from limb, or trampled to death, under the suspicion of being concerned in this anointing of the walls, and even the cathedral benches, with plague-poison; yet no death, that the nun could remember, had ever been traced directly to the compost. It was a mysterious terror which struck deep into the hearts of a frightened people, so that at last, against his better reason, and at the repeated prayer of his flock, the good Archbishop allowed the crystal coffin of St. Carlo Borromeo to be carried in solemn procession, upon the shoulders of Cardinals, from end to end of the city--on which occasion all Milan crowded into the streets, and clustered thick on either side of the pompous train of monks and incense-bearers, priests and acolytes. But soon there fell a deeper despair upon the inhabitants of the doomed city; for within two days after this solemn carrying of the saintly remains the death-rate had tripled and there was scarce a house in which the contagion had not entered. Then it was said that the anointers had been in active work in the midst of the crowd, and had been busiest in the public squares where the bearers of the crystal coffin halted for a space with their sacred load, and where the people clustered thickest. The Archbishop had foreseen the danger of this gathering of the people, many but just recovering from the disease, many infected and unconscious of their state; but his flock saw only the handiwork of the fiend in this increase of evil.

In Protestant London there had been less inclination to superstition; yet even here a comet which, under ordinary circumstances, would have appeared but as other comets, was thought to wear the shape of a fiery sword stretched over the city in awful threatening.

Full of pity and of gravest, saddest thoughts, the lonely girl walked through the lonely town to that part of the city where the streets were narrowest, a labyrinth of lanes and alleys, with a church-tower or steeple rising up amidst the crowded dwellings at almost every point to which the eye looked. Angela wondered at the sight of so many fine churches in this heretical land. Many of these city churches were left open in this day of wrath, so that unhappy souls who had a mind to pray might go in at will, and kneel there. Angela peered in at an old church in a narrow court, holding the door a little way ajar, and looking along the cold grey nave. All was gloom and silence, save for a monotonous and suppressed murmur of one invisible worshipper in a pew near the altar, who varied his supplicatory mutterings with long-drawn sighs.

Angela turned with a shudder from the cold emptiness of the great grey church, with its sombre woodwork, and lack of all those beautiful forms which appeal to the heart and imagination in a Romanist temple. She thought how in Flanders there would have been tapers burning, and censors swinging, and the rolling thunder of the organ pealing along the vaulted roof in the solemn strains of a ***Dies Irae***, lifting the soul of the worshipper into the far-off heaven of the world beyond death, soothing the sorrowful heart with visions of eternal bliss.

She wandered through the maze of streets and lanes, sometimes coming back unawares to a street she had lately traversed, till at last she came to a church that was not silent, for through the open door she heard a voice within, preaching or praying. She hesitated for a few minutes on the threshold, having been taught that it was a sin to enter a Protestant church; and then something within her, some new sense of independence and revolt against old traditions, moved her to enter, and take her place quietly in one of the curious wooden boxes where the sparse congregation were seated, listening to a man in a Geneva gown, who was preaching in a tall oaken pulpit, surmounted by a massive sounding-board, and furnished with a crimson velvet cushion, which the preacher used with great effect during his discourse, now folding his arms upon it and leaning forward to argue familiarly with his flock, now stretching a long, lean arm above it to point a denouncing finger at the sinners below, anon belabouring it severely in the passion of his eloquence.

The flock was small, but devout, consisting for the most part of middle-aged and elderly persons in sombre attire and of Puritanical aspect; for the preacher was one of those Calvinistic clergy of Cromwell's time who had been lately evicted from their pulpits, and prosecuted for assembling congregations under the roofs of private citizens, and had shown a noble perseverance in serving God in circumstances of peculiar difficulty. And now, though the Primate had remained at his post, unfaltering and unafraid, many of the orthodox shepherds had fled and left their sheep, being too careful of their own tender persons to remain in the plague-stricken town and minister to the sick and dying; whereupon the evicted clergy had in some cases taken possession of the deserted pulpits and the silent churches, and were preaching Christ's Gospel to that remnant of the faithful which feared not to assemble in the House of God.

Angela listened to a sermon marked by a rough eloquence which enchained her attention and moved her heart. It was not difficult to utter heart-stirring words or move the tender breast to pity when the Preacher's theme was death; with all its train of attendant agonies; its partings and farewells; its awful suddenness, as shown in this pestilence, where a young man rejoicing in his health and strength at noon-

tide sees, as the sun slopes westward, the death-tokens on his bosom, and is lying
dumb and stark at night-fall; where the joyous maiden is surprised in the midst of
her mirth by the apparition of the plague-spot, and in a few hours is lifeless clay.
The Preacher dwelt upon the sins and follies and vanities of the inhabitants of that
great city; their alacrity in the pursuit of pleasure; their slackness in the service of
God.

"A man who will give twenty shillings for a pair of laced gloves to a pretty
shopwoman at the New Exchange, will grudge a crown for the maintenance of
God's people that are in distress; and one who is not hardy enough to walk half
a mile to church, will stand for a whole afternoon in the pit of a theatre, to see
painted women-actors defile a stage that was evil enough in the late King's time,
but which has in these latter days sunk to a depth of infamy that it befits not me to
speak of in this holy place. Oh, my Brethren, out of that glittering dream which you
have dreamt since his Majesty's return, out of the groves of Baal, where you have
sung and danced, and feasted, worshipping false gods, steeping your benighted souls
in the vices of pagans and image-worshippers, it has pleased the God of Israel to give
you a rough waking. Can you doubt that this plague, which has desolated a city, and
filled many a yawning pit with the promiscuous dead, has been God's way of chas-
tening a profligate people, a people caring only for fleshly pleasures, for rich meats
and strong wines, for fine clothing and jovial company, and despising the spiritual
blessings that the Almighty Father has reserved for them that love Him? Oh, my afflicted Brethren, bethink you that this pestilence is a chastisement upon a blind and
foolish people; and if it strikes the innocent as well as the guilty, if it falls as heavily
upon the spotless virgin as upon the hoary sinner, remember that it is not for us to
measure the workings of Omnipotence with the fathom-line of our earthly intellects; or to say this fair girl should be spared, and that hoary sinner taken. Has not
the Angel of Death ever chosen the fairest blossoms? His business is to people the
skies rather than to depopulate the earth. The innocent are taken, but the warning
is for the guilty; for the sinners whose debaucheries have made this world so polluted a place that God's greatest mercy to the pure is an early death. The call is loud
and instant, a call to repentance and sacrifice. Let each bear his portion of suffering
with patience, as under that wise rule of a score years past each family forewent a
weekly meal to help those who needed bread. Let each acknowledge his debt to

God, and be content to have paid it in a season of universal sorrow."

And then the Preacher turned from that awful image of an angry and avenging God to contemplate Divine compassion in the Redeemer of mankind--godlike power joined with human love. He preached of Christ the Saviour with a fulness and a force which were new to Angela. He held up that commanding, that touching image, unobscured by any other personality. All those surrounding figures which Angela had seen crowded around the godlike form, all those sufferings and virtues of the spotless Mother of God were ignored in that impassioned oration. The preacher held up Christ crucified, Him only, as the fountain of pity and pardon. He reduced Christianity to its simplest elements, primitive as when the memory of the God-man was yet fresh in the minds of those who had seen the Divine countenance and listened to the Divine voice; and Angela felt as she had never felt before the singleness and purity of the Christian's faith.

It was the day of long sermons, when a preacher who measured his discourse by the sands of an hour-glass was deemed moderate. Among the Nonconformists there were those who turned the glass, and let the flood of eloquence flow on far into the second hour. The old man had been preaching a long time when Angela awoke as from a dream, and remembered that sick-chamber where duty called her. She left the church quietly and hurried westward, guided chiefly by the sun, till she found herself once more in the Strand; and very soon afterwards she was ringing the bell at the chief entrance of Fareham House. She returned far more depressed in spirits than she went out, for all the horror of the plague-stricken city was upon her; and, fresh from the spectacle of death, she felt less hopeful of Lord Fareham's recovery.

Thomas Stokes opened the great door to admit that one modest figure, a door which looked as if it should open only to noble visitors, to a procession of courtiers and court beauties, in the fitful light of wind-blown torches. Thomas, when interrogated, was not cheerful in his account of the patient's health during Angela's absence. My lord had been strangely disordered; Mrs. Basset had found the fever increasing, and was "afeared the gentleman was relapsing."

Angela's heart sickened at the thought. The Preacher had dwelt on the sudden alternations of the disease, how apparent recovery was sometimes the precursor of death. She hurried up the stairs, and through the seemingly endless suite of rooms which nobody wanted, which never might be inhabited again perhaps, except by bats and owls, to his lordship's chamber, and found him sitting up in bed, with his eyes fixed on the door by which she entered.

"At last!" he cried. "Why did you inflict such torturing apprehensions upon me? This woman has been telling me of the horrors of the streets where you have been; and I figured you stricken suddenly with this foul malady, creeping into some deserted alley to expire uncared for, dying with your head upon a stone, lying there to be carried off by the dead-cart. You must not leave this house again, save for the coach that shall fetch you to Oxfordshire to join Hyacinth and her children--and that coach shall start to-morrow. I am a madman to have let you stay so long in this infected house."

"You forget that I am plague-proof," she answered, throwing off hood and cloak, and going to his bedside, to the chair in which she had spent many hours watching by him and praying for him.

No, there was no relapse. He had only been restless and uneasy because of her absence. The disease was conquered, the pest-spots were healing fairly, and his nurses had only to contend against the weakness and depression which seemed but the natural sequence of the malady.

Dr. Hodgkin was satisfied with his patient's progress. He had written to Lady Fareham, advising her to send some of her servants with horses for his lordship's coach, and to provide for relays of post-horses between London and Oxfordshire, a matter of easier accomplishment than it would have been in the earlier summer, when the quality were flying to the country, and post-horses were at a premium. Now there were but few people of rank or standing who had the courage to stay in town, like the Archbishop, who had not left Lambeth, or the stout old Duke of Albemarle, at the Cockpit, who feared the pestilence no more than he feared sword or cannon.

Two of his lordship's lackeys, and his Oxfordshire major-domo and clerk of the kitchen, arrived a week after Angela's landing, bringing loving letters from Hyacinth to her husband and sister. The physician had so written as not to scare the wife. She had been told that her husband had been ill, but was in a fair way to recovery, and would post to Oxfordshire as soon as he was strong enough for the journey, carrying his sister-in-law with him, and lying at the accustomed inn at

High Wycombe, or perchance resting two nights and spending three days upon the road.

That was a happy day for Angela when her patient was well enough to start on his journey. She had been longing to see her sister and the children, longing still more intensely to escape from the horror of that house, where death had seemed to lie in ambush behind the tapestry hangings, and where few of her hours had been free from a great fear. Even while Fareham was on the high-road to recovery there had been in her mind the ever-present dread of a relapse. She rejoiced with fear and trembling, and was almost afraid to believe physician and nurse when they assured her that all danger was over.

The pestilence had passed by, and they went out in the sunshine, in the freshness of a September morning, balmy, yet cool, with a scent of flowers from the gardens of Lambeth and Bankside blowing across the river. Even this terrible London, the forsaken city, looked fair in the morning light; her palaces and churches, her streets of heavily timbered houses, their projecting windows enriched with carved wood and wrought iron--streets that recalled the days of the Tudors and even suggested an earlier and rougher age, when the French King rode in all honour, albeit a prisoner, at his conqueror's side; or later, when fallen Richard, shorn of all royal dignity, rode abject and forlorn through the city, and caps were flung up for his usurping cousin. But oh, the horror of closed shops and deserted houses, and pestiferous wretches running by the coach door in their poisonous rags, begging alms, whenever the horses went slowly, in those narrow streets that lay between Fareham House and Westminster!

To Angela's wondering eyes Westminster Hall and the Abbey offered a new idea of magnificence, so grandly placed, so dignified in their antiquity. Fareham watched her eager countenance as the great family coach, which had been sent up from Oxfordshire for his accommodation, moved ponderously westward, past the Chancellor's new palace, and other new mansions, to the Hercules Pillars Inn, past Knightsbridge and Kensington, and then northward by rustic lanes, and through the village of Ealing to the Oxford road.

The family coach was as big as a small parlour, and afforded ample room for the convalescent to recline at his ease on one seat, while Angela and the steward, a confidential servant with the manners of a courtier, sat side by side upon the other.

They had the two spaniels with them, Puck and Ganymede, silky-haired little beasts, black and tan, with bulging foreheads, crowded with intellect, pug noses so short as hardly to count for noses, goggle eyes that expressed shrewdness, greediness, and affection. Puck snuggled cosily in the soft lace of his lordship's shirt; Ganymede sat and blinked at the sunshine from Angela's lap. Both snarled at Mr. Manningtree, the steward, and resented the slightest familiarity on his part.

Lord Fareham's thoughtful face brightened with its rare smile--half amused, half cynical--as he watched Angela's eager looks, devouring every object on the road.

"Those grave eyes look at our London grandeurs with a meek wonder, something as thy namesake an angel might look upon the splendours of Babylon. You can remember nothing of yonder palace, or senate house, or Abbey, I think, child?"

"Yes, I remember the Abbey, though it looked different then. I saw it through a cloud of falling snow. It was all faint and dim there. There were soldiers in the streets, and it was bitter cold; and my father sat in the coach with his elbows on his knees and his face hidden in his hands. And when I spoke to him, and tried to pull his hands away--for I was afraid of that hidden face--he shook me off and groaned aloud. Oh, such a harrowing groan! I should have thought him mad had I known what madness meant; but I know not what I thought. I remember only that I was frightened. And later, when I asked him why he was sorry, he said it was for the King."

"Ay, poor King! We have all supped full of sorrow for his sake. We have cursed and hated his enemies, and drawn and quartered their vile carcases, and have dug them out of the darkness where the worms were eating them. We have been distraught with indignation, cruel in our fury; and I look back to-day, after fifteen years, and see but too clearly now that Charles Stuart's death lies at one man's door."

"At Cromwell's? At Bradshaw's?"

"No, child; at his own. Cromwell would have never been heard of, save in Huntingdon Market-place, as a God-fearing yeoman, had Charles been strong and true. The King's weakness was Cromwell's opportunity. He dug his own grave with false promises, with shilly-shally, with an inimitable talent for always doing the wrong thing and choosing the wrong road. Open not so wide those reproachful eyes. Oh, I grant you, he was a noble king, a king of kings to walk in a royal procession, to sit upon a dais under a velvet and gold canopy, to receive ambassadors, and patronise foreign painters, and fulfil all that is splendid and stately in ideal kingship. He was an adoring husband--confiding to simplicity--a kind father, a fond friend, though never a firm one."

"Oh, surely, surely you loved him?"

"Not as your father loved him, for I never suffered with him. It was those who sacrificed the most who loved him best, those who were with him to the end, long after common sense told them his cause was hopeless; indeed, I believe my father knew as much at Nottingham, when that luckless standard was blown down in the tempest. Those who starved for him, and lay out on barren moors through the cold English nights for him, and wore their clothes threadbare and their shoes into holes for him, and left wife and children, and melted their silver and squandered their gold for him--those are the men who love his memory dearest, and for whose poor sakes we of the younger generation must make believe to think him a saint and a martyr."

"Oh, my lord, say not that you think him a bad man!"

"Bad! Nay, I believe that all his instincts were virtuous and honourable, and that--until the whirlwind of those latter days in which he scarce knew what he was doing--he meant fairly by his people, and had their welfare at heart. He might have done far better for himself and others had he been a brave bad man like Wentworth--audacious, unscrupulous, driving straight to a fixed goal. No, Angela, he was that which is worse for mankind--an obstinate, weak man. A bundle of impulses, some good and some evil; a man who had many chances, and lost them all; who loved foolishly and too well, and let himself be ruled by a wife who could not rule herself. Blind impulse, passionate folly were sailing the State ship through that sea of troubles which could be crossed but by a navigator as politic, profound, and crafty as Richelieu or Mazarin. Who can wonder that the Royal Charles went down?"

"It must seem strange to you, looking back from the Court, as Hyacinth's letters have painted it--to that time of trouble?"

"Strange! I stand in the crowd at Whitehall sometimes, amidst their masking and folly, their frolic schemes, their malice, their jeering wit and riotous merriment, and wonder whether it is all a dream, and I shall wake and see the England of '44, the year Henrietta Maria vanished--a discrowned fugitive, from the scene where she had lived to do harm. I look along the perspective of painted faces and flowing hair, jewels, and gay colours, towards that window through which Charles I. walked to his bloody death, suffered with a kingly grandeur that made the world forget all that was poor and petty in his life; and I wonder does anyone else recall that suffering or reflect upon that doom. Not one! Each has his jest, and his mistress--the eyes he worships, the lips he adores. It is only the rural Put that feels himself lost in the crowd whose thoughts turn sadly to the sad past."

"Yet whatever your lordship may say----"

"Tush, child, I am no lordship to you! Call me brother, or Fareham; and never talk to me as if I were anything else than your brother in affection."

"It is sweet to hear you say so much, sir," she answered gently. "I have often envied my companions at the Ursulines when they talked of their brothers. It was so strange to hear them tell of bickering and ill-will between brother and sister. Had God given me a brother, I would not quarrel with him."

"Nor shall thou quarrel with me, sweetheart; but we will be fast friends always. Do I not owe thee my life?"

"I will not hear you say so; it is blasphemy against your Creator, who relented and spared you."

"What! you think that Omnipotence, in the inaccessible mystery of Heaven, keeps the muster-roll of earth open before Him, and reckons each little life as it drops off the list? That is hardly my notion of Divinity. I see the Almighty rather as the Roman poet saw Him--an inexorable Father, hurling the thunderbolt our folly has deserved from His red right hand, yet merciful to stay that hand when we have taken our punishment meekly. That, Angela, is the nearest my mind can reach to the idea of a personal God. But do not bend those pencilled brows with such a sad perplexity. You know, doubtless, that I come of a Catholic family, and was bred in the old faith. Alas! I have conformed ill to Church discipline. I am no theologian, nor quite an infidel, and should be as much at sea in an argument with Hobbes as with Bossuet. Trouble not thy gentle spirit for my sins of thought or deed. Your tender care has given me time to repent all my errors. You were going to tell my lordship something, when I chid you for excess of ceremony--"

"Nay, sir--brother, I had but to say that this wicked Court, of which my father and you have spoken so ill, can scarcely fail to be turned from its sins by so terrible a visitation. Those who have looked upon the city as I saw it a week ago can scarce return with unchastened hearts to feasting and dancing and idle company."

"But the beaux and belles of Whitehall have not seen the city as my brave girl saw it," cried Fareham.

"They have not met the dead-cart, nor heard the groans of the dying, nor seen the red cross upon the doors. They made off with the first rumour of peril. The roads were crowded with their coaches, their saddle-horses, their furniture and finery; one could scarce command a post-horse for love or money. 'A thousand less this week,' says one. 'We may be going back to town and have the theatres open again in the cold weather.'"

They dined at the Crown, at Uxbridge, which was that "fair house at the end of the town" provided for the meeting of the late King's Commissioners with the representatives of the Parliament in the year '44. Fareham showed his sister-in-law a spacious panelled parlour, which was that "fair room in the middle of the house" that had been handsomely dressed up for the Commissioners to sit in.

They pushed on to High Wycombe before night-fall, and supped *tete-a-tete* in the best room of the inn, with Fareham's faithful Manningtree to bring in the chief dish, and the people of the house to wait upon them. They were very friendly and happy together, Fareham telling his companion much of his adventurous life in France, and how in the first Fronde war he had been on the side of Queen and Minister, and afterwards, for love and admiration of Conde, had joined the party of the Princes.

"Well, it was a time worth living in--a good education for the boy-king, Louis, for it showed him that the hereditary ruler of a great nation has something more to do than to be born, and to exist, and to spend money."

Lord Fareham described the shining lights of that brilliant court with a caustic tongue; but he was more indulgent to the follies of the Palais Royal and the Louvre than he had been to the debaucheries of Whitehall.

"There is a grace even in their vices," he said. "Their wit is lighter, and there is more mind in their follies. Our mirth is vulgar even when it is not bestial. I know of no Parisian adventure so degrading as certain pranks of Buckhurst's, which I would not dare mention in your hearing. We imitate them, and out-herod Herod, but we are never like them. We send to Paris for our clothes, and borrow their newest words--for they are ever inventing some cant phrase to startle dulness--and we make our language a foreign farrago. Why, here is even plain John Evelyn, that most pious of pedants, pleading for the enlistment of a troop of Gallic substantives and adjectives to eke out our native English!"

Fareham told Angela much of his past life during the freedom of that long *tete-a-tete*, talking to her as if she had indeed been a young sister from whom he had been separated since her childhood. That mild, pensive manner promised sympathy and understanding, and he unconsciously inclined to confide his thoughts and opinions to her, as well as the history of his youth.

He had fought at Edgehill as a lad of thirteen, had been with the King at Beverley, York, and Nottingham, and had only left the Court to accompany the Prince of Wales to Jersey, and afterwards to Paris.

"I soon sickened of a Court life and its petty plots and parlour intrigues," he told Angela, "and was glad to join Conde's army, where my father's influence got me a captaincy before I was eighteen. To fight under such a leader as that was to serve under the god of war. I can imagine Mars himself no grander soldier. Oh, my dear, what a man! Nay, I will not call him by that common name. He was something more or less than man--of another species. In the thick of the fight a lion; in his dominion over armies, in his calmness amidst danger, a god. Shall I ever see it again, I wonder--that vulture face, those eyes that flashed Jove's red lightning?"

"Your own face changes when you speak of him," said Angela, awe-stricken at that fierce energy which heroic memories evoked in Fareham's wasted countenance.

"Nay, you should have seen the change in *his* face when he flung off the courtier for the captain. His whole being was transformed. Those who knew Conde at St. Germain, at the Hotel de Rambouillet, at the Palais Royal, knew not the measure or the might of that great nature. He was born to conquer. But you must not think that with him victory meant brute force. It meant thought and patience, the power to foresee and to combine, the rapid apprehension of opposing circumstances, the just measure of his own materials. A strict disciplinarian, a severe master, but willing to work at the lowest details, the humblest offices of war. A soldier, did I say? He was the Genius of modern warfare."

"You talk as if you loved him dearly."

"I loved him as I shall never love any other man. He was my friend as well as my General. But I claim no merit in loving one whom all the world honoured. Could you have seen princes and nobles, as I saw them when I was a boy at Paris, standing on chairs, on tables, kneeling, to drink his health! A demi-god could have received no more fervent adulation. Alas! sister, I look back at those years of foreign service and know they were the best of my life!"

They started early next morning, and were within half a dozen miles of Oxford before the sun was low. They drove by a level road that skirted the river; and now, for the first time, Angela saw that river flowing placidly through a rural landscape, the rich green of marshy meadows in the foreground, and low wooded hills on the opposite bank, while midway across the stream an islet covered with reed and willow cast a shadow over the rosy water painted by the western sun.

"Are we near them now?" she asked eagerly, knowing that her brother-in-law's mansion lay within a few miles of Oxford.

"We are very near," answered Fareham; "I can see the chimneys, and the white stone pillars of the great gate."

He had his head out of the carriage, looking sunward, shading his eyes with his big doe-skin gauntlet as he looked. Those two days on the road, the fresh autumn air, the generous diet, the variety and movement of the journey, had made a new man of him. Lean and gaunt he must needs be for some time to come; but the dark face was no longer bloodless; the eyes had the fire of health.

"I see the gate--and there is more than that in view!" he cried excitedly. "Your sister is coming in a troop to meet us, with her children, and visitors, and servants. Stop the coach, Manningtree, and let us out."

The post-boys pulled up their horses, and the steward opened the coach door and assisted his master to alight. Fareham's footsteps were somewhat uncertain as he walked slowly along the waste grass by the roadside, leaning a little upon Angela's shoulder.

Lady Fareham came running towards them in advance of children and friends, an airy figure in blue and white, her fair hair flying in the wind, her arms stretched out as if to greet them from afar. She clasped her sister to her breast even before she saluted her husband, clasped her and kissed her, laughing between the kisses.

"Welcome, my escaped nun!" she cried. "I never thought they would let thee out of thy prison, or that thou wouldst muster courage to break thy bonds. Welcome, and a hundred times, welcome. And that thou shouldst have nursed and tended my ailing lord! Oh, the wonder of it! While I, within a hundred miles of him, knew not that he was ill, here didst thou come across seas to save him! Why, 'tis a modern fairy tale."

"And she is the good fairy," said Fareham, taking his wife's face between his two hands and bending down to kiss the white forehead under its cloud of pale golden curls, "and you must cherish her for all the rest of your life. But for her I should have died alone in that great gaudy house, and the rats would have eaten me, and then perhaps you would have cared no longer for the mansion, and would have had to build another further west, by my Lord Clarendon's, where all the fine folks are going--and that would have been a pity."

"Oh, Fareham, do not begin with thy irony-stop! I know all your organ tones, from the tenor of your kindness to the bourdon of your displeasure. Do you think I am not glad to have you here safe and sound? Do you think I have not been miserable about you since I knew of your sickness? Monsieur de Malfort will tell you whether I have been unhappy or not."

"Why, Malfort! What wind blew you hither at this perilous season, when Englishmen are going abroad for fear of the pestilence, and when your friend St Evremond has fled from the beauties of Oxford to the malodorous sewers and fusty fraus of the Netherlands?"

"I had no fear of the contagion, and I wanted to see my friends. I am in lodgings in Oxford, where there is almost as much good company as there ever was at Whitehall."

The Comte de Malfort and Fareham clasped hands with a cordiality which bespoke old friendship; and it was only an instinctive recoil on the part of the Englishman which spared him his friend's kisses. They had lived in camps and in courts together, these two, and had much in common, and much that was antagonistic, in temperament and habits, Malfort being lazy and luxurious, when no fighting was on hand; a man whose one business, when not under canvas, was to surpass everybody else in the fashion and folly of the hour, to be quite the finest gentleman in whatever company he found himself.

He was a godson and favourite of Madame de Montrond, who had numbered his father among the army of her devoted admirers. He had been Hyacinth's play-fellow and slave in her early girlhood, and had been *l'ami de la maison* in those brilliant years of the young King's reign, when the Farehams were living in the Marais. To him had been permitted all privileges that a being as harmless and innocent as he was polished and elegant might be allowed, by a husband who had too much confidence in his wife's virtue, and too good an opinion of his own merits to be easily jealous. Nor was Henri de Malfort a man to provoke jealousy by any superior gifts of mind or person. Nature had not been especially kind to him. His features were insignificant, his eyes pale, and he had not escaped that scourge of the seventeenth century, the small-pox. His pale and clear complexion was but slightly pitted, however, and his eyelids had not suffered. Men were inclined to call him ugly; women thought him interesting. His frame was badly built from the athlete's point of view; but it had the suppleness which makes the graceful dancer, and was an elegant scaffolding on which to hang the picturesque costume of the day. For the rest, all that he was he had made himself, during those eighteen years of intelligent self-culture, which had been his engrossing occupation since his fifteenth birthday, when he determined to be one of the finest gentlemen of his epoch.

A fine gentleman at the Court of Louis had to be something more than a figure steeped in perfumes and hung with ribbons. His red-heeled shoes, his periwig and cannon sleeves, were indispensable to fashion, but not enough for fame. The favoured guest of the Hotel de Rambouillet, and of Mademoiselle de Scudery's "Saturdays," must have wit and learning, or at least that capacity for smart speech and pedantic allusion which might pass current for both in a society where the critics were chiefly feminine. Henri de Malfort had graduated in a college of blue-stockings. He had grown up in an atmosphere of gunpowder and ***bouts rimes***. He had stormed the breach at sieges where the assault was led off by a company of violins, in the Spanish fashion. He had fought with distinction under the finest soldiers in Europe, and had seen some of his dearest friends expire at his side.

Unlike Gramont and St. Evremond, he was still in the floodtide of royal favour in his own country; and it seemed a curious caprice that had led him to follow those gentlemen to England, to shine in a duller society, and sparkle at a less magnificent court.

The children hung upon their father, Papillon on one side, Cupid on the other, and it was in them rather than in her sister's friend that Angela was interested. The girl resembled her mother only in the grace and flexibility of her slender form, the quickness of her movements, and the vivacity of her speech. Her hair and eyes were dark, like her father's, and her colouring was that of a brunette, with something of a pale bronze under the delicate carmine of her cheeks. The boy favoured his mother, and was worthy of the sobriquet Rochester had bestowed upon him. His blue eyes, chubby cheeks, cherry lips, and golden hair were like the typical Cupid of Rubens, and might be seen repeated ***ad libitum*** on the ceiling of the Banqueting House.

"I'll warrant this is all flummery," said Fareham, looking down at the girl as she hung upon him. "Thou art not glad to see me."

"I am so glad that I could eat you, as the Giant would have eaten Jack," answered the girl, leaping up to kiss him, her hair flying back like a dark cloud, her nimble legs struggling for freedom in her long brocade petticoat.

"And you are not afraid of the contagion?"

"Afraid! Why, I wanted mother to take me to you as soon as I heard you were ill."

"Well, I have been smoke-dried and pickled in strong waters, until Dr. Hodgkin accounts me safe, or I would not come nigh thee. See, sweetheart, this is your aunt, whom you are to love next best to your mother."

"But not so well as you, sir. You are first," said the child, and then turned to Angela and held up her rosebud mouth to be kissed. "You saved my father's life," she said. "If you ever want anybody to die for you let it be me."

"Gud! what a delicate wit! The sweet child is positively ***tuant***," exclaimed a young lady, who was strolling beside them, and whom Lady Fareham had not taken the trouble to introduce by name to any one, but who was now accounted for as a country neighbour, Mrs. Dorothy Lettsome.

Angela was watching her brother-in-law as they sauntered along, and she saw that the fatigue and agitation of this meeting were beginning to affect him. He was carrying his hat in one hand, while the other caressed Papillon. There were beads of perspiration on his forehead, and his footsteps began to drag a little. Happily the coach had kept a few paces in their rear, and Manningtree was walking beside it; so Angela proposed that his lordship should resume his seat in the vehicle and drive on to his house, while she went on foot with her sister.

"I must go with his lordship," cried Papillon, and leapt into the coach before her father.

Hyacinth put her arm through Angela's, and led her slowly along the grassy walk to the great gates, the Frenchman and Mrs. Lettsome following; and unversed as the convent-bred girl was in the ways of this particular world, she could nevertheless perceive that in the conversation between these two, M. de Malfort was amusing himself at the expense of his fair companion. His own English was by no means despicable, as he had spent more than a year, at the Embassy immediately after the Restoration, to say nothing of his constant intercourse with the Farehams and other English exiles in France; but he was encouraging the young lady to talk to him in French, which was spoken with an affected drawl, that was even more ridiculous than its errors in grammar.

CHAPTER VII.
AT THE TOP OF THE FASHION.

Nothing could have been more cordial than Lady Fareham's welcome to her sister, nor were it easy to imagine a life more delightful than that at Chilton Abbey in that autumnal season, when every stage of the decaying year clothed itself with a variety and brilliancy of colouring which made ruin beautiful, and disguised the approach of winter, as a court harridan might hide age and wrinkles under a yellow satin mask and flame-coloured domino. The Abbey was one of those capacious, irregular buildings in which all that a house was in the past and all that it is in the present are composed into a harmonious whole, and in which past and present are so cunningly interwoven that it would have been difficult for any one but an architect to distinguish where the improvements and additions of yesterday were grafted on to the masonry of the fourteenth century. Here, where the spacious plate-room and pantry began, there were walls massive enough for the immuring of refractory nuns; and this corkscrew Jacobean staircase, which wound with carved balusters up to the garret story, had its foundations in a flight of Cyclopean stone steps that descended to the cellars, where the monks kept their strong liquors and brewed their beer. Half of my lady's drawing-room had been the refectory, and the long dining-parlour still showed the groined roof of an ancient cloister; while the music-room, into which it opened, had been designed by Inigo Jones, and built by the last Lord Fareham. All that there is of the romantic in this kind of architectural patchwork had been enhanced by the collection of old furniture that the present possessors of the Abbey had imported from Lady Fareham's chateau in Normandy, and which was more interesting though less splendid than the furniture of Fareham's town mansion, as it was the result of gradual accumulation in the Montrond family, or of purchase from the wreck of noble houses, ruined in the civil war which had distracted France before the reign of the Bearnais.

To Angela the change from an enclosed convent to such a house as Chilton Abbey, was a change that filled all her days with wonder. The splendour, the air of careless luxury that pervaded her sister's house, and suggested costliness and waste in every detail, could but be distressing to the pupil of Flemish nuns, who had seen even the trenchers scraped to make soup for the poor, and every morsel of bread garnered as if it were gold dust. From that sparse fare of the convent to this Rabelaisian plenty, this plethora of meat and poultry, huge game pies and elaborate confectionery, this perpetual too much of everything, was a transition that startled and shocked her. She heard with wonder of the numerous dinner tables that were spread every day at Chilton. Mr. Manningtree's table, at which the Roman Priest from Oxford dined, except on those rare occasions when he was invited to sit down with the quality; and Mrs. Hubbock's table, where the superior servants dined, and at which Henriette's dancing-master considered it a privilege to over-eat himself; and the two great tables in the servants' hall, twenty at each table; and the *gouvernante*, Mrs. Priscilla Goodman's table in the blue parlour upstairs, at which my lady's English and French waiting-women, and my lord's gentlemen ate, and at which Henriette and her brother were supposed to take their meals, but where they seldom appeared, usually claiming the right to eat with their parents. She wondered as she heard of the fine-drawn distinctions among that rabble of servants, the upper ranks of whom were supplied by the small gentry--of servants who waited upon servants, and again other servants who waited on those, down to that lowest stratum of kitchen sluts and turnspits, who actually made their own beds and scraped their own trenchers. Everywhere there was lavish expenditure--everywhere the abundance which, among that uneducated and unthoughtful class, ever degenerates into wanton waste.

It sickened Angela to see the long dining-table loaded, day after day, with dishes that were many of them left untouched amidst the superabundance, while the massive Cromwellian sideboard seemed to need all the thickness of its gouty legs to sustain the "regalia" of hams and tongues, pasties, salads and jellies. And all this time *The Weekly Gazette* from London told of the unexampled distress in that afflicted city, which was but the natural result of an epidemic that had driven all the well-to-do away, and left neither trade nor employment for the lower classes.

"What becomes of that mountain of food?" Angela asked her sister, after her second dinner at Chilton, by which time she and Hyacinth had become familiar and at ease with each other. "Is it given to the poor?"

"Some of it, perhaps, love; but I'll warrant that most of it is eaten in the offices--with many a handsome sirloin and haunch to boot."

"Oh, sister, it is dreadful to think of such a troop! I am always meeting strange faces. How many servants have you?"

"I have never reckoned them. Manningtree knows, no doubt; for his wages book would tell him. I take it there may be more than fifty, and less than a hundred. Anyhow, we could not exist were they fewer."

"More than fifty people to wait upon four!"

"For our state and importance, *cherie*. We are very ill-waited upon. I nearly died last week before I could get any one to bring me my afternoon chocolate. The men had all rushed off to a bull-baiting, and the women were romping or fighting in the laundry, except my own women, who are too genteel to play with the under-servants, and had taken a holiday to go and see a tragedy at Oxford. I found myself in a deserted house. I might have been burnt alive, or have expired in a fit, for aught any of those over-fed devils cared."

"But could they not be better regulated?"

"They are, when Manningtree is at home. He has them all under his thumb."

"And he is an honest, conscientious man?"

"Who knows? I dare say he robs us, and takes a *pot de vin* wherever 'tis offered. But it is better to be robbed by one than by an army; and if Manningtree keeps others from cheating he is worth his wages."

"And you, dear Hyacinth. Do you keep no accounts?"

"Keep accounts! Why, my dearest simpleton, did you ever hear of a woman of quality keeping accounts--unless it were some lunatic universal genius like her Grace of Newcastle, who rises in the middle of the night to scribble verses, and who might do anything preposterous. Keep accounts! Why, if you was to tell me that two and two make five I couldn't controvert you, from my own knowledge."

"It all seems so strange to me," murmured Angela.

"My aunt supervised all the expenditure of the convent, and was unhappy if she discovered waste in the smallest item."

"Unhappy! Yes, my dear innocent. And do you think if I was to investigate the cost of kitchen and cellar, and calculate how many pounds of meat each of our tall lackeys consumes per diem, I should not speedily be plagued into grey hairs and wrinkles? I hope we are rich enough to support their wastefulness. And if we are not--why, *vogue la galere*--when we are ruined the King must do something for Fareham--make him Lord Chancellor. His Majesty is mighty sick of poor old Clarendon and his lectures. Fareham has a long head, and would do as well as anybody else for Chancellor if he would but show himself at Court oftener, and conform to the fashion of the time, instead of holding himself aloof, with a Puritanical disdain for amusements and people that please his betters. He has taken a leaf out of Lord Southampton's book, and would not allow me to return a visit Lady Castlemaine paid me the other day, in the utmost friendliness: and to slight her is the quickest way to offend his Majesty."

"But, sister, you would not consort with an infamous woman?"

"Infamous! Who told you she is infamous? Your innocency should be ignorant of such trumpery tittle-tattle. And one can be civil without consorting, as you call it."

Angela took her sister's reckless speech for mere sportiveness. Hyacinth might be careless and ignorant of business, but his lordship doubtless knew the extent of his income, and was too grave and experienced a personage to be a spendthrift. He had confessed to seven and thirty, which to the girl of twenty seemed serious middle-age.

There were musicians in her ladyship's household--youths who played lute and viol, and sang the dainty, meaningless songs of the latest ballad-mongers very prettily. The warm weather, which had a bad effect upon the bills of mortality, was so far advantageous that it allowed these gentlemen to sing in the garden while the family were at supper, or on the river while the family were taking their evening airing. Their newest performance was an arrangement of Lord Dorset's lines--"To all you ladies now on land," set as a round. There could scarcely be anything prettier than the dying fall of the refrain that ended every verse:--

> "With a fa, la, la,
> Perhaps permit some happier man
> To kiss your hand or flirt your fan,
> With a fa, la, la."

The last lines died away in the distance of the moonlit garden, as the singers slowly retired, while Henri de Malfort illustrated that final couplet with Hyacinth's fan, as he sat beside her.

"Music, and moonlight, and a garden. You might fancy yourself amidst the grottoes and terraces of St. Germain."

"I note that whenever there is anything meritorious in our English life Malfort is reminded of France, and when he discovers any obnoxious feature in our manners or habits he expatiates on the vast difference between the two nations," said his lordship.

"Dear Fareham, I am a human being. When I am in England I remember all I loved in my own country. I must return to it before I shall understand the worth of all I leave here--and the understanding may be bitter. Call your singers back, and let us have those two last verses again. 'Tis a fine tune, and your fellows perform it with sweetness and brio."

The song was new. The victory which it celebrated was fresh in the minds of men. The disgrace of later Dutch experiences--the ships in the Nore ravaging and insulting--was yet to come. England still believed her floating castles invincible.

To Angela's mind the life at Chilton was full of change and joyous expectancy. No hour of the day but offered some variety of recreation, from battledore and shuttlecock in the *plaisance* to long days with the hounds or the hawks. Angela learnt to ride in less than a month, instructed by the stud-groom, a gentleman of considerable importance in the household; an old campaigner, who had groomed Fareham's horses after many a battle, and many a skirmish, and had suffered scant food and rough quarters without murmuring; and also with considerable assistance and counsel from Lord Fareham, and occasional lectures from Papillon, who was a Diana at ten years old, and rode with her father in the first flight. Angela was soon equal to accompanying her sister in the hunting-field, for Hyacinth liked following the chase after the French rather than the English fashion, affecting no ruder sport than to wait at an opening of the wood, or on the crest of a common, to see hounds and riders sweep by; or, favoured by chance now and then, to signal the villain's whereabouts by a lace handkerchief waved high above her head. This was how a beautiful lady who had hunted in the forests of St. Germain and Fontainebleau understood sport; and such performances as this Angela found easy and agreeable. They had many cavaliers who came to talk with them for a few minutes, to tell them what was doing or not doing yonder where the hounds were hidden in thicket or coppice; but Henri de Malfort was their most constant attendant. He rarely left them, and dawdled through the earlier half of an October day, walking his horse from point to point, or dismounting at sheltered corners to stand and talk at Lady Fareham's side, with a patience that made Angela wonder at the contrast between English headlong eagerness, crashing and splashing through hedge and brook, and French indifference.

"I have not Fareham's passion for mud," he explained to her, when she remarked upon his lack of interest in the chase, even when the music of the hounds was ringing through wood and valley, now close beside them, anon diminishing in the distance, thin in the thin air. "If he comes not home at dark plastered with mire from boots to eyebrows he will cry, like Alexander, 'I have lost a day.'"

Partridge-hawking in the wide fields between Chilton and Nettlebed was more to Malfort's taste, and it was a sport for which Lady Fareham expressed a certain enthusiasm, and for which she attired herself to the perfection of picturesque costume. Her hunting-coats were marvels of embroidery on atlas and smooth cloth; but her smartest velvet and brocade she kept for the sunny mornings, when, with hooded peregrine on wrist, she sallied forth intent on slaughter, Angela, Papillon, and De Malfort for her *cortege*, an easy-paced horse to amble over the grass with her, and the Dutch falconer to tell her the right moment at which to slip her falcon's hood.

The nuns at the Ursuline Convent would scarcely have recognised their quondam pupil in the girl on the grey palfrey, whose hair flew loose under a beaver hat, mingling its tresses with the long ostrich plume, whose trimly fitting jacket had a masculine air which only accentuated the womanliness of the fair face above it, and whose complexion, somewhat too colourless within the convent walls, now glowed with a carnation that brightened and darkened the large grey eyes into new beauty.

That open-air life was a revelation to the cloister-bred girl. Could this earth hold greater bliss than to roam at large over spacious gardens, to cross the river, sculling her boat with strong hands, with her niece Henriette, otherwise Papillon, sitting in the stern to steer, and scream instructions to the novice in navigation; and then to lose themselves in the woods on the further shore, to wander in a labyrinth of reddening beeches, and oaks on which the thick foliage still kept its dusky green; to emerge upon open lawns where the pale gold birches looked like fairy trees, and where amber and crimson toadstools shone like jewels on the skirts of the dense undergrowth of holly and hawthorn? The liberty of it all, the delicious feeling of freedom, the release from convent rules and convent hours, bells ringing for chapel, bells ringing for meals, bells ringing to mark the end of the brief recreation--a perpetual ringing and drilling which had made conventual life a dull machine, working always in the same grooves.

Oh, this liberty, this variety, this beauty in all things around and about her! How the young glad soul, newly escaped from prison, revelled and expatiated in its freedom! Papillon, who at ten years old, had skimmed the cream off all the simple pleasures, appointed herself her aunt's instructress in most things, and taught her to row, with some help from Lord Fareham, who was an expert waterman; and, at the same time, tried to teach her to despise the country, and all rustic pleasures, except hunting--although in her inmost heart the minx preferred the liberty of Oxfordshire woods to the splendour of Fareham House, where she was cooped in a nursery with her *gouvernante* for the greater part of her time, and was only exhibited like a doll to her mother's fine company, or seated upon a cushion to tinkle a saraband and display her precocious talent on the guitar, which she played almost as badly as Lady Fareham herself, at whose feeble endeavours even the courteous De Malfort laughed.

Never was sister kinder than Hyacinth, impelled by that impulsive sweetness which was her chief characteristic, and also, it might be, moved to lavish generosity by some scruples of conscience with regard to her grandmother's will. Her first business was to send for the best milliner in Oxford, a London Madam who had followed her court customers to the university town, and to order everything that was beautiful and seemly for a young person of quality.

"I implore you not to make me too fine, dearest," pleaded Angela, who was more horrified at the milliner's painted face and exuberant figure than charmed by the contents of the baskets which she had brought with her in the spacious leather coach--velvets and brocades, hoods and gloves, silk stockings, fans, perfumes and pulvilios, sweet-bags and scented boxes--all of which the woman spread out upon Lady Fareham's embroidered satin bed, for the young lady's admiration. "I pray you remember that I am accustomed to have only two gowns--a black and a grey. You will make me afraid of my image in the glass if you dress me like--like--"

She glanced from her sister's *decollete* bodice to the far more appalling charms of the milliner, which a gauze kerchief rather emphasised than concealed, and could find no proper conclusion for her sentence.

"Nay, sweetheart, let not thy modesty take fright. Thou shalt be clad as demurely as the nun thou hast escaped being--

'And sable stole of Cyprus lawn   Over thy decent shoulders drawn.'

We will have no blacks, but as much decency as you choose. You will mark the distinction between my sister and your maids of honour, Mrs. Lewin. She is but a *debutante* in our modish world, and must be dressed as modestly as you can contrive, to be consistent with the fashion."

"Oh, my lady, I catch your ladyship's meaning, and your ladyship's instructions shall be carried out as far as can be without making a savage of the young lady. I know what some young ladies are when they first come to Court. I had fuss enough with Miss Hamilton before I could persuade her to have her bodice cut like a Christian. And even the beautiful Miss Brooks were all for high tuckers and modesty-pieces when I began to make for them; but they soon came round. And now with my Lady Denham it is always, 'Gud, Lewin, do you call that the right cut for a bosom? Udsbud, woman, you haven't made the curve half deep enough.' And with my Lady Chesterfield it is, 'Sure, if they say my legs are thick and ugly, I'll let them know my shoulders are worth looking at. Give me your scissors, creature,' and then with her own delicate hand she will scoop me a good inch off the satin, till I am fit to swoon at seeing the cold steel against her milk-white flesh."

Mrs. Lewin talked with but little interruption for the best part of an hour while measuring her new customer, showing her pattern-book, and exhibiting the ready-made wares she had brought, the greater number of which Hyacinth insisted on buying for Angela--who was horrified at the slanderous innuendoes that dropped in casual abundance from the painted lips of the milliner; horrified, too, that her sister could loll back in her armchair and laugh at the woman's coarse and malignant talk.

"Indeed, sister, you are far too generous, and you have overpowered me with gifts," she said, when the milliner had curtsied herself out of the room; "for I fear my own income will never pay for all these costly things. Three pounds, I think she said, was the price of the Mazarine hood alone--and there are stockings and gloves innumerable."

"Mon Ange, while you are with me your own income is but for charities and vails. I will have it spent for nothing else. You know how rich the Marquise has made me--while I believe Fareham is a kind of modern Croesus, though we do not boast of his wealth, for all that is most substantial in his fortune comes from his mother, whose father was a great merchant trading with Spain and the Indies, all through James's reign, and luckier in the hunt for gold than poor Raleigh. Never must you talk to me of obligation. Are we not sisters, and was it not a mere accident that made me the elder, and Madame de Montrond's *protegee*?"

"I have no words to thank you for so much kindness. I will only say I am so happy here that I could never have believed there was such full content on this sinful earth."

"Wait till we are in London, Angelique. Here we endure existence. It is only in London that we live."

"Nay, I believe the country will always please me better than the town. But, sister, do you not hate that Mrs. Lewin--that horrid painted face and evil tongue?"

"My dearest child, one hates a milliner for the spoiling of a bodice or the ill cut of a sleeve--not for her character. I believe Mrs. Lewin's is among the worst, and that she has had as many intrigues as Lady Castlemaine. As for her painting, doubtless she does that to remind her customers that she sells alabaster powder and ceruse."

"Nay, if she wants to disgust them with painted faces she has but to show her own."

"I grant she lays the stuff on badly. I hope, if I live to have as many wrinkles, I shall fill them better than she does. Yet who can tell what a hideous toad she might be in her natural skin? It may be Christian charity that induces her to paint, and so to spare us the sight of a monster. She will make thee a beauty, Ange, be sure of that. For satin or velvet, birthday or gala gowns, nobody can beat her. The wretch has had thousands of my money, so I ought to know. But for thy riding-habit and hawking-jacket we want the firmer grip of a man's hand. Those must be made by Roget."

"A Frenchman?"

"Yes, child. One only accepts British workmanship when a Parisian artist is not to be had. Clever as Lewin is, if I want to eclipse my dearest enemy on any special occasion I send Manningtree across the Channel, or ask De Malfort to let his valet-- who spends his life in transit like a king's messenger--bring me the latest confection from the Rue de Richelieu."

"What infinite trouble about a gown--and for you who would look lovely in anything!"

"Tush, child! You have never seen me in 'anything.' If ever you should surprise me in an ill gown you will see how much the feathers make the bird. Poets and play-wrights may pretend to believe that we need no embellishment from art; but the very men who write all that romantic nonsense are the first to court a well-dressed woman. And there are few of them who could calculate with any exactness the relation of beauty to its surroundings. That is why women go deep into debt to their milliners, and would sooner be dead in well-made graveclothes than alive in an old-fashioned mantua."

Angela could not be in her sister's company for a month without discovering that Lady Fareham's whole life was given up to the worship of the trivial. She was kind, she was amiable, generous, even to recklessness. She was not irreligious, heard Mass and went to confession as often as the hard conditions of an alien and jealously treated Church would allow, had never disputed the truth of any tenet that was taught her--but of serious views, of an earnest consideration of life and death, husband and children, Hyacinth Fareham was as incapable as her ten-year-old daughter. Indeed, it sometimes seemed to Angela that the child had broader and deeper thoughts than the mother, and saw her surroundings with a shrewder and clearer eye, despite the natural frivolity of childhood, and the exuberance of a fine physique.

It was not for the younger sister to teach the elder, nor did Angela deem herself capable of teaching. Her nature was thoughtful and earnest: but she lacked that experience of life which can alone give the thinker a broad and philosophic view of other people's conduct. She was still far from the stage of existence in which to understand all is to pardon all.

She beheld the life about her with wonder and bewilderment. It was so pleasant, so full of beauty and variety; yet things were said and done that shocked her. There was nothing in her sister's own behaviour to alarm her modesty; but to hear her sister talk of other women's conduct outraged all her ideas of decency and virtue. If there were really such wickedness in the world, women so shameless and vile, was it right that good women should know of them, that pure lips should speak of their iniquity?

She was still more shocked when Hyacinth talked of Lady Castlemaine with a good-humoured indulgence.

"There is something fine about her," Lady Fareham said one day, "in spite of her tempers and pranks."

"What!" cried Angela, aghast, having thought these creatures unrecognised by any honest woman, "do you know her--that Lady Castlemaine of whom you have told me such dreadful things?"

"C'est vrai. J'en ai dit des raides. Mon Ange, in town one must needs know everybody, though I doubt that after not returning her visit t'other day, I shall be in her black books, and in somebody else's. She has never been one of my intimates. If I were often at Whitehall, I should have to be friends with her. But Fareham is jealous of Court influences; and I am only allowed to appear on gala nights--perhaps not a half-dozen times in a season. There is a distinction in not showing one's self often; but it is provoking to hear of the frolics and jollities which go on every day and every night, and from which I am banished. It mattered little while the Queen-mother was at Somerset House, for her Court ranked higher--and was certainly more refined in its splendour--than her son's ragamuffin herd. But now she is gone, I shall miss our intellectual *milieu*, and wish myself in the Rue St. Thomas du Louvre, where the Hotel du Rambouillet, even in its decline, offers a finer style of company than anything you will see in England."

"Sister, I fear you left half your heart in France."

"Nay, sweet; perhaps some of it has followed me," answered Hyacinth, with a blush and an enigmatic smile. "*Peste*! I am not a woman to make a fuss about hearts! There is not a grain of tragedy in my composition. I am like that girl in the play we saw at Oxford t'other day. Fletcher's was it, or Shakespeare's? 'A star danced, and under that was I born.' Yes, I was born under a dancing star; and I shall never break my heart--for love."

"But you regret Paris?"

"*Helas*! Paris means my girlhood; and were you to take me back there to-morrow you could not make me seventeen again--and so where's the use? I should see wrinkles in the faces of my friends; and should know that they were seeing the same ugly lines in mine. Indeed, Ange, I think it is my youth I sigh for rather than the friends I lived with. They were such merry days: battles and sieges in the provinces, parliaments disputing here and there; Conde in and out of prison--now the King's loyal servant, now in arms against him; swords clashing, cannon roaring under our very windows; alarm bells pealing, cries of fire, barricades in the streets; and amidst it all, lute and theorbo, *bouts rimes* and madrigals, dancing and play-acting, and foolish practical jests! One could not take the smallest step in life but one of the wits would make a song about it. Oh, it was a boisterous time! And we were all mad, I think; so lightly did we reckon life and death, even when the cannon slew some of our noblest, and the finest saloons were hung with black. You have done less than live, Angelique, not to have lived in that time."

Hyacinth loved to ring the changes on her sister's name. Angela was too English, and sounded too much like the name of a nun; but Angelique suggested one of the most enchanting personalities in that brilliant circle on which Lady Fareham so often rhapsodised. This was the beautiful Angelique Paulet, whose father invented the tax called by his name, La Paulette--a financial measure, which was the main cause of the first Fronde war.

"I only knew her when she was between fifty and sixty," said Lady Fareham, "but she hardly looked forty; and she was still handsome, in spite of her red hair. ***Trop dore***, her admirers called it; but, my love, it was as red as that scullion's we saw in the poultry yard yesterday. She was a reigning beauty at three Courts, and had a crowd of adorers when she was only fourteen. Ah, Papillon, you may open your eyes! What will you be at fourteen? Still playing with your babies, or mad about your shock dogs, I dare swear!"

"I gave my babies to the housekeeper's grand-daughter last year," said Papillon, much offended, "when father gave me the peregrine. I only care for live things now I am old."

"And at fourteen thou wilt be an awkward, long-legged wench that will frighten away all my admirers, yet not be worth the trouble of a compliment on thine own account."

"I want no such stuff!" cried Papillon. "Do you think I would like a French fop always at my elbow as Monsieur de Malfort is ever at yours? I love hunting and hawking, and a man that can ride, and shoot, and row, and fight, like father or Sir Denzil Warner--not a man who thinks more of his ribbons and periwig and cannon-sleeves than of killing his fox or flying his falcon."

"Oh, you are beginning to have opinions!" sighed Hyacinth. "I am indeed an old woman! Go and find yourself something to play with, alive or dead. You are vastly too clever for my company."

"I'll go and saddle Brownie. Will you come for a ride, Aunt Angy?"

"Yes, dear, if her ladyship does not want me at home."

"Her ladyship knows your heart is in the fields and woods. Yes, sweetheart, saddle your pony, and order your aunt's horse and a pair of grooms to take care of you."

The child ran off rejoicing.

"Precocious little devil! She will pick up all our jargon before she is in her teens."

"Dear sister, if you talk so indiscreetly before her----"

"Indiscreet! Am I really so indiscreet? That is Fareham's word. I believe I was born so. But I was telling you about your namesake, Mademoiselle Paulet. She began to reign when Henri was king, and no doubt he was one of her most ardent admirers. Don't look frightened! She was always a model of virtue. Mademoiselle Scudery has devoted pages to painting her perfections under an Oriental alias. She sang, she danced, she talked divinely. She did everything better than everybody else. Priests and Bishops praised her. And after changes and losses and troubles, she died far from Paris, a spinster, nearly sixty years old. It was a paltry finish to a life that began in a blaze of glory."

CHAPTER VIII.
SUPERIOR TO FASHION.

At Oxford Angela was so happy as to be presented to Catharine of Braganza, a little dark woman, whose attire still bore some traces of its original Portuguese heaviness; such a dress--clumsy, ugly, infinitely rich and expensive--as one sees in old portraits of Spanish and Netherlandish matrons, in which every elaborate detail of the costly fabric seems to have been devised in the research of ugliness. She saw the King also; met him casually--she walking with her brother-in-law, while Lady Fareham and her friends ran from shop to shop in the High Street--in Magdalen College grounds, a group of beauties and a family of spaniels fawning upon him as he sauntered slowly, or stopped to feed the swans that swam close by the bank, keeping pace with him, and stretching long necks in greedy solicitation.

The loveliest woman Angela had ever seen--tall, built like a goddess--walked on the King's right hand. She carried a heap of broken bread in the satin petticoat which she held up over one white arm, while with her other hand she gave the pieces one by one to the King. Angela saw that as each hunch changed hands the royal fingers touched the lady's tapering finger-tips and tried to detain them.

Fareham took off his hat, bowed low in a grave and stately salutation, and passed on; but Charles called him back.

"Nay, Fareham, has the world grown so dull that you have nothing to tell us this November morning?"

"Indeed, sir, I fear that my riverside hermitage can afford very little news that could interest your Majesty or these ladies."

"A fox gone to ground, an otter killed among your reeds, or a hawk in the sulks, is an event in the country. Anything would be a relief from the weekly total of London deaths, which is our chief subject of conversation, or the General's complaints that there is no one in town but himself to transact business, or dismal prophecies of a Nonconformist rebellion that is to follow the Five Mile Act."

The group of ladies stared at Angela in a smiling silence, one haughtier than the rest standing a little aloof. She was older, and of a more audacious loveliness than the lady who carried broken bread in her petticoat; but she too was splendidly beautiful as a goddess on a painted ceiling, and as much painted perhaps.

Angela contemplated her with the reverence youth gives to consummate beauty, unaware that she was admiring the notorious Barbara Palmer.

Fareham waited, hat in hand, grave almost to sullenness. It was not for him to do more than reply to his Majesty's remarks, nor could he retire till dismissed.

"You have a strange face at your side, man. Pray introduce the lady," said the King, smiling at Angela, whose vivid blush was as fresh as Miss Stewart's had been a year or two ago, before she had her first quarrel with Lady Castlemaine, or rode in Gramont's glass coach, or gave her classic profile to embellish the coin of the realm--the "common drudge 'tween man and man."

"I have the honour to present my sister-in-law, Mistress Kirkland, to your Majesty." The King shook hands with Angela in the easiest way, as if he had been mortal.

"Welcome to our poor court, Mistress Kirkland. Your father was my father's friend and companion in the evil days. They starved together at Beverley, and rode side by side through the Warwickshire lanes to suffer the insolence of Coventry. I have not forgotten. If I had I have a monitor yonder to remind me," glancing in the direction of a middle-aged gentleman, stately, and sober of attire, who was walking slowly towards them. "The Chancellor is a living chronicle, and his conversation chiefly consists in reminiscences of events I would rather forget"

"Memory is an invention of Old Nick," said Lady Castlemaine. "Who the deuce wants to remember anything, except what cards are out and what are in?"

"Not you, Fairest. You should be the last to cultivate mnemonics for yourself or for your friends. Is your father in England, sweet mistress?"

Angela faltered a negative, as if with somebody else's voice--or so it seemed to her. A swarthy, heavy-browed man, wearing a dark-blue ribbon and a star--a man with whom his intimates jested in shameless freedom--a man whom the town called Rowley, after some ignominious quadruped--a man who had distinguished himself neither in the field nor in the drawing-room by any excellence above the majority, since the wit men praised has resolved itself for posterity into half a dozen happy repartees. Only this! But he was a King, a crowned and anointed King, and even Angela, who was less frivolous and shallow than most women, stood before him abashed and dazzled.

His Majesty bowed a gracious adieu, yawned, flung another crust to the swans, and sauntered on, the Stewart whispering in his ear, the Castlemaine talking loud to her neighbour, Lady Chesterfield, this latter lady very pretty, very bold and mischievous, newly restored to the Court after exile with her jealous husband at his mansion in Wales.

They were gone; Charles to be button-holed by Lord Clarendon, who waited for him at the end of the walk; the ladies to wander as they pleased till the two-o'clock dinner. They were gone, like a dream of beauty and splendour, and Fareham and Angela pursued their walk by the river, grey in the sunless November.

"Well, sister, you have seen the man whom we brought back in a whirlwind of loyalty five years ago, and for whose sake we rebuilt the fabric of monarchical government. Do you think we are much the gainers by that tempest of enthusiasm which blew us home Charles the Second? We had suffered all the trouble of the change to a Republic; a life that should have been sacred had been sacrificed to the principles of liberty. While abhorring the regicides, we might have profited by their crime. We might have been a free state to-day, like the United Provinces. Do you think we are better off with a King like Rowley, to amuse himself at the expense of the nation?"

"I detest the idea of a Republic."

"Youth worships the supernatural in anointed kings. Think not that I am opposed to a constitutional monarchy, so long as it works well for the majority. But when England had with such terrible convulsions shaken off all those shackles and trappings of royalty, and when the ship, so lightened, had sailed so steadily with no ballast but common sense, does it not seem almost a pity to undo what has been done--to begin again the long procession of good kings and bad kings, foolish or wise--for the sake of such a man as yonder saunterer?" with a glance towards the British Sultan and his harem.

"England was never better governed than by Cromwell," he continued. "She was tranquil at home and victorious abroad, admired and feared. Mazarin, while pretending to be the faithful friend of Charles, was the obsequious courtier of Oliver. The finest form of government is a limited despotism. See how France prospered under the sagacious tyrant, Louis the Eleventh, under the soldier-statesman, Sully, under pure reason incarnate in Richelieu. Whether you call your tyrant king or protector, minister or president, matters nothing. It is the man and not the institution, the mind and not the machinery that is wanted."

"I did not know you were a Republican, like Sir Denzil Warner."

"I am nothing now I have left off being a soldier. I have no strong opinions about anything. I am a looker on; and life seems little more real to me than a stage play. Warner is of a different stamp. He is an enthusiastic in politics--godson of Horn's--a disciple of Milton's, the son of a Puritan, and a Puritan himself. A fine nature, Angela, allied to a handsome presence."

Sir Denzil Warner was their neighbour at Chilton, and Angela had met him often enough for them to become friends. He had ridden by her side with hawk and hound, had been one of her instructors in English sport, and had sometimes, by an accident, joined her and Henriette in their boating expeditions, and helped her to perfect herself in the management of a pair of sculls.

"Hyacinth has her fancies about Warner," Fareham said presently, as they strolled along.

There was a significance in his tone that the girl could not mistake; more especially as her sister had not been reticent about those notions to which Fareham alluded.

"Hyacinth has fancies about many things," she said, blushing a little.

Fareham noted the slightness of the blush.

"I verily believe that handsome youth has found you adamant," he said, after a thoughtful silence. "Yet you might easily choose a worse suitor. Your sister has often the strangest whims about marriage-making; but in this fancy I did not oppose her. It would be a very suitable alliance."

"I hope your lordship does not begin to think me a burden on your household," faltered Angela, wounded by his cold-blooded air in disposing of her. "When you and my sister are tired of me I can go back to my convent."

"What! Return to those imprisoning walls; immure your sweet youth in a clois-ter? Not for the Indies. I would not suffer such a sacrifice. Tired of you! I--so deeply bound! I who owe you my life! I who looked up out of a burning hell of pain and madness and saw an angel standing by my bed! Tired of you! Indeed you know me better than to think so badly of me were it but in one flash of thought. You can need no protestations from me. Only, as a young and beautiful woman, living in an age that is full of peril for women, I should like to see you married to a good and true man--such as Denzil Warner."

"I am sorry to disappoint you," Angela answered coldly; "but Papillon and I have agreed that I am always to be her spinster aunt, and am to keep her house when she is married, and wear a linsey gown and a bunch of keys at my girdle, like Mrs. Hubbuck, at Chilton."

"That's just like Henriette. She takes after her mother, and thinks that this globe and all the people upon it were created principally for her pleasure. The Americas to give her chocolate, the Indian isles to sweeten it for her, the ocean tides to bring her feathers and finery. She is her own centre and circumference, like her mother."

"You should not say such an ill thing of your wife, Fareham," said Angela, deeply shocked. "Hyacinth is not one to look into the heart of things. She has too happy a disposition for grave backward-reaching thoughts; but I will swear that she loves you--ay--almost to reverence."

"Yes, to reverence, to over much reverence, perhaps. She might have given a freer, fonder love to a more amiable man. I have some strain of my unhappy kins-man's temper, perhaps--the disposition that keeps a wife at a distance. He managed to make three wives afraid of him; and it was darkly rumoured that he killed one."

"Strafford--a murderer! No, no."

"Not by intent. An accident--only an accident. They who most hated him pre-tended that he pushed her from him somewhat roughly when she was least able to bear roughness, and that the after consequences of the blow were fatal. He was one of the doomed always, you see. He knew that himself, and told his bosom friend that he was not long-lived. The brand of misfortune was upon him even at the height of his power. You may read his destiny in his face."

They walked on in silence for some time, Angela depressed and unhappy. It seemed as if Fareham had lifted a mask and shown her his real countenance, with all the lines that tell a life history. She had suspected that he was not happy; that the joyous existence amidst fairest surroundings which seemed so exquisite to her was dull and vapid for him. She could but think that he was like her father, and that action and danger were necessary to him, and that it was only this rustic tranquillity that weighed upon his spirits.

"Do not for a moment believe that I would speak slightingly of your sister," Fareham resumed, after that silent interval. "It were indeed an ill thing in me-- most of all to disparage her in your hearing. She is lovely, accomplished, learned even, after the fashion of the Rue St. Thomas du Louvre. She used to shine among the brightest at the Scuderys' Saturday parties, which were the most wearisome assemblies I ever ran away from. The match was made for us by others, and I was her betrothed husband before I saw her. Yet I loved her at first sight. Who could help loving a face as fair as morning over the eastward hills, a voice as sweet as the nightingales in the Tuileries garden? She was so young--a child almost; so gentle and confiding. And to see her now with Papillon is to question which is the younger, mother or daughter. Love her? Why, of course I love her. I loved her then. I love her now. Her beauty has but ripened with the passing years; and she has walked the furnace of fine company in two cities, and has never been seared by fire. Love her! Could a man help loving beauty, and frankness, and a natural innocence which cannot be spoiled even by the knowledge of things evil, even by daily contact with sin in high places?"

Again there was a silence, and then, in a deeper tone, after a long sigh, Fareham said--

"I love and honour my wife; I adore my children; yet I am alone, Angela, and I shall be alone till death."

"I don't understand."

"Oh yes, you do; you understand as well as I who suffer. My wife and I love each other dearly. If she have a fit of the vapours, or an aching tooth, I am wretched. But we have never been companions. The things that she loves are charmless for me. She is enchanted with people from whom I run away. Is it companionship, do you think, for me to look on while she walks a coranto or tosses shuttlecocks with De Malfort? Roxalana is as much my companion when I admire her on the stage from my seat in the pit. There are times when my wife seems no nearer to me than a beautiful picture. If I sit in a corner, and listen to her pretty babble about the last fan she bought at the Middle Exchange, or the last witless comedy she saw at the King's Theatre, is that companionship, think you? I may be charmed to-day--as I was charmed ten years ago--with the silvery sweetness of her voice, with the graceful turn of her head, the white roundness of her throat. At least I am constant. There is no change in her or in me. We are just as near and just as far apart as when the priest joined our hands at St. Eustache. And it must be so to the end, I suppose; and I think the fault is in me. I am out of joint with the world I live in. I cannot set myself in tune with their new music. I look back, and remember, and regret; yet hardly know why I remember or what I regret."

Again a silence, briefer than the last, and he went on:--

"Do you think it strange that I talk so freely--to you--who are scarce more than a child, less learned than Henriette in worldly knowledge? It is a comfort sometimes to talk of one's self; of what one has missed as well as of what one has. And you have such an air of being wise beyond your years; wise in all thoughts that are not of the world--thoughts of things of which there is no truck at the Exchanges; which no one buys or sells at Abingdon fair. And you are so near allied to me--a sister! I never had a sister of my own blood, Angela. I was an only child. Solitude was my portion. I lived alone with my tutor and *gouvernante*--a poor relation of my mother's--alone in a house that was mostly deserted, for Lord and Lady Fareham were in London with the King, till the troubles brought the Court to Christchurch, and them to Chilton. I have had few in whom to confide. And you--remember what you have been to me, and do not wonder if I trust you more than others. Thou didst go down to the very grave with me, didst pluck me out of the pit. Corruption could not touch a creature so lovely and so innocent Thou didst walk unharmed through the charnel-house. Remembering this, as I ever must remember, can you wonder that you are nearer to me than all the rest of the world?"

She had seated herself on a bench that commanded a view of the river, and her dreaming eyes were looking far away along the dim perspective of mist and water, bare pollard willows, ragged sedges. Her head drooped a little so that he could not see her face, and one ungloved hand hung listlessly at her side.

He bent down to take the slender hand in his, lifted it to his lips, and quickly let it go; but not before she had felt his tears upon it. She looked up a few minutes later, and the place was empty. Her tears fell thick and fast. Never before had she suffered this exquisite pain--sadness so intense, yet touching so close on joy. She sat alone in the inexpressible melancholy of the late autumn; pale mists rising from the river; dead leaves falling; and Fareham's tears upon her hand.

CHAPTER IX.
IN A PURITAN HOUSE.

How quickly the days passed in that gay household at Chilton! and yet every day of Angela's life held so much of action and emotion that, looking back at Christmas time to the three months that had slipped by since she had brought Fareham from his sick bed to his country home, she could but experience that common feeling of youth in such circumstances. Surely it was half a lifetime that had lapsed; or else she, by some subtle and supernatural change, had become a new creature.

She thought of her life in the Convent, thought of it much and deeply on those Sunday mornings when she and her sister and De Malfort and a score or so of servants crept quietly to a room in the heart of the house where a Priest, who had been fetched from Oxford in, Lady Fareham's coach, said Mass within locked doors. The familiar words of the service, the odour of the incense, brought back the old time--the unforgotten atmosphere, the dull tranquillity of ten years, which had been as one year by reason of their level monotony.

Could she go back to such a life as that? Go back! Leave all she loved? At the mere suggestion her trembling hand was stretched out involuntarily to clasp her niece Henriette, kneeling beside her. Leave them--leave those with whom and for whom she lived? Leave this loving child--her sister--her brother? Fareham had told her to call him "Brother." He had been to her as a brother, with all a brother's kindness, counselling her, confiding in her.

Only with one person at Chilton Abbey had she ever conversed as seriously as with Fareham, and that person was Sir Denzil Warner, who at five and twenty was more serious in his way of looking at serious things than most men of fifty.

"I cannot make a jest of life," he said once, in reply to some flippant speech of De Malfort's; "it is too painful a business for the majority."

"What has that to do with us--the minority? Can we smooth a sick man's pillow by pulling a long face? We shall do him more good by tossing him a crown, if he be poor; or helping to build him a hospital by the sacrifice of a night's winnings at ombre. Long faces help nobody; that is what you Puritans will never consider."

"No; but if the long faces are the faces of men who think, something may come of their thoughts for the good of humanity."

Denzil Warner was the only person who ever spoke to Angela of her religion. With extreme courtesy, and with gentle excuses for his temerity in touching on so delicate a theme, he ventured to express his abhorrence of the superstitions interwoven with the Romanist's creed. He talked as one who had sat at the feet of the blind poet--talked sometimes in the very words of John Milton.

There was much in what he said that appealed to her reason; but there was no charm in that severer form of worship which he offered in exchange for her own. He was frank and generous; he had a fine nature, but was too much given to judging his fellow-men. He had all the arrogance of Puritanism superadded to the natural arrogance of youth that has never known humiliating reverses, that has never been the servant of circumstance. He was Angela's senior by something less than four years; yet it seemed to her that he was in every attribute infinitely her superior. In education, in depth of thought, in resolution for good, and scorn of evil. If he loved her--as Hyacinth insisted upon declaring--there was nothing of youthful impetuosity in his passion. He had, indeed, betrayed his sentiments by no direct speech. He had told her gravely that he was interested in her, and deeply concerned that one so worthy and so amiable should have been brought up in the house of idolaters, should have been taught falsehood instead of truth.

She stood up boldly for the faith of her maternal ancestors.

"I cannot continue your friend if you speak evil of those I love, Sir Denzil," she said. "Could you have seen the lives of those good ladies of the Ursuline Convent, their unselfishness, their charity, you must needs have respected their religion. I cannot think why you love to say hard words of us Catholics; for in all I have ever heard or seen of the lives of the Nonconformists they approach us far more nearly in their principles than the members of the Church of England, who, if my sister does not paint them with too black a brush, practise their religion with a laxity and indifference that would go far to turn religion to a jest."

Whatever Sir Denzil's ideas might be upon the question of creed--and he did not scruple to tell Angela that he thought every Papist foredoomed to everlasting punishment--he showed so much pleasure in her society as to be at Chilton Abbey, and the sharer of her walks and rides, as often as possible. Lady Fareham encouraged his visits, and was always gracious to him. She discovered that he possessed the gift of music, though not in the same remarkable degree as Henri de Malfort, who played the guitar exquisitely, and into whose hands you had but to put a musical instrument for him to extract sweetness from it. Lute or theorbo, viola or viol di gamba, treble or bass, came alike to his hand and ear. Some instruments he had studied; with some his skill came by intuition.

Denzil Warner performed very creditably upon the organ. He had played on John Milton's organ in St. Bride's Church, when he was a boy, and he had played of late in the church at Chalfont St. Giles, where he had visited Milton frequently, since the poet had left his lodgings in Artillery Walk, carrying his family and his books to that sequestered village in the shelter of the hills between Uxbridge and Beaconsfield. Here from the lips of his sometime tutor the Puritan had heard such stories of the Court as made him hourly expectant of exterminating fires. Doubtless the fire would have come, as it came upon Sodom and Gomorrah, but for those righteous lives of the Nonconformists, which redeemed the time; quiet, god-fearing lives in dull old city houses, in streets almost as narrow as those which Milton remembered in his beloved Italy; streets where the sun looked in for an hour, shooting golden arrows down upon the diamond-paned casements, and deepening the shadow of the massive timbers that held up the overlapping stories, looked in and bade "good night" within an hour or so, leaving an atmosphere of sober grey, cool, and quiet, and dull, in those obscure streets and alleys where the great traffic of Cheapside or Ludgate sounded like the murmur of a far-off sea.

Pious men and women worshipped the implacable God of the Puritans in the secret chambers of those narrow streets; and those who gathered together in these days--if they rejected the Liturgy of the Church of England--must indeed be few, and must meet by stealth, as if to pray or preach after their own manner were a crime. Charles, within a year or so of his general amnesty and happy restoration,

had made such worship criminal; and now the Five Mile Act, lately passed at Oxford, had rendered the restrictions and penalties of Nonconformity utterly intolerable. Men were lying in prison here and there about merry England for no greater
offence than preaching the gospel to a handful of God-fearing people. But that a
Puritan tinker should moulder for a dozen years in a damp jail could count for
little against the blessed fact of the Maypole reinstated in the Strand, and five play-
houses in London performing ribald comedies, till but recently, when the plague
shut their doors.

Milton, old and blind, and somewhat soured by domestic disappointments, had
imparted no optimistic philosophy to young Denzil Warner, whose father he had
known and loved. The fight at Hopton Heath had made Denzil fatherless; the Colonel of Warner's horse riding to his death in the last fatal charge of that memorable
day.

Denzil had grown up under the prosperous rule of the Protector, and his boyhood had been spent in the guardianship of a most watchful and serious-minded
mother. He had been somewhat over-cosseted and apron-stringed, it may be, in
that tranquil atmosphere of the rich widow's house; but not all Lady Warner's tenderness could make her son a milksop. Except for a period of two years in London,
when he had lived under the roof of the great Republican, a docile pupil to a stern
but kind master, Denzil had lived mostly under the open sky, was a keen sports-
man, and loved the country with almost as sensitive a love as his quondam master
and present friend, John Milton; and it was perhaps this appreciation of rural beauty which had made a bond of friendship between the great poet and the Puritan
squire.

"You have a knack of painting rural scenes which needs but to be joined with
the gift of music to make you a poet," he said, when Denzil had been expatiating
upon the landscape amidst which he had enjoyed his last bout of falconry, or his
last run with his half-dozen couple of hounds. "You are almost as the power of sight
to me when you describe those downs and valleys whose every shape and shadow I
once knew so well. Alas, that I should be changed so much and they so little!"

"It is one thing, sir, to feel that this world is beautiful, and another to find
golden words and phrases which to a prisoner in the Tower could conjure up as fair
a landscape as Claude Lorraine ever painted. Those sonorous and mellifluous lines

which you were so gracious as to repeat to me, forming part of the great epic which the world is waiting for, bear witness to the power that can turn words into music, and make pictures out of the common tongue. That splendid art, sir, is but given to one man in a century--or in several centuries; since I know but Dante and Virgil who have ever equalled your vision of heaven and hell."

"Do not over-praise me, Denzil, in thy charity to poverty and affliction. It is pleasing to be understood by a youth who loves hawk and hound better than books; for it offers the promise of popular appreciation in years to come. Yet the world is so little athirst for my epic that I doubt if I shall find a bookseller to give me a few pounds for the right to print a work that has cost me years of thought and laborious revision. But at least it has been my consolation in the long blank night of my decay, and has saved me many a heart-ache. For while I am building up my verses, and engraving line after line upon the tablets of memory, I can forget that I am blind, and poor, and neglected, and that the dear saint I loved was snatched from me in the noontide of our happiness."

Denzil talked much of John Milton in his conversations with Angela, during those rides or rambles, in which Papillon was their only chaperon. Lady Fareham sauntered, like her royal master; but she rarely walked a mile at a stretch; and she was pleased to encourage the rural wanderings that brought her sister and War-ner into a closer intimacy, and promised well for the success of her matrimonial scheme.

"I believe they adore each other already," she told Fareham one morning, standing by his side in the great stone porch, to watch those three youthful figures ride away, aunt and niece side by side, on palfrey and pony, with Denzil for their cavalier.

"You are always over-quick to be sure of anything that suits your own fancy, dearest," answered Fareham, watching them to the curve of the avenue; "but I see no signs of favour to that solemn youth in your sister. She suffers his attentions out of pure civility. He is an accomplished horseman, having given all his life to learning how to jump a fence gracefully; and his company is at least better than a groom's."

"How scornfully you jeer at him!"

"Oh, I have no more scorn than the Cavalier's natural contempt for the Roundhead. A hereditary hatred, perhaps."

"You say such hard things of his Majesty that one might often take you to be of Sir Denzil's way of thinking."

"I never think about the King. I only wonder. I may sometimes express my wonderment too freely for a loyal subject."

"I cannot vouch for Angela, but I will wager that he is deep in love," persisted Hyacinth.

"Have it your own way, sweetheart. He is dull enough to be deep in debt, or love, or politics, anything dismal and troublesome," answered his lordship, as he strolled off with his spaniels; not those dainty toy dogs which had been his companions at the gate of death, but the fine liver-and-black shooting dogs that lived in the kennels, and thought it doghood's highest privilege to attend their lord in his walks, whether with or without a gun.

*   *   *   *   *

His lordship kept open Christmas that year at Chilton Abbey, and there was great festivity, chiefly devised and carried out by the household, as Fareham and his wife were too much of the modern fashion, and too cosmopolitan in their ideas, to appreciate the fuss and feasting of an English Christmas. They submitted, however, to the festival as arranged for them by Mr. Manningtree and Mrs. Hubbuck--the copious feasting for servants and dependents, the mummers and carolsingers, the garlands and greenery which disguised the fine old tapestry, and made a bower of the vaulted hall. Everything was done with a lavish plenteousness, and no doubt the household enjoyed the fun and feasting all the more because of that dismal season of a few years back, when all Christmas ceremonies had been denounced as idolatrous, and when the members of the Anglican Church had assembled for their Christmas service secretly in private houses, and as much under the ban of the law as the Nonconformists were now.

Angela was interested in everything in that bright world where all things were new. The children piping Christmas hymns in the clear cold morning enchanted her. She ran down to kiss and fondle the smaller among them, and finding them thinly clad promised to make them warm cloaks and hoods as fast as her fingers could sew. Denzil found her there in the wide snowy space before the porch, prattling with the children, bare-headed, her soft brown hair blown about in the wind; and he was moved, as a man must needs be moved by the aspect of the woman that he loves caressing a small child, melted almost to tears by the thought that in some blessed time to come she might so caress, only more warmly, a child whose existence should be their bond of union.

And yet, being both shy and somewhat cold of temperament, he restrained himself, and greeted her only as a friend; for his mother's influence was holding him back, urging him not to marry a Papist, were she ever so lovely or lovable.

He had known Angela for nearly three months, and his acquaintance with her had reached this point of intimacy, yet Lady Warner had never seen her. This fact distressed him, and he had tried hard to awaken his mother's interest by praises of the Fareham family and of Angela's exquisite character; but the Scarlet Spectre came between the Puritan lady and the house of Fareham.

"There is nothing you can tell me about this girl, upon whom I fear you have foolishly set your affection, which can make me forget that she has been nursed and swaddled in the bondage of a corrupt Church, taught to worship idols, and to cherish lying traditions, while the light of God's holy word has been made dark for her."

"She is young enough to embrace a purer creed, and to walk by the clearer light that leads your footsteps, mother. If she were my wife I should not despair of winning her to think as we do."

"And in all the length of England was there no young woman of right principles fit to be thy wife, that thou must needs fall into the snare of the first Popish witch who set her lure for thee?"

"Popish witch! Oh, mother, how ill you can conceive the image of my dear love, who has no witchcraft but beauty, no charm so potent as her truth and innocency!"

"I know them--these children of the Scarlet Woman--and I know their works, and the fate of those who trust them. The late King--weak and stubborn as he was--might have been alive this day, and reigning over a contented people, but for that fair witch who ruled him. It was the Frenchwoman's sorceries that wrought

Charles's ruin."

"If thou wouldst but see my Angela," pleaded the son, with a caressing arm about his mother's spare shoulders.

"Thine! What! is she thine--pledged and promised already? Then, indeed, these white hairs will go down with sorrow to the grave."

"Mother, I doubt if thou couldst find so much as a single grey hair in that comely head of thine," said the son; and the mother smiled in the midst of her affliction.

"And as for promise--there has been none. I have said no word of love; nor have I been encouraged to speak by any token of liking on the lady's part. I stand aloof and admire, and wonder at so much modesty and intelligence in Lady Fareham's sister. Let me bring her to see you, mother?"

"This is your house, Denzil. Were you to fill it with the sons and daughters of Belial, I could but pray that your eyes might be opened to their iniquity. I could not shut these doors against you or your companions. But I want no Popish women here."

"Ah, you do not know! Wait until you have seen her," urged Denzil, with the lover's confidence in the omnipotence of his mistress's charms.

And now on this Christmas Day there came the opportunity Denzil had been waiting for. The weather was cold and bright, the landscape was blotted out with snow; and the lake in Chilton Park offered a sound surface for the exercise of that novel amusement of skating, an accomplishment which Lord Fareham had acquired while in the Low Countries, and in which he had been Denzil's instructor during the late severe weather. Angela, at her brother-in-law's entreaty, had also adventured herself upon a pair of skates, and had speedily found delight in the swift motion, which seemed to her like the flight of a bird skimming the steely surface of the frozen lake, and incomparable in enjoyment.

"It is even more delightful than a gallop on Zephyr," she told her sister, who stood on the bank with a cluster of gay company, watching the skaters.

"I doubt not that; since there is even more danger of getting your neck broken upon runaway skates than on a runaway horse," answered Hyacinth.

After an hour on the lake, in which Denzil had distinguished himself by his mastery of the new exercise, being always at hand to support his mistress at the slightest indication of peril, she consented to the removal of her skates, at Papillon's earnest entreaty, who wanted her aunt to walk with her before dinner. After dinner there would be the swift-coming December twilight, and Christmas games, snap-dragon and the like, which Papillon, although a little fine lady, reproducing all her mother's likes and dislikes in miniature, could not, as a human child, altogether disregard.

"I don't care about such nonsense as Georgie does," she told her aunt, with condescending reference to her brother; "but I like to see the others amused. Those village children are such funny little savages. They stick their fingers in their mouths and grin at me, and call me 'Your annar,' or 'Your worship,' and say 'Anan' to everything. They are like Audrey in the play you read to me."

Denzil was in attendance upon aunt and niece.

"If you want to come with us, you must invent a pretty walk, Sir Denzil," said Papillon. "I am tired of long lanes and ploughed fields."

"I know of one of the pleasantest rambles in the shire--across the woods to the Grange. And we can rest there for half an hour, if Mrs. Angela will allow us, and take a light refreshment."

"Dear Sir Denzil, that is the very thing," answered Papillon, breathlessly. "I am dying of hunger. And I don't want to go back to the Abbey. Will there be any cakes or mince pies at the Grange?"

"Cakes in plenty, but I fear there will be no mince pies. My mother does not love Christmas dainties."

Henriette wanted to know why. She was always wanting the reason of things. A bright inquiring little mind, perpetually on the alert for novelty; an imitative brain like a monkey's; hands and feet that know not rest; and there you have the Honourable Henrietta Maria Revel, *alias* Papillon.

They crossed the river, Angela and Denzil each taking an oar, while Papillon pretended to steer, a process which she effected chiefly by screaming.

"Another lump of ice!" she shrieked. "We shall be swamped. I believe the river will be frozen before Twelfth Night, and we shall be able to dance upon it. We must have bonfires and roast an ox for the poor people. Mrs. Hubbuck told me they roasted an ox the year King Charles was beheaded. Horrid brutes--to think that they could eat at such a time! If they had been sorry they could not have relished roast beef."

Hadley Grange, commonly known as the Grange, was in every detail the antithesis of Chilton Abbey. At the Abbey the eye was dazzled, the mind was bewildered, by an excess of splendour--an over-much of everything gorgeous or beautiful. At the Grange sight and mind were rested by the low tone of colour, the quaker-like precision of form. All the furniture in the house was Elizabethan, plain, ponderous, the conscientious work of Oxfordshire mechanics. On one side of the house there was a bowling green, on the other a physic garden, where odours of medicinal herbs, camomile, fennel, rosemary, rue, hung ever on the surrounding air. There was nothing modern in Lady Warner's house but the spotless cleanliness; the perfume of last summer's roses and lavender; the polished surface of tables and cabinets, oak chests and oak floors, testifying to the inexorable industry of rustic housemaids. In all other respects the Grange was like a house that had just awakened from a century of sleep.

Lady Warner rose from her high-backed chair by the chimney corner in the oak parlour, and laid aside the book she had been reading, to welcome her son, startled at seeing him followed by a tall, fair girl in a black mantle and hood, and a little slip of a thing, with bright dark eyes and small determined face, pert, pointed, interrogative, framed in swansdown--a small aerial figure in a white cloth cloak, and a scarlet brocade frock, under which two little red shoes danced into the room.

"Mother, I have brought Mrs. Angela Kirkland and her niece to visit you this Christmas morning."

"Mrs. Kirkland and her niece are welcome," and Lady Warner made a deep curtsy, not like one of Lady Fareham's sinking curtseys, as of one near swooning in an ecstasy of politeness, but dignified and inflexible, straight down and straight up again.

"But as for Christmas, 'tis one of those superstitious observances which I have ever associated with a Church I abhor."

Denzil reddened furiously. To have brought this upon his beloved!

Angela drew herself up, and paled at the unexpected assault. The brutality of it was startling, though she knew, from Denzil's opinions, that his mother must be an enemy of her faith.

"Indeed, madam, I am sorry that anybody in England should think it an ill thing to celebrate the birthday of our Redeemer and Lord," she said.

"Do you think, young lady, that foolish romping games, and huge chines of beef, and smoking ale made luscious with spices and roasted pippins, and carol-singing and play-acting, can be the proper honouring of Him who was God first and for ever, and Man only for one brief interval in His eternal existence? To keep God's birthday with drunken rioting! What blasphemy! If you can think that there is not more profaneness than piety in such sensual revelries--why, it is that you do not know how to think. You would have learnt to reason better had you known that sweet poet and musician, and true thinker, Mr. John Milton, with whom it was my privilege to converse frequently during my husband's lifetime, and afterwards when he condescended to accept my son for his pupil, and spent three days and nights under this roof."

"Mr. Milton is still at Chalfont, mother. So you may hope to see him again with a less journey than to London," said Denzil, seizing the first chance of a change in the conversation; "and here is a little Miss to whom I have promised a light collation, with some of your Jersey milk."

"Mistress Kirkland and her niece shall have the best I can provide. The larder will furnish something acceptable, I doubt not, although I and my household observe this day as a fast."

"What, madam, are you sorry that Jesus Christ was born to-day?" asked Papillon.

"I am sorry for my sins, little mistress, and for the sins of all mankind, which nothing but His blood could wash away. To remember His birth is to remember that He died for us; and that is why I spend the twenty-fifth of December in fasting and prayer."

"Are you not glad you are to dine at the Abbey to-day, Sir Denzil?" asked Papillon, by way of commentary.

"Nay, I put no restraint on my son. He can serve God after his own manner, and veer with every wind of passion or fancy, if he will. But you shall have your cake and draught of milk, little lady, and you too, Mistress Kirkland, will, I hope, taste our Jersey milk, unless you would prefer a glass of Malmsey wine."

"Mrs. Kirkland is as much an anchorite as yourself, mother. She takes no wine."

Lady Warner was the soul of hospitality, and particularly proud of her dairy. When kept clear of theology and politics she was not an ill-natured woman. But to be a Puritan in the year of the Five Mile Act was not to think kindly of the Government under which she lived; while her sense of her own wrongs was intensified by rumours of over-indulgence shown to Papists, and the broad assertion that King and Duke were Roman Catholic at heart, and waited only the convenient hour to reforge the fetters that had bound England to Rome.

She was fond of children, most of all of little girls, never having had a daughter. She bent down to kiss Henriette, and then turned to Angela with her kindest smile--

"And this is Lady Fareham's daughter? She is as pretty as a picture."

"And I am as good as a picture--sometimes, madam," chirped Papillon. "Mother says I am ***douce comme un image.***"

"When thou hast been silent or still for five minutes," said Angela, "and that is but seldom."

A loud hand-bell summoned the butler, and an Arcadian meal was speedily set out on a table in the hall, where a great fire of logs burnt as merrily as if it had been designed to enliven a Christmas-keeping household. Indeed there was nothing miserly or sparing about the housekeeping at the Grange, which harmonised with the sombre richness of Lady Warner's grey brocade gown, from the old-fashioned silk mercer's at the sign of the Flower-de-luce, in Cheapside. There was liberality without waste, and a certain quiet refinement in every detail, which reminded Angela of the convent parlour and her aunt's room--and contrasted curiously with the elegant disorder of her sister's surroundings.

Papillon clapped her hands at sight of the large plum cake, the jug of milk, and bowl of blackberry conserve.

"I was so hungry," she said, apologetically, after Denzil had supplied her with generous slices of cake, and large spoonfuls of jam. "I did not know that Nonconformists had such nice things to eat."

"Did you think we all lay in gaol to suffer cold and hunger for the faith that is in us, like that poor preacher at Bedford?" asked Lady Warner, bitterly. "It will come to that some day, perhaps, under the new Act."

"Will you show Mistress Kirkland your house, mother, and your dairy?" Denzil asked hurriedly. "I know she would like to see one of the neatest dairies in Oxford-shire."

No request could be more acceptable to Lady Warner, who was a housekeeper first and a controversialist afterwards. Inclined as she was to rail against the Church of Rome--partly because she had made up her mind upon hearsay, chiefly Milto-nian, that Roman Catholicism was only another name for image-worship and mar-tyr-burning, and partly on account of the favour that had been shown to Papists, as compared with the cruel treatment of Nonconformists--still there was a charm in Angela's gentle beauty against which the daughterless matron could not steel her heart. She melted in the space of a quarter of an hour, while Denzil was encourag-ing Henriette to over-eat herself, and trying to persuade Angela to taste this or that dainty, or reproaching her for taking so little; and by the time the child had finished her copious meal, Lady Warner was telling herself how dearly she might have loved this girl for a daughter-in-law, were it not for that fatal objection of a corrupt and pernicious creed.

No! Lovely as she was, modest, refined, and in all things worthy to be loved, the question of creed must be a stumbling-block. And then there were other objections. Rural gossip, the loose talk of servants, had brought a highly coloured description of Lady Fareham's household to her neighbour's ears. The extravagant splendour, the waste and idleness, the late hours, the worship of pleasure, the visiting, the singing, and dancing, and junketing, and worst of all, the too-indulgent friendship shown to a Parisian fopling, had formed the subject of conversation in many an assembly of pious ladies, and hands and eyebrows had been uplifted at the iniquities of Chilton Abbey, as second only to the monstrous goings-on of the Court at Oxford.

Almost ever since the Restoration Lady Warner had been living in meek expec-tancy of fire from heaven; and the chastisement of this memorable year had seemed to her the inevitable realisation of her fears. The fiery rain had come down--impal-pable, invisible, leaving its deadly tokens in burning plague spots, the forerunners of death. That the contagion had mostly visited that humbler class of persons who had been strangers to the excesses and pleasures of the Court made nothing against Lady Warner's conviction that this scourge was Heaven's vengeance upon fashion-able vice. Her son had brought her stories of the life at Whitehall, terrible pictures of iniquity, conveyed in the scathing words of one who sat apart, in a humble lodging, where for him the light of day came not, and heard with disgust and horror of that wave of debauchery which had swept over the city he loved, since the triumph of the Royalists. And Lady Warner had heard the words of Milton, and had listened with a reverence as profound as if the blind poet had been the prophet of Israel, alone in his place of hiding, holding himself aloof from an idolatrous monarch and a wicked people.

And now her son had brought her this fair girl, upon whom he had set his foolish hopes, a Papist, and the sister of a woman whose ways were the ways of--! A favourite scriptural substantive closed the sentence in Lady Warner's mind.

No; it might not be. Whatever power she had over her son must be used against his Papistical syren. She would treat her with courtesy, show her house and dairy, and there an end. And so they repaired to the offices, with Papillon running backwards and forwards as they went along, exclaiming and questioning, delighted with the shining oak floors and great oak chests in the corridor, and the armour in the hall, where, as the sacred and central object, hung the breastplate Sir George Warner wore when he fell at Hopton Heath, dinted by sword and pike, as the enemy's horse rode him down in the *melee*. His orange scarf, soiled and torn, was looped across the steel cuirass. Papillon admired everything, most of all the great cool dairy, which had once been a chapel, and where the piscina was converted to a niche for a polished brass milk-can, to the horror of Angela, who could say no word in praise of a place that had been created by the profanation of holy things. A chapel turned into a storehouse for milk and butter! Was this how Protestants valued consecrated places? An awe-stricken silence came upon her, and she was glad when Denzil remembered that they would have barely time to walk back to the Abbey before the two o'clock dinner.

"You keep Court hours even in the country," said Lady Warner. "I dined half an hour before you came."

"I don't care if I have no dinner to-day," said Papillon; "but I hope I shall be able to eat a mince pie. Why don't you love mince pies, madam? He"--pointing to Denzil--"says you do not."

CHAPTER X.
THE PRIEST'S HOLE.

Denzil dined at the Abbey, where he was always made welcome. Lady Fareham had been warmly insistent upon his presence at their Christmas gaieties.

"We want to show you a Cavalier's Christmas," she told him at dinner, he seated at her side in the place of honour, while Angela sat at the other end of the table between Fareham and De Malfort. "For ourselves we care little for such simple sports: but for the poor folk and the children Yule should be a season to be remembered for good cheer and merriment through all their slow, dull year. Poor wretches! I think of their hard life sometimes, and wonder they don't either drown themselves or massacre us."

"They are like the beasts of the field, Lady Fareham. They have learnt patience from the habit of suffering. They are born poor, and they die poor. It is happy for us that they are not learned enough to consider the inequalities of fortune, or we should have the rising of want against abundance, a bitterer strife, perhaps, than the strife of adverse creeds, which made Ireland so bloody a spectacle for the world's wonder thirty years ago."

"Well, we shall make them all happy this afternoon; and there will be a supper in the great stone barn which will acquaint them with abundance for this one evening at least," answered Hyacinth, gaily.

"We are going to play games after dinner!" cried Henriette, from her place at her father's elbow.

His lordship was the only person who ever reproved her seriously, yet she loved him best of all her kindred or friends.

"Aunt Angy is going to play hide-and-seek with us. Will you play, Sir Denzil?"

"I shall think myself privileged if I may join in your amusements."

"What a courteous speech! You will be cutting off your pretty curly hair, and putting on a French perruque, like his"--pointing to De Malfort. "Please do not. You would be like everybody else in London--and now you are only like yourself--and vastly handsome."

"Hush, Henriette! you are much too pert," remonstrated Fareham.

"But 'tis the very truth, father. All the women who visit mother paint their faces, so that they are all alike; and all the men talk alike, so that I don't know one from t'other, except Lord Rochester, who is impudenter and younger than the others, and gives me more sugar-plums and pays me prettier compliments than anybody else."

"Hold your tongue, mistress! A dinner-table is no place for pert children. Thy brother there has better manners," said her father, pointing to the cherubic son and heir, whose ideas were concentrated upon a loaded plate of red-deer pasty.

"You mean that he is greedier than I," retorted Papillon. "He will eat till he won't be able to run about with us after dinner; and then he will sprawl upon mother's satin train by the fire, with Ganymede and Phosphor, and she will tell everybody how good and gentle he is, and how much better bred than his sister. And now, if people are *ever* going to leave off eating, we may as well begin our games before it is quite dark. Perhaps *you* are ready, auntie, if nobody else is."

Dinner may have ended a little quicker for this speech, although Papillon was sternly suppressed, and bade to keep silence or leave the table. She obeyed so far as to make no further remarks, but expressed her contempt for the gluttony of her elders by several loud yawns, and bounced up out of her seat, like a ball from a racket, directly the little gentleman in black sitting near his lordship had murmured a discreet thanksgiving. This gentleman was the Roman Catholic priest from Oxford, who had said Mass early that morning in the muniment room, and had been invited to his lordship's table in honour of the festival.

Papillon led all the games, and ordered everybody about. Mrs. Dorothy Lettsome, the young lady who was sorry she had not had the honour to be born in France, was of the party, with her brother, honest Dan Lettsome, an Oxfordshire squire, who had been in London only once in his life, to see the Coronation, and had nearly lost his life, as well as his purse and jewellery, in a tavern, after that august ceremonial. This bitter experience had given him a distaste for the pleasures of the town which his poor sister deplored exceedingly; since she was dependent upon his coffers, and subject to his authority, and had no hope of leaving Oxfordshire unless she were fortunate enough to find a town-bred husband.

These two joined in the sports with ardour, Squire Dan glad to be moving about, rather than to sit still and listen to music which he hated, or to conversation to which he could contribute neither wit nor sense, unless the kennel or the gun-room were the topic under discussion. The talk of a lady and gentleman who had graduated in the salons of the Hotel de Rambouillet was a foreign language to him; and he told his sister that it was all one to him whether Lady Fareham and the Mounseer talked French or English, since it was quite as hard to understand 'em in one language as in t'other.

Papillon, this rustic youth adored. He knew no greater pleasure than to break and train a pony for her, to teach her the true knack of clearing a hedge, to explain the habits and nature of those vermin in whose lawless lives she was deeply interested--rats, weasels, badgers, and such-like--to attend her when she hunted, or flew her peregrine.

"If you will marry me, sweetheart, when you are of the marrying age, I would rather wait half a dozen years for you than have the best woman in Oxfordshire that I know of at this present."

"Marry you!" cried Lord Fareham's daughter. "Why, I shall marry no one under an earl; and I hope it will be a duke or a marquis. Marchioness is a pretty title: it sounds better than duchess, because it is in three syllables--mar-chion-ess," with an affected drawl. "I am going to be very beautiful. Mrs. Hubbuck says so, and mother's own woman; and I heard that painted old wretch, Mrs. Lewin, tell mother so. 'Eh, gud, your la'ship, the young miss will be almost as great a beauty as your la'ship's self!' Mrs. Lewin always begins her speeches with 'Eh, gud!' or 'What devil!' But I hope I shall be handsomer than *mother*" concluded Papillon, in a tone which implied a poor opinion of the maternal charms.

And now on this Christmas evening, in the thickening twilight of the rambling old house, through long galleries, crooked passages, queer little turns at right angles, rooms opening out of rooms, half a dozen in succession, Squire Dan led the games, ordered about all the time by Papillon, whom he talked of admiringly as a high-mettled filly, declaring that she had more tricks than the running-horse he was training for Abingdon races.

De Malfort, after assisting in their sports for a quarter of an hour with considerable spirit, had deserted them, and sneaked off to the great saloon, where he sat on the Turkey carpet at Lady Fareham's feet, singing chansonettes to his guitar, while George and the spaniels sprawled beside him, the whole group making a picture of indolent enjoyment, fitfully lighted by the blaze of a yule log that filled the width of the chimney. Fareham and the Priest were playing chess at the other end of the long low room, by the light of a single candle.

Papillon ran in at the door and ejaculated her disgust at De Malfort's desertion.

"Was there ever such laziness? It's bad enough in Georgie to be so idle; but then, *he* has over-eaten himself."

"And how do you know that I haven't over-eaten myself, mistress?" asked De Malfort.

"You never do that; but you often drink too much--much, much, much too much!"

"That's a slanderous thing to say of your mother's most devoted servant," laughed De Malfort. "And pray how does a baby-girl like you know when a gentleman has been more thirsty than discreet?"

"By the way you talk--always French. Jarni! ch'dame, n'savons joui d' n'belle s'ree--n'fam-partie d'ombre. Moi j'ai p'du n'belle f'tune, p'rol'd'nneur! You clip your words to nothing. Aren't you coming to play hide-and-seek?"

"Not I, fair slanderer. I am a salamander, and love the fire."

"Is that a kind of Turk? Good-bye. I'm going to hide."

"Beware of the chests in the gallery, sweetheart," said her father, who heard only this last sentence, as his daughter ran past him towards the door. "When I was in Italy I was told of a bride who hid herself in an old dower-chest, on her wedding-day--and the lid clapped to with a spring and kept her there for half a century."

"There's no spring that ever locksmith wrought that will keep down Papillon," cried De Malfort, sounding a light accompaniment to his words on the guitar strings, with delicatest touch, like fairy music.

"I know of better hiding-places," answered the child, and vanished, banging the great door behind her.

She found her aunt with Dorothy Lettsome and her brother and Denzil in the gallery above stairs, walking up and down, and listening with every indication of weariness to the Squire's discourse about his hunters and running-horses.

"Now we are going to have real good sport!" cried Papillon. "Aunt Angy and I are to hide, and you three are to look for us. You must stop in this gallery for ten minutes by the French clock yonder--with the door shut. You must give us ten minutes' law, Mr. Lettsome, as you did the hare the other day, when I was out with you--and then you may begin to look for us. Promise."

"Stay, little miss, you will be outside the house belike, roaming lord knows where; in the shrubberies, or the barns, or halfway to Oxford--while we are made fools of here."

"No, no. We will be inside the house."

"Do you promise that, pretty lady?"

"Yes, I promise."

Mrs. Dorothy suggested that there had been enough of childish play, and that it would be pleasanter to sit in the saloon with her ladyship, and hear Monsieur de Malfort sing.

"I'll wager he was singing when you saw him just now."

"Yes, he is always singing foolish French songs--and I'm sure you can't understand 'em."

"I've learnt the French ever since I was as old as you, Mistress Henriette."

"Ah! that was too late to begin. People who learn French out of books know what it looks like, but not what it sounds like."

"I should be very sorry if I could not understand a French ballad, little miss."

"Would you--would you, really?" cried Papillon, her face alight with impish mirth. "Then, of course, you understand this--

　　　Oh, la d'moiselle, comme elle est sot-te,　　Eh, je me moque de sa sot-ti-se! Eh, la d'moiselle, comme elle est be-te,　　Eh, je m'ris de sa be-ti-se!"

She sang this impromptu nonsense *prestissimo* as she danced out of the room, leaving the accomplished Dorothy vexed and perplexed at not having understood a single word.

It was nearly an hour later when Denzil entered the saloon hurriedly, pale and perturbed of aspect, with Dorothy and her brother following him.

"We have been hunting all over the house for Mrs. Angela and Henriette," Denzil said, and Fareham started up from the chess-table, scared at the young man's agitated tone and pallid countenance. "We have looked in every room--"

"In every closet," interrupted Dorothy.

"In every corner of the staircases and passages," said Squire Dan.

"Can your lordship help us? There may be places you know of which we do not know?" said Denzil, his voice trembling a little. "It is alarming that they should be so long in concealment. We have called to them in every part of the house."

Fareham hurried to the door, taking instant alarm--anxious, pale, alert.

"Come!" he said to the others. "The oak chests in the music-room--the great Florentine coffer in the gallery? Have you looked in those?"

"Yes; we have opened every chest."

"Faith, to see Sir Denzil turn over piles of tapestries, you would have thought he was looking for a fairy that could hide in the folds of a curtain!" said Lettsome.

"It is no theme for jesting. I hate these tricks of hiding in strange corners," said Fareham. "Now, show me where they left you."

"In the long gallery."

"They have gone up to the roof, perhaps."

"We have been in the roof," said Denzil.

"I have scarcely recovered my senses after the cracked skull I got from one of your tie-beams," added Lettsome; and Fareham saw that both men had their doublets coated with dust and cobwebs, in a manner which indicated a remorseless searching of places unvisited by housemaids and brooms.

Mrs. Dorothy, with a due regard for her dainty lace kerchief and ruffles, and her cherry silk petticoat, had avoided these loathly places, the abode of darkness, haunted by the fear of rats.

Fareham tramped the house from cellar to garret, Denzil alone accompanying him.

"We want no posse comitatus," he had said, somewhat discourteously. "You, Squire, had best go and mend your cracked head in the eating-parlour with a brimmer or two of clary wine; and you, Mrs. Dorothy, can go and keep her ladyship company. But not a word of our fright. Swoons and screaming would only hinder us."

He took Mrs. Lettsome's arm, and led her to the staircase, pushing the Squire after her, and then turned his anxious countenance to Denzil.

"If they are not to be found in the house, they must be found outside the house.

Oh, the folly, the madness of it! A December night--snow on the ground--a rising wind--another fall of snow, perhaps--and those two afoot and alone!"

"I do not believe they are out-of-doors," Denzil answered. "Your daughter promised that they would not leave the house."

"My daughter tells the truth. It is her chief virtue."

"And yet we have hunted in every hole and corner," said Denzil, dejectedly.

"Hole!" cried Fareham, almost in a shout. "Thou hast hit it, man! That one word is a flash of lightning. The Priest's Hole! Come this way. Bring your candle!" snatching up that which he had himself set down on a table, when he stood still to deliberate. "The Priest's Hole? The child knew the secret of it--fool that I was ever to show her. God! what a place to hide in on a winter night!"

He was halfway up the staircase to the second story before he had uttered the last of these exclamations, Denzil following him.

Suddenly, through the stillness of the house, there sounded a faint far-off cry, the shrill thin sound of a child's voice. Fareham and Warner would hardly have heard it had they not been sportsmen, with ears trained to listen for distant sounds. No view-hallo sounding across miles of wood and valley was ever fainter or more ethereal.

"You hear them?" cried Fareham. "Quick, quick!"

He led the way along a narrow gallery, about eight feet high, where people had danced in Elizabeth's time, when the house was newly converted to secular uses; and then into a room in which there were several iron chests, the muniment room, where a sliding panel, of which the master of the house knew the trick, revealed an opening in the wall. Fareham squeezed himself through the gap, still carrying the tall iron candlestick, with flaring candle, and vanished. Denzil followed, and found himself descending a narrow stone staircase, very steep, built into an angle of the great chimney, while as if from the bowels of the earth there came, louder at every step, that shrill cry of distress, in a voice he could not doubt was Henriette's.

"The other is mute," groaned Fareham; "scared to death, perhaps, like a frightened bird." And then he called, "I am coming. You are safe, love; safe, safe!" And then he groaned aloud, "Oh, the madness, the folly of it!"

Halfway down the staircase there was a sudden gap of six feet, down which Fareham dropped with his hands on the lowest stair, Denzil following; a break in

the continuity of the descent planned for the discomfiture of strangers and the protection of the family hiding-place.

Fareham and Denzil were on a narrow stone landing at the bottom of the
house; and the child's wail of anguish changed to a joyous shriek, "Father, father!"
close in their ears. Fareham set his shoulder against the heavy oak door, and it burst
inwards. There had been no question of secret spring or complicated machinery;
but the great, clumsy door dragged upon its rusty hinges, and the united strength
of the two girls had not served to pull it open, though Papillon, in her eagerness for
concealment in the first fever of hiding, had been strong enough to push the door
till she had jammed it, and thus made all after efforts vain.

"Father!" she cried, leaping into his arms, as he came into the room, large
enough to hold six-men standing upright; but a hideous den in which to perish
alone in the dark. "Oh, father! I thought no one would ever find us. I was afraid we
should have died like the Italian lady--and people would have found our skeletons
and wondered about us. I never was afraid before. Not when the great horse reared
as high as a house--and her ladyship screamed. I only laughed then--but to-night I
have been afraid."

Fareham put her aside without looking at her.

"Angela! Great God! She is dead!"

No, she was not dead, only in a half swoon, leaning against the angle of the
wall, ghastly white in the flare of the candles. She was not quite unconscious. She
knew whose strong arms were holding her, whose lips were so near her own, whose
head bent suddenly upon her breast, leaning against the lace kerchief, to listen for
the beating of her heart.

She made a great effort to relieve his fear, understanding dimly that he thought
her dead; but could only murmur broken syllables, till he carried her up three or
four stairs, to a secret door that opened into the garden. There in the wintry air,
under the steely light of wintry stars, her senses came back to her. She opened her
eyes and looked at him.

"I am sorry I have not Papillon's courage," she said.

"Tu m'as donne une affreuse peur--je te croyais morte," muttered Fareham, letting his arms drop like lead as she released herself from their support.

Denzil and Henriette were close to them. They had come to the open door for fresh air, after the charnel-like chill and closeness of the small underground chamber.

"Father is angry with me," said the girl; "he won't speak to me."

"Angry! no, no;" and he bent to kiss her. "But oh, child, the folly of it! She might have died--you too--found just an hour too late."

"It would have taken a long time to kill me," said Papillon; "but I was very cold, and my teeth were chattering, and I should soon have been hungry. Have you had supper yet?"

"Nobody has even thought of supper."

"I am glad of that. And I may have supper with you, mayn't I, and eat what I like, because it's Christmas, and because I might have been starved to death in the Priest's Hole. But it was a good hiding-place, tout de meme. Who guessed at last?"

"The only person who knew of the place, child. And now, remember, the secret is to be kept. Your dungeon may some day save an honest man's life. You must tell nobody where you were hid."

"But what shall I say when they ask me? I must not tell them a story."

"Say you were hidden in the great chimney--which is truth; for the Priest's Hole is but a recess at the back of the chimney. And you, Warner," turning to Denzil, who had not spoken since the opening of the door, "I know you'll keep the secret."

"Yes. I will keep your secret," Denzil answered, cold as ice; and said no word more.

They walked slowly round the house by the terrace, where the clipped yews stood out like obelisks against the bleak bright sky. Papillon ran and skipped at her father's side, clinging to him, expatiating upon her sufferings in the dust and darkness. Denzil followed with, Angela, in a dead silence.

CHAPTER XI.
LIGHTER THAN VANITY.

"I think father must be a witch," Henriette said at dinner next day, "or why did he tell me of the Italian lady who was shut in the dower-chest, just before Angela and I were lost in"--she checked herself at a look from his lordship--"in the chimney?"

"It wants no witch to tell that little girls are foolish and mischievous," answered Fareham.

"You ladies must have been vastly black when you came out of your hiding-place," said De Malfort. "I should have been sorry to see so much beauty disguised in soot. Perhaps Mrs. Kirkland means to appear in the character of a chimney at our next Court masquerade. She would cause as great a stir as Lady Muskerry, in all her Babylonian splendour; but for other reasons. Nothing could mitigate the Muskerry's ugliness; and no disguise could hide Mrs. Angela's beauty."

"What would the costume be?" asked Papillon.

"Oh, something simple. A long black satin gown, and a brick-dust velvet hat, tall and curiously twisted, like your Tudor chimney; and a cluster of grey feathers on the top, to represent smoke."

"Monsieur le Comte makes a joke of everything. But what would father have said if we had never been found?"

"I should have said that they are right who swear there is a curse upon all property taken from the Church, and that the ban fell black and bitter upon Chilton Abbey," answered his lordship's grave deep voice from the end of the table, where he sat somewhat apart from the rest, gloomy and silent, save when directly addressed.

Her ladyship and De Malfort had always plenty to talk about. They had the past as well as the present for their discourse, and were always sighing for the vanished glories of their youth--at Paris, at Fontainebleau, at St. Germain. Nor were they restricted to the realities of the present and the memories of the past; they had that wider world of unreality in which to circulate; they had the Scudery language at the tips of their tongues, the fantastic sentimentalism of that marvellous old maid who invented the seventeenth-century hero and heroine; or who crystallised the vanishing figures of that brilliant age and made them immortal. All that little language of toyshop platonics had become a natural form of speech with these two, bred and educated in the Marais, while it was still the select and aristocratic quarter of Paris.

To-day Hyacinth and her old playfellow had been chattering like children, or birds in an aviary, and with little more sense in their conversation; but at this talk of the Church's ban, Hyacinth stopped in her prattle and was almost serious.

"I sometimes think we shall have bad luck in this house," she said, "or that we shall see the ghosts of the wicked monks who were turned out to make room for Fareham's great-grandfather."

"Tush, child! what do you know of their wickedness, after a century?"

"They were very wicked, I believe, for it was one of those quiet little monasteries where the monks could do all manner of evil things, and raise the devil, if they liked, without anybody knowing. And when Henry the Eighth sent his Commissioners, they were taken by surprise; and the altar at which they worshipped Beelzebub was found in a side chapel, and a wax figure of the King stuck with arrows, like St. Sebastian. The Abbot pretended it **was** St. Sebastian; but nobody believed him."

"Nobody wanted to believe him," said Fareham. "King Henry made an example of Chilton Abbey, and gave it to my worthy ancestor, who was a fourth cousin of Jane Seymour's, and had turned Protestant to please his royal master. He went back to the Church of Rome on his death-bed, and we Revels have been Papists ever since. I wish the Church joy of us!"

"The Church has neither profit nor honour from you," said his wife, shaking her fan at him. "You seldom go to Mass; you never go to confession."

"I would rather keep my sins to myself, and atone for them by the pangs of a wounded conscience. That is too easy a religion which shifts the burden of guilt on to the shoulders of a stipendiary priest, and walks away from the confessional absolved by the payment of a few extra prayers."

"I believe you are either an infidel or a Puritan."

"A cross between the two, perhaps--a mongrel in religion, as I am a mongrel in politics."

Angela looked up at him with sad eyes--reproachful, yet full of pity. She remembered his wild talk, semi-delirious some of it, all feverish and excited, during his illness, and how she had listened with aching heart to the ravings of one so near death, and so unfit to die. And now that the pestilence had passed him by, now that he was a strong man again, with half a lifetime before him, her heart was still heavy for him. She who sat in the theatre of life as a spectator had discovered that her sister's husband was not happy. The trifles that delighted Hyacinth left Fareham unamused and discontented; and his wife knew not that there was anything wanting to his felicity. She could go on prattling like a child, could be in a fever about a fan or a bunch of ribbons, could talk for an hour of a new play or the contents of the French *Gazette*, while he sat gloomy and apart.

The sympathy, the companionship that should be in marriage was wanting here. Angela saw and deplored this distance, scarce daring to touch so delicate a theme, fearful lest she, the younger, should seem to sermonise the elder; and yet she could not be silent for ever while duty and religion urged her to speak.

At Chilton Abbey the sisters were rarely alone. Papillon was almost always with them; and De Malfort spent more of his life in attendance upon Lady Fareham than at Oxford, where he was supposed to be living. Mrs. Lettsome and her brother were frequent guests; and coach-loads of fine people came over from the court almost every day. Indeed, it was only Fareham's character--austere as Clarendon's or Southampton's--which kept the finest of all company at a distance. Lady Castlemaine had called at Chilton in her coach-and-four early in July; and her visit had not been returned--a slight which the proud beauty bitterly resented: and from that time she had lost no opportunity of depreciating Lady Fareham. Happily her jests, not over refined in quality, had not been repeated to Hyacinth's husband.

One January afternoon the longed-for opportunity came. The sisters were sitting alone in front of the vast mediaeval chimney, where the Abbots of old had burnt their surplus timber--Angela busy with her embroidery frame, working a satin coverlet for her niece's bed; Hyacinth yawning over a volume of Cyrus; in whose stately pages she loved to recognise the portraits of her dearest friends, and for which she was a living key. Angela was now familiar with the famous romance, which she had read with deepest interest, enlightened by her sister. As an eastern story--a record of battles and sieges evolved from a clever spinster's brain, an account of men and women who had never lived--the book might have seemed passing dull; but the story of actual lives, of living, breathing beauty, and valour that still burnt in warrior breasts, the keen and clever analysis of men and women who were making history, could not fail to interest an intelligent girl, to whom all things in life were new.

Angela read of the siege of Dunkirk, where Fareham had fought; of the tem-

pestuous weather; the camp in the midst of salt marshes and quicksands, and all the
sufferings and perils of life in the trenches. He had been in more than one of those
battles which mademoiselle's conscientious pen depicted with such graphic power,
the **Gazette** at her elbow as she wrote. The names of battles, sieges, Generals, had
been on his lips in his delirious ravings. He had talked of the taking of Charenton,
the key to Paris, a stronghold dominating Seine and Marne; of Clanleu, the brave
defender of the fortress; of Chatillon, who led the charge--both killed there--Cha-
tillon, the friend of Conde, who wept bitterest tears for a loss that poisoned victory.
Read by these lights, the "Grand Cyrus" was a book to be pored over, a book to bend
over in the grey winter dusk, reading by the broad blaze of the logs that flamed and
crackled on wrought-iron standards. Just as merrily the blaze had spread its ruddy
light over the room when it was a monkish refectory, and when the droning of a
youthful brother reading aloud to the fraternity as they ate their supper was the
only sound, except the clattering of knives and grinding of jaws.

Now the room was her ladyship's drawing-room, bright with Gobelins tapestry, dazzling with Venetian mirrors, gaudy with gold and colour, the black oak
floor enlivened by many-hued carpets from our new colony of Tangiers. Fareham
told his wife that her Moorish carpets had cost the country fifty times the price she
had paid for them, and were associated with an irrevocable evil in the existence of
a childless Queen; but that piece of malice, Hyacinth told him, had no foundation
but his hatred of the Duke, who had always been perfectly civil to him.

"Of two profligate brothers I prefer the bolder sinner," said Fareham. "Bigotry
and debauchery are an ill mixture."

"I doubt if his Majesty frets for the want of an heir," remarked De Malfort. "He
is not a family man."

"He is not a one family man, Count," answered Fareham.

Fareham and De Malfort were both away on this January evening. Papillon
was taking a dancing lesson from a wizened old Frenchman, who brought himself
and his fiddle from Oxford twice a week for the damsel's instruction. Mrs. Priscilla,
nurse and **gouvernante**, attended these lessons, at which the Honourable Henrietta
Maria Revel gave herself prodigious airs, and was indeed so rude to the poor old
professor that her aunt had declined to assist at any more performances.

"Has his lordship gone to Oxford?" Angela asked, after a silence broken only by her sister's yawns.

"I doubt he is anywhere rather than in such good company," Hyacinth answered, carelessly. "He hates the King, and would like to preach at him, as John Knox did at his great-grandmother. Fareham is riding, or roving with his dogs, I dare say. He has a gloomy taste for solitude."

"Hyacinth, do you not see that he is unhappy?" Angela asked, suddenly, and the pain in her voice startled her sister from the contemplation of the sublime Mandane.

"Unhappy, child! What reason has he to be unhappy?"

"Ah, dearest, it is that I would have you discover. 'Tis a wife's business to know what grieves her husband."

"Unless it be Mrs. Lewin's bill--who is an inexorable harpy--I know of no act of mine that can afflict him."

"I did not mean that his gloom was caused by any act of yours, sister. I only urge you to discover why he is so sad."

"Sad? Sullen, you mean. He has a fine, generous nature. I am sure it is not Lewin's charges that trouble him. But he had always a sullen temper--by fits and starts."

"But of late he has been always silent and gloomy."

"How the child watches him! Ma tres chere, that silence is natural. There are but two things Fareham loves--the first, war; the second, sport. If he cannot be storming a town, he loves to be killing a fox. This fireside life of ours--our books and music, our idle talk of plays and dances--wearies him. You may see how he avoids us--except out-of-doors."

"Dear Hyacinth, forgive me!" Angela began, falteringly, leaving her embroidery frame and moving to the other side of the hearth, where she dropped on her knees by her ladyship's chair, and was almost swallowed up in the ample folds of her brocade train. "Is it not possible that Lord Fareham is pained to see you so much gayer and more familiar with Monsieur de Malfort than you ever are with him?"

"Gayer! more familiar!" cried Hyacinth. "Can you conceive any creature gay and familiar with Fareham? One could as soon be gay with Don Quixote; indeed, there is much in common between the knight of the rueful countenance and my husband. Gay and familiar! And pray, mistress, why should I not take life pleasantly with a man who understands me, and in whose friendship I have grown up almost as if we were brother and sister? Do you forget that I have known Henri ever since I was ten years old--that we played battledore and shuttlecock together in our dear garden in the Rue de Touraine, next the bowling-green, when he was at school with the Jesuit Fathers, and used to spend all his holiday afternoons with the Marquise? I think I only learnt to know the saints' days because they brought me my playfellow. And when I was old enough to attend the Court--and, indeed, I was but a child when I first appeared there--it was Henri who sang my praises, and brought a crowd of admirers about me. Ah, what a life it was! Love in the city, and war at the gates: plots, battles, barricades! How happy we all were! except when there came the news of some great man killed, and walls were hung with black, where there had been a thousand wax candles and a crowd of dancers. Chatillon, Chabot, Laval! *Helas*, those were sad losses!"

"Dear sister, I can understand your affection for an old friend, but I would not have you place him above your husband; least of all would I have his lordship suspect that you preferred the friend to the husband----"

"Suspect! Fareham! Are you afraid I shall make Fareham jealous, because I sing duets and cudgel these poor brains to make *bouts rimes* with De Malfort? Ah, child, how little those watchful eyes of yours have discovered the man's character! Fareham jealous! Why, at St. Germain he has seen me surrounded by adorers; the subject of more madrigals than would fill a big book. At the Louvre he has seen me the--what is that Mr. What's-his-name, your friend's old school-master, the Republican poet, calls it--'the cynosure of neighbouring eyes.' Don't think me vain, ma mie. I am an old woman now, and I hate my looking-glass ever since it has shown me my first wrinkle; but in those days I had almost as many admirers as Madame Henriette, or the Princess Palatine, or the fair-haired Duchess. I was called la belle Anglaise."

It was difficult to sound a warning-note in ears so obstinately deaf to all serious things. Papillon came bounding in after her dancing-lesson-- exuberant, loquacious.

"The little beast has taught me a new step in the coranto. See, mother," and the slim small figure was drawn up to its fullest, and the thin little lithe arms were curved with a studied grace, as Papillon slid and tripped across the room, her dainty little features illumined by a smirk of ineffable conceit.

"Henriette, you are an ill-bred child to call your master so rude a name," remonstrated her mother, languidly.

"'Tis the name you called him last week when his dirty shoes left marks on the stairs. He changes his shoes in my presence," added Papillon, disgustedly. "I saw a hole in his stocking. Monsieur de Malfort calls him Cut-Caper."

CHAPTER XII.
LADY FAREHAM'S DAY.

A month later the ***Oxford Gazette*** brought Lady Fareham the welcomest news that she had read for ever so long. The London death-rate had decreased, and his Majesty had gone to Hampton Court, attended by the Duke and Prince Rupert, Lord Clarendon, and his other indispensable advisers, and a retinue of servants, to be within easy distance of that sturdy soldier Albemarle, who had remained in London, unafraid of the pestilence; and who declared that while it was essential for him to be in frequent communication with his Majesty, it would be perilous to the interests of the State for him to absent himself from London; for the Dutch war had gone drivelling on ever since the victory in June, and that victory was not to be supposed final. Indeed, according to the General, there was need of speedy action and a considerable increase of our naval strength.

Windsor had been thought of in the first place as a residence for the King; but the law courts had been transferred there, and the judges and their following had overrun the town, while there was a report of an infected house there. So it had been resolved that his Majesty should make a brief residence at Hampton Court, leaving the Queen, the Duchess, and their belongings at Oxford, whither he could return as soon as the business of providing for the setting out of the fleet had been arranged between him and the General, who could travel in a day backwards and forwards between the Cockpit and Wolsey's palace.

When this news came they were snowed up at Chilton. Sport of all kinds had been stopped, and Fareham, who, in his wife's parlance, lived in his boots all the winter, had to amuse himself without the aid of horse and hound; while even walking was made difficult by the snowdrifts that blocked the lanes, and reduced the face of Nature to one muffled and monotonous whiteness, while all the edges of the landscape were outlined vaguely against the misty greyness of the sky.

Hyacinth spent her days half in yawning and sighing, and half in idle laughter and childish games with Henriette and De Malfort. When she was gay she was as much a child as her daughter; when she was fretful and hipped, it was a childish discontent.

They played battledore and shuttlecock in the picture-gallery, and my lady laughed when her volant struck some reverend judge or venerable bishop a rap on the nose. They sat for hours twanging guitars, Hyacinth taking her music-lesson from De Malfort, whose exquisite taste and touch made a guitar seem a different instrument from that on which his pupil's delicate fingers nipped a wiry melody, more suggestive of finger-nails than music.

He taught her, and took all possible pains in the teaching, and laughed at her, and told her plainly that she had no talent for music. He told her that in her hands the finest lute Laux Maler ever made, mellowed by three centuries, would be but wood and catgut.

"It is the prettiest head in the world, and a forehead as white as Queen Anne's," he said one day, with a light touch on the ringletted brow, "but there is nothing inside. I wonder if there is anything here?" and the same light touch fluttered for an instant against her brocade bodice, at the spot where fancy locates the faculty of loving and suffering.

She laughed at his rude speeches, just as she laughed at his flatteries--as if there were safety in that atmosphere of idle mirth. Angela heard and wondered, wondering most perhaps what occupied and interested Lord Fareham in those white winter days, when he lived for the greater part alone in his own rooms, or pacing the long walks from which the gardeners had cleared the snow. He spent some of his time indoors, deep in a book. She knew as much as that. He had allowed Angela to read some of his favourites, though he would not permit any of the new comedies, which everybody at Court was reading, to enter his house, much to Lady Fareham's annoyance.

"I am half a century behind all my friends in intelligence," she said, "because of your Puritanism. One tires of your everlasting gloomy tragedies--your ***Broken***

Hearts and *Philasters*. I am all for the genius of comedy."

"Then satisfy your inclinations, and read Moliere. He is second only to Shakespeare."

"I have him by heart already."

The **Broken Heart** and **Philaster** delighted Angela; indeed, she had read the latter play so often, and with such deep interest, that many passages in it had engraved themselves on her memory, and recurred to her sometimes in the silence of wakeful nights.

That character of Bellario touched her as no heroine of the "Grand Cyrus" had power to move her. How elaborately artificial seemed the Scudery's polished tirades, her refinements and quintessences of the grand passion, as compared with the fervid simplicity of the woman-page--a love so humble, so intense, so unselfish!

Sir Denzil came to Chilton nearly every day, and was always graciously received by her ladyship. His Puritan gravity fell away from him like a pilgrim's cloak, in the light air of Hyacinth's amusements. He seemed to grow younger; and Henriette's sharp eyes discovered an improvement in his dress.

"This is your second new suit since Christmas," she said, "and I'll swear it is made by the King's tailor. Regardez done, madame! What exquisite embroidery, silver and gold thread intermixed with little sparks of garnets sewn in the pattern! It is better than anything of his lordship's. I wish I had a father who dressed well. I'm sure mine must be the shabbiest lord at Whitehall. You have no right to be more modish than monsieur mon pere, Sir Denzil."

"Hold that insolent tongue, p'tit drole!" cried the mother. "Sir Denzil is younger by a dozen years than his lordship, and has his reputation to make at Court, and with the ladies he will meet there. I hope you are coming to London, Denzil. You shall have a seat in one of our coaches as soon as the death-rate diminishes, and this odious weather breaks up."

"Your ladyship is all goodness. I shall go where my lode-star leads," answered Denzil, looking at Angela, and blushing at the audacity of his speech.

He was one of those modest lovers who rarely bring a blush to the cheek of the beloved object, but are so poor-spirited as to do most of the blushing themselves.

A week later Lady Fareham could do nothing but praise that severe weather which she had pronounced odious, for her husband, coming in from Oxford after a ride along the road, deep with melting snow, brought the news of a considerable diminution in the London death-rate; and the more startling news that his Majesty had removed to Whitehall for the quicker despatch of business with the Duke of Albemarle, albeit the bills of mortality recorded fifteen hundred deaths from the pestilence in the previous week, and although not a carriage appeared in the deserted streets of the metropolis except those in his Majesty's train.

"How brave, how admirable!" cried Hyacinth, clapping her hands in the exuberance of her joy. "Then we can go to London to-morrow, if horses and coaches can be made ready. Give your orders at once, Fareham, I beseech you. The thaw has set in. There will be no snow to stop us."

"There will be floods which may make fords impassable."

"We can avoid every ford--there is always a *detour* by the lanes."

"Have you any idea what the lanes will be like after two feet deep of snow? Be sure, my love, you are happier twanging your lute by this fireside than you would be stuck in a quagmire, perishing with cold in a windy coach."

"I will risk the quagmires and the windy coach. Oh, my lord, if you ever loved me let us set out to-morrow. I languish for Fareham House--my basset-table, my friends, my watermen to waft me to and fro between Blackfriars and Westminster, the mercers in St. Paul's Churchyard, the Middle Exchange. I have not bought myself anything pretty since Christmas. Let us go to-morrow."

"And risk spoiling the prettiest thing you own--your face--by a plague-spot."

"The King is there--the plague is ended."

"Do you think he is a God, that the pestilence will flee at his coming?"

"I think his courage is godlike. To be the first to return to that abandoned city."

"What of Monk and the Archbishop, who never left it?"

"A rough old soldier! A Churchman! Such lives were meant to face danger. But his Majesty! A man for whom existence should be one long holiday?"

"He has done his best to make it so; but the pestilence has shown him that there are grim realities in life. Don't fret, dearest. We will go to town as soon as it is prudent to make the move. Kings must brave great hazards; and there is no reason that little people like us should risk our lives because the necessities of State compel his

Majesty to imperil his."

"We shall be laughed at if we do not hasten after him."

"Let them laugh who please. I have passed through the ordeal, Hyacinth. I don't want a second attack of the sickness; nor would I for worlds that you or your sister should run into the mouth of danger. Besides, you can lose little pleasure by being absent; for the play-houses are all closed, and the Court is in mourning for the French Queen-mother."

"Poor Queen Anne!" sighed Hyacinth. "She was always kind to me. And to die of a cancer--after out-living those she most loved! King Louis would scarcely believe she was seriously ill, till she was at the point of death. But we know what mourning means at Whitehall--Lady Castlemaine in black velvet, with forty thousand pounds in diamonds to enliven it; a concert instead of a play, perhaps; and the King sitting in a corner whispering with Mrs. Stewart. But as for the contagion, you will see that everybody will rush back to London, and that you and I will be laughing-stocks."

The next week justified Lady Fareham's assertion. As soon as it was known that the King had established himself at Whitehall, the great people came back to their London houses, and the town began to fill. It was as if a God had smiled upon the smitten city, and that healing and happiness radiated from the golden halo round that anointed head. Was not this the monarch of whom the most eloquent preacher of the age had written, "In the arms of whose justice and wisdom we lie down in safety"?

London flung off her cerements--erased her plague-marks. The dead-cart's dreadful bell no longer sounded in the silence of an afflicted city. Coffins no longer stood at every other door; the pits at Finsbury, in Tothill Fields, at Islington, were all filled up and trampled down; and the grass was beginning to grow over the forgotten dead. The Judges came back to Westminster. London was alive again--alive and healed; basking in the sunshine of Royalty.

Nowhere was London more alive in the month of March than at Fareham House on the Thames, where the Fareham liveries of green and gold showed conspicuous upon his lordship's watermen, lounging about the stone steps that led down to the water, or waiting in the terraced garden, which was one of the finest on the river. Wherries of various weights and sizes filled one spacious boathouse, and in another handsome stone edifice with a vaulted roof Lord Fareham's barge lay in state, glorious in cream colour and gold, with green velvet cushions and Oriental carpets, as splendid as that blue-and-gold barge which Charles had sent as a present to Madame, a vessel to out-glitter Cleopatra's galley, when her ladyship and her friends and their singing-boys and musicians filled it for a voyage to Hampton Court.

The barge was used on festive occasions, or for country voyages, as to Hampton or Greenwich; the wherries were in constant requisition. Along that shining waterway rank and fashion, commerce and business, were moving backwards and forwards all day long. That more novel mode of transit, the hackney coach, was only resorted to in foul weather; for the Legislature had handicapped the coaching trade in the interests of the watermen, and coaches were few and dear.

If Angela had loved the country, she was not less charmed with London under its altered aspect. All this gaiety and splendour, this movement and brightness, astonished and dazzled her.

"I am afraid I am very shallow-minded," she told Denzil when he asked her opinion of London. "It seems an enchanted place, and I can scarcely believe it is the same dreadful city I saw a few months ago, when the dead were lying in the streets. Oh, how clearly it comes back to me--those empty streets, the smoke of the fires, the wretched ragged creatures begging for bread! I looked down a narrow court, and saw a corpse lying there, and a child wailing over it; and a little way farther on a woman flung up a window, and screamed out, 'Dead, dead! The last of my children is dead! Has God no relenting mercy?'"

"It is curious," said Hyacinth, "how little the town seems changed after all those horrors. I miss nobody I know."

"Nay, madam," said Denzil, "there have only died one hundred and sixty thousand people, mostly of the lower classes; or at least that is the record of the bills; but I am told the mortality has been twice as much, for people have had a secret way of dying and burying their dead. If your ladyship could have heard the account that Mr. Milton gave me this morning of the sufferings he saw before he left London, you would not think the visitation a light one."

"I wonder you consort with such a rebellious subject as Mr. Milton," said Hyacinth. "A creature of Cromwell's, who wrote with hideous malevolence and disrespect of the murdered King, who was in hiding for ever so long after his Majesty's return, and who now escapes a prison only by the royal clemency."

"The King lacks only that culminating distinction of having persecuted the greatest poet of the age in order to stand equal to the bigots who murdered Giordano Bruno," said Denzil.

"The greatest poet! Sure you would not compare Milton with Waller?"

"Indeed I would not, Lady Fareham."

"Nor with Cowley, nor Denham--dear cracked-brained Denham?"

"Nor with Denham. To my fancy he stands as high above them as the pole-star over your ladyship's garden lamps."

"A pamphleteer who has scribbled schoolboy Latin verses, and a few short poems; and, let me see, a masque--yes, a masque that he wrote for Lord Bridgewater's children before the troubles. I have heard my father talk of it. I think he called the thing *Comus*."

"A name that will live, Lady Fareham, when Waller and Denham are shadows, remembered only for an occasional couplet."

"Oh, but who cares what people will think two or three hundred years hence? Waller's verses please us now. The people who come after me can please themselves, and may read *Comus* to their hearts' content. I know his lordship reads Milton, as he does Shakespeare, and all the cramped old play-wrights of Elizabeth's time. Henri, sing us that song of Waller's, 'Go, lovely rose.' I would give all Mr. Milton has written for that perfection."

They were sitting on the terrace above the river in the golden light of an afternoon that was fair and warm as May, though by the calendar 'twas March. The capricious climate had changed from austere winter to smiling spring. Skylarks were singing over the fields at Hampstead, and over the plague-pits at Islington, and all London was rejoicing in blue skies and sunshine. Trade was awakening from a death-like sleep. The theatres were closed; but there were plays acted now and then at Court. The New and the Middle Exchange were alive with beribboned fops and painted belles.

It was Lady Fareham's visiting-day. The tall windows of her saloon were open to the terrace, French windows that reached from ceiling to floor, like those at the Hotel de Rambouillet, and which Hyacinth had substituted for the small Jacobean casements, when she took possession of her husband's ancestral mansion. Saloon and terrace were one on a balmy afternoon like this; and her ladyship's guests wandered in and out at their pleasure. Her lackeys, handing chocolate and cakes on silver or gold salvers, were so many as to seem ubiquitous; and in the saloon, presided over by Angela, there was a still choicer refreshment to be obtained at a tea-table, where tiny cups of the new China drink were dispensed to those who cared for exotic novelties.

"Prythee, take your guitar and sing to us, were it but to change the conversation," cried Hyacinth; and De Malfort took up his guitar and began, in the sweetest of tenors, "Go, lovely rose."

He had all her ladyship's visitors, chiefly feminine, round him before he had finished the first verse. That gift of song, that exquisite touch upon the Spanish guitar, were irresistible.

Lord Fareham landed at the lower flight of steps as the song ended, and came slowly along the terrace, saluting his wife's friends with a grave courtesy. He brought an atmosphere of silence and restraint with him, it seemed to some of his wife's visitors, for the babble that usually follows the end of a song was wanting.

Most of Lady Fareham's friends affected literature, and professed familiarity with two books which had caught the public taste on opposite sides of the Channel. In London people quoted Butler, and vowed there was no wit so racy as the wit in "Hudibras." In Paris the cultured were all striving to talk like Rochefoucauld's "Maxims," which had lately delighted the Gallic mind by the frank cynicism that drew everybody's attention to somebody else's failings.

"Himself the vainest of men, 'tis scarce wonderful that he takes vanity to be the mainspring that moves the human species," said De Malfort, when some one had found fault with the Duke's analysis.

"Oh, now we shall hear nothing but stale Rochefoucauldisms, sneers at love and friendship, disparagement of our ill-used sex! Where has my grave husband been, I wonder?" said Hyacinth. "Upon my honour, Fareham, your brow looks as sombre as if it were burdened with the care of the nation."

"I have been with one who has to carry the greater part of that burden, my lady, and my spirits may have caught some touch of his uneasiness."

"You have been prosing with that pragmatical personage at Dunkirk--nay, I beg the Lord Chancellor's pardon, Clarendon House. Are not his marbles and tapestries much finer than ours? And yet he began life as a sneaking lawyer, the younger son of a small Wiltshire squire----"

"Lady Fareham, you allow your tongue too much licence----"

"Nay, I speak but the common feeling. Everybody is tired of a Minister who is a hundred years behind the age. He should have lived under Elizabeth."

"A pretty woman should never talk politics, Hyacinth."

"Of what else can I talk when the theatres are closed, and you deny me the privilege of seeing the last comedy performed at Whitehall? Is it not rank tyranny in his lordship, Lady Sarah?" turning to one of her intimates, a lady who had been a beauty at the court of Henrietta Maria in the beginning of the troubles, and who from old habit still thought herself lovely and beloved. "I appeal to your ladyship's common sense. Is it not monstrous to deprive me of the only real diversion in the town? I was not allowed to enter a theatre at all last year, except when his favourite Shakespeare or Fletcher was acted, and that was but a dozen times, I believe."

"Oh, hang Shakespeare!" cried a gentleman whose periwig occupied nearly as much space against the blue of a vernal sky as all the rest of his dapper little person. "Gud, my lord, it is vastly old-fashioned in your lordship to taste Shakespeare!" protested Sir Ralph Masaroon, shaking a cloud of pulvilio out of his cataract of curls. "There was a pretty enough play concocted t'other day out of two of his--a tragedy and comedy--*Measure for Measure* and *Much Ado about Nothing*, the interstices filled in with the utmost ingenuity. But Shakespeare unadulterated--faugh!"

"I am a fantastical person, perhaps, Sir Ralph; but I would rather my wife saw ten of Shakespeare's plays--in spite of their occasional coarseness--than one of your modern comedies."

"I should revolt against such tyranny," said Lady Sarah. "I have always appreciated Shakespeare, but I adore a witty comedy, and I never allowed my husband to dictate to me on a question of taste."

"Plays which her Majesty patronises can scarcely be unfit entertainment for her subjects," remarked another lady.

"Our Portuguese Queen is an excellent judge of the niceties of our language," said Fareham. "I question if she understands five sentences in as many acts."

"Nor should *I* understand anything low or vulgar," said Hyacinth.

"Then, madam, you are best at home, for the whole entertainment would be Hebrew to you."

"That cannot be," protested Lady Sarah; "for all our plays are written by gentlemen. The hack writers of King James's time have been shoved aside. It is the mark of a man of quality to write a comedy."

"It is a pity that fine gentlemen should write foul jests. Nay, it is a subject I can scarce speak of with patience, when I remember what the English stage has been, and hear what it is; when I recall what Lord Clarendon has told me of his Majesty's father, for whom Shakespeare was a closet companion, who loved all that was noblest in the drama of the Elizabethan age. Time, which should have refined and improved the stage, has sunk it in ignominy. We stand alone among nations in our worship of the obscene. You have seen plays enough in Paris, Hyacinth. Recall the themes that pleased you at the Marais and the Hotel de Bourgogne; the stories of classic heroism, of Christian fortitude, of manhood and womanhood lifted to the sublime. You who, in your girlhood, were familiar with the austere genius of Corneille----"

"I am sick of that Frenchman's name," interjected Lady Sarah. "St. Evremond was always praising him, and had the audacity to pronounce him superior to Dryden; to compare *Cinna* with the *Indian Queen*."

"A comparison which makes one sorry for Mr. Dryden," said Fareham. "I have heard that Conde, when a young man, was affected to tears at the scene between Augustus and his foe."

"He must have been very young," said Lady Fareham. "But I am not going to depreciate Corneille, or to pretend that the French theatre is not vastly superior to our own. I would only protest that if our laughter-loving King prefers farce to tragedy, and rhyme to blankverse, his subjects should accommodate themselves to his taste, and enjoy the plays he likes. It is a foolish prejudice that deprives me of such a pleasure. I could always go in a mask."

"Can you put a mask upon your mind, and preserve that unstained in an atmosphere of corruption? Indeed, your ladyship does not know what you are asking for. To sit and simper through a comedy in which the filthiest subjects are discussed in the vilest language; to see all that is foolish or lascivious in your own sex exaggerated with a malignant licence, which makes a young and beautiful woman an epitome of all the vices, uniting the extreme of masculine profligacy with the extreme of feminine silliness. Will you encourage by your presence the wretches who libel your sex? Will you sit smiling to see your sisters in the pillory of satire?"

"I should smile as at a fairy tale. There are no such women among my friends----"

"And if the satire hits an enemy, it is all the more pungent," said Lady Sarah.

"An enemy! The man who can so write of women is your worst enemy. The day will come, perhaps, long after we are dust, when the women in *Epsom Wells* will be thought pictures from life. 'Such an one,' people will say, as they stand to read your epitaph, 'was this Lady Sarah, whose virtues are recorded here in Latin superlatives. We know her better in the pages of Shadwell.'"

Lady Sarah paled under her rouge at that image of a tomb, as Fareham's falcon eye singled her out in the light-hearted group of which De Malfort was the central figure, sitting on the marble balustrade, in an easy impertinent attitude, swinging his legs, and dandling his guitar. She was less concerned at the thought of what posterity might say of her morals than at the idea that she must inevitably die.

"Not a word against Shad," protested Sir Ralph. "I have roared with laughter at his last play. Never did any one so hit the follies of town and country. His rural Put is perfection; his London rook is to the very life."

"And if the generality of his female characters conduct themselves badly there is always one heroine of irreproachable morals," said Lady Sarah.

"Who talks like a moral dragoon," said Fareham.

"Oh, dem, we must have the play-houses!" cried Masaroon. "Consider how dull town is without them. They are the only assemblies that please quality and riffraff alike. Sure 'tis the nature of wit to bubble into licentiousness, as champagne foams over the rim of a glass; and, after all, who listens to the play? Half the time one is talking to some adventurous miss, who will swallow a compliment from a stranger if he offer it with a china orange. Or, perhaps, there is quarrelling; and all our eyes and ears are on the scufflers. One may ogle a pretty actress on the stage; but who listens to the play, except the cits and commonalty?"

"And even they are more eyes than ears," said Lady Sarah, "and are gazing at the King and Queen, or the Duke and Duchess, when they should be 'following an intrigue by Shadwell or Dryden."

"Pardieu!" exclaimed De Malfort, "there are tragedies and comedies in the boxes deeper and more human than anything that is acted on the stage. To watch the

Queen, sitting silent and melancholy, while Madame Barbara lolls across half a dozen people to talk to his Majesty, dazzling him with her brilliant eyes, bewildering him by her daring speech. Or, on other nights to see the same lady out of favour, sitting apart, with an ivory shoulder turned towards Royalty, scowling at the audience like a thunder-cloud."

"Well, it is but natural, perhaps, that such a Court should inspire such a stage," returned Fareham, "and that for the heroic drama of Beaumont and Fletcher, Webster, Massinger, and Ford, we should have a gross caricature of our own follies and our own vices. Nay, so essential is foulness to the modern stage that when the manager ventures a serious play, he takes care to introduce it with some filthy prologue, and to spice the finish with a filthier epilogue."

"Zounds, Fareham!" cried Masaroon, "when one has yawned or slept through five acts of dull heroics, one needs to be stung into wakefulness by a high-spiced epilogue. For my taste your epilogue can't be too pungent to give a flavour to my oysters and Rhenish. Gud, my lord, we must have something to talk about when we leave the play-house!"

"His lordship is spoilt; we are all spoilt for London after having lived in the most exquisite city in the world," drawled Mrs. Danville, one of Lady Fareham's particular friends, who had been educated at the Visitandines with the Princess Henrietta, now Duchess of Orleans. "Who can tolerate the coarse manners and sea-coal fires of London after the smokeless skies and exquisite courtesies of Parisian good company in the Rue St. Thomas du Louvre--a society so refined that a fault in grammar shocks as much as a slit nose at Charing Cross? I shudder when I recall the Saturdays in the Rue du Temple, and compare the conversations there, the play of wit and fancy, the elaborate arguments upon platonic love, the graceful raillery, with any assembly in London--except yours, Hyacinth. At Fareham House we breathe a finer air, although his lordship's esprit moqueur will not allow us any superiority to the coarse English mob."

"Indeed, Mrs. Danville, even your prejudice cannot deny London fine gentlemen and wits," remonstrated Sir Ralph. "A court that can boast a Buckhurst, a Rochester, an Etherege, a Sedley----"

"There is not one of them can compare with Voiture or Godeau, with Bussy or St. Evremond, still less with Scarron or Moliere," said De Malfort. "I have heard more wit in one evening at Scarron's than in a week at Whitehall. Wit in France has its basis in thought and erudition. Here it is the sparkle and froth of empty minds, a trick of speech, a knack of saying brutal things under a pretence of humour, varnishing real impertinence with mock wit. I have heard Rowley laugh at insolences which, addressed to Louis, would have ensured the speaker a year in the Bastille."

"I would not exchange our easy-tempered King for your graceful despot," said Fareham. "Pride is the mainspring that moves Louis' self-absorbed soul. His mother instilled it into his mind almost before he could speak. He was bred in the belief that he has no more parallel or fellow than the sun which he has chosen for his emblem. And then, for moral worth, he is little better than his cousin, Louis has all Charles's elegant vices, plus tyranny."

"Louis is every inch a King. Your easy-tempered gentleman at Whitehall is only a tradition," answered De Malfort. "He is but an extravagantly paid official, whose office is a sinecure, and who sells something of his prerogative every session for a new grant of money. I dare adventure, by the end of his reign, Charles will have done more than Cromwell to increase the liberty of the subject and to demonstrate the insignificance of kings."

"I doubt the easy-tempered sinecurist who trusts the business of the State to the nation's representatives will wear longer than your officious tyrant, who wants to hold all the strings in his own fingers."

"He may do that safely, so long as he has men like Colbert for puppets----"

"Men!" cried Fareham. "A man of so rare an honesty must not be thought of in the plural. Colbert's talent, probity, and honour constitute a phoenix that appears once in a century; and, given those rare qualities in the man, it needs a Richelieu to inspire the minister, and a Mazarin to teach him his craft, and to prepare him for double-dealing in others which his own direct mind could never have imagined. Trained first by one of the greatest, and next by one of the subtlest statesmen the world has ever seen, the provincial woollen-draper's son has all the qualities needed to raise France to the pinnacle of fortune, if his master will but give him a free hand."

"At any rate, he will make Jacques Bonhomme pay handsomely for his Majesty's new palaces and new loves," said De Malfort. "Colbert adores the King, and is blind to his follies, which are no more economical than the vulgar pleasures of your jovial Rowley."

"Who takes four shillings in every country gentleman's pound to spend on the pleasures of London," interjected Masaroon. "Royalty is plaguey expensive."

The company sighed a melancholy assent.

"And one can never tell whether the money they squeeze out of us goes to build a new ship, or to pay Lady Castlemaine's gambling debts," said Lady Sarah.

"Oh, no doubt the lady, as Hyde calls her, has her tithes," said De Malfort. "I have observed she always flames in new jewels after a subsidy."

"Royal accounts should be kept so that every tax-payer could look into them," said Masaroon. "The King has spent millions. We were all so foolishly fond of him in the joyful day of his restoration that we allowed him to wallow in extravagance, and asked no questions; and for a man who had worn threadbare velvet and tarnished gold, and lived upon loans and gratuities from foreign princes and particulars, it was a new sensation to draw *ad libitum* upon a national exchequer."

"The exchequer Rowley draws upon should be as deep and wide as the river Pactolus; for he is a spendthrift by instinct," said Fareham.

"Yet his largest expenditure can hardly equal his cousin's drain upon the revenue. Mansart is spending millions on Versailles, with his bastard Italian architecture, his bloated garlands and festoons, his stone lilies and pomegranates. Charles builds no palaces, initiates no war----"

"And will leave neither palace nor monument; will have lived only to have diminished the dignity and importance of his country. Restored to kingdom and power as if by a miracle, he makes it his chief business to show Englishmen how well they could have done without him," said Denzil Warner, who had been hanging over Angela's tea-table until just now, when they both sauntered on to the terrace, the lady's office being fulfilled, the little Chinese teapot emptied of its costly contents, and the tiny tea-cups distributed among the modish few who relished, or pretended to relish, the new drink.

"You are a Republican, Sir Denzil, fostered by an arrant demagogue!" exclaimed Masaroon, with a contemptuous shake of his shoulder ribbons. "You hate the King because he is a King."

"No, sir, I despise him because he is so much less than a King. Nobody could hate Charles the Second. He is not big enough."

"Oh, dem, we want no meddlesome Kings to quarrel with their neighbours, and set Europe by the ears! The treaty of the Pyrenees may be a fine thing for France; but how many noble gentlemen's lives it cost, to say nothing of the common people! Rowley is the finest gentleman in his kingdom, and the most good-natured. Eh, gud, sirs! what more would you have?"

"A MAN--like Henry the Fifth, or Oliver Cromwell, or Elizabeth."

"Faith, she had need possess the manly virtues, for she must have been an untowardly female--a sour, lantern-jawed spinster, with all the inclinations but none of the qualities of a coquette."

"Greatness has the privilege of small failings, or it would scarce be human. Elizabeth and Julius Caesar might be excused some harmless vanities."

*   *   *   *   *

The spring evenings were now mild enough for promenading St. James's Park, and the Mall was crowded night after night by the finest company in London. Hyacinth walked in the Mall, and appeared occasionally in her coach in Hyde Park; but she repeatedly reminded her friends how inferior was the mill-round of the Ring to the procession of open carriages along the Cours la Reine, by the side of the Seine; the splendour of the women's dress, outshone sometimes by the extravagant decoration of their coaches and the richness of their liveries; the crowds of horsemen, the finest gentlemen in France, riding at the coach doors, and bandying jests and compliments with Beauty, enthroned in her triumphal chariot. Gay, joyous sunsets; light laughter; delicate feasting in Renard's garden, hard by the Tuileries. To remember that fairer and different scene was to recall the freshness of youth, the romance of a first love.

Here in the Mall there was gaiety enough and to spare. A crowd of fine people that sometimes thickened to a mob, hustled by the cits and starveling poets who came to stare at them.

Yet, since St. James's Park was fashion's favourite promenade, Lady Fareham affected it, and took a turn or two nearly every evening, alighting from her chair at one gate and returning to it at another, on her way to rout or dance. She took Angela with her; and De Malfort and Sir Denzil were generally in attendance upon them, Denzil's devotion stopping at nothing except a proposal of marriage, for which he had not mustered courage in a friendship that had lasted half a year.

"Because there was one so favoured as Endymion, am I to hope for the moon to come down and give herself to me?" he said one day, when Lady Fareham rebuked him for his reticence. "I know your sister does not love me; yet I hang on, hoping that love will come suddenly, like the coming of spring, which is ever a surprise. And even if I am never to win her, it is happiness to see her and to talk with her. I will not spoil my chance by rashness; I will not hazard banishment from her dear company."

"She is lucky in such an admirer," sighed Hyacinth. "A silent, respectful passion is the rarest thing nowadays. Well, you deserve to conquer, Denzil; and if my sister were not of the coldest nature I ever met in woman she would have returned your passion ages ago, when you were so much in her company at Chilton."

"I can afford to wait as long as the Greeks waited before Troy," said Denzil; "and I will be as constant as they were. If I cannot be her lover I can be her friend, and her protector."

"Protector! Nay, surely she needs no protector out-of-doors, when she has Fareham and me within!"

"Beauty has always need of defenders."

"Not such beauty as Angela's. In the first place, her charms are of no dazzling order; and in the second, she has a coldness of temper and an old-fashioned wisdom which would safeguard her amidst the rabble rout of Comus."

"There I believe you are right, Lady Fareham. Temptation could not touch her. Sin, even the subtlest, could not so disguise itself that her purity would not take alarm. Yes; she is like Milton's lady. The tempter could not touch the freedom of her mind. Sinful love would wither at a look from those pure eyes."

He turned away suddenly and walked to the window.

"Denzil! Why, what is the matter? You are weeping!"

"Forgive me!" he said, recovering himself. "Indeed, I am not ashamed of a tributary tear to virtue and beauty like your sister's."

"Dear friend, I shall not be happy till I call you brother."

She gave him both her hands, and he bent down to kiss them.

"I swear you are losing all your Anabaptist stiffness," she said, laughingly. "You will be ruffling it in Covent Garden with Buckhurst and his crew before long."

CHAPTER XIII.
THE SAGE OF SAYES COURT.

One of Angela's letters to her convent companion, the chosen friend and confidante of childhood and girlhood, Leonie de Ville, now married to the Baron de Beaulieu, and established in a fine house in the Place Royale, will best depict her life and thoughts and feelings during her first London season.

"You tell me, chere, that this London, which I have painted in somewhat brilliant colours, must be a poor place compared with your exquisite city; but, indeed, despite all you say of the Cours la Reine, and your splendour of gilded coaches, fine ladies, and noble gentlemen, who ride at your coach windows, talking to you as they rein in their spirited horses, I cannot think that your fashionable promenade can so much surpass our Ring in Hyde Park, where the Court airs itself daily in the new glass coaches, or outvie for gaiety our Mall in St. James's Park, where all the world of beauty and wit is to be met walking up and down in the gayest, easiest way, everybody familiar and acquainted, with the exception of a few women in masks, who are never to be spoken to or spoken about. Indeed, my sister and I have acquired the art of appearing neither to see nor to hear objectionable company, and pass close beside fine flaunting masks, rub shoulders with them even--and all as if we saw them not. It is for this that Lord Fareham hates London. Here, he says, vice takes the highest place, and flaunts in the sun, while virtue blushes, and steals by with averted head. But though I wonder at this Court of Whitehall, and the wicked woman who reigns empress there, and the neglected Queen, and the ladies of honour, whose bad conduct is on every one's lips, I wonder more at the people and the life you describe at the Louvre, and St. Germain, and Fontainebleau, and your new palace of Versailles.

"Indeed, Leonie, the world must be in a strange way when vice can put on all the grace and dignity of virtue, and hold an honourable place among good and noble women. My sister says that Madame de Montausier is a woman of stainless character, and her husband the proudest of men; yet you tell me that both husband and wife are full of kindness and favours for that unhappy Mlle. de la Valliere, whose position at Court is an open insult to your Queen. Have Queens often been so unhappy, I wonder, as her Majesty here, and your own royal mistress? One at least was not. The martyred King was of all husbands the most constant and affectionate, and, in the opinion of many, lost his kingdom chiefly through his fatal indulgence of Queen Henrietta's caprices, and his willingness to be governed by her opinions in circumstances of difficulty, where only the wisest heads in the land should have counselled him. But how I am wandering from my defence of this beautiful city against your assertion of its inferiority! I hope, chere, that you will cross the sea some day, and allow my sister to lodge you in this house where I write; and when you look out upon our delightful river, with its gay traffic of boats and barges passing to and fro, and its palaces, rising from gardens and Italian terraces on either side of the stream; when you see our ancient cathedral of St. Paul; and the Abbey of St. Peter, lying a little back from the water, grand and ancient, and somewhat gloomy in its massive bulk; and eastward, the old fortress-prison, with its four towers; and the ships lying in the Pool; and fertile Bermondsey with its gardens; and all the beauty of verdant shores and citizens' houses between the bridge and Greenwich, you will own that London and its adjacent villages can compare favourably with any metropolis in the world.

"The only complaint one hears is of its rapid growth, which is fast encroaching upon the pleasant fields and rustic lanes behind the Lambs Conduit and Southampton House; and on the western side spreading so rapidly that there will soon be no country left between London and Knightsbridge.

"How I wish thou couldst see our river-terrace on my sister's visiting-day, when De Malfort is lolling on the marble balustrade, singing one of your favourite chansons to the guitar which he touches so exquisitely, and when Hyacinth's fine lady friends and foppish admirers are sitting about in the sunshine! Thou wouldst confess that even Renard's garden can show no gayer scene.

"It was only last Tuesday that I had the opportunity of seeing more of the city than I had seen previously--and at its best advantage, as seen from the river. Mr. Evelyn, of Sayes Court, had invited my sister and her husband to visit his house and gardens. He is a great gardener and arboriculturist, as you may have heard, for he has travelled much on the Continent, and acquired a world-wide reputation for his knowledge of trees and flowers.

"We were all invited--the Farehams, and my niece Henriette; and even I, whom Mr. Evelyn had seen but once, was included in the invitation. We were to travel by water, in his lordship's barge, and Mr. Evelyn's coach was to meet us at a landing-place not far from his house. We were to start in the morning, dine with him, and return to Fareham House before dark. Henriette was enchanted, and I found her at prayers on Monday night praying St. Swithin, whom she believes to have care of the weather, to allow no rain on Tuesday.

"She looked so pretty next morning, dressed for the journey, in a light blue cloth cloak embroidered with silver, and a hood of the same; but she brought me bad news--my sister had a feverish headache, and begged us to go without her. I went to Hyacinth's room to try to persuade her to go with us, in the hope that the fresh air along the river would cure her headache; but she had been at a dance over-night, and was tired, and would do nothing but rest in a dark room all day--at least, that was her resolve in the morning; but later she remembered that it was Lady Lucretia Topham's visiting-day, and, feeling better, ordered her chair and went off to Bloomsbury Square, where she met all the wits, full of a new play which had been acted at Whitehall, the public theatres being still closed on account of the late contagion.

"They do not act their plays here as often as Moliere is acted at the Hotel de Bourgogne. The town is constant in nothing but wanting perpetual variety, and the stir and bustle of a new play, which gives something for the wits to dispute about. I think we must have three play-wrights to one of yours; but I doubt if there is wit enough in a dozen of our writers to equal your Moliere, whose last comedy seems to surpass all that has gone before. His lordship had a copy from Paris last week, and read the play to us in the evening. He has no accent, and reads French beautifully, with spirit and fire, and in the passionate scenes his great deep voice has a fine effect.

"We left Fareham House at nine o'clock on a lovely morning, worthy this month of May. The lessening of fires in the city since the warmer weather has freed our skies from sea-coal smoke, and the sky last Tuesday was bluer than the river.

"The cream-coloured and gold barge, with twelve rowers in the Fareham green velvet liveries, would have pleased your eyes, which have ever loved splendour; but you might have thought the master of this splendid barge too sombre in dress and aspect to become a scene which recalled Cleopatra's galley. To me there is much that is interesting in that severe and serious face, with its olive complexion and dark eyes, shadowed by the strong, thoughtful brow. People who knew Lord Stafford say that my brother-in-law has a look of that great, unfortunate man--sacrificed to stem the rising flood of rebellion, and sacrificed in vain. Fareham is his kinsman on the mother's side, and may have perhaps something of his powerful mind, together with the rugged grandeur of his features and the bent carriage of his shoulders, which some one the other day called the Stratford stoop.

"I have been reading some of Lord Stafford's letters, and the account of his trial. Indeed he was an ill-used man, and the victim of private hatred--from the Vanes and others--as much as of public faction. His trial and condemnation were scarce less unfair--though the form and tribunal may have been legal--than his master's, and indeed did but forecast that most unwarrantable judgment. Is it not strange, Leonie, to consider how much of tragical history you and I have lived through that are yet so young? But to me it is strangest of all to see the people in this city, who abandon themselves as freely to a life of idle pleasures and sinful folly--at least, the majority of them--as if England had never seen the tragedy of the late monarch's murder, or been visited by death in his most horrible aspect, only the year last past. My sister tells every one, smiling, that she misses no one from the circle of her friends. She never saw the red cross on almost every door, the coffins, and the uncoffined dead, as I saw them one stifling summer day, nor heard the shrieks of the mourners in houses where death was master. Nor does she suspect how near she was to missing her husband, who was hanging between life and death when I found him, forsaken and alone. He never talks to me of those days of sickness and slow recovery; yet I think the memory of them must be in his mind as it is in mine, and that this serves as a link to draw us nearer than many a real brother and sister. I am sending you a little picture which I made of him from memory, for he has one of those striking faces that paint themselves easily upon the mind. Tell me how you, who are clever at reading faces, interpret this one.

"Helas, how I wander from our excursion! My pen winds like the river which carried us to Deptford. Pardon, cherie, si je m'oublie trop; mais c'est si doux de causer avec une amie d'enfance.

"At the Tower stairs we stopped to take on board a gentleman in a very fine peach-blossom suit, and with a huge periwig, at which Papillon began to laugh, and had to be chid somewhat harshly. He was a very civil-spoken, friendly person, and he brought with him a lad carrying a viol. He is an officer of the Admiralty, called Pepys, and, Fareham tells me, a useful, indefatigable person. My sister met him at Clarendon House two years ago, and wrote to me about him somewhat scornfully; but my brother respects him as shrewd and capable, and more honest than such persons usually are. We were to fetch him to Sayes Court, where he also was invited by Mr. Evelyn; and in talking to Henriette and me, he expressed great regret that his wife had not been included, and he paid my niece compliments upon her grace and beauty which I could but think very fulsome and showing want of judgment in addressing a child. And then, seeing me vexed, he hoped I was not jealous; at which I could hardly command my anger, and rose in a huff and left him. But he was a person not easy to keep at a distance, and was following me to the prow of the boat, when Fareham took hold of him by his cannon sleeve and led him to a seat, where he kept him talking of the navy and the great ships now a-building to replace those that have been lost in the Dutch War.

"When we had passed the Pool, and the busy trading ships, and all the noise of sailors and labourers shipping or unloading cargo, and the traffic of small boats hastening to and fro, and were out on a broad reach of the river with the green country on either side, the lad tuned his viol, and played a pretty, pensive air, and he and Mr. Pepys sang some verses by Herrick, one of our favourite English poets, set for two voices--

"'Gather ye rosebuds while ye may,
Old Time still is a-flying;
And this same flower that smiles to-day,
To-morrow will be dying."

The boy had a voice like Mere Ursule's lovely soprano, and Mr. Pepys a pretty tenor; and you can imagine nothing more silvery sweet than the union of the two voices to the staccato notes of the viol, dropping in here and there like music whispered. The setting was Mr. Pepys' own, and he seemed overcome with pride when we praised it. When the song was over, Fareham came to the bench where Papillon and I were sitting, and asked me what I thought of this fine Admiralty gentleman, whereupon I confessed I liked the song better than the singer, who at that moment was strutting on the deck like a peacock, looking at every vessel we passed as if he were Neptune, and could sink navies with a nod.

"Misericorde! how my letter grows! But I love to prattle to you. My sister is all goodness to me; but she has her ideas and I have mine; and though I love her none the less because our fancies pull us in opposite directions, I cannot talk to her as I can write to you; and if I plague you with too much of my own history you must not fear to tell me so. Yet if I dare judge by my own feelings, who am never weary of your letters--nay, can never hear enough of your thoughts and doings--I think you will bear with my expatiations, and not deem them too impertinent.

"Mr. Evelyn's coach was waiting at the landing-stage; and that good gentleman received us at his hall door. He is not young, and has gone through much affliction in the loss of his dear children--one, who died of a fever during that wicked reign of the Usurper Cromwell, was a boy of gifts and capacities that seemed almost miraculous, and had more scholarship at five years old than my poor woman's mind could compass were I to live till fifty. Mr. Evelyn took a kind of sad delight in talking to Henriette and me of this gifted child, asking her what she knew of this and that subject, and comparing her extensive ignorance at eleven with his lamented son's vast knowledge at five. I was more sorry for him than I dared to say; for I could but think this dear overtaught child might have died from a perpetual fever of the brain as likely as from a four days' fever of the body; and afterwards when Mr. Evelyn talked to us of a manner of forcing fruits to grow in strange shapes--a process in which he was greatly interested--I thought that this dear infant's mind had been constrained and directed, like the fruits, into a form unnatural to childhood. Picture to yourself, Leonie, at an age when he should have been chasing butterflies or making himself a garden of cut-flowers stuck in the ground, this child was labouring over Greek and Latin, and all his dreams must have been filled with the toilsome perplexities of his daily tasks. It is happy for the bereaved father that he takes a different view, and that his pride in the child's learning is even greater than his grief at having lost him.

"At dinner the conversation was chiefly of public affairs--the navy, the war, the King, the Duke, and the General. Mr. Evelyn told Fareham much of his embarrassments last year, when he had the Dutch prisoners, and the sick and wounded from the fleet, in his charge; and when there was so terrible a scarcity of provision for these poor wretches that he was constrained to draw largely on his own private means in order to keep them from starving.

"Later, during the long dinner, Mr. Pepys made allusions to an unhappy passion of his master and patron, Lord Sandwich, that had diverted his mind from public business, and was likely to bring him to disgrace. Nothing was said plainly about this matter, but rather in hints and innuendoes, and my brother's brow darkened as the conversation went on; and then, at last, after sitting silent for some time while Mr. Evelyn and Mr. Pepys conversed, he broke up their discourse in a rough, abrupt way he has when greatly moved.

"'He is a wretch--a guilty wretch--to love where he should not, to hazard the world's esteem, to grieve his wife, and to dishonour his name! And yet, I wonder, is he happier in his sinful indulgence than if he had played a Roman part, or, like the Spartan lad we read of, had let the wild-beast passion gnaw his heart out, and yet made no sign? To suffer and die, that is virtue, I take it, Mr. Evelyn; and you Christian sages assure us that virtue is happiness. A strange kind of happiness!'

"'The Christian's law is a law of sacrifice,' Mr. Evelyn said, in his melancholic way. 'The harvest of surrender here is to be garnered in a better world.'

"'But if Sandwich does not believe in the everlasting joys of the heavenly Jerusalem--and prefers to anticipate his harvest of joy!' said Fareham.

"'Then he is the more to be pitied,' interrupted Mr. Evelyn.

"'He is as God made him. Nothing can come out of a man but what his Maker put in him. Your gold vase there will not turn vicious and produce copper--nor can all your alchemy turn copper to gold. There are some of us who believe that a man can live only once, and love only once, and be happy only once in that pitiful span of infirmities which we call life; and that he is wisest who gathers his roses while he may--as Mr. Pepys sang to us this morning.'

"Mr. Evelyn sighed, and looked at my brother with mild reproof.

"'If in this life only we have hope in Christ, we are of all men most miserable,' he said. 'My lord, when those you love people the Heavenly City, you will begin to believe and hope as I do.'

"I have transcribed this conversation at full length, Leonie, because it gives you the keynote to Fareham's character, and accounts for much that is strange in his conduct. Alas, that I must say it of so noble a man! He is an infidel! Bred in our Church, he has faith neither in the Church nor in its Divine Founder. His favourite books are metaphysical works by Descartes, Hobbes, Spinoza. I have discovered him reading those pernicious writings whose chief tendency is to make us question the most blessed truths our Church has taught us, or to confuse the mind by leading us to doubt even of our own existence. I was curious to know what there could be in books that so interested a man of his intelligence, and asked to be allowed to read them; but the perusal only served to make me unhappy. This daring attempt to reduce all the mysteries of life to a simple sum in arithmetic, and to make God a mere attribute in the mind of man, disturbed and depressed me. Indeed, there can be no more unhappy moment in any life than that in which for the first time a terrible 'if' flashes upon the mind. *If* God is not the God I have worshipped, and in whose goodness I rest all my hopes of future bliss; *if* in the place of an all-powerful Creator, who gave me my life and governs it, and will renew it after the grave, there is nothing but a quality of my mind, which makes it necessary to me to invent a Superior Being, and to worship the product of my own imagination! Oh, Leonie, beware of these modern thinkers, who assail the creed that has been the stronghold and comfort of humanity for sixteen hundred years, and who employ the reason which God has given them to disprove the existence of their Maker. Fareham insists that Spinoza is a religious man--and has beautiful ideas about God; but I found only doubt and despair in his pages; and I ascribe my poor brother's melancholic disposition in some part to his study of such philosophers.

"I wonder what you would think of Fareham, did you see him daily and hourly, almost, as I do. Would you like or dislike, admire or scorn him? I cannot tell. His manners have none of the velvet softness which is the fashion in London--where all the fine gentlemen shape themselves upon the Parisian model; yet he is courteous, after his graver mode, to all women, and kind and thoughtful of our happiness. To my sister he is all beneficence; and if he has a fault it is over-much indulgence of her whims and extravagances--though Hyacinth, poor soul, thinks him a tyrant because he forbids her some places of amusement to which other women of quality resort freely. Were he my husband, I should honour him for his desire to spare me all evil sounds and profligate company; and so would Hyacinth, perhaps, had she leisure for reflection. But in her London life, surrounded ever with a bevy of friends, moving like a star amidst a galaxy of great ladies, there is little time for the free exercise of a sound judgment, and she can but think as others bid her, who swear that her husband is a despot.

"Mrs. Evelyn was absent from home on a visit; so after dinner Henriette and I, having no hostess to entertain us, walked with our host, who showed us all the curiosities and beauties of his garden, and condescended to instruct us upon many interesting particulars relating to trees and flowers, and the methods of cultivation pursued in various countries. His fig trees are as fine as those in the convent garden at Louvain; and, indeed, walking with him in a long alley, shut in by holly hedges of which he is especially proud, and with orchard trees on either side, I was taken back in fancy to the old pathway along which you and I have paced so often with Mother Agnes, talking of the time when we should go out into the world. You have been more than three years in that world of which you then knew so little, but it lacks still a quarter of one year since I left that quiet and so monotonous life; and already I look back and wonder if I ever really lived there. I cannot picture myself within those walls. I cannot call back my own feelings or my own image at the time when I had never seen London, when my sister was almost a stranger to me, and my sister's husband only a name. Yet a day of sorrow might come when I should be fain to find a tranquil retreat in that sober place, and to spend my declining years in prayer and meditation, as my dear aunt did spend nearly all her life. May God maintain us in the true faith, sweet friend, so that we may ever have that sanctuary of holy seclusion and prayer to fly to--and, oh, how deep should be our pity for a soul like Fareham's, which knows not the consolations nor the strength of religion, for whom there is no armour against the arrows of death, no City of Refuge in the day of mourning!

"Indeed he is not happy. I question and perplex myself to find a reason for his melancholy. He is rich in money and in powerful friends; has a wife whom all the world admires; houses which might lodge Royalty. Perhaps it is because his life has been over prosperous that he sickens of it, like one who flings away from a banquet table, satiated by feasting. Life to him may be like the weariness of our

English dinners, where one mountain of food is carried away to make room on the board for another; and where after people have sat eating and drinking for over an hour comes a roasted swan, or a peacock, or some other fantastical dish, which the company praise as a pretty surprise. Often, in the midst of such a dinner, I recall our sparing meals in the convent; our soup maigre and snow eggs, our cool salads and black bread--and regret that simple food, while the reeking joints and hecatombs of fowl nauseate my senses.

"It was late in the afternoon when we returned to the barge, for Mr. Pepys had business to transact with our host, and spent an hour with him in his study, signing papers, and looking at accounts, while Papillon and I roamed about the garden with his lordship, conversing upon various subjects, and about Mr. Evelyn, and his opinions and politics.

"'The good man has a pretty trivial taste that will keep him amused and happy till he drops into the grave--but, lord! what insipid trash it all seems to the heart on fire with passion!' Fareham said in his impetuous way, as if he despised Mr. Evelyn for taking pleasure in bagatelles.

"The sun was setting as we passed Greenwich, and I thought of those who had lived and made history in the old palace--Queen Elizabeth, so great, so lonely; Shakespeare, whom his lordship honours; Bacon, said to be one of the wisest men who have lived since the Seven of Greece; Raleigh, so brave, so adventurous, so unhappy! Surely men and women must have been made of another stuff a century ago; for what will those who come after us remember of the wits and beauties of Whitehall, except that they lived and died?

"Mr. Pepys was somewhat noisy on the evening voyage, and I was very glad when he left the barge. He paid me ridiculous compliments mixed with scraps of French and Spanish, and, finding his conversation distasteful, he insisted upon attempting several songs--not one of which he was able to finish, and at last began one which for some reason made his lordship angry, who gave him a cuff on his head that scattered all the scented powder in his wig; on which, instead of starting up furious to return the blow, as I feared to see him, Mr. Pepys gave a little whimpering laugh, muttered something to the effect that his lordship was vastly nice, and sank down in a corner of the cushioned seat, where he almost instantly fell asleep.

"Henriette and I were spectators of this scene at some distance, I am glad to say, for all the length of the barge divided us from the noisy singer.

"The sun went down, and the stars stole out of the deep blue vault, and trembled between us and those vast fields of heaven. Papillon watched their reflection in the river, or looked at the houses along the shore, few and far apart, where a solitary candle showed here and there. Fareham came and seated himself near us, but talked little. We drew our cloaks closer, for the air was cold, and Papillon nestled beside me and dropped asleep. Even the dipping of the oars had a ghostly sound in the night stillness; and we seemed so melancholy in this silence, and so far away from one another, that I could but think of Charon's boat laden with the souls of the dead.

"Write to me soon, dearest, and as long a letter as I have written to you.

"A toi de coeur,

"ANGELA."

CHAPTER XIV.
THE MILLBANK GHOST.

One of the greatest charms of London has ever been the facility of getting away from it to some adjacent rustic or pseudo-rustic spot; and in 1666, though many people declared that the city had outgrown all reason, and was eating up the country, a two-mile journey would carry the Londoner from bricks and mortar to rusticity, and while the tower of St Paul's Cathedral was still within sight he might lie on the grass on a wild hillside, and hear the skylark warbling in the blue arch above him, and scent the hawthorn blowing in untrimmed hedge-rows. And then there were the fashionable resorts--the gardens or the fields which the town had marked as its own. Beauty and wit had their choice of such meeting-grounds between Westminster and Barn Elms, where in the remote solitudes along the river murder might be done in strict accordance with etiquette, and was too seldom punished by law.

Among the rendezvous of fashion there was one retired spot less widely known than Fox Hall or the Mulberry Garden, but which possessed a certain repute, and was affected rather by the exclusives than by the crowd. It was a dilapidated building of immemorial age, known as the "haunted Abbey," being, in fact, the refectory of a Cistercian monastery, of which all other remains had disappeared long ago. The Abbey had flourished in the lifetime of Sir Thomas More, and was mentioned in some of his familiar epistles. The ruined building had been used as a granary in the time of Charles the First; and it was only within the last decade that it had been redeemed from that degraded use, and had been in some measure restored and made habitable for the occupation of an old couple, who owned the surrounding fields, and who had a small dairy farm from which they sent fresh milk into London every morning.

The ghostly repute of the place and the attraction of new milk, cheese cakes, and syllabubs, had drawn a certain number of those satiated pleasure-seekers who were ever on the alert for a new sensation, among whom there was none more active or more noisy than Lady Sarah Tewkesbury. She had made the haunted Abbey in a manner her own, had invited her friends to midnight parties to watch for the ghost, and to morning parties to eat syllabubs and dance on the grass. She had brought a shower of gold into the lap of the miserly freeholder, and had husband and wife completely under her thumb.

Doler, the husband, had fought in the civil war, and Mrs. Doler had been a cook in the Fairfax household; but both had scrupulously sunk all Cromwellian associations since his Majesty's return, and in boasting, as he often did boast, of having fought desperately and been left for dead at the battle of Brentford, Mr. Doler had been careful to suppress the fact that he was a hireling soldier of the Parliament. He would weep for the martyred King, and tell the story of his own wounds, until it is possible he had forgotten which side he had fought for, in remembering his personal prowess and sufferings.

So far there had been disappointment as to the ghost. Sounds had been heard of a most satisfying grimness, during those midnight and early morning watchings; rappings, and scrapings, and scratching on the wall, groanings and meanings, sighings and whisperings behind the wainscote; but nothing spectral had been seen; and Mrs. Doler had been severely reprimanded by her patrons and patronesses for the unwarrantable conduct of a spectre which she professed to have seen as often as she had fingers and toes.

It was the phantom of a nun--a woman of exceeding beauty, but white as the linen which banded her cheek and brow. There was a dark story of violated oaths, priestly sin, and the sleepless conscience of the dead, who could not rest even in that dreadful grave where the sinner had been immured alive, but must needs haunt the footsteps of the living, a wandering shade. Some there were who disbelieved in the traditions of that living grave, and who even went so far as to doubt the ghost; but the spectre had an established repute of more than a century, was firmly believed in by all the children and old women of the neighbourhood, and had been written about by students of the unseen.

One of Lady Sarah's parties took place at full moon, not long after the visit to Deptford, and Lord Fareham's barge was again employed, this time on a nocturnal expedition up the river to the fields near the haunted Abbey, to carry Hyacinth, her sister, De Malfort, Lord Rochester, Sir Ralph Masaroon, Sir Denzil Warner, and a bevy of wits and beauties--beauties who had, some of them, been carrying on the beauty-business and trading in eyes and complexion for more than one decade, and who loved that night season when paint might be laid on thicker than in the glare of day.

The barge wore a much more festive aspect under her ladyship's management than when used by his lordship for a daylight voyage like the trip to Deptford. Satin coverlets and tapestry curtains had been brought from Lady Fareham's own apartments, to be flung with studied carelessness over benches and tabourets. Her ladyship's singing-boys and musicians were grouped picturesquely under a silken canopy in the bows, and a row of lanterns hung on chains festooned from stem to stern, pretty gew-gaws, that had no illuminating power under that all-potent moon, but which glittered with coloured light like jewels, and twinkled and trembled in the summer air.

A table in the stern was spread with a light collation, which gave an excuse for the display of parcel-gilt cups, silver tankards, and Venetian wine-flasks. A miniature fountain played perfumed waters in the midst of this splendour; and it amused the ladies to pull off their long gloves, dip them in the scented water, and flap them in the faces of their beaux.

The distance was only too short, since Lady Fareham's friends declared the voyage was by far the pleasanter part of the entertainment. Denzil, among others, was of this opinion, for it was his good fortune to have secured the seat next Angela, and to be able to interest her by his account of the buildings they passed, whose historical associations were much better known to him than to most young men of his epoch. He had sat at the feet of a man who scoffed at Pope and King, and hated Episcopacy, but who revered all that was noble and excellent in England's past.

"Flams, mere flams!" cried Hyacinth, acknowledging the praises bestowed on her barge; "but if you like clary wine better than skimmed milk you had best drink a brimmer or two before you leave the barge, since 'tis odds you'll get nothing but syllabubs and gingerbread from Lady Sarah."

"A substantial supper might frighten away the ghost, who doubtless parted with sensual propensities when she died," said De Malfort. "How do we watch for her? In a severe silence, as if we were at church?"

"Aw would keep silence for a week o' Sawbaths gin Aw was sure o' seeing a bogle," said Lady Euphemia Dubbin, a Scotch marquess's daughter, who had married a wealthy cit, and made it the chief endeavour of her life to ignore her husband and keep him at a distance.

She hated the man only a little less than his plebeian name, which she had not succeeded in persuading him to change, because, forsooth, there had been Dubbins in Mark Lane for many generations. All previous Dubbins had lived over their warehouses and offices; but her ladyship had brought Thomas Dubbin from Mark Lane to my Lord Bedford's Piazza in the Convent Garden, where he endured the tedium of existence in a fine new house in which he was afraid of his fine new servants, and never had anything to eat that he liked, his gastronomic taste being for dishes the very names of which were intolerable to persons of quality.

This evening Mr. Dubbin had been incorrigible, and had insisted on intruding his clumsy person upon Lady Fareham's party, arguing with a dull persistence that his name was on her ladyship's billet of invitation.

"Your name is on a great many invitations only because it is my misfortune to be called by it," his wife told him. "To sit on a barge after ten o'clock at night in June--the coarsest month in summer--is to court lumbago; and all I hope is ye'll not be punished by a worse attack than common."

Mr. Dubbin had refused to be discouraged, even by this churlishness from his lady, and appeared in attendance upon her, wearing a magnificent birthday suit of crimson velvet and green brocade, which he meant to present to his favourite actor at the Duke's Theatre, after he had exhibited himself in it half a dozen times at

Whitehall, for the benefit of the great world, and at the Mulberry Garden for the admiration of the **bona-robas**. He was a fat, double-chinned little man, the essence of good nature, and perfectly unconscious of being an offence to fine people.

Although not a wit himself, Mr. Dubbin was occasionally the cause of wit in others, if the practice of bubbling an innocent rustic or citizen can be called wit. Rochester and Sir Ralph Masaroon, and one Jerry Spavinger, a gentleman jockey, who was a nobody in town, but a shining light at Newmarket, took it upon themselves to draw the harmless citizen, and, as a preliminary to making him ridiculous, essayed to make him drunk.

They were clustered together in a little group somewhat apart from the rest of the company, and were attended upon by a lackey who brought a full tankard at the first whistle on the empty one, and whom Mr. Dubbin, after a rapid succession of brimmers, insisted on calling "drawer." It was very seldom that Rochester condescended to take part in any entertainment on which the royal sun shone not, unless it were some post-midnight marauding with Buckhurst, Sedley, and a band of wild coursers from the purlieus of Drury Lane. He could see no pleasure in any medium between Whitehall and Alsatia.

"If I am not fooling on the steps of the throne, let me sprawl in the gutter with pamphleteers and orange-girls," said this precocious profligate. "I abhor a reputable party among your petty nobility, and if I had not been in love with Lady Fareham off and on, ever since I cut my second teeth, I would have no hand in such a humdrum business as this."

"There's not a neater filly in the London stable than her ladyship," said Jerry, "and I don't blame your taste. I was side-glassing her yesterday in Hi' Park, but she didn't seem to relish the manoeuvre, though I was wearing a Chedreux peruke that ought to strike 'em dead."

"You don't give your peruke a chance, Jerry, while you frame that ugly phiz in it."

"Why not buffle the whole company, my lord?" said Masaroon, while Mr. Dubbin talked apart with Lady Euphemia, who had come from the other end of the barge to warn her husband against excess in Rhenish or Burgundy. "You are good at disguises. Why not act the ghost and frighten everybody out of their senses?"

"Il n'y a pas de quoi, Ralph. The creatures have no sense to be robbed of. They are second-rate fashion, which is only worked by machinery. They imitate us as monkeys do, without knowing what they aim at. Their women have virtuous instincts, but turn wanton rather than not be like the maids of honour; and because we have our duels their men murder each other for a shrugged shoulder or a casual word. No, I'll not chalk my face or smear myself with phosphorus to amuse such trumpery. It was worth my pains to disguise myself as a German Nostradamus, in order to fool the lovely Jennings and her friend Price--who won't easily forget their adventures as orange-girls in the heart of the city. But I have done with all such follies."

"You are growing old, Wilmot. The years are telling upon your spirits."

"I was nineteen last birthday, and 'tis fit I should feel the burden of time, and think of virtue and a rich wife."

"Like Mrs. Mallet, for example."

"Faith, a man might do worse than win so much beauty and wealth. But the creature is arrogant, and calls me 'child;' and half the peerage is after her. But we'll have our jest with the city scrub, Ralph; not because I bear him malice, but because I hate his wife. And we'll have our masquerading some time after midnight; if you can borrow a little finery."

Mr. Dubbin was released from his lady's *sotto voce* lecture at this instant, and Lord Rochester continued his communication in a whisper, the Honourable Jeremiah assenting with nods and chucklings, while Masaroon whistled for a fresh tankard, and plied the honest merchant with a glass which he never allowed to be empty.

The taste for masquerading was a fashion of the time, as much as combing a periwig, or flirting a fan. While Rochester was planning a trick upon the citizen, Lady Fareham was whispering to De Malfort under cover of the fiddles, which were playing an Italian pazzemano, an air beloved by Henrietta of Orleans, who danced to that music with her royal brother-in-law, in one of the sumptuous ballets at St. Cloud.

"Why should they be disappointed of their ghost," said Hyacinth, "when it would be so easy for me to dress up as the nun and scare them all? This white satin gown of mine, with a few yards of white lawn arranged on my head and shoulders----"

"Ah, but you have not the lawn at hand to-night, or your woman to arrange your head," interjected De Malfort quickly. "It would be a capital joke; but it must be for another occasion and choicer company. The rabble you have to-night is not worth it. Besides, there is Rochester, who is past-master in disguises, and would smoke you at a glance. Let me arrange it some night before the end of the summer--when there is a waning moon. It were a pity the thing were done ill."

"Will you really plan a party for me, and let me appear to them on the stroke of one, with my face whitened? I have as slender a shape as most women."

"There is no such sylph in London."

"And I can make myself look ethereal. Will you draw the nun's habit for me? and I will give your picture to Lewin to copy."

"I will do more. I will get you a real habit."

"But there are no nuns so white as the ghost."

"True, but you may rely upon me. The nun's robes shall be there, the phosphorous, the blue fire, and a selection of the choicest company to tremble at you. Leave the whole business to my care. It will amuse me to plan so exquisite a jest for so lovely a jester."

He bent down to kiss her hand, till his forehead almost touched her knee, and in the few moments that passed before he raised it, she heard him laughing softly to himself, as if with irrepressible delight.

"What a child you are," she said, "to be pleased with such folly!"

"What children we both are, Hyacinth! My sweet soul, let us always be childish, and find pleasure in follies. Life is such a poor thing, that if we had leisure to appraise its value we should have a contagion of suicide that would number more deaths than the plague. Indeed, the wonder is, not that any man should commit *felo de se*, but that so many of us should take the trouble to live."

Lady Sarah received them at the landing-stage, with an escort of fops and fine ladies; and the festival promised to be a success. There was a better supper, and more wine than people expected from her ladyship; and after supper a good many of those who pretended to have come to see the ghost, wandered off in couples to saunter along the willow-shaded bank, while only the more earnest spirits were content to wait and watch and listen in the great vaulted hall, with no light but the moon which sent a flood of silver through the high Gothic window, from which every vestige of glass had long vanished.

There were stone benches along the two side walls, and Lady Sarah's *prevoyance* had secured cushions or carpets for her guests to sit upon; and here the superstitious sat in patient weariness, Angela among them, with Denzil still at her side, scornful of credulous folly, but loving to be with her he adored. Lady Fareham had been tempted out-of-doors by De Malfort to look at the moonlight on the river, and had not returned. Rochester and his crew had also vanished directly after supper; and for company Angela had on her left hand Mr. Dubbin, far advanced in liquor, and trembling at every breath of summer wind that fluttered the ivy round the ruined window, and at every shadow that moved upon the moonlit wall. His wife was on the other side of the hall, whispering with Lady Sarah, and both so deep in a court scandal--in which the "K" and the "D" recurred very often--that they had almost forgotten the purpose of that moonlight sitting.

Suddenly in the distance there sounded a long shrill wailing, as of a soul in agony, whereupon Mr. Dubbin, after clinging wildly to Angela, and being somewhat roughly flung aside by Denzil, collapsed altogether, and rolled upon the ground.

"Lady Euphemia," cried Mrs. Townshend, a young lady who had been sitting next the obnoxious citizen, "be pleased to look after your drunken husband. If you take the low-bred sot into company, you should at least charge yourself with the care of his manners."

The damsel had started to her feet, and indignantly snatched her satin petticoat from contact with the citizen's porpoise figure.

"I hate mixed company," she told Angela, "and old maids who marry tallow-chandlers. If a woman of rank marries a shopkeeper she ought never to be allowed west of Temple Bar."

This young lady was no believer in ghosts; but others of the company were too scared for speech. All had risen, and were staring in the direction whence that dismal shriek had come. A trick, perhaps, since anybody with strong lungs--dairymaid or cowboy--could shriek. They all wanted to *see* something, a real manifestation of the supernatural.

The unearthly sound was repeated, and the next moment a spectral shape, in flowing white garments, rushed through the great window, and crossed the hall, followed by three other shapes in dark loose robes, with hooded heads. One carried a rope, another a pickaxe, the third a trowel and hod of mortar. They crossed the hall with flying footsteps--shadowlike--the pale shape in distracted flight, the dark shapes pursuing, and came to a stop close against the wall, which had been vacated by the scared assembly, scattering as if the king of terrors had appeared among them--yet with fascinated eyes fixed on those fearsome figures.

"It is the nun herself!" cried Lady Sarah, apprehension and triumph contending in her agitated spirits; for it was surely a feather in her ladyship's cap to have produced such a phantasmal train at her party. "The nun and her executioners!"

The company fell back from the ghostly troop, recoiling till they were all clustered against the opposite wall, leaving a clear space in front of the spectres, whence they looked on, shuddering, at the tragedy of the erring Sister's fate, repeated in dumb show. The white-robed figure knelt and grovelled at the feet of those hooded executioners. One seized and bound her, with strange automatic action, unlike the movements of living creatures, and another smote the wall with a pickaxe that made no sound, while the third waited with his trowel and mortar. It was a gruesome sight to those who knew the story--a gruesome, yet an enjoyable spectacle; since, as Lady Sarah's friends had not had the pleasure of knowing the sinning Sister in the flesh, they watched this ghostly representation of her suffering with as keen an interest as they would have felt had they been privileged to see Claud Duval swing at Tyburn.

The person most terrified by this ghostly show was the only one who had the hardihood to tackle the performers. This was Mr. Dubbin, who sat on the ground watching the shadowy figures, sobered by fear, and his shrewd city senses gradually returning to a brain bemused by Burgundy.

"Look at her boots!" he cried suddenly, scrambling to his feet, and pointing to the nun, who, in sprawling and writhing at the feet of her executioner, had revealed more leg and foot than were consistent with her spectral whiteness. "She wears yaller boots, as substantial as any shoe leather among the company. I'll swear to them yaller boots."

A chorus of laughter followed this attack--laughter which found a smothered echo among the ghosts. The spell was broken; disillusion followed the exquisite thrill of fear; and all Lady Sarah's male visitors made a rush upon the guilty nun. The loose white robe was stripped off, and little Jerry Spavinger, gentleman jock, famous on the Heath, and at Doncaster, stood revealed, in his shirt and breeches, and those light riding-boots which he rarely exchanged for a more courtly chaussure.

The monks, hustled out of their disguise, were Rochester, Masaroon, and Lady Sarah's young brother, George Saddington.

"From my Lord Rochester I expect nothing but pot-house buffoonery; but I take it vastly ill on your part, George, to join in making me a laughing-stock," remonstrated Lady Sarah.

"Indeed, sister, you have to thank his light-headed lordship for giving a spirited end to your assembly. Could you conceive how preposterous you and your friends looked sitting against the walls, mute as stockfish, and suggesting nothing but a Quaker's meeting, you would make us your lowest curtsy, and thank us kindly for having helped you out of a dilemma."

Lady Sarah, who was too much of a woman of the world to quarrel seriously with a Court favourite, furled the fan with which she had been cooling her indignation, and tapped young Wilmot playfully on that oval cheek where the beard had scarce begun to grow.

"Thou art the most incorrigible wretch of thy years in London," she said, "and it is impossible to help being angry with thee or to help forgiving thee."

The saunterers on the willow-shadowed banks came strolling in. Lady Fareham's cornets and fiddles sounded a March in Alceste; and the party broke up in laughter and good temper, Mr. Dubbin being much complimented upon his having detected Spavinger's boots.

"I ought to know 'em," he answered ruefully. "I lost a hundred meggs on him Toosday se'nnight, at Windsor races; and I had time to take the pattern of them boots while he was crawling in, a bad third."

CHAPTER XV.
FALCON AND DOVE.

"Has your ladyship any commands for Paris?" Lord Fareham asked, one August afternoon, when the ghost party at Millbank was almost forgotten amid a succession of entertainments on land and river; a fortnight at Epsom to drink the waters;

and a fortnight at Tunbridge--where the Queen and Court were spending the close of summer--to neutralise the bad effects of Epsom chalybeates with a regimen of Kentish sulphur. If nobody at either resort drank deeper of the medicinal springs than Hyacinth--who had ordered her physician to order her that treatment--the risk of harm or the possibility of benefit was of the smallest. But at Epsom there had been a good deal of gay company, and a greater liberty of manners than in London; for, indeed, as Rochester assured Lady Fareham, "the freedom of Epsom allowed almost nothing to be scandalous." And at Tunbridge there were dances by torchlight on the common. "And at the worst," Lady Fareham told her friends, "a fortnight or so at the Wells helps to shorten the summer."

It was the middle of August when they went back to Fareham House, hot, dry weather, and London seemed to be living on the Thames, so thick was the throng of boats going up and down the river, so that with an afternoon tide running up it seemed as if barges, luggers, and wherries were moving in one solid block into the sunset sky.

De Malfort had been attached to her ladyship's party at Epsom, and at Tunbridge Wells. He had his own lodgings, but seldom occupied them, except in that period between four or five in the morning and two in the afternoon, which Rochester and he called night. His days were passed chiefly in attendance upon Lady Fareham--singing and playing, fetching and carrying combing her favourite spaniel with the same ivory pocket-comb that arranged his own waterfall curls; or reading a French romance to her, or teaching her the newest game of cards, or the last dancing-step imported from Fontainebleau or St. Cloud, or some new grace or fashion in dancing, the holding of the hand lower or higher; the latest manner of passaging in a bransle or a coranto, as performed by the French King and Madame Henriette, the two finest dancers in France; Conde, once so famous for his dancing, now appearing in those gay scenes but seldom.

"Have you any commands for Paris, Hyacinth?" repeated Lord Fareham, his wife being for the moment too surprised to answer him. "Or have you, sister? I am starting for France to-morrow. I shall ride to Dover--lying a night at Sittingbourne, perhaps--and cross by the Packet that goes twice a week to Calais."

"Paris! And pray, my lord, what business takes you to Paris?"

"There is a great collection of books to be sold there next week. The library of your old admirer, Nicolas Fouquet, whom you knew in his splendour, but who has been a prisoner at Pignerol for a year and a half."

"Poor wretch!" cried De Malfort, "I was at the Chamber with Madame de Sevigne very often during his long tedious trial. Mon dieu! what courage, what talent he showed in defending himself! Every safeguard of the law was violated in order to silence him and prove him guilty; his papers seized in his absence, no friend or servant allowed to protect his interest, no inventory taken--documents suppressed that might have served for his defence, forgeries inserted by his foes. He had an implacable enemy, and he the highest in the land. He was the scapegoat of the past, and had to answer for a system of plunder that made Mazarin the richest man in France."

"I don't wonder that Louis was angry with a servant who had the insolence to entertain his Majesty with a splendour that surpassed his own," said Lady Fareham. "I should like to have been at those fetes at Vaux. But although Fareham talks so lightly of travelling to Paris to choose a few dusty books, he has always discouraged me from going there to see old friends, and my own house--which I grieve to think of--abandoned to the carelessness of servants."

"Dearest, the cleverest woman in the world cannot be in two places at once; and it seems to me you have ever had your days here so full of agreeable engagements that you can have scarcely desired to leave London," answered Fareham, with his grave smile.

"To leave London--no! But there have been long moping months in Oxfordshire when it would have been a relief to change the scene."

"Then, indeed, had you been very earnest in wanting such a change, I am sure you would have taken it. I have never forbidden your going to Paris, nor refused to accompany you there. You may go with me to-morrow, if you can be ready."

"Which you know I cannot, or you would scarce make so liberal an offer."

"Tres chere, you are pleased to be petulant. But I repeat my question. Is there anything you want at Paris?"

"Anything? A million things! Everything! But they are things which you would not be able to choose--except, perhaps, some of the new lace. I might trust you to buy that, though I'll wager you will bring me a hideous pattern--and some white Cypress powder--and a piece of the ash-coloured velvet Madame wore last winter.

I have friends who can choose for you, if I write to them; and you will have but to bring the goods, and see they suffer no harm on the voyage. And you can go to the Rue de Tourain and see whether my servants are keeping the house in tolerable order."

"With your ladyship's permission I will lodge there while I am in Paris, which will be but long enough to attend the sale of books, and see some old friends. If I am detained it will be by finding my friends out of town, and having to make a journey to see them. I shall not go beyond Fontainebleau at furthest."

"Dear Fontainebleau! It is of all French palaces my favourite. I always envy Diana of Poitiers for having her cypher emblazoned all over that lovely gallery--Henri and Diane! Diane and Henri! Ah, me!"

"You envy her a kind of notoriety which I do not covet for my wife!"

"You always take one au pied de la lettre; but seriously, Madame de Breze was an honest woman compared with the lady who lodges by the Holbein Gate."

"I admit that sin wears a bolder front than it did in the last century. Angela, can I find nothing for you in Paris?"

"No; I thank your lordship. You and sister are both so generous to me that I have lost the capacity to wish for anything."

"And as Lewin crosses the Channel three or four times a year, I doubt we positively have the Paris fashions as soon as the Parisians themselves," added Hyacinth.

"That is an agreeable hallucination with which Englishwomen have ever consoled themselves for not being French," said De Malfort, who sat lolling against the marble balustrade, nursing the guitar on which he had been playing when Fareham interrupted their noontide idleness; "but your ladyship may be sure that London milliners are ever a twelvemonth in the rear of Paris fashions. It is not that they do not see the new mode. They see it, and think it hideous; and it takes a year to teach them that it is the one perfect style possible."

"I was not thinking of kerchiefs or petticoats," said Fareham. "You are a book-lover, sister, like myself. Can I bring you no books you wish for?"

"If there were a new comedy by Moliere; but I fear it is wrong to read him, since in his late play, performed before the King at Versailles, he is so cruel an enemy to our Church."

"A foe only to hypocrites and pretenders, Angela. I will bring you his ***Tartuffe***, if it is printed; or still better, ***Le Misanthrope***, which I am told is the finest comedy that was ever written; and the latest romance, in twenty volumes or so, by one of those lady authors Hyacinth so admires, but which I own to finding as tedious as the divine Orinda's verses."

"You can jeer at that poor lady's poetry, yet take pleasure in such balderdash as Hudibras!"

"I love wit, dearest; though I am not witty. But as for your Princesse de Cleves, I find her ineffably dull."

"That is because you do not take the trouble to discover for whom the characters are meant. You lack the key to the imbroglio," said his wife, with a superior air.

"I do not care for a book that is a series of enigmas. Don Quixote needs no such guess-work. Shakespeare's characters are painted not from the petty models of yesterday and to-day, but from mankind in every age and every climate. Moliere's and Calderon's personages stand on as solid a basis. In less than half a century your 'Grand Cyrus' will be insufferable jargon."

"Not more so than your ***Hamlet*** or ***Othello***. Shakespeare was but kept in fashion during the late King's reign because his Majesty loved him--and will soon be forgotten, now that we have so many gayer and brisker dramatists."

"Whoever quotes Shakespeare, nowadays?" asked Lady Sarah Tewkesbury, who had been showing a rustic niece the beauties of the river, as seen from Fareham House. "Even Mr. Taylor, whose sermons bristle with elegant allusions, never points one of his passionate climaxes with a Shakespearian line. And yet there are some very fine lines in ***Hamlet*** and ***Macbeth***, which would scarce sound amiss from the pulpit," added her ladyship, condescendingly. "I have read all the plays, some of them twice over. And I doubt that though Shakespeare cannot hold the stage in our more enlightened age, and will be less and less acted as the town grows more refined, his works will always be tasted by scholars; among whom, in my modest way, I dare reckon myself."

*   *   *   *   *

Lord Fareham left London on horseback, with but one servant, in the early

August dawn, before the rest of the household were stirring. Hyacinth lay nearly as late of a morning as Henrietta Maria, whom Charles used sometimes to reproach for not being up in time for the noonday office at her own chapel. Lady Fareham had not Portuguese Catherine's fervour, who was often at Mass at seven o'clock; but she did usually contrive to be present at High Mass at the Queen's chapel; and this was the beginning of her day. By that time Angela and her niece and nephew had spent hours on the river, or in the meadows at Chiswick, or on Putney Heath, ever glad to escape from the great overgrown city, which was now licking up every stretch of green sward, and every flowery hedgerow west of St. James's Street. Soon there would be no country between the Haymarket and "The Pillars of Hercules."

Denzil sometimes enjoyed the privilege of accompanying Angela, children, and *gouvernante*, on these rural expeditions by the great waterway; and on such occasions he and Angela would each take an oar and row the boat for some part of the voyage, while the watermen rested, and in this manner Angela, instructed by Sir Denzil, considerably advanced her power as an oarswoman. It was an exercise she loved, as indeed she loved all out-of-door exercises, from riding with hawks and hounds to battledore and shuttlecock. But most of all, perhaps, she loved the river, and the rhythmical dip of oars in the fresh morning air, when every curve of the fertile shores seemed to reveal new beauty.

It had been a hot, dry summer, and the grass in the parks was burnt to a dull brown--had, indeed, almost ceased to be grass--while the atmosphere in town had a fiery taste, and was heavy with the dust which whitened all the roadways, and which the faintest breath of wind dispersed. Here on the flowing tide there was coolness, and the long rank grass upon those low sedgy shores was still green.

Lady Fareham supported the August heats sitting on her terrace, with a cluster of friends about her, and her musicians and singing-boys grouped in the distance, ready to perform at her bidding; but Henriette and her brother soon tired of that luxurious repose, and would urge their aunt to assist in a river expedition. The *gouvernante* was fat and lazy and good-tempered, had attended upon Henriette from babyhood, and always did as she was told.

"Her ladyship says I must have some clever person instead of Priscilla before I am a year older," Henriette told her aunt; "but I have promised poor old Prissy to hate the new person consumedly."

Angela and Denzil laughed as they rowed past the ruined abbey, seen dimly across the low water-meadow, where cows of the same colour were all lying in the same attitude, chewing the cud.

"I think Mr. Spavinger's trick must have cured your sister's fine friends of all belief in ghosts," he said.

"I doubt they would be as ready to believe--or to pretend to believe--to-morrow," answered Angela. "They think of nothing from morning till night but how to amuse themselves; and when every pleasure has been exhausted, I suppose fear comes in as a form of entertainment, and they want the shock of seeing a ghost."

"There have been no more midnight parties since Lady Sarah's assembly, I think?"

"Not among people of quality, perhaps; but there have been citizens' parties. I heard Monsieur de Malfort telling my sister about a supper given by a wealthy wine-cooper's lady from Aldersgate. The city people copy everything that their superiors wear or do."

"Even to their morals," said Denzil. "'Twere happy if the so-called superiors would remember that, and upon what a fertile ground they sow the seed of new vices. It is like the importation of a new weed or a new insect, which, beginning with an accident, may end in ruined crops and a country's famine."

Without deliberate disobedience to her husband, Lady Fareham made the best use of her time during his absence in Paris. The public theatres had not yet re-opened after the horror of the plague. Whitehall was a desert, the King and his chief following being at Tunbridge. It was the dullest season of the year, and the recrudescence of the contagion in the low-lying towns along the Thames--Deptford, Greenwich, and the neighbourhood--together with some isolated cases in London, made people more serious than usual, despite of the so-called victory over the Dutch, which, although a mixed benefit, was celebrated piously by a day of General Thanksgiving.

Hyacinth, disgusted at the dulness of the town, was for ordering her coaches and retiring to Chilton.

"It is mortal dull at the Abbey," she said, "but at least we have the hawks, and breezy hills to ride over, instead of this sickly city atmosphere, which to my nostrils smells of the pestilence."

Henri de Malfort argued against such a retreat.

"It were a deliberate suicide," he said. "London, when everybody has left--all the bodies we count worthy to live, *par exemple*--is a more delightful place than you can imagine. There are a host of vulgar amusements which you would not dare to visit when your friends are in town; and which are ten times as amusing as the pleasures you know by heart. Have you ever been to the Bear Garden? I'll warrant you no, though 'tis but across the river at Bankside. We'll go there this afternoon, if you like, and see how the common people taste life. Then there are the gardens at Islington. There are mountebanks, and palmists, and fortune-tellers, who will frighten you out of your wits for a shilling. There's a man at Clerkenwell, a jeweller's journeyman from Venice, who pretends to practise the transmutation of metals, and to make gold. He squeezed hundreds out of that old miser Denham, who was afraid to have the law of him for imposture, lest all London should laugh at his own credulity and applaud the cheat. And you have not seen the Italian puppet-play, which is vastly entertaining. I could find you novelty and amusement for a month."

"Find anything new, even if it fail to amuse me. I am sick of everything I know."

"And then there is our midnight party at Millbank, the ghost-party, at which you are to frighten your dearest friends out of their poor little wits."

"Most of my dearest friends are in the country."

"Nay, there is Lady Lucretia Topham, whom I know you hate; and Lady Sarah and the Dubbins are still in Covent Garden."

"I will have no Dubbin--a toping wretch--and she is a too incongruous mixture, with her Edinburgh lingo and her Whitehall arrogance. Besides, the whole notion of a mock ghost was vulgarised by Wilmot's foolery, who ought to have been born a saltimbanque, and spent his life in a fair. No, I have abandoned the scheme."

"What! after I have been taxing my invention to produce the most terrible illusion that was ever witnessed? Will you let a clown like Spavinger--a well-born stable-boy--baulk us of our triumph? I am sending to Paris for a powder to burn in a corner of the room, which will throw the ghastliest pallor upon your countenance. When I devise a ghost, it shall be no impromptu spectre in yellow riding-boots, but a vision so awful, so true an image of a being returned from the dead, that the stoutest nerves will thrill and tremble at the apparition. The nun's habit is coming from Paris. I have asked my cousin, Madame de Fiesque, to obtain it for me at the Carmelites."

"You are taking a vast deal of trouble. But what kind of assembly can we muster at this dead season?" "Leave all in my hands. I will find you some of the choicest spirits. It is to be *my* party. I will not even tell you what night I fix upon, till all is ready. So make no engagements for your evenings, and tell nobody anything."

"Who invented that powder?"

"A French chemist. He has it of all colours, and can flood a scene in golden light, or the rose of dawn, or the crimson of sunset, or a pale silvery blueness that you would swear was moonshine. It has been used in all the Court ballets. I saw Madame once look as ghastly as death itself, and all the Court was seized with terror. Some blundering fool had burnt the wrong powder, which cast a greenish tint over the faces, and Henriette's long thin features had a look of death. It seemed the forecast of an early grave; and some of us shuddered, as at a prophecy of evil."

"You might expect the worst in her case, knowing the wretched life she leads with Monsieur."

"Yes, when she is with him; but that is not always. There are compensations."

"If you mean scandal, I will not hear a word. She is adorable. The most sympathetic person I know--good even to her enemies--who are legion."

"You had better not say that, for I doubt she has only one kind of enemy."

"As how?"

"The admirers she has encouraged and disappointed. Yes, she is adorable, wofully thin, and, I fear, consumptive, but royal: and adorable, 'douceur et lumiere,' as Bossuet calls her. But to return to my ghost-party."

"If you were wise, you would abandon the notion. I doubt that in spite of your powders your friends will never believe in a ghost."

"Oh yes, they will. It shall be my business to get them in the proper temper."

That idea of figuring in a picturesque habit, and in a halo of churchyard light, was irresistible. Hyacinth promised to conform to Malfort's plans, and to be ready to assume her phantom *role* whenever she was called upon.

Angela knew something of the scheme, and that there was to be another assembly at Millbank; but her sister had seemed disinclined to talk of the plan in her presence--a curious reticence in one whose sentiments and caprices were usually given to the world at large with perfect freedom. For once in her life Hyacinth had a secret air, and checked herself suddenly in the midst of her light babble at a look from De Malfort, who had urged her to keep her sister out of their midnight party.

"I pledge my honour that there shall be nothing to offend," he told her, "but I hope to have the wittiest coxcombs in London, and we want no prudes to strangle every jest with a long-drawn lip and an alarmed eye. Your sister has a pale, fragile prettiness which pleases an eye satiated with the exuberant charms of your Rubens and Titian women; but she is not handsome enough to give herself airs; and she is a little inclined that way. By the faith of a gentleman, I have suffered scowls from her that I would scarce have endured from Barbara!"

"Barbara! You are vastly free with her ladyship's name."

"Not freer than she has ever been with her friendship."

"Henri, if I thought----"

"What, dearest?"

"That you had ever cared for that--wanton----"

"Could you think it, when you know my life in England has been one long tragedy of loving in vain--of sighing only to be denied--of secret tears--and public submission."

"Do not talk so," she exclaimed, starting up from her low tabouret, and moving hastily to the open window, to fresh air and sunshine, rippling river and blue sky, escaping from an atmosphere that had become feverish.

"De Malfort, you know I must not listen to foolish raptures."

"I know you have been refusing to hear for the last two years."

They were on the terrace now, she leaning on the broad marble balustrade, he standing beside her, and all the traffic of London moving with the tide below them.

"To return to our party," she said, in a lighter tone, for that spurt of jealousy had betrayed her into seriousness. "It will be very awkward not to invite my sister to go with me."

"If you did she would refuse, belike, for she is under Fareham's thumb; and he disapproves of everything human."

"Under Fareham's thumb! What nonsense! Indeed I must invite her. She would think it so strange to be omitted."

"Not if you manage things cleverly. The party is to be a surprise. You can tell her next morning you knew nothing about it beforehand."

"But she will hear me order the barge--or will see me start."

"There will be no barge. I shall carry you to Millbank in my coach, after your evening's entertainment, wherever that may be."

"I had better take my own carriage at least, or my chair."

"You can have a chair, if you are too prudish to use my coach, but it shall be got for you at the moment. We won't have your own chairman and links to chatter and betray you before you have played the ghost. Remember you come to my party not as a guest, but as a performer. If they ask why Lady Fareham is absent I shall say you refused to take part in our foolery."

"Oh, you must invent some better excuse. They will never believe anything rational of me. Say I was disappointed of a hat or a mantua. Well, it shall be as you wish. Angela is apt to be tiresome. I hate a disapproving carriage, especially in a younger sister."

Angela was puzzled by Hyacinth's demeanour. A want of frankness in one so frank by nature aroused her fears. She was puzzled and anxious, and longed for Fareham's return, lest his giddy-pated wife should be guilty of some innocent indiscretion that might vex him.

"Oh! if she but valued him at his just worth she would value his opinion second only to the approval of conscience," she thought, sadly, ever regretful of her sister's too obvious indifference towards so kind a husband.

CHAPTER XVI.
WHICH WAS THE FIERCER FIRE?

It was Saturday, the first of September, and the hot dry weather having continued with but trifling changes throughout the month, the atmosphere was at its sultriest, and the burnt grass in the parks looked as if even the dews of morning and evening had ceased to moisten it, while the arid and dusty foliage gave no feeling of coolness, and the very shadows cast upon that parched ground seemed hot. Morning was sultry as noon; evening brought but little refreshment; while the night was hotter than the day. People complained that the season was even more sickly than in the plague year, and prophesied a new and worse outbreak of the pestilence. Was not this the fatal year about which there had been darkest prophecies? 1666! Something awful, something tragical was to make this triplicate of sixes for ever memorable. Sixty-five had been terrible, sixty-six was to bring a greater horror; doubtless a recrudescence of that dire malady which had desolated London.

"And this time," says one modish raven, "'twill be the quality that will suffer. The lower 'classis' has paid its penalty, and only the strong and hardy are left. We. have plenty of weaklings and corrupt constitutions that will take fire at a spark. I should not wonder were the contagion to rage worst at Whitehall. The buildings lie low, and there is ever a nucleus of fever somewhere in that conglomeration of slaughter-houses, bakeries, kitchens, stables, cider-houses, coal-yards, and over-crowded servants' lodgings."

"One gets but casual whiffs from their private butcheries and bakeries," says another. "What I complain of is the atmosphere of his Majesty's apartments, where one can scarce breathe for the stench of those cursed spaniels he so delights in."

Every one agreed that the long dry summer menaced some catastrophic change which should surprise this easy-going age as the plague had done last year. But oh, how lightly that widespread calamity had touched those light minds! and, if Providence had designed to warn or to punish, how vain had been the warning, and how soon forgotten the penalty that had left the worst offenders unstricken!

There was to be a play at Whitehall that evening, his Majesty and the Court having returned from Tunbridge Wells, the business of the navy calling Charles to council with his faithful General--*the* General *par excellence*, George Monk, Duke of Albemarle, and his Lord High Admiral and brother--*par excellence* the Duke. Even in briefest residence, and on sternest business intent, with the welfare and honour of the nation contingent on their consultations, to build or not to build warships of the first magnitude, the ball of pleasure must be kept rolling. So Killigrew was to produce a new version of an old comedy, written in the forties, but now polished up to the modern style of wit. This new-old play, *The Parson's Widow*, was said to be all froth and sparkle and current interest, fresh as the last *London Gazette*, and spiced with allusions to the late sickness, an admirable subject, and allowing a wide field for the ridiculous.

Hyacinth was to be present at this Court function; but not a word was to be said to Angela about the entertainment.

"She would only preach me a sermon upon Fareham's tastes and wishes, and urge me to stay away because he abhors a fashionable comedy," she told De Malfort, "I shall say I am going to Lady Sarah's to play basset. Ange hates cards, and will not desire to go with me. She is always happy with the children, who adore her."

"Faute de mieux."

"You are so ready to jeer! Yes, I know I am a neglectful mother. But what would you have?"

"I would have you as you are," he answered, "and only as you are; or for choice a trifle worse than you are; and so much nearer my own level."

"Oh, I know you! It is the wicked women you admire--like Madame Palmer."

"Always harping upon Barbara. 'My mother had a maid called Barbara.' His Majesty has--a lady of the same melodious name. Well, I have a world of engagements between now and nine o'clock, when the play begins. I shall be at the door to lift you out of your chair. Cover yourself with your richest jewels--or at least those you love best--so that you may blaze like the sun when you cast off the nun's habit. All the town will be there to admire you."

"All the town! Why, there is no one in London!"

"Indeed, you mistake. Travelling is so easy nowadays. People tear to and fro between Tunbridge and St James's as often as they once circulated betwixt London and Chelsea. Were it not for the highwaymen we should be always on the road."

Angela and her niece were on the terrace in the evening coolness. The atmosphere was less oppressive here by the flowing tide than anywhere else in London; but even here there was a heaviness in the night air, and Henriette sprawled her long thin legs wearily on the cushioned bench where she lay, and vowed that it would be sheer folly for Priscilla to insist upon her going to bed at her usual hour of nine, when everybody knew she could not sleep.

"I scarce closed my eyes last night," she protested, "and I had half a mind to put on a petticoat and come down to the terrace. I could have come through the yellow drawing-room, where the men usually forget to close the shutters. And I should have brought my theorbo and serenaded you. Should you have taken me for a fairy, chere, if you had heard me singing?"

"I should have taken you for a very silly little person who wanted to frighten her friends by catching an inflammation of the lungs."

"Well, you see, I thought better of it, though it would have been impossible to catch cold on such a stifling night I heard every clock strike in Westminster and London. It was light at five, yet the night seemed endless. I would have welcomed even a mouse behind the wainscot. Priscilla is an odious tyrant," making a face at the easy-tempered gouvernante sitting by; "she won't let me have my dogs in my room at night."

"Your ladyship knows that dogs in a bed-chamber are unwholesome," said Priscilla.

"No, you foolish old thing; my ladyship knows the contrary; for his Majesty's bed-chamber swarms with them, and he has them on his bed even--whole families--mothers and their puppies. Why can't I have a few dear little mischievous innocents to amuse me in the long dreary nights?"

By dint of clamour and expostulation the honourable Henriette contrived to stay up till ten o'clock was belled with solemn tone from St. Paul's Cathedral, which magnificent church was speedily to be put in hand for restoration, at a great expenditure. The wooden scaffolding which had been necessary for a careful examination of the building was still up. Until the striking of the great city clock, Papillon had resolutely disputed the lateness of the hour, putting forward her own timekeeper as infallible--a little fat round purple enamel watch with diamond figures, and gold hands much bent from being pushed backwards and forwards, to bring recorded time into unison with the young lady's desires--a watch to which no sensible person could give the slightest credit. The clocks of London having demonstrated the futility of any reference to that ill-used Geneva toy, she consented to retire, but was reluctant to the last.

"I am going to bed," she told her aunt, "because this absurd old Prissy insists upon it, but I don't expect a quarter of an hour's sleep between now and morning; and most of the time I shall be looking out of the window, watching for the turn of the tide, to see the barges and boats swinging round."

"You will do nothing of the kind, Mrs. Henriette; for I shall sit in your room till you are sound asleep," said Priscilla.

"Then you will have to sit there all night; and I shall have somebody to talk to."

"I shall not allow you to talk."

"Will you gag me, or put a pillow over my face, like the Blackamoor in the play?"

The minx and her governess retired, still disputing, after Angela had been desperately hugged by Henriette, who brimmed over with warmest affection in the midst of her insolence. They were gone, their voices sounding in the stillness on the terrace, and then on the staircase, and through the great empty rooms, where the windows were open to the sultry night, while the host of idle servants caroused in the basement, in a spacious room with a vaulted roof, like a college hall, where they were free to be as noisy or as drunken as they pleased. My lady was out, had taken only her chair, and running footmen, and had sent chairmen and footmen back from Whitehall, with an intimation that they would be wanted no more that night.

Angela lingered on the terrace in the sultry summer gloom, watching solitary boats moving to and fro, shadowy as Charon's. She dreaded the stillness of silent rooms, and to be alone with her own thoughts, which were not of the happiest. Her sister's relations with De Malfort troubled her, innocent as they doubtless were: innocent as that close friendship of Henrietta of England with her cousin of France, when they two spent the fair midsummer nights roaming in palace gardens, close as lovers, but only fast friends. Malicious tongues had babbled even of that innocent friendship; and there were those who said that if Monsieur behaved liked a brute to his lovely young wife, it was because he had good reason for jealousy of Louis in the past, as well as of De Guiche in the present. These innocent friendships are ever the cause of uneasiness to the lookers-on. It is like seeing children at play on the edge of a cliff. They are too near danger and destruction.

Hyacinth, being about as able to carry a secret as to carry an elephant, had betrayed by a hundred indications that a plot of some kind was being hatched between her and De Malfort. And to-night, before going out, she had made too much fuss about so simple a matter as a basset-party at Lady Sarah's, who had her basset-table every night, and was popularly supposed to keep house upon her winnings, and to have no higher code of honour than De Gramont had when he invited a brother officer to supper on purpose to rook him.

Mr. Killigrew's comedy had been discussed in Angela's hearing. People who had been deprived of the theatre for over a year were greedy and eager spectators of all the plays produced at Court; but this production was an exceptional event. Killigrew's wit and impudence and impecuniosity were the talk of the town, and anything written by that audacious jester was sure to be worth hearing.

Had her sister gone to Whitehall to see the new comedy, in direct disobedience to her husband, instead of to so accustomed an entertainment as Lady Sarah's basset-table? And was that the only mystery between Hyacinth and De Malfort? Or was there something else--some ghost-party, such as they had planned and talked about openly till a fortnight ago, and had suddenly dropped altogether, as if the notion were abandoned and forgotten? It was so unlike Hyacinth to be secret about anything; and her sister feared, therefore, that there was some plot of De Malfort's contriving--De Malfort, whom she regarded with distrust and even repugnance; for she could recall no sentiment of his that did not make for evil. Beneath that gossamer veil of airy language which he flung over vicious theories, the conscienceless, unrelenting character of the man had been discovered by those clear eyes of the meditative onlooker. Alas! what a man to be her sister's closest friend, claiming privileges by long association, which Hyacinth would have been the last to grant her dissolute admirers of yesterday, but which were only the more perilous for those memories of childhood that justified a so dangerous friendship.

She was startled from these painful reflections by the clatter of horses' hoofs on the paved courtyard east of the house, and the jingle of sword-belt and bit, sounds instantly followed by the ringing of the bell at the principal door.

Was it her sister coming home so early? No, Lady Fareham had gone out in her chair. Was it his lordship returning unannounced? He had stated no time for his return, telling his wife only that, on his business in Paris being finished, he would come back without delay. Indeed, Hyacinth had debated the chances of his arrival this very evening with half a dozen of her particular friends, who knew that she was going to see Mr. Killigrew's play.

"Fate cannot be so perverse as to bring him back on the only night when his return would be troublesome," she said.

"Fate is always perverse, and a husband is very lucky if there is but one day out of seven on which his return would be troublesome," answered one of her gossips.

Fate had been perverse, for Angela heard her brother-in-law's deep strong voice talking in the hall, and presently he came down the marble steps to the terrace, and came towards her, white with Kentish dust, and carrying an open letter in his hand. She had risen at the sound of the bell, and was hurrying to the house as he met her. He came close up to her, scarcely according her the civility of greeting. Never had she seen his countenance more gloomy.

"You can tell me truer than those drunken devils below stairs," he said. "Where is your sister?"

"At Lady Sarah Tewkesbury's."

"So her major-domo swears; but her chairmen, whom I found asleep in the hall, say they set her down at the palace."

"At Whitehall?"

"Yes, at Whitehall. There is a modish performance there to-night, I hear; but I doubt it is over, for the Strand was crowded with hackney coaches moving eastward. I passed a pair of handsome eyes in a gilded chair, that flashed fury at me as I rode by, which I'll swear were Mrs. Palmer's; and, waiting for me in the hall, I found this letter, that had just been handed in by a link, who doubtless belonged to the same lady. Read, Angela; the contents are scarce long enough to weary you."

She took the letter from him with a hand that trembled so that she could hardly hold the sheet of paper.

"Watch! There is an intrigue afoot this night; and you must be a greater dullard than I think you if you cannot unmask a deceitful----"

The final word was one which modern manners forbid in speech or printed page. Angela's pallid cheek flushed crimson at the sight of the vile epithet. Oh, insane lightness of conduct which made such an insult possible! Standing there, confronting the angry husband, with that detestable paper in her hand, she felt a pang of compunction at the thought that she might have been more strenuous in her arguments with her sister, more earnest and constant in reproof. When the peace and good repute of two lives were at stake, was it for her to consider any question of older or younger, or to be restrained by the fear of offending a sister who had been so generous and indulgent to her?

Fareham saw her distress, and looked at her with angry suspicion.

"Come," he said, "I scarce expected a lying answer from you; and yet you join with servants to deceive me. You know your sister is not at Lady Sarah's."

"I know nothing, except that, wherever she is, I will vouch that she is innocently employed, and has done nothing to deserve that infamous aspersion," giving him back the letter.

"Innocently employed! You carry matters with a high hand. Innocently employed, in a company of she-profligates, listening to Killigrew's ribald jokes--Killigrew, the profanest of them all, who can turn the greatest calamity this city ever suffered to horseplay and jeering. Innocently employed, in direct disobedience to her husband! So innocently employed that she makes her servants--and her sister--tell lies to cover her innocence!"

"Hector as much as you please, I have told your lordship no lies; and, with your permission, I will leave you to recover your temper before my sister's return, which I doubt will happen within the next hour."

She moved quickly past him towards the house.

"Angela, forgive me----" he began, trying to detain her; but she hurried on through the open French window, and ran upstairs to her room, where she locked herself in.

For some minutes she walked up and down, profoundly agitated, thinking out the position of affairs. To Fareham she had carried matters with a high hand, but she was full of fear. The play was over, and her sister, who doubtless had been among the audience, had not come home. Was she staying at the palace, gossiping with the maids-of-honour, shining among that brilliant, unscrupulous crowd, where intrigue was in the very air, where no woman was credited with virtue, and every man was remorseless?

The anonymous letter scarcely influenced Angela's thoughts in these agitated moments--that was but a foul assault on character by a foul-minded woman. But the furtive confabulations of the past week must have had some motive; and her sister's fluttered manner before leaving the house had marked this night as the crisis of the plot.

Angela could imagine nothing but that ghostly masquerading which had, in the first place, been discussed freely in her presence; and she could but wonder that De Malfort and her sister should have made a mystery about a plan which she had known in its inception. The more deeply she considered all the circumstances, the more she inclined to suspect some evil intention on De Malfort's part, of which Hyacinth, so frank, so shallow, might be too easy a dupe.

"I do little good doubting and suspecting and wondering here," she said to herself; and after hastily lighting the candles on her toilet-table, she began to unlace the bodice of her light-coloured silk mantua, and in a few minutes had changed her elegant evening attire for a dark cloth gown, short in the skirt, and loose in the sleeves, which had been made for her to wear upon the river. In this costume she could handle a pair of sculls as freely as a waterman.

When she had put on a little black silk hood, she extinguished her candles, pulled aside the curtain which obscured the open window, and looked out on the terrace. There was just light enough to show her that the coast was clear. The iron gate at the top of the water-stairs was seldom locked, nor were the boat-houses often shut, as boats were being taken in and out at all hours, and, for the rest, neglect and carelessness might always be reckoned upon in the Fareham household.

She ran lightly down a side staircase, and so by an obscure door to the river-front. No, the gate was not locked, and there was not a creature within sight to observe or impede her movements. She went down the steps to the paved quay below the garden terrace. The house where the wherries were kept was wide open, and, better still, there was a skiff moored by the side of the steps, as if waiting for her; and she had but to take a pair of sculls from the rack and step into the boat, unmoor and away westward, with swiftly dipping oars, in the soft summer silence, broken now and then by sounds of singing--a tipsy, unmelodious strain, perhaps, were it heard too near, but musical in the distance--as the rise and fall of voices crept along a reach of running water.

The night was hot and oppressive, even on the river. But it was better here than anywhere else; and Angela breathed more freely as she bent over her sculls, rowing with all her might, intent upon reaching that landing-stage she knew of in the very shortest possible time. The boat was heavy, but she had the incoming tide to help her.

Was Fareham hunting for his wife, she wondered? Would he go to Lady Sarah's lodgings, in the first place; and, not finding Hyacinth there, to Whitehall? And then, would he remember the assembly at Millbank, in which he had taken no part, and apparently no interest? And would he extend his search to the ruined abbey?

At the worst, Angela would be there before him, to prepare her sister for the angry suspicions which she would have to meet. He was not likely to think of that place till he had exhausted all other chances.

It was not much more than a mile from Fareham House to that desolate bit of country betwixt Westminster and Chelsea, where the modern dairy-farm occupied the old monkish pastures. As Angela ran her boat inshore, she expected to see Venetian lanterns, and to hear music and voices, and all the indications of a gay assembly; but there were only silence and darkness, save for one lighted window in the dairyman's dwelling-house, and she thought that she had come upon a futile errand, and had been mistaken in her conjectures.

She moored her boat to the wooden landing-stage, and went on shore to examine the premises. The revelry might be designed for a later hour, though it was now near midnight, and Lady Sarah's party had assembled at eleven. She walked across a meadow, where the dewy grass was cool under her feet, and so to the open space in front of the dairyman's house--a shabby building attached like a wen to the ruined refectory.

She started at hearing the snort of a horse, and the jingling of bit and curbchain, and came suddenly upon a coach-and-four, with a couple of post-boys standing beside their team.

"Whose coach is this?" she asked.

"Mr. Malfy's, your ladyship."

"The French gentleman from St. James's Street, my lady," explained the other man.

"Did you bring Monsieur de Malfort here?"

"No, madam. We was told to be here at eleven, with horses as fresh as fire; and the poor tits be mighty impatient to be moving. Steady, Champion! You'll have work enough this side Dartford,"--to the near leader, who was shaking his head vehemently, and pawing the gravel.

Angela waited to ask no further questions, but made straight for the unglazed window, through which Mr. Spavinger and his companions had entered.

There was no light in the great vaulted room, save the faint light of summer stars, and two figures were there in the dimness--a woman standing straight and tall in a satin gown, whose pale sheen reflected the starlight; a woman whose right arm was flung above her head, bare and white, her hand clasping her brow distractedly; and a man, who knelt at her feet, grasping the hand that hung at her side, looking up at her, and talking eagerly, with passionate gestures.

Her voice was clearer than his; and Angela heard her repeating with a piteous shrillness, "No, no, no! No, Henri, no!"

She stayed to hear no more, but sprang through the opening between the broken mullions, and rushed to her sister's side; and as De Malfort started to his feet, she thrust him vehemently aside, and clasped Hyacinth in her arms.

"You here, Mistress Kill-joy?" he muttered, in a surly tone. "May I ask what business brought you? For I'll swear you wasn't invited."

"I have come to save my sister from a villain, sir. But oh, my sweet, I little dreamt thou hadst such need of me!"

"Nay, love, thou didst ever make tragedies out of nothing," said Hyacinth, struggling to disguise hysterical tears with airy laughter. "But I am right glad all the same that you are come; for this gentleman has put a scurvy trick upon me, and brought me here on pretence of a gay assembly that has no existence."

"He is a villain and a traitor," said Angela, in deep, indignant tones. "Dear love, thou hast been in danger I dare scarce think of. Fareham is searching for you."

"Fareham! In London?"

"Returned an hour ago. Hark!"

She lifted her finger warningly as a bell rang, and the well-known voice sounded outside the house, calling to some one to open the door.

"He is here!" cried Hyacinth, distractedly. "For God's sake, hide me from him! Not for worlds--not for worlds would I meet him!"

"Nay, you have nothing to fear. It is Monsieur de Malfort who has to answer for what he has done."

"Henri, he will kill you! Alas, you know not what he is in anger! I have seen him, once in Paris, when he thought a man was insolent to me. God! The thunder of his voice, the blackness of his brow! He will kill you! Oh, if you love me--if you ever loved me--come out of his way! He is fatal with his sword!"

"And am I such a tyro at fence, or such a poltroon as to be afraid to meet him? No, Hyacinth, I go with you to Dover, or I stand my ground and face him."

"You shall not!" sobbed Hyacinth. "I will not have your blood on my head!

Come, come--by the garden--by the river!"

She dragged him towards the window; he pretending to resist, as Angela thought, yet letting himself be led as she pleased to lead him. They had but just crossed the yawning gap between the mullions and vanished into the night, when Fareham burst into the room with his sword drawn, and came towards Angela, who stood in shadow, her face half hidden in her close-fitting hood.

"So, madam, I have found you at last," he said; "and in time to stop your journey, though not to save myself the dishonour of a wanton wife! But it is your paramour I am looking for, not you. Where is that craven hiding?"

He went back to the inhabited part of the house, and returned after a hasty examination of the premises, carrying the lamp which had lighted his search, only to find the same solitary figure in the vast bare room. Angela had moved nearer the window, and had sunk exhausted upon a large carved oak chair, which might be a relic of the monkish occupation. Fareham came to her with the lamp in his hand.

"He has given me a clean pair of heels," he said; "but I know where to find him. It is but a pleasure postponed. And now, woman, you had best return to the house your folly, or your sin, has disgraced. For to-night, at least, it must needs shelter you. Come!"

The hooded figure rose at his bidding, and he saw the face in the lamplight.

"You!" he gasped. "You!"

"Yes, Fareham, it is I. Cannot you take a kind view of a foolish business, and believe there has been only folly and no dishonour in the purpose that brought me here?"

"You!" he repeated. "You!"

His bearing was that of a man who staggers under a crushing blow, a stroke so unexpected that he can but wonder and suffer. He set down the lamp with a shaking hand, then took two or three hurried turns up and down the room; then stopped abruptly by the lamp, snatched the anonymous letter from his breast, and read the lines over again.

"'An intrigue on foot----' No name. And I took it for granted my wife was meant. I looked for folly from her; but wisdom, honour, purity, all the virtues from you. Oh, what was the use of my fortitude, what the motive of self-conquest here," striking himself upon the breast, "if you were unchaste? Angela, you have broken my heart."

There was a long pause before she answered, and her face was turned from him to hide her streaming tears. At last she was able to reply calmly--

"Indeed, Fareham, you do wrong to take this matter so passionately. You may trust my sister and me. On my honour, you have no cause to be angry with either of us."

"And when I gave you this letter to read," he went on, disregarding her protestations, "you knew that you were coming here to meet a lover. You hurried away from me, dissembler as you were, to steal to this lonely place at midnight, to fling yourself into his arms. Tell me where he is hiding, that I may kill him; now, while I pant for vengeance. Such rage as mine cannot wait for idle forms. Now, now, now, is the time to reckon with your seducer!"

"Fareham, you cover me with insults!"

He had rushed to the door, still carrying his naked sword; but he turned back as she spoke, and stood looking at her from head to foot with a savage scornfulness.

"Insult!" he cried. "You have sunk too low for insult. There are no words that I know vile enough to stigmatise such disgrace as yours! Do you know what you have been to me, Angela? A saint--a star; ineffably pure, ineffably remote; a creature to worship at a distance; for whose sake it was scarce a sacrifice to repress all that is common to the base heart of man; from whom a kind word was enough for happiness--so pure, so far away, so detached from this vile age we live in. God, how that saintly face has cheated me! Mock saint, mock nun; a creature of passions like my own but more stealthy; from top to toe an incarnate lie!"

He flung out of the room, and she heard his footsteps about the house, and heard doors opened and shut. She waited for no more; but, being sure by this time that her sister had left the premises, her own desire was to return to Farebam House as soon as possible, counting upon finding Hyacinth there; yet with a sick fear that the seducer might take base advantage of her sister's terror and confused spirits, and hustle her off upon the fatal journey he had planned.

The boat lay where she had moored it, at the foot of the wooden stair, and she was stepping into it when Fareham ran hastily to the bank.

"Your paramour has got clear off," he said; and then asked curtly, "How came you by that boat?"

"I brought it from Fareham House."

"What! you came here alone by water at so late an hour! You heaven-born adventuress! Other women need education in vice; but to you it comes by nature."

He pulled off his doublet as he stepped into the boat; then seated himself and took the sculls.

"Has your lordship not left a horse waiting for you?" Angela inquired hesitatingly.

"My lordship's horse will find his stables before morning with the groom that has him in charge. I am going to row you home. Love expectant is bold; but disappointed love may lack courage for a solitary jaunt after midnight. Come, mistress, let us have no ceremony. We have done with that for ever--as we have done with friendship. There are thousands of women in England, all much of a pattern; and you are one of them. That is the end of our romance."

He bent to his work, and rowed with a steady stroke, and in a stubborn silence, which lasted till it was more strangely broken than such angry silence is apt to be.

The tide was still running up, and it was as much as the single oarsman could do, in that heavy boat, to hold his own against the stream.

Angela sat watching him, with her gaze rooted to that dark countenance and bare head, on which the iron-grey hair waved thick and strong, for Fareham had never consented to envelop his neck and shoulders in a mantle of dead men's tresses, and wore his own hair after the fashion of Charles the First's time. So intent was her watch, that the objects on either shore passed her like shadows in a dream. The Primate's palace on her right hand, as the boat swept round that great bend which the river makes opposite Lambeth Marsh; on her left, as they neared London, the stern grandeur of the Abbey and St. Margaret's. It was only as they approached Whitehall that she became aware of a light upon the water which was not the reflection of daybreak, and, looking suddenly up, she saw the fierce glare of a conflagration in the eastern sky, and cried--

"There is a fire, my lord!--a great fire, I doubt, in the city."

The long roof and massive tower of St Paul's stood dark against the vivid splendour of that sky, and every timber in the scaffolding showed like a black lattice across the crimson and sulphur of raging flames.

Fareham looked round, without moving his sculls from the rowlocks.

"A great fire in verity, mistress! Would God it meant the fulfilment of prophecy!"

"What prophecy, sir?"

"The end of the world, with which we are threatened in this year. God, how the flames rage and mount! Would it were the great fire, and He had come to judge us, and to empty the vials of His wrath upon profligates and seducers!"

He looked at the face opposite, radiant with reflected rose and gold, supernal in that strange light, and, oh, so calm in every line and feature, the large dark eyes meeting his with a gaze that seemed to him half indignant, half reproachful.

"Oh, what hypocrites these women are!" he told himself. "And all alike--all alike. What comedians! For acting one need not go to the Duke's or the King's. One may see it at one's own board, by one's own hearth. Acting, nothing but acting! And I thought that in the universal mass of falsehood and folly there were some rare stars, dwelling apart here and there, and that she was one of them. An idle dream! Nature has made them all in one mould, and it is but by means and opportunity that they differ."

Higher and higher rose that vast sheet of vivid colour; and now every tower and steeple was bathed in rosy light, or else stood black against the radiant sky-- towers illuminated, towers in densest shadow; the slim spars of ships showing as if drawn with pen and ink on a sulphur background--a scene of surpassing splendour and terror. Fareham had seen Flemish villages blazing, Flemish citadels exploding, their fragments hurled skyward in a blue flame of gunpowder; but never this vast arch of crimson, glowing and growing before his astonished gaze, as he paddled the boat inshore, and stood up to watch the great disaster.

"God has remembered the new Sodom," he said savagely. "He punished us with pestilence, and we took no heed. And now He tries us with fire. But if it come not yonder," pointing to Whitehall, which was immediately above them, for their boat lay close to the King's landing-stage--"if, like the contagion, it stays in the east and only the citizens suffer, why, vive la bagatelle! We--and our concubines--have no part in the punishment. We, who call down the fire, do not suffer it"

Spellbound by that strange spectacle, Fareham stood and gazed, and Angela was afraid to urge him to take the boat on to Fareham House, anxious as she was to span those few hundred yards of distance, to be assured of her sister's safety.

They waited thus nearly an hour, the sky ever increasing in brilliancy, and the sounds of voices and tramp of hurrying feet growing with every minute. Whitehall was now all alive--men and women, in a careless undress, at every window, some of them hanging half out of the window to talk to people in the court below. Shrieks of terror or of wonder, ejaculations, and oaths sounding on every side; while Fareham, who had moored the boat to an iron ring in the wall by his Majesty's stairs, stood gloomy and motionless, and made no further comment, only watched the conflagration in dismal silence, fascinated by that prodigious ruin.

It was but the beginning of that stupendous destruction, yet it was already great enough to seem like the end of all things.

"And last night, in the Court theatre, Killigrew's players were making a jest of a pestilence that filled the grave-pits by thousands," Fareham muttered, as if awaking from a dream. "Well, the wits will have a new subject for their mirth--London in flames."

He untied the rope, took his seat and rowed out into the stream. Within that hour in which they had waited, the Thames had covered itself with traffic; boats were moving westward, loaded with frightened souls in casual attire, and with heaps of humble goods and chattels. Some whose houses were nearest the river had been quick enough to save a portion of their poor possessions, and to get them packed on barges; but these were the wise minority. The greater number of the sufferers were stupefied by the suddenness of the calamity, the rapidity with which destruction rushed upon them, the flames leaping from house to house, spanning chasms of emptiness, darting hither and thither like lizards or winged scorpions, or breaking out mysteriously in fresh places, so that already the cry of arson had arisen, and the ever-growing fire was set down to fiendish creatures labouring secretly at a work of universal destruction.

Most of the sufferers looked on at the ruin of their homes, paralysed by horror, unable to help themselves or to mitigate their losses by energetic action of any kind. Dumb and helpless as sheep, they saw their property destroyed, their children's lives imperilled, and could only thank Providence, and those few brave men who helped them in their helplessness, for escape from a fiery death. Panic and ruin prevailed within a mile eastward of Fareham House, when the boat ground against the edge of the marble landing-stage, and Angela alighted and ran quickly up the stairs, and made her way straight to the house. The door stood wide open, and candles were burning in the vestibule. The servants were at the eastern end of the terrace watching the fire, too much engrossed to see their master and his companion land at the western steps.

At the foot of the great staircase Angela heard herself called by a crystalline voice, and, looking up, saw Henriette hanging over the banister rail.

"Auntie, where have you been?"

"Is your mother with you?" Angela asked.

"Mother is locked in her bed-chamber, and mighty sullen. She told me to go to bed. As if anybody could lie quietly in bed with London burning!" added Papillon, her tone implying that a great city in flames was a kind of entertainment that could not be too highly appreciated.

She came flying downstairs in her pretty silken deshabille, with her hair streaming, and flung her arm round her aunt's neck.

"Ma chatte, where have you been?"

"On the terrace."

"Fi donc, menteuse! I saw you and my father land at the west stairs, five minutes ago."

"We had been looking at the fire."

"And never offered to take me with you! What a greedy pig!"

"Indeed, dearest, it is no scene for little girls to look upon."

"And when I am grown up what shall I have to talk about if I miss all the great sights?"

"Come to your room, love. You will see only too much from your windows. I am going to your mother."

"Ce n'est pas la peine. She is in one of her tempers, and has locked herself in."

"No matter. She will see me."

"Je m'en doute. She came home in a coach-and-four nearly two hours ago, with Monsieur de Malfort; and I think they must have quarrelled. They bade each other good night so uncivilly; but he was more huffed than mother."

"Where were you that you know so much?"

"In the gallery. Did I not tell you I shouldn't be able to sleep? I went into the gallery for coolness, and then I heard the coach in the courtyard, and the doors opened, and I listened."

"Inquisitive child!"

"No, I was not inquisitive. I was only vastly hipped for want of knowing what to do with myself. And I ran to bid her ladyship good morning, for it was close upon one o'clock; but she frowned at me, and pushed me aside with a 'Go to your bed, troublesome imp! What business have you up at this hour?' 'As much business as you have riding about in your coach,' I had a mind to say, mais je me tenais coy; and made her ladyship la belle Jennings' curtsy instead. She sinks lower and rises straighter than any of the other ladies. I watched her on mother's visiting-day. Lord, auntie, how white you are! One might take you for a ghost!"

Angela put the little prattler aside, more gently, perhaps, than the mother had done, and passed hurriedly on to Lady Fareham's room. The door was still locked, but she would take no denial.

"I must speak with you," she said.

CHAPTER XVII.
THE MOTIVE--MURDER.

For Lady Fareham and her sister September and October made a blank interval in the story of life--uneventful as the empty page at the end of a chapter. They spent those months at Fareham, a house which Hyacinth detested, a neighbourhood where she had never condescended to make friends. She condemned the local gentry as a collection of nobodies, and had never taken the trouble to please the three or four great families within a twenty-mile drive, because, though they had rank and consequence, they had not fashion. The ***haut gout*** of Paris and London was wanting to them.

Lord Fareham had insisted upon leaving London on the third of September, and had, his wife declared, out of pure malignity, taken his family to Fareham, a place she hated, rather than to Chilton, a place she loved, at least as much as any civilised mortal could love the country. Never, Hyacinth protested, had her husband been so sullen and ferocious.

"He is not like an angry man," she told Angela, "but like a wounded lion; and yet, since your goodness took all the blame of my unlucky escapade upon your shoulders, and he knows nothing of De Malfort's insolent attempt to carry me off, I see no reason why he should have become such a gloomy savage."

She accepted her sister's sacrifice with an amiable lightness. How could it harm Angela to be thought to have run out at midnight for a frolic rendezvous? The maids of honour had some such adventure half a dozen times in a season, and were found out, and laughed at, and laughed again, and wound up their tempestuous careers by marrying great noblemen.

"If you can but get yourself talked about you may marry as high as you choose," Lady Fareham told her sister.

*   *   *   *   *

Early in November they went back to London, and though all Hyacinth's fine people protested that the town stank of burnt wood, smoked oil, and resin, and was altogether odious, they rejoiced not the less to be back again. Lady Fareham plunged with renewed eagerness into the whirlpool of pleasure, and tried to drag Angela with her; but it was a surprise to both, and to one a cause for uneasiness, when his lordship began to show himself in scenes which he had for the most part avoided as well as reviled. For some unexplained reason he became now a frequent attendant at the evening festivities at Whitehall, and without even the pretence of being interested or amused there.

Fareham's appearance at Court caused more surprise than pleasure in that brilliant circle. The statue of the Comandante would scarcely have seemed a grimmer guest. He was there in the midst of laughter and delight, with never a smile upon his stern features. He was silent for the most part, or if badgered into talking by some of his more familiar acquaintances, would vent his spleen in a tirade that startled them, as the pleasant chirpings of a poultry-yard are startled by the raid of a dog. They laughed at his conversation behind his back; but in his presence, under the angry light of those grey eyes, the gloom of those bent brows, they were chilled into submission and civility. He had a dignity which made his Puritanical plainness more patrician than Rochester's finery, more impressive than Buckingham's graceful splendour. The force and vigour of his countenance were more striking than Sedley's beauty. The eyes of strangers singled him out in that gay throng, and people wanted to know who he was and what he had done for fame.

A soldier, yes, cela saute aux yeux. He could be nothing else than a soldier. A cavalier of the old school. Albeit younger by half a lifetime than Southampton and Clarendon, and the other ghosts of the troubles.

Charles treated him with chill civility.

"Why does the man come here without his wife?" he asked De Malfort. "There is a sister, too, fresher and fairer than her ladyship. Why are we to have the shadow without the sun? Yet it is as well, perhaps, they keep away; for I have heard of a visit which was not returned--a condescension from a woman of the highest rank slighted by a trumpery baron's wife--and after an offence of that kind she could only have brought us trouble. Why do women quarrel, Wilmot?"

"Why are there any men in the world, sir? If there were none, women would live together like lambs in a meadow. It is only about us they fight. As for Lady Fareham, she is adorable, though no longer young. I believe she will be thirty on her next birthday."

"And the sister? She had a wild-rose prettiness, I thought, when I saw her at Oxford. She looked like a lily till I spoke to her, and then flamed like a red rose. So fresh, so easily startled. 'Tis pity that shyness of youthful purity wears off in a week. I dare swear by this time Mrs. Kirkland is as brazen as the boldest of our young houris yonder," with a glance in the direction of the maids of honour, the Queen's and the Duchess's, a bevy of chatterers, waving fans, giggling, whispering, shoulder to shoulder with the impudentest men in his Majesty's kingdom; the men who gave their mornings to writing comedies coarser than Dryden or Etherege, and their nights to cards, dice, and strong drink; roving the streets half clad, dishevelled, wanton; beating the watch, and insulting decent pedestrians; with occasional vicious outbreaks which would have been revolting in a company of inebriated coalheavers, and which brought these fine gentlemen before a too lenient magistrate. But were not these the manners of which St. Evremond lightly sang--

"'La douce erreur ne s'appelait point crime;   Les vices delicats se nommaient des plaisirs.'"

"Mistress Kirkland has an inexorable modesty which would outlive even a week at Whitehall, sir," answered Rochester. "If I did not adore the matron I should worship the maid. Happily for the wretch who loves her I am otherwise engaged!"

"Thou insolent brat! To be eighteen years of age and think thyself irresistible!"

"Does your Majesty suppose I shall be more attractive at six and thirty?"

"Yes, villain; for at my age thou wilt have experience."

"And a reputation for incorrigible vice. No woman of taste can resist that."

"And pray who is Mrs. Kirkland's lover?"

"A Puritan baronet. One Denzil Warner."

"There was a Warner killed at Hoptown Heath."

"His son, sir. A fellow who believes in extempore prayer and republican government; and swears England was never so happy or prosperous as under Cromwell."

"And the lady favours this psalm-singing rebel?"

"I know not. For all I have seen of the two she has been barely civil to him. That he adores her is obvious; and I know Lady Fareham's heart is set upon the match."

"Why did not Lady Fareham return the Countess's visit?"

There was no need to ask what Countess.

"Be sure, sir, the husband was to blame, if there was want of respect for that lovely lady. I can answer for Lady Fareham's right feeling in that matter."

"The husband takes a leaf out of Hyde's book, and forgets that what may be passed over in the Lord Chancellor, and a man of prodigious usefulness, is intolerable in a person of Fareham's insignificance."

"Nay, sir, insignificance is scarcely the word. I would as soon call a thunderstorm insignificant. The man is a volcano, and may explode at any provocation."

"We want no such suppressed fires at Whitehall. Nor do we want long faces; as Clarendon may discover some day, if his sermons grow too troublesome."

"The Chancellor is a domestic man; as your Majesty may infer from the size and splendour of his new house."

"He is an expensive man, Wilmot I believe he got more by the sale of Dunkirk than his master did."

"In that case your Majesty cannot do better than shift all the disgrace of the transaction on to his shoulders. Dunkirk will be a sure card to play when Clarendon has to go overboard."

That incivility of Lady Fareham's in the matter of an unreturned visit had rankled deep in the bosom of the King's imperious mistress. To sin more boldly than woman ever sinned, and yet to claim all the privileges and honours due to virtue was but a trifling inconsistency in a mind so fortified by pride that it scarce knew how to reckon with shame. That she, in her supremacy of beauty and splendour, a fortune sparkling in either ear, the price of a landed estate on her neck--that she, Barbara, Countess of Castlemaine, should have driven in a windowless coach through dusty lanes, eating dirt, as it were, with her train of court gallants on horseback at her coach doors, her ladies in a carriage in the rear, to visit a person of Lady Fareham's petty quality, a Buckinghamshire Knight's daughter married to a Baron of Henry the Eighth's creation! And that this amazing condescension--received with a smiling and curtsying civility--should have been unacknowledged by any reciprocal courtesy was an affront that could hardly be wiped out with blood. Indeed, it could never be atoned for. The wound was poisoned, and would rankle and fester to the end of that proud life.

Yet on Fareham's appearance at Whitehall Lady Castlemaine distinguished with a marked civility, and even condescended, smilingly, as if there were no cause of quarrel, to inquire after his wife.

"Her ladyship is as pretty as ever, though we are all growing old," she said. "We exchanged curtsies at Tunbridge Wells the other day. I wonder how it is we never get further than smiles and curtsies? I should like to show the dear woman some more substantial civility. She is buried alive in your stately house by the river, for the want of an influential friend to show her the world we live in."

"Indeed, madam, my wife has all the pleasure she desires--her visiting-day, her friends."

"And her admirers. Rochester is always hanging about your garden, or landing from his wherry, when I go by; or, if he himself be not visible, there are a couple of his watermen on your steps."

"My Lord Rochester has a precocious wit which amuses my wife and her sister."

"And then there is De Malfort--an impertinent, second only to Gramont. He and Lady Fareham are twin stars. I have seldom seen them apart."

"Since De Malfort has the honour of being somewhat intimate with your lady-ship, he has doubtless given you full particulars of his friendship for my wife. I assure you it will bear being talked about. There are no secrets in it."

"Really; I thought I had heard something about a sedan which took the wrong road after Killigrew's play. But that was the night before the fire. Good God! my lord, your face darkens as if a man had struck you. Whatever happened before the fire should have been burnt out of our memories by this time."

"I see his Majesty looking this way, madam, and I have not yet paid my respects to him," Fareham said, moving away, but a dazzling hand on his sleeve arrested him.

"Oh, your respects will keep; he has Miss Stewart giggling at his elbow. Strange, is it not, that a woman with as much brain as a pigeon can amuse a man who reckons himself both wise and witty?"

"It is not the lady who amuses the gentleman, madam. She has the good sense to pretend that he amuses her."

"And no more understands a jest than she does Hebrew."

"She is conscious of pretty teeth and an enchanting smile. Wit or understanding would be superfluous," answered Fareham, bowing his adieu to the Sultana in chief.

There was a great assembly, with music and dancing, on the Queen's birthday, to which Lord and Lady Fareham and Mistress Kirkland were invited; and again Angela saw and wondered at the splendid scene, and at this brilliant world, which calamity could not touch. Pestilence had ravaged the city, flames had devoured it-- yet here there were only smiling people, gorgeous dress, incomparable jewels. The plague had not touched them, and the fire had not reached them. Such afflictions are for the common herd. Angela promenaded with De Malfort in the spacious banqueting-hall, with its ceiling of such prodigious height that the apotheosis of King James, and all the emblematical figures, triumphal cars, lions, bears and rams, corn-sheaves and baskets of fruit, which filled the panels, might as well have been executed by a sign-painter's rough-and-ready brush, as by the pencil of the great Fleming.

"We are a little kinder to Rubens at the Louvre," said De Malfort, noting her upward gaze; "for we allow his elaborate glorification of his Majesty's grandfather and grandmother about half a mile of wall. But I forgot, you have not seen Paris, nor those acres of gaudy colouring which Henri's vanity inflicted upon us. Florentine Marie, with her carnation cheeks and opulent shoulders--the Roman-nosed Bear-nais, with his pointed beard and stiff ruff. Mon Dieu, how the world has changed since Ravaillac's knife snapped that valiant life! And you have never seen Paris? You look about you with wide-open eyes, and take this crowd, this ceiling, those candlebra for splendour."

"Can there be a scene more splendid?" asked Angela, pleased to keep him by her side, rather than see him devote himself to her sister; grateful for his attention in that crowd where most people were strangers, and where Lord Fareham had not vouchsafed the slightest notice of her.

"When you have seen the Louvre, you will wonder that any King, with a sense of his own consequence in the world, can inhabit such a hovel as Whitehall--this congeries of shabby apartments, the offices of servants, the lodgings of followers and dependents, soldiers and civilians--huddled in a confused labyrinth of brick and stone--redeemed from squalor only by one fine room. Could you see the grand proportions, the colossal majesty of the great Henri's palace--that palace whose costly completion sat heavy upon Sully's careful soul! Henri loved to build--and his grandson, Louis, inherits that Augustan taste."

"You were telling us of a new palace at Versailles----"

"A royal city in stone--white--dazzling--grandiose. The mortar was scarcely dry when I was there in March; but you should have seen the mi-careme ball. The finest masquerade that was ever beheld in Europe. All Paris came in masks to see that magnificent spectacle. His Majesty allowed entrance to all--and those who came were feasted at a banquet which only Rabelais could fairly describe. And then with our splendour there is an elegant restraint--a decency unknown here. Compare these women--Lady Shrewsbury yonder, Lady Chesterfield, the fat woman in sea-green and silver--Lady Castlemaine, brazen in orange velvet and emeralds--compare them with Conde's sister, with the Duchesse de Bouillon, the Princess Palatine----"

"Are those such good women?"

"Humph! They are ladies. These are the kind of women King Charles admires.

They are as distinct a race as the dogs that lie in his bed-chamber, and follow him in his walks, a species of his own creation. They do not even affect modesty. But I am turning preacher, like Fareham. Come, there is to be an entertainment in the theatre. Roxalana has returned to the stage--and Jacob Hall, the rope-dancer, is to perform."

They followed the crowd, and De Malfort remained at Angela's side till the end of the performance, and attended her to the supper-table afterwards. Fareham watched them from his place in the background. He stood ever aloof from the royal focus, the beauty, and the wit, the most dazzling jewels, the most splendid raiment. He was amidst the Court, but not of it.

Yes; the passion which these two entertained for each other was patent to every eye; but had it been an honourable attachment upon De Malfort's side, he would have declared himself before now. He would not have abandoned the field to such a sober suitor as Denzil. Henri de Malfort loved her, and she fed his passion with her sweetest smiles, the low and tender tones of the most musical voice Fareham had ever listened to.

"The voice that came to me in my desolation--the sweetest sound that ever fell on a dying man's ear," he thought, recalling those solitary days and nights in the plague year, recalling those vanished hours with a fond longing, "that arm which shows dazzling white against the purple velvet of his sleeve is the arm that held up my aching head, in the dawn of returning reason; those are the eyes that looked down upon mine, so pitiful, so anxious for my recovery. Oh, lovely angel, I would be a leper again, a plague-stricken wretch, only to drink a cup of water from that dear hand--only to feel the touch of those light fingers on my forehead! There was a magic in that touch that surpassed the healing powers of kings. There was a light as of heaven in those benignant eyes. But, oh, she is changed since then. She is plague-stricken with the contagion of a profligate age. Her wings are scorched by the fire of this modish Tophet She has been taught to dress and look like the women around her--a little more modest--but after the same fashion. The nun I worshipped is no more."

Some one tapped him on the shoulder with an ostrich fan. He turned, and saw Lady Castlemaine close at his elbow.

"Image of gloom, will you lead me to my rooms?" she asked, in a curious voice, her dark blue eyes deepened by the pallor that showed through her rouge.

"I shall esteem myself too much honoured by that office," he answered, as she took his arm and moved quickly, with hurried footsteps, through the lessening throng.

"Oh, there is no one to dispute the honour with you. Sometimes I have a mob to hustle me to my lodgings, borne on the current of their adulation--sometimes I move through a desert, as I do to-night. Your face attracted me--for I believe it is the only one at Whitehall as gloomy as my own--unless there are some of my creditors, men to whom I owe gaming debts."

It was curious to note that subtle change in the faces of those they passed, which Barbara Palmer knew so well--faces that changed, obedient to the weathercock of royal caprice--the countenances of courtiers who even yet had not learnt justly to weigh the influence of that imperial favourite, or to understand that she ruled their King with a power which no transient fancy for newer faces could undermine. A day or two in the sulks, frowns and mournful looks for gossip Pepys to jot down in his diary, and the next day the sun would be shining again, and the King would be at supper with "the lady."

Perhaps Lady Castlemaine knew that her empire was secure; but she took these transient fancies *moult serieusement*. Her jealous soul could tolerate no rival--or it may be that she really loved the King. He had given himself to her in the flush of his triumphant return, while he was still young enough to feel a genuine passion. For her sake he had been a cruel husband, an insolent tyrant to an inoffensive wife; for her sake he had squandered his people's money, and outraged every moral law; and it may be that she remembered these things, and hated him the more fiercely for them when he was inconstant. She was a woman of extremes, in whose tropical temperament there was no medium between hatred and love.

"You will sup with me, Fareham?" she said, as he waited on the threshold of her lodgings, which were in a detached pile of buildings, near the Holbein Gateway, and looking upon an enclosed and somewhat gloomy garden.

"Your ladyship will excuse me. I am expected at home."

"What devil! Perhaps you think I am inviting you to a *tete-a-tete*. I shall have some company, though the drove have gone to the Stewarts' in a hope of getting asked to supper--which but a few of them can realise in her mean lodgings. You had better stay. I may have Buckhurst, Sedley, De Malfort, and a few more of the pretty fellows--enough to empty your pockets at basset."

"Your ladyship is all goodness," said Fareham, quickly.

De Malfort's name had decided him. He followed his hostess through a crowd of lackeys, a splendour of wax candles, to her saloon, where she turned and flashed upon him a glorious picture of mature loveliness, her complexion the peach in its ripest bloom, the orange sheen of her velvet mantua shining out against a background of purple damask curtains embroidered with gold.

The logs blazed and roared in the wide chimney. Warmth, opulence, hospitality, were all expressed in the brilliantly lighted room, where luxurious fauteuils, after the new French fashion, stood about, ready to receive her ladyship's guests.

These were not long waited for. There was no crowd. Less than twenty men, and about a dozen women, were enough to add an air of living gaiety to the brilliancy of light and colour. De Malfort was the last who entered. He kissed her ladyship's hand, looked about him, and recognised Fareham with open wonder.

"An Israelite in the house of Dagon!" he said, ***sotto voce***, as he approached him. "What, Fareham, have you given your neck to the yoke? Do you yield to the charm which has subjugated such lighter natures as Villiers and Buckhurst?"

"It is only human to love variety. You have discovered the charm of youth and innocence."

"Do you think it needs a modish Columbus to discover that? We all worship innocence, were it but for its rarity, as we esteem a black pearl or a yellow diamond above a white one. Jarni, but I am pleased to see you here! It is the most human thing I have known of you since you recovered of the contagion; for you have been a gloomier man from that time."

"Be assured I am altogether human--at least upon the worser side of humanity."

"How dismal you look! Upon my soul, Fareham, you should fight against that melancholic habit. Her ladyship is in the black sulks. We are in for a pleasant evening. Yet, if we were to go away, she would storm at us to-morrow; call us sycophants and time-servers, swear she would hold no further commerce with any manjack among our detestable crew. Well, she is a magnificent termagant. If Cleopatra was half as handsome, I can forgive Antony for following her to ruin at Actium."

"There is supper in the music-room, gentlemen," said Lady Castlemaine, who was standing near the fire in the midst of a knot of whispering women.

They had been abusing the fair Frances, and ridiculing old Rowley, to gratify their hostess. She knew them by heart--their falsehood and hollowness. She knew that they were ready, every one of them, to steal her royal lover, had they but the chance of such a conquest; yet it solaced her soreness to hear Miss Stewart depreciated even by those false lips--"She was too tall." "Her Britannia profile looked as if it was cut out of wood." "She was bold, bad, designing." "It was she who would have the King, not the King who would have her."

"You are too malicious, my dearest Price," said Lady Castlemaine, with more good humour than had been seen in her countenance that evening. "Buckhurst, will you take Mrs. Price to supper? There are cards in the gallery. Pray amuse yourselves."

"But will your ladyship neither sup nor play?" asked Sedley.

"My ladyship has a raging headache. What devil! Did I not lose enough to some of you blackguards last night? Do you want to rook me again? Pray amuse yourselves, friends. No doubt his Majesty is being exquisitely entertained where he is; but I doubt if he will get as good a supper as you will find in the next room."

The significant laugh which concluded her speech was too angry for mirth, and the blackness of her brow forbade questioning. All the town knew next day that she had contrived to get the royal supper intercepted and carried off, on its way from the King's kitchen to Miss Stewart's lodgings, and that his Majesty had a Barmecide feast at the table of beauty. It was a joke quite in the humour of the age.

The company melted out of the room; all but Fareham, who watched Lady Castlemaine as she stood by the hearth in an attitude of hopeless self-forgetfulness, leaning against the lofty sculptured chimney-piece, one slender foot in gold-embroidered slipper and transparent stocking poised on the brazen fender, and her proud eyelids lowered as if there was nothing in this world worth looking at but the pile of ship's timber, burning with many-coloured flames upon the silver andirons.

In spite of that sullen downward gaze she was conscious of Fareham's lingering.

"Why do you stay, my lord?" she asked, without looking up. "If your purse is heavy there are friends of mine yonder who will lighten it for you, fairly or foully.

I have never made up my mind how far a gentleman may be a rogue with impunity. If you don't love losing money you had best eat a good supper and begone."

"I thank you, madam. I am more in the mood for cards than for feasting."

She did not answer him, but clasped her hands suddenly before her face and gave a heart-breaking sigh. Fareham paused on the threshold of the gallery, watching her, and then went slowly back, bent down to take the hand that had dropped at her side, and pressed his lips upon it, silently, respectfully, with a kind of homage that had become strange of late years to Barbara Palmer. Adorers she had and to spare, toadeaters and flatterers, a regiment of mercenaries; but these all wanted something of her--kisses, smiles, influence, money. Disinterested respect was new.

"I thought you were a Puritan, Lord Fareham."

"I am a man; and I know what it is to suffer the hell-fire of jealousy."

"Jealousy, yes! I never was good at hiding my feelings. He treats me shamefully. Come, now, you take me for an abandoned profligate woman, a callous wanton. That is what the world takes me for; and, perhaps, I have deserved no better of the world. But whatever I am 'twas he made me so. If he had been true, I could have been constant. It is the insolence of abandonment that stings; the careless slights, scarce conscious that he wounds. Before the eyes of the world, too, before wretches that grin and whisper, and prophesy the day when my pride shall be in the dust. It is treat ment such as this that makes women desperate; and if we cannot keep him we love, we make believe to love some one else, and flaunt our fancy in the deceiver's face. Do you think I cared for Buckingham, with his heart of ice; or for such a snipe as Jermyn; or for a low-born rope-dancer? No, Fareham; there has been more of rage and hate than of passion in my caprices. And he is with Frances Stewart to-night. She sets up for a model of chastity, and is to marry Richmond next month. But we know, Fareham, we know. Women who ride in glass coaches should not throw stones. I will have Charles at my feet again. I will have my foot upon his neck again. I cannot use him too ill for the pain he gives me. There, go--go! Why did you tempt me to lay my heart bare?"

"Dearest lady, believe me, I respect your candour. My heart bleeds for your wrongs. So beautiful, so high above all other women in the capacity to charm! Ah, be sure such loveliness has its responsibilities. It is a gift from Heaven, and to hold it cheap is a sin."

"There is nothing in this life can be held too cheap. Beauty, love--all trumpery! You would make life a tragedy. It is a farce, Fareham, a farce; and all our pleasures and diversions only serve to make us forget what worms we are. There, go--to cards--to supper--as you please. I am going to my bed-chamber to rest this throbbing head. I may return and take a hand at cards by-and-by, perhaps. Those fellows will game and booze till daylight."

Fareham opened the door for her, as she went out, regal in port and air. She had moved him to compassion, even while she owned herself a wanton. To love passionately--and to see another preferred! There is a brotherhood in agony, that brings even opposite natures into sympathy. He passed into the gallery, a long low room, hung with modern tapestries, richly coloured, voluptuous in design. Clusters of wax tapers in gilded sconces lit up those Paphian pictures. There were several tables, at which the mixed company were sitting. Piles of the new guineas, fresh from his Majesty's Mint, shone in the candle-light. At some tables there was a silent absorption in the game, which argued high play, and the true gambler's spirit; at others mirth reigned--talk, laughter, animated looks. One of the noisiest was the table at which De Malfort was the most conspicuous figure; his periwig the highest, his dress the most sumptuous, his breast glittering with orders. His companions were Sir Ralph Masaroon, Colonel Dangerfield, an old Malignant, who had hibernated during the Protectorate, and had never left his own country, and Lady Lucretia Topham, a visiting acquaintance of Hyacinth's.

"Come here, Fareham," cried De Malfort; "there is plenty of room for you. I'll wager Lady Lucretia will pass you her hand, and thank you for taking it."

"Lady Lucretia is glad to be quit of such dishonest company," said the lady, tossing her cards upon the table, and rising in a cloud of powder and perfume, and a flutter of lace and brocade. "If I were ill-humoured I would say you marked the cards! but as I'm the soul of good nature, I'll only swear you are the luckiest dog in London."

"You are the soul of good nature, and I am the luckiest dog in the universe when you smile upon me," answered De Malfort, without looking up from his cards, as the lady posed herself gracefully at the back of his chair, leaning over his shoulder to watch his play. "I would not limit the area to any city, however big."

Fareham seated himself in the chair the lady had vacated, and gathered up the cards she had abandoned. He took a handful of gold from his pocket, and put it on the table at his elbow, all with a somewhat churlish silence, that escaped notice where everybody was loquacious. De Malfort went on fooling with Lady Lucretia, whose lovely hand and arm, her strongest point, descended upon a card now and then, to indicate the play she deemed wisest.

Once he caught the hand and kissed it in transit.

"Wert thou as wise as this hand is fair it should direct my play; but it is only a woman's hand, and points the way to perdition."

Fareham had been losing steadily from the moment he took up Lady Lucretia's cards; and his pile of jacobuses had been gradually passed over to De Malfort's side of the table. He had emptied his pockets, and had scrawled two or three I.O.U.'s upon scraps of paper torn from a note-book. Yet he went on playing, with the same immovable countenance. The room had emptied itself, the rest of the visitors leaving earlier than their usual hour in that hospitable house. Perhaps because the hostess was missing; perhaps because the royal sun was shining elsewhere.

Lackeys handed their salvers of Burgundy and Bordeaux, and the players refreshed themselves occasionally with a brimmer of clary; but no wine brightened Fareham's scowling brow, or changed the glooiay intensity of his outlook.

"My cards have brought your lordship bad luck," said Lady Lucretia, who watched De Malfort's winnings with an air of personal interest.

"I knew my risk before I took them, madam. When an Englishman plays against a Frenchman he is a fool if he is not prepared to be rooked."

"Fareham, are you mad?" cried De Malfort, starting to his feet. "To insult your friend's country, and, by basest implication, your friend."

"I see no friend here. I say that you Frenchmen cheat at cards--on principle--and are proud of being cheats! I have heard De Gramont brag of having lured a man to his tent, and fed him, and wined him, and fleeced him while he was drunk." He took a goblet of claret from the lackey who brought his salver, emptied it, and went on, hoarse with passion. "To the marrow of your bones you are false, all of you! You do not cog your dice, perhaps, but you bubble your friends with finesses, and are as much sharpers at heart as the lowest tat-mongers in Alsatia. You empty our purses, and cozen our women with twanging guitars and jingling rhymes, and laugh at us because we are honest and trust you. Seducers, tricksters, poltroons!"

The footman was at De Malfort's elbow now. He snatched a tankard from the salver, and flung the contents across the table, straight at Fareham's face.

"This bully forces me to spoil his Point de Venise," he said coolly, as he set down the tankard. "There should be a law for chaining up rabid curs that have run mad without provocation."

Fareham sprang to his feet, black and terrible, but with a savage exultation in his countenance. The wine poured in a red stream from his point-lace cravat, but had not touched his face.

"There shall be something redder than Burgundy spilt before we have done!" he said.

"Sacre nom, nous sommes tombes dans un antre de betes sauvages!" exclaimed Masaroon, starting up, and anxiously examining the skirts of his brocade coat, lest that sudden deluge had caught him.

"None of your ---- French to show your fine breeding!" growled the old cavalier. "Fareham, you deserved the insult; but one red will wash out another. I'm with your lordship."

"And I'm with De Malfort," said Masaroon. "He had more than enough provocation."

"Gentlemen, gentlemen, no bloodshed!" cried Lady Lucretia; "or, if you are going to be uncivil to each other, for God's sake get me to my chair. I have a husband who would never forgive me if it were said you fought for my sake."

"We will see you safely disposed of, madam, before we begin our business," said Colonel Dangerfield, bluntly. "Fareham, you can take the lady to her chair, while Masaroon and I discuss particulars."

"There is no need of a discussion," interrupted Fareham, hotly. "We have nothing to arrange--nothing to wait for. Time, the present; place, the garden, under these windows; weapons, the swords we wear. We shall have no witnesses but the moon and stars. It is the dead middle of the night, and we have the world all to ourselves."

"Give me your rapier, then, that I may compare it with the Count's. You are satisfied, monsieur? 'Tis you that are the offender, and Lord Fareham has the choice of weapons."

"Let him choose. I will fight him with cannon--or with soap-bubbles," answered De Malfort, lolling back in his chair, tilted at an angle of forty-five, and drumming a gay dance tune with his finger-tips on the table. "'Tis a foolish imbroglio from first to last: and only his lordship and I know how foolish. He came here to provoke a quarrel, and I must indulge him. Come, Lady Lucretia"--he turned to his fair friend, as he unbuckled his sword and flung it on the table--"it is my place to lead you to your chair. Colonel, you and your friend will find me below stairs in front of the Holbein Gate."

"You are forgetting your winnings," remonstrated the lady, pointing to the pile of gold.

"The lackeys will not forget them when they clear the room," answered De Malfort, putting her hand through his arm, and leaving the money on the table.

Ten minutes later Fareham and De Malfort were standing front to front in the glare of four torches, held by a brace of her ladyship's lackeys who had been impressed into the service, and the colder light of a moon that rode high in the blue-black of a wintry heaven. There was not a sound but the ripple of the unseen river, and the distant cry of a watchman in Petty France, till the clash of swords began.

It was decided after a brief parley that the principals only should fight. The quarrel was private. The seconds placed their men on a piece of level turf, five paces apart. They were bare-headed, and without coat or vest, the lace ruffles of their shirt-sleeves rolled back to the elbow, their naked arms ghastly white, their faces suggesting ghost or devil as the spectral moonlight or the flame of the flambeaux shone upon them.

"You mean business, so we may sink the parade of the fencing saloon," said Dangerfield. "Advance, gentlemen."

"A pity," murmured Masaroon, "there is nothing prettier than the salute *a la Francaise*."

Dangerfield handed the men their swords. They were nearly similar in fashion, both flat-grooved blades, with needle points, and no cutting edge, furnished with shell-guards and cross-bars in the Italian style, and were about of a length.

The word was given, and the business of engagement proceeded slowly and warily, for a few moments that seemed minutes; and then the blades were firmly joined in carte, and a series of rapid feints began, De Malfort having a slight advantage in the neatness of his circles, and the swiftness of his wrist play. But in these preliminary lounges and parries, he soon found he needed all his skill to dodge his opponent's point; for Fareham's blade followed his own, steadily and strongly, through every turn.

De Malfort had begun the fight with an insolent smile upon his lips, the smile of a man who believes himself invincible, while Fareham's countenance never changed from the black anger that had darkened it all that night. It was a face that meant death. A man who had never been a duellist, who had raised his voice sternly against the practice of duelling, stood there intent upon bloodshed. There could be no mistake as to his purpose. The quarrel was an artificial quarrel--the object was murder.

De Malfort, provoked at the unexpected strength of Fareham's fence, attempted a partial disarmament, after the deadly Continental method. Joining his opponent's blade near the point, from a wide circular parry, he made a rapid thrust in seconde, carrying his forte the entire length of Fareham's blade, almost wrenching the sword from his grasp; and then, in the next instant, reaching forward to his fullest stretch, he lunged at his enemy's breast, aiming at the vital region of the heart; a thrust that must have proved fatal had not Fareham sprung aside, and so received the blow where the sword only grazed his ribs, inflicting a flesh-wound that showed red upon the whiteness of his shirt. Dangerfield tore off his cravat, and wanted to bind it round his principal's waist; but Fareham repulsed him, and lashed into hot fury by the Frenchman's uncavalier-like ruse, met his adversary's thrusts with a deadly purpose, which drove De Malfort to reckless lunging and riposting, and the play grew fast and fierce, while the rattle of steel seemed never likely to end. Suddenly, timing his attack to the fraction of a second, Fareham dropped on his left knee, and planting his left hand upon the ground, sent a murderous thrust home under De Malfort's guard, whose blade passed harmlessly over his adversary's head as he crouched on the sward.

De Malfort fell heavily in the arms of the two seconds, who both sprang to his assistance.

"Is it fatal?" asked Fareham, standing motionless as stone, while the other men knelt on either side of De Malfort.

"I'll run for a surgeon," said Masaroon. "There's a fellow I know of this side the Abbey--mends bloody noses and paints black eyes," and he was off, running across the grass to the nearest gate.

"It looks plaguily like a coffin," Dangerfield answered, with his hand on the wounded man's breast. "There's throbbing here yet; but he may bleed to death, like poor Lindsey, before surgery can help him. You had better run, Fareham. Take horse to Dover, and get across to Calais or Ostend. You were devilish provoking. It might go hard with you if he was to die."

"I shall not budge, Dangerfield. Didn't you hear me say I wanted to kill him? You might guess I didn't care a cast of the dice for my life when I said as much. Let them find it murder, and hang me. I wanted him out of the world, and don't care how soon I follow."

"You are mad--stark, staring mad!"

The wounded man raised himself on his elbow, groaning aloud in the agony of movement, and beckoned Fareham, who knelt down beside him, all of a piece, like a stone figure.

"Fareham, you had better run; I have powerful friends. There'll be an ugly stir if I die of this bout. Kiss me, mon ami. I forgive you. I know what wound rankled; 'twas for your wife's sister you fought--not the cards."

He sank into Dangerfield's arms, swooning from loss of blood, as Masaroon came back at a run, bringing a surgeon, an elderly man of that Alsatian class which is to be found out of bed in the small hours. He brought styptics and bandages, and at once set about staunching the wound.

While this was happening a curtain had been suddenly pulled aside at an upper window in Lady Castlemaine's lodgings, showing a light within. The window was thrown open, and a figure appeared, clad in a white satin night-gown that glistened in the moonlight, with a deep collar of ermine, from which the handsomest face in London looked across the garden, to the spot where Fareham, the seconds, and the surgeon were grouped about De Malfort.

It was Lady Castlemaine. She leant out of the window and called to them.

"What has happened? Is any one hurt? I'll wager a thousand pounds you devils have been fighting."

"De Malfort is stabbed!" Masaroon answered.

"Not dead?" she shrieked, leaning farther out of the window.

"No; but it looks dangerous."

"Bring him into my house this instant! I'll send my fellows to help. Have you sent for a surgeon?"

"The surgeon is here."

The radiant figure vanished like a vision in the skies; and in three minutes a door was heard opening, and a voice calling, "John, William, Hugh, Peter, every manjack of you. Lazy devils! There's been no time for you to fall asleep since the company left. Stir yourselves, vermin, and out with you!"

"We had best levant, Fareham," muttered Dangerfield, and drew away his principal, who went with him, silent and unresisting, having no more to do there; not to fly the country, however, but to walk quietly home to Fareham House, and to let himself in at the garden door, known to the household as his lordship's.

CHAPTER XVIII.
REVELATIONS.

Lord Fareham stayed in his own house by the Thames, and nobody interfered with his liberty, though Henri de Malfort lay for nearly a fortnight between life and death, and it was only in the beginning of December that he was pronounced out of danger, and was able to be removed from Lady Castlemaine's luxurious rooms to his own lodgings. Scandal-mongers might have made much talk of his lying ill in her ladyship's house, and being tenderly nursed by her, had not Lady Castlemaine outlived the possibility of slander. It would have been as difficult for her name to acquire any blacker stain as for a damaged reputation to wash itself white. The secret of the encounter had been faithfully kept by principals and seconds, De Malfort behaving with a chivalrous generosity. He appeared, indeed, as anxious for his antagonist's safety as for his own recovery.

"It was a mistake," he said, when Masaroon pressed him with home questions. "Every man is mad once in his life. Fareham's madness took an angry turn against an old friend. Why, we slept under the same blanket in the trenches before Dunkirk; we rode shoulder to shoulder through the rain of bullets at Chitillon; and to pick a trumpery quarrel with a brother-in-arms!"

"I wonder the quarrel was not picked earlier," Masaroon answered bluntly.

"Your courtship of the gentleman's wife has been notorious for the last five years."

"Call it not courtship, Ralph. Lady Fareham and I are old playfellows. We were reared in the **pays du tendre**, Loveland--the kingdom of innocent attachments and pure penchants, that country of which Mademoiselle Scudery has given us laws and a map. Your vulgar London lover cannot understand platonics--the affection which is satisfied with a smile or a madrigal. Fareham knows his wife and me better than to doubt us."

"And yet he acted like a man who was madly jealous. His rudeness at the card-table was obvious malice afore-thought. He came resolved to quarrel."

"Ay, he came to quarrel--but not about his wife."

Pressed to explain this dubious phrase, De Malfort affected a fit of languor, and would talk no more.

The town was told that the Comte de Malfort was ill of a quartain fever, and much was said about his sufferings during the Fronde, his exposure to damp and cold in the sea-marshes by Dunkirk, his rough fare and hard riding through the war of the Princes. This fever, which hung about him so long, was an after-consequence of hardship suffered in his youth--privations faced with a boyish recklessness, and which he had paid for with an impaired constitution. Fine ladies in gilded chairs, and vizard-masks in hackney coaches, called frequently at his lodgings in St. James's Street to inquire about his progress. Lady Fareham's private messenger was at his door every morning, and brought a note, or a book, or a piece of new music from her ladyship, who had been sternly forbidden to visit her old friend in person.

"You grow every day a gloomier tyrant!" Hyacinth protested, with more passion in her voice and mien than ever her husband had known. "Why should I not go to him when he is ill--dangerously ill--dying perhaps? He is my old, old friend. I remember no joy in life that he did not share. Why should I not go to him in his sorrow?"

"Because you are my wife, and I forbid you. I cannot understand this passion. I thought you suffered the company of that empty-headed fop as you suffered your lap-dogs--the trivial appendage of a fine lady's state. Had I supposed that there was anything serious in your liking--that you could think him worth anger or tears--should have ordered your life differently, and he would have had no place in it."

"Tyrant! tyrant!"

"You astound me, Hyacinth! Would you dispute the favours of a fop with your young sister?"

"With my sister!" she cried, scornfully.

"Ay, with your sister, whom he has courted assiduously; but with no honourable motive! I have seen his designs."

"Well, perhaps you are right. He may care for Angela--and think her too poor to marry."

"He is a traitor and a villain----"

"Oh, what fury! Marry my sister to Sir Denzil, and then she will be safe from all pursuit! He will bury her alive in Oxfordshire--withdraw her for ever from this wicked town--like poor Lady Yarborough in Cornwall."

"I will never ask her to marry a man she cannot love."

"Why not? Are not you and I a happy couple? And how much love had we for each other before we married? Why I scarce knew the colour of your eyes; and if I had met you in the street, I doubt if I should have recognised you! And now, after thirteen years of matrimony, we are at our first quarrel, and that no lasting one. Come, Fareham, be pleasant and yielding. Let me go and see my old playfellow. I am heartbroken for lack of his company, for fear of his death."

She hung upon him coaxingly, the bright blue eyes looking up at him--eyes that had so often been compared to Madame de Longueville's, eyes that had smiled and beamed in many a song and madrigal by the parlour poets of the Hotel de Rambouillet. She was exquisitely pretty in her youthful colouring of lilies and roses, blue eyes, and pale gold hair, and retained at thirty almost all the charms and graces of eighteen.

Fareham took her by both hands and held her away from him, severely scrutinising a face which he had always been able to admire as calmly as if it had been on canvas.

"You look like an innocent woman," he said, "and I have always believed you a good woman; and have trusted my honour in your keeping--have seen that man fawning at your feet, singing and sighing in your ear, and have thought no evil. But now that you have told me, as plainly as woman can speak to man, that this is the man you love, and have loved all your life, there must needs come an end to the sighing and singing. You and Henri de Malfort must meet no more. Nay, look not such angry scorn. I impute no guilt; but between innocence and guilt there need be but one passionate hour. The wife goes out an honest woman, able to look her husband in the face as you are looking at me; the wanton comes home, and the rest of her life is a shameful lie. And the husband awakes some day from his dream of domestic peace to discover that he has been long the laughing-stock of the town. I will be no such fatuous husband, Hyacinth. I will wait for no second warning."

Lady Fareham submitted in silence, and with deep resentment. She had never before experienced a husband's authority sternly exercised. She had been forbidden the free run of London play-houses, and some of the pleasures of Court society; but then she had been denied with all kindness, and had been allowed so many counterbalancing extravagances, pleasures, and follies, that it would have been difficult for her to think herself ill-used.

She submitted angrily, passionately regretting the man whose presence had long been the brightest element in her life. Her cheek paled; she grew indifferent to the amusements which had been her sole occupation; she sulked in her rooms, equally avoiding her children and their aunt; and, indeed, seemed to care for no one's society except Mrs. Lewin's. The Court milliner had business with her ladyship every day, and was regaled with cakes and liqueurs in her ladyship's dressing-room.

"You must be very busy about new gowns, Hyacinth," her husband said to her one day at dinner. "I meet the harridan from Covent Garden on the stairs every morning."

"She is not a harridan, whatever that elegant word may mean. And as for gowns, it would be wiser for me to order no new ones, since it is but likely I shall soon have to wear mourning for an old friend."

She looked at her husband, defying him. He rose from the table with a sigh, and walked out of the room. There was war between them, or at best an armed neutrality. He looked back, and saw that he had been blind to the things he should have seen, dull and unobservant where he should have had sense and understanding.

"I did not care enough for my honour," he thought. "Was it because I cared too little for my wife? It is indifference, and not love, that is blind."

Angela saw the cloud that overshadowed Fareham House with deepest distress; and yet felt herself powerless to bring back sunshine. Her sister met her remonstrances with scorn.

"Do you take the part of a tyrant against your own flesh and blood?" she asked. "I have been too tame a slave. To keep me away from the Court while I was young and worth looking at--to deny me amusements and admiration which are the privilege of every woman of quality--to forbid me the play-house, and make a country cousin of me by keeping me ignorant of modern wit. I am ashamed of my compliance."

"Nay, dearest, was it not an evidence of his love that he should desire you to keep your mind pure as well as your face fair?"

"No, he has never loved me. It is only a churlish jealousy that would shut me up in a harem like a Turk's wife, and part me from the friend I like best in the world-- with the purest platonic affection."

"Hyacinth, don't be angry with me for being out of the fashion; but indeed I cannot think it right for a wife to care for the company of any other man but her husband."

"And my husband is so entertaining! Sure any woman might be content with such gay company--such flashes of wit--such light raillery!" cried Hyacinth, scornfully, walking up and down the room, plucking at the lace upon her sleeves with restless hands, her bosom heaving, her eyes steel-bright with anger. "Since his sickness last year, he has been the image of melancholy; he has held himself aloof from me as if *I* had had the pestilence. I was content that it should be so. I had my children and you, and one who loved me better, in his light way, than any of you--and I could do without Lord Fareham. But now he forbids me to see an old friend that is dangerously ill, and every drop of blood in my veins boils in rebellion against his tyranny!"

It was in the early dusk, an hour or so after dinner. Angela sat silent in the shadow of a bay window, quite as heavy-hearted as her sister--sorry for Hyacinth, but still sorrier for Hyacinth's husband, yet feeling that there was treachery and unkindness in making him first in her thoughts. But surely, surely he deserved a better wife than this! Surely he deserved a wife's love--this man who stood alone among the men she knew, hating all evil things, honouring all things good and noble! He had been unkind to her--cold and cruel--since that fatal night. He had let her understand that all friendship between them was at an end for ever, and that she had become despicable in his sight; and she had submitted to be scorned by him, since it was impossible that she should clear herself. She had made her sisterly sacrifice for a sister who regarded it very lightly; to whose light fancy that night and all it involved counted but as a scene in a comedy; and she could not unmake it. But having so sacrificed his good opinion whose esteem she valued, she wanted to see some happy result, and to save this splendid home from shipwreck.

Suddenly, with a passionate impulse, she went to her sister, and put her arms round her and kissed her.

"Hyacinth, you shall not continue in this folly," she cried, "to fret for that shallow idler, whose love is lighter than thistledown, whose element is the ruelle of one of those libertine French duchesses he is ever talking about. To rebel against the noblest gentleman in England! Oh, sister, you must know him better than I do; and yet I, who am nothing to him, am wretched when I see him ill-used. Indeed, Hyacinth, you are acting like a wicked wife. You should never have wished to see De Malfort again, after the peril of that night. You should have known that he had no esteem for you, that he was a traitor--that his design was the wickedest, cruellest----"

"I don't pretend to know a man's mind as well as you--neither De Malfort's nor my husband's. You have needed but the experience of a year to make you wise enough in the world's ways to instruct your elders. I am not going to be preached to----Hark!" she cried, running to the nearest window, and looking out at the river, "that is better than your sermons."

It was the sound of fiddles playing the symphony of a song she knew well--one of De Malfort's, a French chanson, her latest favourite, the words adapted from a little poem by Voiture, "Pour vos beaux yeux."

She opened the casement, and Angela stood beside her looking down at a boat in which several muffled figures were seated, and which was moored to the terrace wall.

There were three violins and a 'cello, and a quartette of singing-boys with fair young faces smiling in the light of the lamps that hung in front of Fareham's house.

The evening was still, and mild as early autumn, and the plash of oars passing up and down the river sounded like a part of the music--

"Love in her sunny eyes doth basking play,   Love walks the pleasant mazes of her hair,   Love does on both her lips for ever stray,   And sows and reaps a thousand kisses there;   In all her outward parts love's always seen;   But, oh, he never went within."

It was a song of Cowley's, which De Malfort had lately set to music, and to a melody which Hyacinth especially admired.

"A serenade! Only De Malfort could have thought of such a thing. Lying ill and alone, he sends me the sweetest token of his regard--my favourite air, his own setting--the last song I ever heard him sing. And you wonder that I value so pure, so disinterested a love!" protested Hyacinth to her sister, in the silence at the end of the song.

"Sing again, sweet boys, sing again!" she cried, snatching a purse from her pocket, and flinging it with impetuous aim into the boat.

It hit one of the fiddlers on the head, and there was a laugh, and in a trice the largesse was divided and pocketed.

"They are from his Majesty's choir; I know their voices," said Hyacinth, "so fresh, and pure. They are the prettiest singers in the chapel. That little monkey with the cherub's voice is Purcell--Dr. Blow's favourite pupil--and a rare genius."

They sang another song from De Malfort's repertoire, an Italian serenade, which Hyacinth had heard in the brilliant days before her marriage, when the Italian Opera was still a new thing in Paris. The melody brought back the memory of her happy girlhood with a rush of sudden tears.

The little concert lasted for something less than an hour, with intervals of light music, dances and marches, between the singing. Boats passed and repassed. Strange voices joined in a refrain now and then, and the sisters stood at the open window enthralled by the charm of the music and the scene. London lay in ruins yonder to the east, and Sir Matthew Hale and other judges were sitting at Clifford's Inn to decide questions of title and boundary, and the obligation to rebuild; but here in this western London there were long ranges of lighted windows shining through the wintry mists, wherries passing up and down with lanterns at their prows, an air of life and gaiety hanging over that river which had carried so many a noble victim to his doom yonder, where the four towers stood black against the starlit greyness, unscathed by fire, and untouched by time.

The last notes of a good-night song dwindled and died, to the accompaniment of dipping oars, as the boat moved slowly along the tideway, and lost itself among other boats--jovial cits going eastward, from an afternoon at the King's theatre, modish gallants voyaging westward from play-house or tavern, some going home to domesticity, others intent upon pleasure and intrigue, as the darkness came down, and the hour for supper and deeper drinking drew near. And who would have thought, watching the lighted windows of palace and tavern, hearing those joyous sounds of glee or catch trolled by voices that reeked of wine--who would have thought of the dead-cart, and the unnumbered dead lying in the pest pits yonder, or the city in ruins, or the King enslaved to a foreign power, and pledged to a hated Church? London, gay, splendid, and prosperous, the queen-city of the world as she seemed to those who loved her--could rise glorious from the ashes of a fire unparalleled in modern history, and to Charles and Wren it might be given to realise a boast which in Augustus had been little more than an imperial phrase.

CHAPTER XIX.
DIDO.

The armed neutrality between man and wife continued, and the domestic sky at Fareham House was dark and depressing. Lady Fareham, who had hitherto been remarkable for a girlish amiability of speech which went well with her girlish beauty, became now the height of the mode for acidity and slander. The worst of the evil speakers on her ladyship's visiting-day flavoured the China tea with no bitterer allusions than those that fell from the rosy lips of the hostess. And, for the colouring of those lips, which once owed their vermeil tint only to nature, Lady Fareham was now dependent upon Mrs. Lewin, as well as for the carnation of cheeks that looked pallid and sunken in the glass which reflected the sad mourning face.

Mrs. Lewin brought roses and lilies in her queer little china pots and powder boxes, pencils and brushes, perfumes and washes without number. It cost as much to keep a complexion as to keep a horse. And Mrs. Lewin was infinitely useful at this juncture, since she called every day at St. James's Street, to carry a lace cravat, or a ribbon, or a flask of essence to the invalid languishing in lodgings there, and visited by all the town, except Fareham and his wife. De Malfort had lain for a fortnight at Lady Castlemaine's house, alternately petted and neglected by his fair hostess, as the fit took her, since she showed herself ever of the chameleon breed, and hovered betwixt angel and devil. His surgeon told him in confidence that when once his wound was healed enough to allow his removal, the sooner he quitted that feverish company the better it would be for his chance of a speedy convalescence. So, at the end of the second week, he was moved in a covered litter to his own lodgings, where his faithful valet, who had followed his fortunes since he came to man's estate, was quite capable of nursing him.

The town soon discovered the breach between Lord Fareham and his friend--a breach commented upon with many shoulder-shrugs, and not a few coarse innuendoes. Lady Lucretia Topham insisted upon making her way to the sick man's room, in the teeth of messages delivered by his valet, which, even to a less intelligent mind than Lady Lucretia's, might have conveyed the fact that she was not wanted. She flung herself on her knees by De Malfort's bed, and wept and raved at the brutality which had deprived the world of his charming company--and herself of the only man she had ever loved. De Malfort, fevered and vexed at her intrusion, and at this renewal of fires long burnt out, had yet discretion enough to threaten her with his dire displeasure if she betrayed the secret of his illness.

"I have sworn Dangerfield and Masaroon to silence," he said. "Except servants, who have been paid to keep mute, you are the only other witness of our quarrel; and if the story becomes town talk, I shall know whose busy tongue set it going-- and then--well, there are things I might tell that your ladyship would hardly like the world to know."

"Traitor! If your purse has accommodated me once in a way when luck has been adverse----"

"Oh, madam, you cannot think me base enough to blab of a money transaction with a lady. There are secrets more tender--more romantic."

"Those secrets can be easily denied, wretch. However, I know you would not injure me with a husband so odious and tyrannical that I stood excused in advance for inconstancy when I stooped to wed country manners and stubborn ignorance. Indeed, mon ami, if you will but take pains to recover, I will never breathe a word about the duel; but if--if--" a sob indicated the tragic possibility which Lady Lucretia dared not put into words--"I will do all that a weak woman can do to get Fareham hanged for murder. There has never been a peer hanged in England, I believe. He should be the first."

"Dear soul, there need be no hanging! I have been on the mending hand for a week, or my doctors would not have let you upstairs. There, go, my pretty Lucrece; but if your milliner or your shoemaker is pressing, there are a few jacobuses in the right-hand drawer of yonder escritoire, and you may as well take them as leave them for my valet to steal. He is one of those excellent old servants who make no distinctions, and he robs me as freely as he robbed my father before me."

"Mrs. Lewin is always pressing," sighed Lady Lucretia. "She made me a gown like that of Lady Fareham's, for which you were all eyes. I ordered the brocade to please you; and now I am wearing it when you are not at Whitehall. Well, as you are so kind, I will be your debtor for another trifling loan. It is wicked to leave money where it tempts a good servant to dishonesty. Ah, Henri"--she was pocketing the gold as she talked--"if ten years of my life could save you ten days of pain and fever, how gladly would I give them to you!"

"Ah, douce, if there were a market for the exchange of such commodities, what a roaring trade would be done there! I never loved a woman yet but she offered me her life, or an instalment of it."

"I have emptied your drawer," laughing coyly. "There is just enough to keep Lewin in good humour till you are well again, and we can be partners at basset."

"It will be very long before I play basset in London."

"Oh, but indeed you will soon be well."

"Well enough to change the scene, I hope. It needs change of places and persons to make life bearable. I long to be at the Louvre again, to see a play by Moliere's company, as only they can act, instead of the loathsome translations we get here, in which all that there is of wit and charm in the original is transmuted to coarseness and vulgarity. When I leave this bed, Lucrece, it will be for Paris."

"Why, it will be ages before you are strong enough for such a journey."

"Oh, I will risk that. I hate London so badly, that to escape from it will work a miraculous cure for me."

*   *   *   *   *

An armed neutrality! Even the children felt the change in the atmosphere of home, and nestled closer to their aunt, who never changed to them.

"Father mostly looks angry," Henriette complained, "and mother is always unhappy, if she is not laughing and talking in the midst of company; and neither of them ever seems to want me. I wish I was grown up, so that I could be maid of honour to the Queen or the Duchess, and live at Whitehall. Mademoiselle told me that there is always life and pleasure at Court."

"Your father does not love the Court, dearest, and mademoiselle should be wiser than to talk to you of such things, when she is here to teach you dancing and French literature."

"Mademoiselle" was a governess lately imported from Paris, recommended by Mademoiselle Scudery, and full of high-flown ideas expressed in high-flown language. All Paris had laughed at Moliere's *Precieuses Ridicules*; but the Precieuses themselves, and their friends, protested that the popular farce was aimed only at the low-born imitators of those great ladies who had originated the school of superfine culture and romantic aspirations.

"Sapho" herself, in tracing her own portrait with a careful and elaborate pencil, told the world how shamefully she had been imitated by the spurious middle-class Saphos, who set up their salons, and vied with the sacred house of Rambouillet, and the privileged coterie of the Rue de Temple.

Lady Fareham had not ceased to believe in her dear, plain, witty Scudery, and was delighted to secure a governess of her choosing, whereby Papillon, who loved freedom and idleness, and hated lessons of all kinds, was set down to write themes upon chivalry, politeness, benevolence, pride, war, and other abstractions; or to fill in bouts-rimes, by way of enlarging her acquaintance with the French language, which she had chattered freely all her life. Mademoiselle insisted upon all the niceties of phraseology as discussed in the Rue Saint Thomas du Louvre.

There had been a change of late in Fareham's manner to his sister-in-law, a change refreshing to her troubled spirit as mercy, that gentle dew from heaven, to the criminal. He had been kinder; and though he spent very few of his hours with the women of his household, he had talked to Angela somewhat in the friendly tone of those fondly remembered days at Chilton, when he had taught her to row and ride, to manage a spirited palfrey and fly a falcon, and had been in all things her mentor and friend. He seemed less oppressed with gloom as time went on, but had his sullen fits still, and, after being kind and courteous to wife and sister, and playful with his children, would leave them suddenly, and return no more to the saloon or drawing-room that evening. Yet on the whole the sky was lightening. He ignored Hyacinth's resentment, endured her pettishness, and was studiously polite to her.

*   *   *   *   *

It was on Lady Fareham's visiting-day, deep in that very severe winter, that some news was told her which came like a thunder-clap, and which it needed all the weak soul's power of self-repression to suffer without swooning or hysterics.

Lady Sarah Tewkesbury, gorgeous in velvet and fur, her thickly painted countenance framed in a furred hood, entered fussily upon a little coterie in which Masaroon, vapouring about the last performance at the King's theatre, was the principal figure.

"There was a little woman spoke the epilogue," he said, "a little creature in a monstrous big hat, as large and as round as a cart-wheel, which vastly amused his Majesty."

"The hat?"

"Nay, it was woman and hat. The thing is so small it might have been scarce noticed without the hat, but it has a pretty little, insignificant, crumpled face, and laughs all over its face till it has no eyes, and then stops laughing suddenly, and the eyes shine out, twinkling and dancing like stars reflected in running water, and it stamps its little foot upon the stage in a comic passion--and--***nous verrons***. It sold oranges in the pit, folks tell me, a year ago. It may be selling sinecures and captaincies in a year or two, and putting another shilling in the pound upon land."

"Is it that brazen little comedy actress you are talking of, Masaroon?" Lady Sarah asked, when she had exchanged curtsies with the ladies of the company, and established herself on the most comfortable tabouret, near Lady Fareham's tea-table; "Mrs. Glyn--Wynn--Gwyn? I wonder a man of wit can notice such a vulgar creature, a she-jack-pudden, fit only to please the rabble in the gallery."

"Ay, but there is a finer sort of rabble--a rabble of quality--beginning with his Majesty, that are always pleased with anything new. And this little creature is as fresh as a spring morning. To see her laugh, to hear the ring of it, clear and sweet as a skylark's song! On my life, madam, the town has a new toy; and Mrs. Gwyn will be the rage in high quarters. You should have seen Castlemaine's scowl when Rowley laughed, and ducked under the box almost, in an ecstasy of amusement at the huge hat."

"Lady Castlemaine's brow would thunder-cloud if his Majesty looked at a fly on a window-pane. But she has something else to provoke her frowns to-day."

"What is that, chere dame?" asked Hyacinth, snatching a favourite fan from Sir Ralph, who was teasing one of the Blenheims with African feathers that were almost priceless.

"The desertion of an old friend. The Comte de Malfort has left England."

Lady Fareham turned livid under her rouge. Angela ran to her and leant over her, upon a pretence of rescuing the fan and chiding the dogs; and so contrived to screen her sister's change of complexion from the malignity of her dearest friends.

"Left England! Why, he is confined to his bed with a fever!" Hyacinth said faintly, when she had somewhat recovered from the shock.

"Nay, it seems that he began to go abroad last week, but would see no company, except a confidential friend or so. He left London this morning for Dover."

"No doubt he has business in Burgundy, where his estate is, and at Paris, where he is of importance at the Court," said Hyacinth, as lightly as she could; "but I'll wager anything anybody likes that he will be in London again in a month."

"I'll take you for those black pearls in your ears, ma mie," said Lady Sarah. "His furniture is to be sold by auction next week. I saw a bill on the house this afternoon. It is sudden! Perhaps the Castlemaine had become too exacting!"

"Castlemaine!" faltered Hyacinth, agitated beyond her power of self-control. "Why, what is she to him more than she is to other men?"

"Very little, perhaps," said Sir Ralph, and then everybody laughed, and Hyacinth felt herself sitting among them like a child, understanding nothing of their smiles and shrugs, the malice in their sly interchange of glances.

She sat among them feeling as if her heart were turned to stone. He had left the country without even bidding her farewell--her faithful slave, upon whose devotion she counted as surely as upon the rising of the sun. Whatever her husband might do to separate her from this friend of her girlhood, she had feared no defection upon

De Malfort's part. He would always be near at hand, waiting and watching for the happier days that were to smile upon their innocent loves. She had written to him every day during his illness. Good Mrs. Lewin had taken the letters to him, and had brought her his replies. He had not written so often, or at such length, as she, and had pleaded the languor of convalescence as his excuse; but all his billets-doux had been in the same delicious hyperbole, the language of the Pays du Tendre. She sat silent while her visitors talked about him, plucking a reputation as mercilessly as a kitchen wench plucks a fowl. He was gone. He had left the country deep in debt. It was his landlord who had stuck up that notice of a sale by auction. Tailors and shoemakers, perruquiers and perfumers were bewailing his flight.

So much for the sordid side of things. But what of those numerous affairs of the heart--those entanglements which had made his life one long intrigue?

Lady Sarah sat simpering and nodding as Masaroon whispered close in her ear.

Barbara? Oh, that was almost as old as the story of Antony and Cleopatra. She had paid his debts--and he had paid hers. Their purse had been in common. And the handsome maid of honour? Ah, poor silly soul! That was a horrid, ugly business, and his Majesty's part in it the horridest. And Mrs. Levington, the rich silk mercer's wife? That was a serious attachment. It was said that the husband attempted poison, when De Malfort refused him the satisfaction of a gentleman. And the poor woman was sent to die of *ennui* and rheumatism in a castle among the Irish bogs, where her citizen husband had set up as a landed squire.

The fine company discussed all these foul stories with gusto, insinuating much more than they expressed in words. Never until to-day had they spoken so freely of De Malfort in Lady Fareham's presence; but the story had got about of a breach between Hyacinth and her admirer, and it was supposed that any abuse of the defaulter would be pleasant in her ears. And then, he was ruined and gone; and there is no vulture's feast sweeter than to banquet upon a departed rival's character.

Hyacinth listened in dull silence, as if her sensations were suddenly benumbed. She felt nothing but a horrible surprise. Her lover--her platonic lover--that other half of her mind and heart--with whom she had been in such tender sympathy, in unison of spirit, so subtle that the same thoughts sprang up simultaneously in the minds of each, the same language leapt to their lips, and they laughed to find their words alike. It had been only a shallow woman's shallow love--but trivial woes are tragedies for trivial minds; and when her guests had gradually melted away, dispersing themselves with reciprocal curtsies and airy compliments, elegant in their modish iniquity as a troop of vicious fairies--Hyacinth stood on the hearth where they had left her, a statue of despair.

Angela went to her, when the stately double doors had closed on the last of the gossips and lackeys, and they two were alone amidst the spacious splendour. The younger sister hugged the elder to her breast, and kissed her, and cried over her, like a mother comforting her disappointed child.

"Don't heed that shameful talk, dearest. No character is safe with them. Be sure Monsieur de Malfort is not the reprobate they would make him. You have known him nearly all your life. You know him too well to judge him by the idle talk of the town."

"No, no; I have never known him. He has always worn a mask. He is as false as Satan. Don't talk to me--don't kiss me, child. You have smeared my face horribly with your kisses and tears. Your pity drives me mad. How can you understand these things--you who have never loved any one? What can you know of what women feel? There, silly fool! you are trembling as if I had hit you," as Angela withdrew her arms suddenly, and stood aloof. "I have been a virtuous wife, sister, in a town where scarce one woman in ten is true to her marriage vows. I have never sinned against my husband; but I have never loved him. Henri had my heart before I knew what the word, love meant; and in all these years we have loved each other with the purest, noblest affection--at least he made me believe my love was reciprocated. We have enjoyed a most exquisite communion of thought and feeling. His letters-- you shall read his letters some day--so noble, so brilliant--all poetry, and chivalry, and wit. I lived upon his letters when fate parted us. And when he followed us to England, I thought it was for my sake that he came--only for me. And to hear that he was her lover--hers--that woman! To know that he came to me--with sweetest words upon his lips--knelt to kiss the tips of my fingers--as if it were a privilege to die for--from her arms, from her caresses--the wickedest woman in England--and the loveliest!"

"Dear Hyacinth, it was a childish dream--and you have awakened! You will live to be glad of being recalled from falsehood to truth. Your husband is worth fifty

De Malforts, did you but know it. Oh, dearest, give him your heart who ought to be its only master. Indeed he is worthy. He stands apart--an honourable, nobly thinking man in a world that is full of libertines. Be sure he deserves your love."

"Don't preach to me, child! If you could give me a sleeping-draught that would blot out memory for ever--make me forget my childhood in the Marais--my youth at St. Germain--the dances at the Louvre--all the days when I was happiest: why, then, perhaps, you might make me in love with Lord Fareham."

"You will begin a new life, sister, now De Malfort is gone."

"I will never forgive him for going!" cried Hyacinth, passionately. "Never--never! To give me no note of warning! To sneak away like a thief who had stolen my diamonds! To fly for debt, too, and not come to me for money! Why have I a fortune, if not to help those I love? But--if he was that woman's lover--I will never see his face again--never speak his name--never--from the moment I am convinced of that hellish treason--never! Her lover! Lady Castlemaine's! We have laughed at her, together! Her lover! And there were other women those spiteful wretches talked about just now--a tradesman's wife! Oh, how hateful, how hateful it all is! Angela, if it is true, I shall go mad!"

"Dearest, to you he was but a friend--and though you may be sorry he was so great a sinner, his sins cannot concern your happiness----"

"What! not to know him a profligate? The man to whom I gave a chaste woman's love! Angela, that night, in the ruined abbey, I let him kiss me. Yes, for one moment I was in his arms--and his lips were on mine. And he had kissed her--the same night perhaps. Her tainted kisses were on his lips. And it was you who saved me! Dear sister, I owe you more than life--I might have given myself to everlasting shame that night. God knows! I was in his power--her lover--judging all women, perhaps, by his knowledge of that----"

The epithet which closed the sentence was not a word for a woman's lips; but it was wrung from the soreness of a woman's wounded heart.

Hyacinth flung herself distractedly into her sister's arms.

"You saved me!" she cried, hysterically. "He wanted me to go to Dover with him--back to France--where we were so happy. He knelt to me, and I refused him; but he prayed me again and again; and if you had not come to rescue me, should I have gone on saying no? God knows if my courage would have held out. There were tears in his eyes. He swore that he had never loved any one upon this earth as he loved me. Hypocrite! Deceiver--liar! He loved that woman! Twenty times handsomer than ever I was--a hundred times more wicked. It is the wicked women that are best loved, Angela, remember that. Oh, bless you for coming to save me! You saved Fareham's life in the plague year. You saved me from everlasting misery. You are our guardian angel!"

"Ah, dearest, if love could guard you, I might deserve that name----"

*   *   *   *   *

It was late in the same evening that Lady Fareham's maid came to her bedchamber to inquire if she would be pleased to see Mrs. Lewin, who had brought a pattern of a new French bodice, with her humble apologies for waiting on her ladyship so late.

Her ladyship would see Mrs. Lewin. She started up from the sofa where she had been lying, her forehead bound with a handkerchief steeped in Hungary water. She was all excitement.

"Bring her here instantly!" she said, and the interval necessary to conduct the milliner up the grand staircase and along the gallery seemed an age to Hyacinth's impatience.

"Well? Have you a letter for me?" she asked, when her woman had retired, and Mrs. Lewin had bustled and curtsied across the room.

"In truly, my lady; and I have to ask your ladyship's pardon for not bringing it early this morning, when his honour gave it to me with his own hand out of 'his travelling carriage. And very white and wasted he looked, dear gentleman, not fit for a voyage to France in this severe weather. And I was to carry you his letter immediately; but, eh, gud! your ladyship, there was never such a business as mine for surprises. I was putting on my cloak to step out with your ladyship's letter, when a coach, with a footman in the royal undress livery, sets down at my door, and one of the Duchess's women had come to fetch me to her Highness; and there I was kept in her Highness's chamber half the morning, disputing over a paduasoy for the Shrove Tuesday masquerade--for her Highness gets somewhat bulky, and is not easy to dress to her advantage or to my credit--though she is a beauty compared with the Queen, who still hankers after her hideous Portuguese fashions----"

"And employs your rival, Madame Marifleur----"

"Marifleur! If your ladyship knew the creature as well as I do, you'd call her Sally Cramp."

"I never can remember a low English name. Marifleur seems to promise all that there is of the most graceful and airy in a ruffled sleeve and a ribbon shoulder-knot."

"I am glad to see your ladyship is in such good spirits," said the milliner, wondering at Lady Fareham's flushed cheeks and brilliant eyes.

They were brilliant with a somewhat glassy brightness, and there was a touch of hysteria in her manner. Mrs. Lewin thought she had been drinking. Many of her customers ended that way--took to cognac and ratafia, when choicer pleasures were exhausted and wrinkles began to show through their paint.

Hyacinth was reading De Malfort's letter as she talked, moving about the room a little, and then stopping in front of the fireplace, where the light from two clusters of wax candles shone down upon the finely written page.

Mrs. Lewin watched her for a few minutes, and then produced some pieces of silk out of her muff.

"I made so bold as to bring your ladyship some patterns of Italian silks which only came to hand this morning," she said. "There is a cherry-red that would become your ladyship to the T."

"Make me a gown of it, my excellent Lewin--and good night to you."

"But sure your ladyship will look at the colour? There is a pattern of amber with gold thread might please you better. Lady Castlemaine has ordered a Court mantua----"

Lady Fareham rang her hand-bell with a vehemence that suggested anger.

"Show Mrs. Lewin to her coach," she said shortly, when her woman appeared. "When you have done that you may go to bed; I want nothing more to-night."

"Mrs. Kirkland has been asking to see your ladyship."

"I will see no one to-night. Tell Mrs. Kirkland so, with my love."

She ran to the door when the maid and milliner were gone, and locked it, and then ran back to the fireplace, and flung herself down upon the rug to read her letter.

"Cherie, when this is handed to you, I shall be sitting in my coach on the dull Dover road, with frost-clouded windows and a heart heavier than your leaden skies. Loveliest of women, all things must end; and, despite your childlike trust in man's virtue, you could scarce hope for eternity to a bond that was too strong for friendship and too weak for love. Dearest, had you given yourself that claim upon love and honour which we have talked of, and which you have ever refused, no lesser power than death should have parted us. I would have dared all, conquered all, for my dear mistress. But you would not. It was not for lack of fervid prayers that the statue remained a statue; but a man cannot go on worshipping a statue for ever. If the Holy Mother did not sometimes vouchsafe a sign of human feeling, even good Catholics would have left off kneeling to her image.

"Or, shall I say, rather, that the child remains a child--fresh, and pure, and innocent, and candid, as in the days when we played our *jeu de volant* in your grandmother's garden--fit emblem of the light love of our future years. You remained a child, Hyacinth, and asked childish love-making from a man. Dearest, accept a cruel truth from a man of the world--it is only the love you call guilty that lasts. There is a stimulus in sin and mystery that will fan the flame of passion and keep love alive even for an inferior object. The ugly women know this, and make lax morals a substitute for beauty. An innocent intrigue, a butterfly affection like ours, will seldom outlive the butterfly's brief day. Indeed, I sometimes admire at myself as a marvel of constancy for having kept faith so long with a mistress who has rewarded me so sparingly.

"So, my angel, I am leaving your foggy island, my cramped London lodgings, and extortionate London tradesmen, on whom I have squandered so much of my fortune that they ought to forgive me for leaving a margin of debt, which I hope to pay the extortioners hereafter for the honour of my name. I doubt if I shall ever revisit England. I have tasted all London pleasures, till familiarity has taken the taste out of them; and though Paris may be only London with a difference, that difference includes bluer skies, brighter streets and gardens, and all the originals of which you have here the copies. There, at least, I shall have the fashion of my peruke and my speech at first hand. Here you only adopt a mode when Paris begins to tire of it.

"Farewell, then, dearest lady, but let it be no tragical or eternal parting, since your fine house in the Rue de Touraine will doubtless be honoured with your presence some day. You have only to open a salon there in order to be the top of the mode. Some really patrician milieu is needed to replace the antique court of the dear old Marquise, and to extinguish the Scudery, whose Saturdays grow more vulgar every week. Yes, you will come to Paris, bringing that human lily, Mrs. Angela, in your train; and I promise to make you the fashion before your house has been open a month. The wits and Court favourites will go where I bid them. And though your dearest friend, Madame de Longueville, has retired from the world in which she was more queenly than the Queen, you will find Mademoiselle de Montpensier as faithful as ever to mundane pleasures, and, after having refused kings and princes, slavishly devoted to a colonel of dragoons who does not care a straw for her.

"Louise de Bourbon, a woman who can head a revolt and fire a cannon, would think no sacrifice too great for a cold-hearted schemer like Lauzun--yet you who swore you loved me, when the coach was waiting that would have carried me to paradise, and made us one for all this life, could suffer a foolish girl to separate us in the very moment of triumphant union. You were mine, Hyacinth; heart and mind were consenting, when your convent-bred sister surprised us, and all my hopes of bliss expired in a sermon. And now I can but say, with that witty rhymester, whom everybody in London quotes--

'Love in your heart as idly burns,   As fire in antique Roman urns.'

"Good-bye, which means 'God be with you.' I know not if the fear of Him was in your mind when you sacrificed your lover to that icy abstraction women call virtue. The Romans had but one virtue, which meant the courage that dares; and to me the highest type of woman would be one whose bold spirit dared and defied the world for love's sake. These are the women history remembers, and whom the men who live after them worship. Cleopatra, Mary Stuart, Diana of Poictiers, Marguerite de Valois, la Chevreuse, la Montbazon! Think you that these became famous by keeping their lovers at a distance?

"'Go, lovely rose!'

"How often I have sung those lines, and you have listened, and nothing has come of it; except time wasted, smiles, sighs, and tears, that ever promised, and ever denied. Beauty, too choice to be kind, adieu!

"DE MALFORT."

When she had read these last words, she crushed the letter in her palm, clenching her fingers over it till the nails wounded the delicate flesh; and then she opened her hand, and employed herself in smoothing out the crumpled paper, as if her life depended on making the letter readable again. But her pains could not undo what her passion had done; and finding this, she tossed the ragged paper into the flames, and began to walk about the room in a distracted fashion, giving a little hysterical cry every now and then, and clasping her hands upon her forehead.

Anger, humiliation, wounded love, wounded vanity, disappointment, disillusion, were all in that cry, and in the passionate beating of her heart, her stifled breath, her clenched hands.

"He was laughing when he wrote that letter--I am sure he was laughing. There was not one serious moment, not one pang at leaving me! He has been laughing at me ever since he came to London. I have been his fool, his amusement. Other women have had his love, the guilty love that he praises! He has come to me straight from their wicked houses, their feasting, and riot, and drunkenness--has come and pretended to love poetry, and Scudery's romances, and music, and innocent conversation--come to rest himself after dissolute pleasures, bringing me the leavings of that hellish company! And I have reviled such women, and he has pretended an equal horror of them; and he was their slave all the time, and went from me to them, and made a jest of me for their amusement I know his biting raillery. And he was at the play-house day after day, where I could not go, sitting side by side with his Jezebels, laughing at filthy comedies, and at me that was forbidden to appear there. He had pleasures of which I knew nothing; and when I fancied our inmost souls moved in harmony, his thoughts were full of wanton women and their wanton jests, and he smiled at my childishness, and fooled me as children are fooled."

The thought was distraction. She plucked out handfuls of her pale gold hair, the pretty blonde hair which had been almost as famous in Paris as Beaufort's or Madame de Longueville's yellow locks. The thought of De Malfort's ridicule cut her like a whalebone whip. She had fancied herself his Beatrice, his Laura, his Stella--a being to be worshipped as reverently as the stars, to make her lover happy with smiles and kindly words, to stand for ever a little way off, like a goddess in her temple, yet near enough to be adored.

And fondly believing this to be her mission, having posed for the character, and filled it to her own fancy, she found that she had only been a dissolute man's dupe all the time; and no doubt had been the laughing-stock of her acquaintance, who looked at the game.

"And I was so proud of his devotion--I carried my slave everywhere with me. Oh, fool, fool, fool!"

And then--the poor little brains being disordered by passionate regrets--wickedest ideas ran riot in the confusion of a mind not wide enough to hold life's large passions. She began to be sorry that she was not like those other women--to hate the modesty that had lost her a lover.

To be like Barbara Castlemaine! That was woman's only royalty. To rule with sovereign power over the hearts and senses of men. A King for her lover, constant in inconstancy, always going back to her from every transient fancy--her property, her chattel; and the foremost wits and dandies of the age for her servants, her Court of adorers, whom she ruled with frowns or smiles, as her humour prompted. To be daring, profuse, reckless, tyrannical; to suffer no control of heaven or men--yes, that was, indeed, to be a Queen! And compared with such empire, the poor authority of the Precieuse, dictating the choice of adjectives, condemning pronouns, theorising upon feelings and passions of which in practice she knows nothing, was a thing for scornfullest laughter.

CHAPTER XX.
PHILASTER.

January was nearly over, the memorial service for the martyred King was drawing near, and royalty and fashion had deserted Whitehall for Hampton Court; yet the Farehams lingered at their riverside mansion. His lordship had business in London, while Sir Denzil Warner, who came to Fareham House daily, was also detained in the city by some special attraction, which made hawk and hound, and even his worthy mother's company, indifferent to him.

Lady Fareham had an air of caring for neither town nor country, but on the whole preferred town.

"London has become a positive desert--and the smoke from the smouldering ruins poisons the garden and terrace whenever there is an east wind," she complained. "But Oxfordshire would be a worse desert--and I believe I should die of the spleen in a week, if I trusted myself in that great rambling Abbey. I can just suffer life in London; so I suppose I had best stay till his lordship has finished his business, about which he is so secret and mysterious."

Denzil was more devoted, more solicitous to please than ever; and had a better chance of pleasing now that most of her ladyship's fine visitors had left town. He read aloud to Hyacinth and her sister as they worked--or pretended to work-- at their embroidery frames. He played the organ, and sang duets with Angela. He walked with her on the terrace, in the cold, bleak afternoon, and told her the news of the town--not the scandals and trivialities which alone interested Lady Fareham, but the graver facts connected with the state and the public welfare--the prospects of war or peace, the outlook towards France and Spain, Holland and Sweden, Andrew Marvel's last speech, or the last grant to the King, who might be relied on to oppose no popular measure when his lieges were about to provide a handsome subsidy or an increase of his revenue.

"We are winning our liberties from him," Denzil said.

"For the mess of pottage we give, the money he squanders on libertine pleasures, England is buying freedom. Yet why, in the name of common sense, maintain this phantom King, this Court which shocks and outrages every decent Englishman's sense of right, and maintains an ever-widening hotbed of corruption, so that habits and extravagances once unknown beyond that focus of all vice, are now spreading as fast as London; and wherever there are bricks and mortar there are profligacy and irreligion? Can you wonder that all the best and wisest in this city regret Cromwell's iron rule, the rule of the strongest, and deplore that so bold a stroke for liberty should have ended in such foolish subservience to a King of whom we knew nothing when we begged him to come and reign over us?"

"But if you win liberty while he is King, if wise laws are established--"

"Yes; but we might have been noble as well as free. There is something so petty in our resumed bondage. Figure to yourself a thoroughbred horse that had kicked off the traces, and stood free upon the open plain with arched neck and lifted nostrils, sniffing the morning air! and behold he creeps back to his harness, and makes himself again a slave! We had done with the Stuarts, at the cost of a tragedy, and in ten years we call them back again, and put on the old shackles; and for common sense, religion, and freedom, we have the orgies of Whitehall, and the extravagance of Lady Castlemaine. It will not last, Angela; it cannot last. I was with his lordship in Artillery Row last night, and we talked with the blind sage who would sacrifice the remnant of his darkened days in the cause of liberty."

"Sir Denzil, I hope you are not plotting mischief--you and my brother," Angela said anxiously. "You are so often together; and his lordship has such a preoccupied air."

"No, no, there is no conspiring; but there is plenty of discontent. It would need but little to fire the train. Can any man in his senses be happy when he sees his country, which ten years ago was at the pinnacle of power and renown, sinking to the appanage of a foreign sovereign; England threatened with a return to Rome; honest men forbidden to preach the gospel; and innocent seekers after truth hounded off to gaol, to rot among malefactors, because they have dared to worship God after their own fashion?"

"Where was your liberty of conscience under the Protectorate, when the Liturgy was forbidden as if it were an unholy thing, when the Anglican priests were turned out of their pulpits, and the Anglican service tolerated in only one church in all this vast London?" Angela asked indignantly.

"That was a revolt of deep thinkers against a service which has all the mechanical artifice of Romanism without its strong appeal to the heart and the senses--dry, empty, rigid--a repetition of vain phrases. If I am ever to bow my neck beneath the Church's yoke, let me swallow the warm-blooded errors of Papacy rather than the heartless formalism of English Episcopacy."

"But what can you or Fareham--or a few good men like you--do to change established things? Remember Venner's plot, and how many lives were wasted on that foolish, futile attempt. You can only hazard your lives, die on the scaffold. Or would you like to see civil war again; the nation divided into opposite camps; Englishmen fighting with Englishmen? Can you forget that dreadful last year of the Rebellion? I was only a little child; but it is branded deep on my memory. Can you forget the murder of the King? He was murdered; let Mr. Milton defend the deed as he can with his riches of big words. I have wept over the royal martyr's own account of his sufferings."

"Over Dr. Gauden's account, that is to say. 'Eikon Basilike' was no more written by Charles than by Cromwell. It was a doctored composition--a churchman's spurious history, trumped up by Charles's friends and partisans, possibly with the approval of the King himself. It is a fine piece of special pleading in a bad cause."

"You make me hate you when you talk so slightingly of that so ill-used King. You will make me hate you more if you lead Fareham into danger by underhand work against the present King."

"Lies Fareham's safety so very near your heart?"

"It lies in my heart," she answered, looking at him, and defying him with straight, clear gaze. "Is he not my sister's husband, and to me as a brother? Do you expect me to be careless about his fate? I know you are leading him into danger. Some mischief must come of these visits to Mr. Milton, a Republican outlaw, who has escaped the penalty of his treasonous pamphlets only because he is blind and old and poor. I doubt there is danger in all such conferences. Fareham is at heart a Republican. It would need little persuasion to make him a traitor to the King."

"You have it in your power to make me so much your slave, that I would sacrifice every patriotic aspiration at your bidding, Angela," Denzil answered gravely.

"I know not if this be the time to speak, or if, after waiting more than a year, I may not even now be premature. Dearest girl, you know that I love you--that I haunt this house only because you live here; that I am in London only because my star shines there; that above all public interests you rule my life. I have exercised a prodigious patience, only because I have a prodigious resolution. Is it not time for me to reap my reward?"

"Oh, Denzil, you fill me with sorrow! Have I not said everything to discourage you?"

"And have I not refused to be discouraged? Angela, I am resolved to discover the reason of your coldness. Was there ever a young and lovely woman who shut love out of her heart? History has no record of such an one. I am of an appropriate age, of good birth and good means, not under-educated, not brutish, or of repulsive face and figure. If your heart is free I ought to be able to win it. If you will not favour my suit, it must be because there is some one else, some one who came before me, or who has crossed my path, and to whom your heart has been secretly given."

She had turned from red to pale as he spoke. She stood before him in the winter light, with her colour changing, her hands tightly clasped, her eyes cast down, and tears trembling on the long dark lashes.

"You have no right to question me. It is enough for you to have my honest answer. I esteem you, but I do not love you; and it distresses me when you talk of love."

"There is some one else, then! I knew it. There is some one else. For me you are marble. You are fire for him. He is in your heart. You have said it"

"How dare you----" she began.

"Why should I shrink from warning you of your danger? It is Fareham you love. I have seen you tremble at his touch--start at the sound of his footstep--that step you know so well. His footstep? Why, the very air he breathes carries to you the consciousness of his approach. Oh, I have watched you both, Angela; and I know, I know. Jealous pangs have racked me, day after day; yet I have hung on. I have been very patient. 'She knows not the sinful impulses of her own heart,' I said, 'knows not in her purity how near she goes to a fall. Here, in her sister's house, passionately loved by her sister's husband! She calls him 'brother,' whose eyes can-not look at her without telling their story of wicked love. She walks on the edge of a precipice--self-deceived. Were I to abandon her she might fall. My affection is her only safeguard; and by winning her to myself I shall snatch her from the pit of hell.'"

It was the truth he was telling her. Yes; even when Fareham was harshest, she had been dimly conscious that love was at the root of his unkindness. The coldness that had held them apart since that midnight meeting had been ice over fire. It was jealousy that had made him so angry. No word of love, directly spoken, had ever offended her ear; but there had been many a speech of double meaning that had set her wondering and thinking.

And, oh! the guilt of it, when an honourable man like Denzil set her sin before her, in plain language. She stood aghast at her own wickedness. That which had been a sin of thought only, a secret sorrow, wrestled with in many an hour of heart-felt prayer, with all the labour of a soul that sought heavenly aid against earthly temptation, was conjured into hideous reality by Denzil's plain speech. To love her sister's husband, to suffer his guilty love, to know gladness only in his company, to be exquisitely happy were he but in the same room with her--to sink to profound-est melancholy when he was absent. Oh, the sin of it! In what degree did her guilt differ from that of the women of the Court, who had each her open secret in some base intrigue that all the world knew and laughed at? She had been kept aloof from that libertine crew; but was she any better than they? Was Fareham, who openly scorned the royal debauchee, was he any better than the King?

She remembered how he had talked of Lord Sandwich, making excuses for a perverted love. She had heard him speak of other offenders in the same strain. He had been ever ready to recognise fatality where a good Catholic would have per-ceived only sin.

"Angela, believe me, you are drifting helmless in perilous waters," Denzil urged, while she stood beside him in mute distress. "Let me be your strong rock. Only give me the promise of your hand. I can be patient still. I will give time for love to grow. Grant me but the right to guard you from the danger of an unholy passion that is always near you in this house."

"You pretend to be his lordship's friend, and you speak slander of him."

"I am his friend. I could find it in my heart to pity him for loving you. Indeed, it has been in friendship that I have tried to interest him in a great national question--to wean him from his darling sin. But were you my wife he should never cross our threshold. The day that made us one should make you and Fareham strangers. It is for you to choose, Angela, between two men who love you--one near your own age, free, God-fearing; the other nearly old enough to be your father, bound by the tie which your Church deems indissoluble, whose love is insult and pollution, and can but end in shame and despair. It is for you to choose between honest and dishonest love."

"There is a nobler choice open to me," she said, more calmly than she had yet spoken, and with a pale dignity in her countenance that awed him. A thrill of ad-miration and fear ran along his nerves as he looked at her. She seemed transfigured. "There is a higher and better love," she said. "This is not the first time that I have considered a sure way out of all my difficulties. I can go back to the convent where, in my dear Aunt Anastasia, I saw so splendid an example of a holy life hidden from the world."

"Life buried in a living grave!" cried Denzil, horror-stricken at the idea of such a sacrifice. "Free-will and reason obscured in a cloud of incense! All the great uses of a noble life brought down to petty observances and childish mummeries, prayers and genuflections before waxen relics and dressed-up madonnas. Oh, my dearest girl, next worst only to the dominion of sin is the slavery of a false religion. I would have thee free as air--free and enlightened--released from the trammels of Rome, happy in thyself and useful to thy fellow-creatures."

"You see, Sir Denzil, even if we loved each other, we could never think alike," Angela said, with a gentle sadness. "Our minds would always dwell far apart. Things that are dear and sacred to me are hateful to you."

"If you love me I could win you to my way of thinking," he said.

"You mean that if I loved you I should love you better than I love God?"

"Not so, dear. But you would open your mind to the truth. St. Paul sanctified union between Christian and pagan, and deemed the unbelieving wife sanctified by the believing husband. There can be no sin, therefore, despite my poor mother's violent opinions, in the union of those who worship the same God, and whose creed differs only in particulars. 'How knowest thou, O man, whether thou shalt save thy wife?' Indeed, love, I doubt not my power to wean you from the errors of your early education."

"Cannot you see how wide apart we are? Every word you say widens the gulf betwixt us. Indeed, Sir Denzil, you had best remain my friend. You can be nothing else."

She turned from him almost impatiently. Young, handsome, of a frank and generous nature, he yet lacked the gifts that charm women; or at least this one woman was cold to him. It might be that in his own nature there was a coldness, a something wanting, the fire we miss in that great poet of the age, whose verse could rise to themes transcendent, but never burnt with the white heat of human passion.

Papillon came flying along the terrace, her skirts and waving tresses spread wide in the wind, a welcome intruder.

"What are you and Sir Denzil doing in the cold? I have news for my dear, dearest auntie. My lord is in a good humour, and *Philaster* is to be acted by the Duke's servants, and her ladyship's footmen are keeping places for us in the boxes. I have only seen three plays in my life, and they were all sad ones. I wish *Philaster* was a comedy. I should like to see ***Love in a Tub***. That must be full of drollery. But his honour likes only grave plays. Be brisk, auntie! The coach will be at the door directly. Come and put on your hood. His lordship says we need no masks. I should have loved to wear a mask. Are you coming to the play, Sir Denzil?"

"I know not if I am bidden, or if there be a place for me."

"Why, you can stand with the fops in the pit, and you can buy us some China oranges. I heard Lady Sarah tell my mother that the new little actress with the pretty feet was once an orange-girl, who lived with Lord Buckhurst. Why did he have an orange-girl to live with him? He must be vastly fond of oranges. I should love to sell oranges in the pit, if I could be an actress afterwards. I would rather be an actress than a duchess. Mademoiselle taught me Chimene's tirades in Corneille's ***Cid***. I learn quicker than any pupil she ever had. Monsieur de Malfort once said I was a born actress," pursued Papillon, as they walked to the house.

Philaster! That story of unhappy love--so pure, patient, melancholy, disinterested. How often Angela had hung over the page, in the solitude of her own chamber! And to hear the lines spoken to-day, when a tempest of emotion had been raised in her breast, with Fareham by her side; to meet his glances at this or that moment of the play, when the devoted girl was revealing the secret of her passionate heart. Yet never was love freer from taint of sin, and the end of the play was in no wise tragic. That pure affection was encouraged and sanctified by the happy bride. Bellario was not to be banished, but sheltered.

Alas! yes; but this was love unreturned. There was no answering warmth on Philaster's part, no fire of passion to scathe and destroy; only a gentle gratitude for the girl's devotion--a brother's, not a lover's regard.

She found Fareham and her sister in the hall, ready to step into the coach.

"I saw the name of your favourite play on the posts as I walked home," he said; "and as Hyacinth is always teasing me for denying her the play-house, I thought this was a good opportunity for pleasing you both."

"You would have pleased me more if you had offered me the chance of seeing a new comedy," his wife retorted, pettishly.

"Ah, dearest, let us not resume an old quarrel. The play-wrights of Elizabeth's age were poets and gentlemen. The men who write for us are blackguards and empty-headed fops. We have novelty, which is all most of us want, a hundred new plays in a year, of which scarce one will be remembered after the year is out."

"Who wants to remember? The highest merit in a play is that it should be a reflection of to-day; and who minds if it be stale to-morrow? To hold the mirror up to nature, doesn't your Shakespeare say? And what more transient than the image in a glass? A comedy should be like one's hat or one's gown, the top of the mode to-day, and cast off and forgotten, in a week."

"That is what our fine gentlemen think; who are satisfied if their wit gets three days' acceptance, and some substantial compliment from the patron to whom they dedicate their trash."

His lordship's liveries and four grey horses made a stir in Lincoln's Inn Fields, and startled the crowd at the doors of the New Theatre; and within the house Lady Fareham and her sister divided the attention of the pit with their royal highnesses the Duke and Duchess, who no longer amused or scandalised the audience by those honeymoon coquetries which had distinguished their earlier appearances in public. Duchess Anne was growing stout, and fast losing her beauty, and Duke James was imitating his brother's infidelities, after his own stealthy fashion; so it may be that Clarendon's daughter was no more happy than her sister-in-law the Queen, nor than her father the Chancellor, over whom the shadows of royal disfavour were darkening.

Lady Fareham lolled languidly back in her box, and let all the audience see her indifference to Fletcher's poetic dialogue. Angela sat motionless, her hands clasped in her lap, entranced by that romantic story, and the acting which gave life and reality to that poetic fable, as well it might when the incomparable Betterton played Philaster. Fareham stood beside his wife, looking down at the stage, and sometimes, as Angela looked up, their eyes met in one swift flash of responsive thought; met and glanced away, as if each knew the peril of such meetings--

> "If it be love
> To forget all respect of his own friends
> In thinking on your face."

Was it by chance that Fareham sighed as those lines were spoken? And again--

"If, when he goes to rest (which will not be),
'Twixt every prayer he says he names you once."

And again, was it chance that brought that swift, half-angry, questioning look upon her from those severe eyes in the midst of Philaster's tirade?--

"How heaven is in your eyes, but in your hearts
More hell than hell has; how your tongues, like scorpions,
Both heal and poison; how your thoughts are woven
With thousand changes in one subtle web,
And worn so by you. How that foolish man
That reads the story of a woman's face,
And dies believing it is lost for ever."

It was Angela whose eyes unconsciously sought his when that passage occurred which had written itself upon her heart long ago at Chilton when she first read the play--

"Alas, my lord, my life is not a thing
Worthy your noble thoughts; 'tis not a life,
'Tis but a piece of childhood thrown away."

What was her poor life worth--so lonely even in her sister's house--so desolate when his eyes looked not upon her in kindness? After having lived for two brief summers and winters in his cherished company, having learnt to know what a proud, honourable man was like, his disdain of vice, his indifference to Court favour, his aspirations for liberty; after having known him, and loved him with silent and secret love, what better could she do than bury herself within convent walls, and spend the rest of her days in praying for those she loved? Alas, he had such need that some faithful soul should soar heavenward in supplication for him who had himself so weak a hold upon the skies! Alas, to think of him as unbelieving, putting his trust in the opinions of infidels like Hobbes and Spinoza, rather than leaning on that Rock of Ages the Church of St. Peter.

If she could not live for him--if it were a sin even to dwell under the same roof with him--she could at least die for him--die to the world of pleasure and folly, of beauty and splendour, die to friendship and love; sink all individuality under the monastic rule; cease to be, except as a part in a great organisation, an atom acting and acted upon by higher powers; surrendering every desire and every hope that distinguished her from the multitude of women vowed to a holy life.

"Never, sir, will I   Marry; it is a thing within my vow."

The voice of the actress sounded silver-clear as Bellario spoke her last speech, finishing her story of a love which can submit to take the lower place, and asks but little of fate.

"It is a thing within my vow."

The line repeated itself in Angela's mind as Denzil met them at the door, and handed her into the coach.

Should she prove of weaker stuff than the sad Eufrasia, and accept a husband she did not love? This humdrum modern age allowed of no romance. She could not stain her face with walnut juice, and disguise herself as a footboy, and live unknown in his service, to wait upon him when he was weary, to nurse him when he was sick. Such a life she would have deemed exquisitely happy; but the hard everyday world had no room for such dreams. In this unromantic age Dion's daughter would be recognised within twenty-four hours of her putting on male attire. The golden days of poetry were dead. Una would find no lion to fawn at her feet. She would be mobbed in the Strand.

"Oh, that it could have been!" thought Angela, as the coach jolted and rumbled through the narrow ways, and shaved awkward corners with its ponderous wheels, and got its horses entangled with other noble teams, to the provocation of much ill-language from postillions, and flunkeys, and linkmen, for it was dark when they came out of the theatre, and a thick mist was rising from the river, and flambeaux were flaring up and down the dim narrow thoroughfares.

"They light the streets better in Paris," complained Hyacinth. "In the Rue de Touraine we had a lamp to every house."

"I like to see the links moving up and down," said Papillon; "'tis ever so much prettier than lanterns that stand still--like that one at the corner."

She pointed to a small round lamp that made a bubble of light in an abyss of gloom.

"Here the lamps stink more than they light," said Hyacinth. "How the coach rocks--those blockheads will end by upsetting it. I should have been twice as well in my chair."

Angela sat in her place, lost in thought, and hardly conscious of the jolting coach, or of Papillon's prattle, who would not be satisfied till she had dragged her aunt into the conversation.

"Did you not love the play, and would you not love to be a princess like Arethusa, and to wear such a necklace? Mother's diamonds are not half as big."

"Pshaw, child, 'twas absolute glass--arrant trumpery."

"But her gown was not trumpery. It was Lady Castlemaine's last birthday gown. I heard a lady telling her friend about it in the seat next mine. Lady Castlemaine gave it to the actress; and it cost three hundred pounds--and Lady Castlemaine is all that there is of the most extravagant, the lady said, and old Rowley has to pay her debts--(who is old Rowley, and why does he pay people's debts?)--though she is the most unscrupulous--I forget the word--in London."

"You see, madam, what a good school the play-house is for your child," said Fareham grimly.

"I never asked you to take our child there."

"Nay, Hyacinth; but a mother should enter no scene unfit for her daughter's innocence."

"Oh, my lord, your opinions are of the Protectorate. You would be better in New England--tilling your fields reclaimed from the waste."

"Yes, I might be better there, reclaimed from the waste--of London life. Strange that your talk should hit upon New England. I was thinking of that New World not an hour ago at the play--thinking what a happy innocent life a man might lead there, were he but young and free, with one he loved."

"Innocent, yes; happy, no; unless he were a savage or a peasant," Hyacinth exclaimed disdainfully. "We that have known the grace and beauty of life cannot go back to the habits of our ancestors, to eat without forks, and cover our floors with rushes instead of Persian carpets."

"The beauty and grace of life--houses that are whited sepulchres, banquets where there is no love."

The coach stopped before the tall Italian doorway, and Fareham handed out his wife and sister in silence; but there was one of the party to whom it was unnatural to be mute.

Papillon sprang off the coach step into her father's arms.

"Sweetheart, why are you so sad?" she asked. "You look more unhappy than Philaster when he thought his lady loved him not."

She would not be put off, but hung about him all the length of the corridor, to the door of his room, where he parted from her with a kiss on her forehead.

"How your lips burn!" she cried. "I hope you are not sickening for the plague. I dreamt last night that the contagion had come back; and that our new glass coach was going about with a bell collecting the dead."

"Thou hadst eaten too much supper, sweet. Such dreams are warnings against excess of pies and jellies. Go, love; I have business."

"You have always business now. You used to let me stay with you--even when you was busy," Henriette remonstrated, dejectedly, as the sonorous oak door closed against her.

Fareham flung himself into his chair in front of the large table, with its heaped-up books and litter of papers. Straight before him there lay Milton's pamphlet--a publication of ten years ago; but he had been reading it only that morning--"The Doctrine and Discipline of Divorce."

There were sentences which seemed to him to stand out upon the page, almost as if written in fire; and to these he recurred again and again, brooding over and weighing every word. "....Neither can this law be of force to engage a blameless creature to his own perpetual sorrow, mistaken for his expected solace, without suffering charity to step in and do a confessed good work of parting those whom nothing holds together but this of God's joining, falsely supposed against the express end of his own ordinance.... 'It is not good,' said He, 'that man should be alone; I will make him a helpmeet for him.' From which words, so plain, less cannot be concluded, nor is by any learned interpreter, than that in God's intention a meet and happy conversation is the chiefest and noblest end of marriage.... Again, where the mind is unsatisfied, the solitariness of man, which God had namely and principally ordered to prevent by marriage, hath no remedy, but lies in a worse condition than the loneliest single life; for in single life the absence and remoteness of a helper might inure him to expect his own comforts out of himself, or to seek with hope; but here the continual sight of his deluded thoughts, without cure, must needs be to him, if especially his complexion incline him to melancholy, a daily trouble and pain of loss, in some degree like that which reprobates feel."

He closed the book, and started up to pace the long, lofty room, full of shadow, betwixt the light of the fire and that one pair of candles on his reading desk.

"Reprobate! Yes. Am not I a reprobate, and the worst, plotting against innocence? New England," he repeated to himself. "How much the name promises. A new world, a new life, and old fetters struck off. God, if it could be done! It would hurt no one--no one--except perhaps those children, who might suffer a brief sorrow--and it would make two lives happy that must be blighted else. Two lives! Am I so sure of her? Yes, if eyes speak true. Sure as of my own fond passion. The contagion, quotha! I have suffered that, sweet, and know its icy sweats and parching heats; but 'tis not so fierce a fever as that devilish disease, the longing for your company."

CHAPTER XXI.
GOOD-BYE, LONDON.

Sitting in her own room before supper, a letter was brought to Angela--a long letter, closely written, in a neat, firm hand she knew very well.

It was from Denzil Warner; a letter full of earnest thought and warm feeling, in which he pursued the subject of their morning's discourse.

"We were interrupted before I had time to open my heart to you, dearest," he wrote; "and at a moment when we had touched on the most delicate point in our friendship--the difference in our religious education and observance. Oh, my beloved, let not difference in particulars divide two hearts that worship the same God, or make a barrier between two minds that think alike upon essentials. The Christ who died for you is not less my Saviour because I love not to obtrude the dressed-up image of His earthly mother between His Godhead and my prayers. In the regeneration of baptism, in the sanctity of marriage, in the resurrection of the body, and the life of the world to come, in the reality of sin and the necessity for repentance, I believe as truly as any Papist living. Let our lives be but once united, who knows how the future may shape and modify our minds and our faith? I may be brought to your way of thinking, or you to mine. I will pledge myself never to be guilty of disrespect to your religion, or to unkindly urge you to any change in your observances. I am not one of those who have exchanged one tyranny for another, and who, released from the dominion of Rome, have become the slave of the Covenant. I have been taught by one who, himself deeply religious, would have all men free to worship God by the light of their own conscience; and to my wife, that dearer half of my soul, I would allow perfect freedom. I suffer from the lack of poetic phrases with which to embellish the plain reality of my love; but be sure, Angela, that you may travel far through the world, and receive many a flowery compliment to your beauty, yet meet none who will love you as faithfully as I have loved you for this year last past, and as I doubt I shall love you--happy or unfortunate in my wooing--for all the rest of my life. Think, dearest, whether it were not wise on your part to accept the chaste and respectful homage of a suitor who is free to love and cherish you, and thus to shield yourself from the sinful pursuit of one who offends Heaven and dishonours you whenever he looks at you with the eyes of a lover. I would not write harshly of a man whose very sin I pity, and whom I believe not wholly vile; but for him, as for me, that were a happy day which should make you my wife, and thus end the madness of unholy hopes. I would again urge that Lady Fareham desires our union with all a sister's concern for you, and more than a friend's tenderness to me.

"I beseech your pardon and indulgence for my rough words of this morning. God forbid that I should impute one unworthy thought to her whose virtues I honour above all earthly merit. If your heart inclines towards one whom it were misery for you to love, I know that it must be with an affection pure and ethereal as the love of the disguised girl in Fletcher's play. But, ah, dearest angel, you know not the peril in which you walk. Your innocent mind cannot conceive the audacious height to which unholy love may climb in a man's fiery nature. You cannot fathom the black depths of such a character as Fareham--a man as capable of greatness in evil as of distinction in good. Forget not whose fierce blood runs in those veins. Can you doubt his audacity in wrong-doing, when you remember that he comes of the same stock which produced that renegade and tyrant, Thomas Wentworth--a man who would have waded deep in the blood of a nation to reach his desired goal, all the history of whose life was expressed by him in one word--'thorough'?

"Do you consider what that word means to a man over whose heart sin has taken the upper hand? Thorough! How resolute in evil, how undaunted and without limit in baseness, is he who takes that word for his motto! Oh, my love, there are dragons and lions about thy innocent footsteps--the dragons of lust, the lions of presumptuous love. Flee from thy worst enemy, dearest, to the shelter of a heart which adores thee; lean upon a breast whose pulses beat for thee with a truth that time cannot change.

"Thine till death,

"WARNER."

Angela tore up the letter in anger. How dared he write thus of Lord Fareham? To impute sinful passions, guilty desires--to enter into another man's mind, and read the secret cipher of his thoughts and wishes with an assumed key, which might be false? His letter was a bundle of false assumptions. What right had he to insist that her brother-in-law cared for her with more than the affection authorised by affinity? He had no right. She hated him for his insolent letter. She scorned the protection of his love. She had her refuge and her shelter in a holier love than his. The doors of the old home would open to her at a word.

She sat on a low stool in front of the hearth, while the pile of ship timber on the andirons burnt itself out and turned from red to grey. She sat looking into the dying fire and recalling the pictures of the past; the dull grey convent rooms and formal convent garden; the petty rules and restrictions; the so-frequent functions--low mass and high, benedictions, vespers--the recurrent sound of the chapel bell. The few dull books, permitted in the hour of so-called recreation; the sombre grey gown, which was the only relief from perpetual black; the limitations of that colourless life. She had been happy with the Ursulines under her kinswoman's gentle sway. But could she be happy with the present Superior, whose domineering temper she knew? She had been happy in her ignorance of the outer world; but could she be happy again in that grey seclusion--she who had sat at the banquet of life, who had seen the beauty and the variety of her native land? To be an exile for the rest of her days, in the hopeless gloom of a Flemish convent, among the heavy faces of Flemish nuns!

In the intensity of introspective thought she had forgotten one who had forbidden that gloomy seclusion, and to whom it would be as natural for her to look for protection and refuge as to convent or husband. From her thoughts to-night the image of her wandering father had been absent. His appearances in her life had been so rare and so brief, his influence on her destiny so slight, that she was forgetful of him now in this crisis of her fate.

*   *   *   *   *

It was within a week of that evening that the sisters were startled by the arrival of their father, unannounced, in the dusk of the winter afternoon. He had come by slow stages from Spain, riding the greater part of the journey--like Howell, fifty years earlier--attended only by one faithful soldier-servant, and enduring no small suffering, and running no slight risk, upon the road.

"The wolves had our provender on more than one occasion," he told them. "The wonder is they never had us or our hackneys. I left Madrid in July, not long after the death of my poor friend Fanshawe. Indeed, it was his friendship and his good lady's unvarying courtesy that took me to the capital. We had last met at Hampton Court, with the King, shortly before his Majesty's so ill-advised flight; and we were bosom-friends then. And so, he being dead of a fever early in the summer, I had no more to do but to travel slowly homeward, to end my days in my own chimney-corner, and to claim thy promise, Angela, that thou wouldst keep my house, and comfort my declining years."

"Dear father!" Angela murmured, hanging over him as he sat in the high-backed velvet chair by the fire, while her ladyship's footmen set a table near him, with wine and provisions for an impromptu meal, Lady Fareham directing them, and coming between-whiles to embrace her father in a flutter of spirits, the fire-light shining on her flame-coloured velvet gown and primrose taffety petticoat, her pretty golden curls and sparkling Sevigne, her ruby necklace and earrings, and her bright restless eyes.

While the elder sister was all movement and agitation, the younger stood calm and still beside her father's chair, her hands clasped in his, her thoughtful eyes looking down at him as he talked, stopping now and then in his story of adventures to eat and drink.

He looked much older than when he surprised her in the Convent garden. His hair and beard, then iron grey, were now silver white. He wore his own hair, which was abundant, and a beard cut after the fashion she knew in the portraits of Henri Quatre. His clothes also were of that style, which lived now only in the paintings of Vandyke and his school.

"How the girl looks at me!" Sir John said, surprising his daughter's earnest gaze. "Does she take me for a ghost?"

"Indeed, sir, she may well fancy you have come back from the other world while you wear that antique suit," said Hyacinth. "I hope your first business to-morrow will be to replenish your wardrobe by the assistance of Lord Rochester's tailor. He is a German, and has the best cut for a justau-corps in all the West End. Fareham is shabby enough to make a wife ashamed of him; but his clothes are only too plain for his condition. Your Spanish cloak and steeple hat are fitter for a travelling quack doctor than for a gentleman of quality, and your doublet and vest might have come out of the ark."

"If I change them, it will be but to humour your vanity, sweetheart," answered her father. "I bought the suit in Paris three years ago, and I swore I would cast them back upon the snip's hands if he gave me any new-fangled finery. But a riding-suit that has crossed the Pyrenees and stood a winter's wear at Montpelier--where I have been living since October--can scarce do credit to a fine lady's saloon; and thou art finest, I'll wager, Hyacinth, where all are fine."

"You would not say that if you had seen Lady Castlemaine's rooms. I would wager that her gold and silver tapestry cost more than the contents of my house."

"Thou shouldst not envy sin in high places, Hyacinth."

"Envy! I envy a----"

"Nay, love, no bad names! 'Tis a sorry pass England has come to when the most conspicuous personage at her Court is the King's mistress. I was with Queen Henrietta at Paris, who received me mighty kindly, and bewailed with me over the contrast betwixt her never-to-be-forgotten husband and his sons. They have nothing of their father, she told me, neither in person nor in mind. 'I know not whence their folly comes to them!' she cried. It would have been uncivil to remind her that her own father, hero as he was, had set no saintly example to royal husbands; and that it is possible our princes take more of their character from their grandfather Henry than from the martyr Charles. Poor lady, I am told she left London deep in debt, after squandering her noble income of these latter years, and that she has sunk in the esteem of the French court by her alliance with Jermyn."

"I can but wonder that she, above all women, should ever cease to be a widow."

"She comes of a light-minded race and nation, Angela; and it is easy to her to forget; or she would not easily forget that so-adoring husband whose fortunes she ruined. His most fatal errors came from his subservience to her. When I saw her in her new splendour at Somerset House, all smiles and gaiety, with youth and beauty revived in the sunshine of restored fortune, I could but remember all he was, in dignity and manly affection, proud and pure as King Arthur in the old romance, and all she cost him by womanish tyrannies and prejudices, and difficult commands laid upon him at a juncture of so exceeding difficulty."

The sisters listened in respectful silence. The old cavalier cut a fresh slice of chine, sighed, and continued his sermon.

"I doubt that while we, the lookers on, remember, they, the actors, forget; for could the son of such a noble victim wallow in a profligate court, surrender himself to the devilish necromancies of vicious women and viler men, if he remembered his father's character, and his father's death? No; memory must be a blank, and we, who suffered with our royal master, are fools to prate of ingratitude or neglect, since the son who can forget such a father may well forget his father's servants and friends. But we will not talk of public matters in the first hour of our greeting. Nor need I prate of the King, since I have not come back to England to clap a periwig over my grey hairs, and play waiter upon Court favour, and wear out the back of my coat against the tapestry at Whitehall, standing in the rear of the crowd, to have my toes trampled upon by the sharp heels of Court ladies, and an elbow in my stomach more often than not. I am come, like Wolsey, girls, to lay my old bones among you. Art thou ready, Angela? Hast thou had enough of London, and play-houses, and parks; and wilt thou share thy father's solitude in Buckinghamshire?"

"With all my heart, sir."

"What! never a sigh for London pleasures? Thou hast the great lady's air and carriage in that brave blue taffety. The nun I knew three years ago has vanished. Can you so lightly renounce the splendour of this house, and your sister's company, to make a prosing old father happy?"

"Indeed, sir, I am ready to go with you."

"How she says that--with what a countenance of woeful resignation! But I will not make the Manor Moat too severe a prison, dearest. You shall visit London, and your sister, when you will. There shall be a coach and a team of stout roadsters to pull it when they are not wanted for the plough. And the Vale of Aylesbury is but a long day's journey from London, while 'tis no more than a morning's ride to Chilton."

"I could not bear for her to be long away from me," said Hyacinth. "She is the only companion I have in the world."

"Except your husband."

"Husbands such as mine are poor company. Fareham has a moody brow, and a mind stuffed with public matters. He dines with Clarendon one day, and with Albemarle another; or he goes to Deptford to grumble with Mr. Evelyn; or he creeps away to some obscure quarter of the town to hob-nob with Milton, and with Marvel, the member for Hull. I doubt they are all of one mind in abusing his Majesty, and conspiring against him. If I lose my sister I shall have no one."

"What, no one; when you have Henriette, who even three years ago had shrewdness enough to keep an old grandfather amused with her impertinent prattle?"

"Grandfathers are easily amused by children they see as seldom as you have seen Papillon. To have her about you all day, with her everlasting chatter, and questions, and remarks, and opinions (a brat of twelve with opinions), would soon give you the vapours."

"I am not so subject to vapours as you, child. Let me look at you, now the candles are lighted."

The footmen had lighted clusters of wax candles on either side the tall chimney-piece.

Sir John drew his elder daughter to the light, and scrutinised her face with a father's privilege of uncompromising survey.

"You paint thick enough, i' conscience' name, though not quite so thick as the

Spanish senoras. They are browner than you, and need a heavier hand with white and red. But you are haggard under all your red. You are not the woman I left in '65."

"I am near two years older than the woman you left; and as for paint, there is not a woman over twenty in London who uses as little red and white as I do."

"What has become of Fareham to-night?" Sir John asked presently, when Hyacinth had picked up her favourite spaniel to nurse and fondle, while Angela had resumed her occupation at an embroidery frame, and a reposeful air as of a long-established domesticity had fallen upon the scene.

"He is at Chilton. When he is not plotting he rushes off to Oxfordshire for the hunting and shooting. He loves buglehorns and yelping curs, and huntsmen's cracked voices, far before the company of ladies or the conversation of wits."

"A man was never meant to sit in a velvet chair and talk fine. It is all one for a French Abbe and a few old women in men's clothing to sit round the room and chop logic with a learned spinster like Mademoiselle Scudery; but men must live *sub Jove*, unless they are statesmen or clerks. They must have horses and hounds, gun and spaniel, hawk or rod. I am glad Fareham loves sport. And as for that talk of conspiring, let me not hear it from thee, Hyacinth. 'Tis a perilous discourse to but hint at treason; and your husband is a loyal gentleman who loves, and"--with a wry face--"reveres--his King."

"Oh, I was only jesting. But, indeed, a man who so disparages the things other people love must needs be a rebel at heart. Did you hear of Monsieur de Malfort while you were at Paris?"

The inquiry was made with that over-acted carelessness which betrays hidden pain; but the soldier's senses had been blunted by the rough-and-tumble of an adventurer's life, and he was not on the alert for shades of feeling.

Angela accepted her father's return, with the new duties it imposed upon her, as if it had been a decree of Heaven. She put aside all consideration of that refuge which would have meant so complete a renunciation and farewell. On her knees that night, in the midst of fervent prayers, her tears streamed fast at the thought that, secure in the shelter of her father's love, in the peaceful solitude of her native valley, she could look to a far-off future when she and Fareham might meet without fear of sin, when no cloud of passion should darken his brotherly affection for her; when his heart, now estranged from holy things, would have returned to the faith of his ancestors, reconciled to God and the Church. She could but think of him now as a fallen angel--a wanderer who had strayed far from the only light and guide of human life, and was thus a mark for the tempter. What lesser power than Satan's could have so turned good to evil; the friendship of a brother to the base passion which had made so wide a gulf between them; and which must keep them strangers till he was cured of his sin? Only to diabolical possession could she ascribe the change that had come over him since those happy days when she had watched the slow dawn of health upon his sunken cheeks, when he and she had travelled together through the rich autumn woods, along the pleasant English roads, and when, in the leisure of the slow journey, he had poured out his thoughts to her, the story of his life, his opinions, expatiating in fraternal confidence upon the things he loved and the things he hated. And at Chilton, she looked back and remembered his goodness to her, the pains he had taken in choosing horses for her to ride, their long mornings on the river with Henriette, their hawking parties, and in all his tender brotherly care of her. The change in him had come about by almost imperceptible degrees: but it had been chiefly marked by a fitful temper that had cut her to the quick; now kind; now barely civil; courting her company to-day; to-morrow avoiding her, as if there were contagion in her presence. Then, after the meeting at Millbank, there had come a coldness so icy, a sarcasm so cutting, that for a long time she had thought he hated as much as he despised her. She had withered in his contempt. His unkindness had overshadowed every hour of her life, and the longing to cry out to him "Indeed, sir, your thoughts wrong me. I am not the wretch you think," had been almost too much for her fortitude. She had felt that she must exculpate herself, even though in so doing she should betray her sister. But honour, and affection for Hyacinth, had prevailed; and she had bent her shoulders to the burden of undeserved shame. She had sat silent and abashed in his presence, like a guilty creature.

Sir John Kirkland spent a week at Fareham House, employed in choosing a team of horses, suitable alike for the road and the plough, looking out, among the coachmakers, for a second-hand travelling carriage, and eventually buying a coach of Lady Fanshawe's, which had been brought from Madrid with the rest of her very extensive goods and chattels.

One need scarce remark that it was not one of the late Ambassador's state carriages, his ruby velvet coach, with fringes that cost three hundred pounds, or his brocade carriage, but a coach that had been built for the everyday use of his suite.

Sir John also bought a little plain silver, in place of that fine collection of silver and parcel-gilt which had been so willingly sacrificed to royal necessities; and though he breathed no sigh over past losses, some bitter thoughts may have come across his cheerfulness as he heard of the splendour and superabundance of Lady Castlemaine's plate and jewels, or of the ring worth six hundred pounds lately presented to a pretty actress.

In a week he was ready for Buckinghamshire; and Angela had her trunks packed, and had bid good-bye to her London friends, amidst the chatter of Lady Fareham's visiting-day, and the clear, bell-like clash of delicate china tea-cups-- miniature bowls of egg-shell porcelain, without handles, and to be held daintily between the tips of high-bred fingers.

There was a chorus of courteous bewailing at the notion of Mrs. Kirkland's departure.

Sir Ralph Masaroon pretended to be in despair.

"Is it not bad enough to have had the coldest winter my youth can remember? But you must needs take the sun from our spring. Why, the maids of honour will count for handsome when you are gone. What's that Butler says?--

'The twinkling stars begin to muster,   And glitter with their borrowed lustre.'

But what's to become of me without the sun? I shall have no one to side-glass in the Ring."

"Indeed, Sir Ralph, I did not know that you ever side-glassed me!"

"What, you have suffered my devotion to pass unperceived? When I have broken half a dozen coach windows in your service, rattling a glass down with a vehemence which would have startled a Venus in marble to turn and recognise an adorer! Round and round the Ring I have driven for hours, on the chance of a look. Nay, marble is not so coy as froward beauty! And at the Queen's chapel have I not knelt at the Mass morning after morning, at the risk of being thought a Papist, for the sake of seeing you at prayers; and have envied the Romish dog who handed you the aspersoir as you went out? And you to be unconscious all the time!"

"Nay, 'tis so much happier for me, Sir Ralph, since you have given me a reserve of gratified vanity that will last me a year in the country, where I shall see nothing but ploughmen and bird-boys."

"Look out for the scarecrows in Sir John's fields, for the odds are you will see me some day disguised as one."

"Why disguised?" asked his friend Mr. Penington, who had lately produced a comedy that had been acted three afternoons at the Duke's Theatre, and one evening at Court, which may be taken as a prosperous run for a new play.

Lady Sarah Tewkesbury held forth on the pleasures of a country life, and lamented that family connections and the necessity of standing well with the Court constrained her to spend the greater part of her existence in town.

"I am like Milton," she said. "I adore a rural life. To hear the cock--

'From his watchtower in the skies,   When the horse and hound do rise.'

Oh, I love buttercups and daisies above all the Paris finery in the Exchange; and to steep one's complexion in May-dew, and to sup on a syllabub or a dish of frumenty--so cheap, too, while it costs a fortune but to scrape along in London."

"The country is well enough for a month at hay-making, to romp with a bevy of London beauties in the meadows near Tunbridge Wells, or to dance to a couple of fiddles on the Common by moonlight," said Mr. Penington; whereupon all agreed that Tunbridge Wells, Epsom, Doncaster, and Newmarket were the only country possible to people of intellect.

"I would never go further than Epsom, if I had my will," said Sir Ralph; "for I see no pleasure in Newmarket for a man who keeps no running-horses, and has no more interest in the upshot of a race than he might have in a maggot match on his own dining-table, did he stake high enough on the result."

"But my sister is not to be buried in Buckinghamshire all the year round," explained Hyacinth. "I shall fetch her here half a dozen times in a season; and her shortest visits must be long enough to take the country freshness out of her complexion, and save her from becoming a milkmaid."

"Gud, to see her freckled!" cried Penington. "I could as soon imagine Helen with a hump. That London pallor is the choicest charm in a girl of quality--a refined sickliness that appeals to the heart of a man of feeling, an 'if-you-don't-lend-me-your-arm-I-shall-swoon' sort of air. Your country hoyden, with her roses-and-cream complexion, and open-air manners, is more shocking than Medusa to a man of taste."

The talk drifted to other topics at the mention of Buckingham, who had but lately been let out of the Tower, where he and Lord Dorchester had been committed for scuffling and quarrelling at the Canary Conference.

"Has your ladyship seen the Duke and Lord Dorchester since they came out of the house of bondage?" asked Lady Sarah. "I think Buckingham was never so gay and handsome, and takes his imprisonment as the best joke that ever was, and is as great at Court as ever."

"His Majesty is but too indulgent," said Masaroon, "and encourages the Duke to be insolent and careless of ceremony. He had the impertinence to show himself at chapel before he had waited on his Majesty."

"Who was very angry and forbade him the Court," said Penington. "But Buckingham sent the King one of his foolish, jesting letters, capped with a rhyme or two; and if you can make Charles Stuart laugh you may pick his pocket----"

"Or seduce his mistress----"

"Oh, he will forgive much to wit and gaiety. He learnt the knack of taking life easily, while he led that queer, shifting life in exile. He was a cosmopolitan and a soldier of fortune before he was a King *de facto;* and still wears the loose garments of those easy, beggarly days, when he had neither money nor care. Be sure he regrets that roving life--Madrid, Paris, the Hague--and will never love a son as well as little Monmouth, the child of his youth."

"What would he not give to make that base-born brat Prince of Wales? Strange that while Lord Ross is trying to make his offspring illegitimate by Act of Parliament, his master's anxieties should all tend the other way."

"Don't talk to me of Parliament!" cried Lady Sarah; "the tyranny of the Rump was nothing to them. Look at the tax upon French wines, which will make it almost impossible for a lady of small means to entertain her friends. And an Act for burying us all in woollen, for the benefit of the English trade in wool."

"But, indeed, Lady Sarah, it is we of the old faith who have most need to complain," said Lady Fareham, "since these wretches make us pay a double poll-tax; and all our foreign friends are being driven away for the same reason--just because the foolish and the ignorant must needs put down the fire to the Catholics."

"Indeed, your ladyship, the Papists have had an unlucky knack at lighting fires, as Smithfield and Oxford can testify," said Penington; "and perhaps, having no more opportunity of roasting martyrs, it may please some of your creed to burn Protestant houses, with the chance of cooking a few Protestants inside 'em."

*   *   *   *   *

Angela had drawn away from the little knot of fine ladies and finer gentlemen, and was sitting in the bay window of an ante-room, with Henriette and the boy, who were sorely dejected at the prospect of losing her. The best consolation she could offer was to promise that they should be invited to the Manor Moat as soon as she and her father had settled themselves comfortably there--if their mother could spare them.

Henriette laughed outright at this final clause.

"Spare us!" she cried. "Does she ever want us? I don't think she knows when we are in the room, unless we tread upon her gown, when she screams out 'Little viper!' and hits us with her fan."

"The lightest touch, Papillon; not so hard as you strike your favourite baby."

"Oh, she doesn't hurt me; but the disrespect of it! Her only daughter, and nearly as high as she is!"

"You are an ungrateful puss to complain, when her ladyship is so kind as to let you be here to see all her fine company."

"I am sick of her company, almost always the same, and always talking about the same things. The King, and the Duke, and the General, and the navy; or Lady Castlemaine's jewels, or the last new head from Paris, or her ladyship's Flanders lace. It is all as dull as ditch-water now Monsieur de Malfort is gone. He was always pleasant, and he let me play on his guitar, though he swore it excruciated him. And he taught me the new Versailles coranto. There's no pleasure for any one since he fell ill and left England."

"You shall come to the Manor. It will be a change, even though you hate the country and love London."

"I have left off loving London. I have had too much of it. If his lordship let us go to the play-house often it would be different. Oh, how I loved Philaster--and that exquisite page! Do you think I could act that character, auntie, if his lordship's tailor made me such a dress?"

"I think thou hast impudence for anything, dearest."

"I would rather act that page than Pauline in **Polyeucte**, though Mademoiselle swears I speak her tirades nearly as well as an actress she once saw at the Marais, who was too old and fat for the character. How I should love to be an actress, and to play tragedy and comedy, and make people cry and laugh! Indeed, I would rather be anything than a lady--unless I could be exactly like Lady Castlemaine."

"Ah, Heaven forbid!"

"But why not? I heard Sir Ralph tell mother that, let her behave as badly as she may, she will always be atop of the tree, and that the young sparks at the Chapel Royal hardly look at their prayer-books for gazing at her, and that the King----"

"Ah, sweetheart, I want to hear no more of her!"

"Why, don't you like her? I thought you did not know her. She never comes here."

"Are there any staghounds in the Vale of Aylesbury?" asked the boy, who had been looking out of the window, watching the boats go by, unheeding his sister's babble.

"I know not, love; but there shall be dogs enough for you to play with, I'll warrant, and a pony for you to ride. Grandfather shall get them for his dearest."

Sir John was fond of Henriette, whom he looked upon as a marvel of precocious brightness; but the boy was his favourite, whom he loved with an old man's half-melancholy affection for the creature which is to live and act a part in the world when he, the greybeard, shall be dust.

CHAPTER XXII.
AT THE MANOR MOAT.

Solid, grave, and sober, grey with a quarter of a century's neglect, the Manor House, in the valley below Brill, differed in every detail from the historical Chilton Abbey. It was a moated manor house, the typical house of the typical English

squire; an E-shaped house, with a capacious roof that lodged all the household servants, and clustered chimney-stacks that accommodated a great company of swallows. It had been built in the reign of Henry the Seventh, and was coeval with its
distinguished neighbour, the house of the Verneys, at Middle Claydon, and it had
never served any other purpose than to shelter Englishmen of good repute in the
land. Souvenirs of Bosworth field--a pair of huge jack-boots, a two-handed sword,
and a battered helmet--hung over the chimney-piece in the low-ceiled hall; but
the end of the civil war was but a memory when the Manor House was built. After
Bosworth a slumberous peace had fallen on the land, and in the stillness of this
secluded valley, sheltered from every bleak wind by surrounding hills and woods,
the gardens of the Manor Moat had grown into a settled beauty that made the chief
attraction of a country seat which boasted so little of architectural dignity, or of expensive fantasy in moulded brick and carved stone. Plain, sombre, with brick walls
and heavy stone mullions to low-browed windows, the Manor House stood in the
midst of gardens such as the modern millionaire may long for, but which only the
grey old gardener Time can create.

There was more than a mile of yew hedge, eight feet high, and three feet broad,
walling in flower garden and physic garden, the latter the particular care of the
house-mothers of previous generations, the former a paradise of those old flowers
which bloom and breathe sweet odours in the pages of Shakespeare, and jewel the
verse of Milton. The fritillary here opened its dusky spotted petals to drink the dews
of May; and here, against a wall of darkest green, daffodils bloomed unruffled by
March winds.

Verily a garden of gardens; but when Angela came there in the chill February
there were no flowers to welcome her, only the long, straight walks beside those
walls of yew, and the dark shining waters of the moat and the fish-pond, reflecting
the winter sun; and over all the scene a quiet as of the grave.

A little colony of old servants had been left in the house, which had escaped
confiscation, albeit the property of a notorious Malignant, perhaps chiefly on account of its insignificance, the bulk of the estate having been sold by Sir John in '44,
when the king's condition was waxing desperate, and money was worth twice its
value to those who clung to hope, and were ready to sacrifice their last jacobus in
the royal cause. The poor little property--shrunk to a home-farm of ninety acres, a

humble homestead, and the Manor House--may have been thought hardly worth selling; or Sir John's rights may have been respected out of regard for his son-in-law, who, on the maternal side, had kindred in high places under the Commonwealth, a fact of which Hyacinth occasionally reminded her husband, telling him that he was by hereditary instinct a rebel and a king-slayer.

The farm had been taken to by Sir John's steward, a man who in politics was of the same easy temper as the Vicar of Bray in religion, and was a staunch Cromwellian so long as Oliver or Richard sat at Whitehall, or would have tossed up his cap and cheered for Monk, as Captain-General of Great Britain, had he been called upon to till his fields and rear his stock under a military despotism. It mattered little to any man living at ease in a fat Buckinghamshire valley what King or Commonwealth ruled in London, so long as there was a ready market at Aylesbury or Thame for all the farm could produce, and civil war planted neither drake nor culverin on Brill Hill.

The old servants had vegetated as best they might in the old house, their wages of the scantiest; but to live and die within familiar walls was better than to fare through a world which had no need of them. The younger members of the household had scattered, and found new homes; but the grey-haired cook was still in her kitchen; the old butler still wept over his pantry, where a dozen or so of spoons, and one battered tankard of Heriot's make, were all that remained of that store of gold and silver which had been his pride forty years ago, when Charles was bringing home his fair French bride, and old Thames at London was alight with fire-works and torches, and alive with music and singing, as the city welcomed its young Queen, and when Reuben Holden was a lad in the pantry, learning to polish a salver or a goblet, and sorely hectored by his uncle the butler.

Reuben, and Marjory, the old cook, famous in her day as any *cordon-bleu*, were the sole representatives of the once respectable household; but a couple of stout wenches had been hired from the cluster of labourers' hovels that called itself a village; and these had been made to drudge as they had never drudged before in the few days of warning which prepared Reuben for his master's return.

Fires had been lighted in rooms where mould and mildew had long prevailed; wainscots had been scrubbed and polished till the whole house reeked of bees-wax and turpentine, to a degree that almost overpowered those pervading odours of damp and dry rot, which can curiously exist together. The old furniture had been made as bright as faded fabrics and worm-eaten wood could be made by labour; and the leaping light of blazing logs, reflected on the black oak panelling, gave a transient air of cheerfulness to the spacious dining-parlour where Sir John and his daughter took their first meal in the old home. And if to Angela's eye, accustomed to the Italian loftiness of the noble mansions on the Thames, the broad oak cross-beams seemed coming down upon her head, there was at least an air of homely snugness in the low darkly coloured room.

On that first evening there had been much to interest and engage her. She had the old house to explore, and dim childish memories to recall. Here was the room where her mother died, the room in which she herself had first seen the light--perhaps not until a month or so after her birth, since the seventeenth-century baby was not flung open-eyed into her birthday sunshine, but was swaddled and muffled in a dismal apprenticeship to life. The chamber had been hung with "blacks" for a twelvemonth, Reuben told her, as he escorted her over the house, and unlocked the doors of disused rooms.

The tall bedstead with its red and yellow stamped velvet curtains and carved ebony posts looked like an Indian temple. One might expect to see Buddha squatting on the embroidered counterpane--the work of half a lifetime. When the curtains were drawn back, a huge moth flew out of the darkness, and spun and wheeled round the room with an awful humming noise, and to the superstitious mind might have suggested a human soul embodied in this phantasmal greyness, with power of sound in such excess of its bulk.

"Sir John never used the room after her ladyship's death," Reuben explained, "though 'tis the best bed-chamber. He has always slept in the blue room, which is at the furthest end of the gallery from the room that has been prepared for madam. We call that the garden room, and it is mighty pretty in summer."

In summer! How far it seemed to summer-time in Angela's thoughts! What a long gulf of nothingness to be bridged over, what a dull level plain to cross, before June and the roses could come round again, bringing with them the memory of last summer; and the days she had lived under the same roof with Fareham, and the evenings when they had sat in the same room, or loitered on the terrace, pausing now and then beside an Italian vase of gaudy flowers to look at this or that, or to watch the mob on the river; and those rare golden days, like that at Sayes Court, which she had spent in some excursion with Fareham and Henriette.

"I hope madam likes the chamber we have prepared for her?" the old man said, as she stood dreaming.

"Yes, my good friend, it is very comfortable. My woman complained of the smoky chimney in her chamber; but no doubt we shall mend that by-and-by."

"It would be strange if a gentlewoman's servant found not something to grumble about," said Reuben; "they have ever less work to do than any one else in the house, and ever make more trouble than their mistresses. I'll settle the hussy, with madam's leave."

"Nay, pray, Mr. Reuben, no harshness. She is a willing, kind-hearted girl, and we shall find plenty of work for her in this big house where there are so few servants."

"Oh, there's work enough for sure, if she'll do it, and is no fine city madam that will scream at sight of a mouse, belike."

"She is a girl I had out of Oxfordshire."

"Oh, if she comes out of Oxfordshire, from his lordship's estate, I dare swear she is a good girl. I hate your London trash; and I think the great fire would have been a blessing in disguise if it had swept away most of such trumpery."

"Oh, sir, if a Romanist were to say as much as that!" said Angela, laughing.

"Oh, madam, I am not one of they fools that say because half London was burnt the Papishes must have set it on fire. What good would the burning of it do 'em, poor souls? And now they are to pay double taxes, as if it was a sure thing their faggots kindled the blaze. I know how kind and sweet a soul a Papish may be, though she do worship idols; for I had the honour to serve your ladyship's mother from the hour she first entered this house till the day I smuggled the French priest by the back stairs to carry her the holy oils. Ah! she was a noble and lovely lady. Madam's eyes are of her colour; and, indeed, madam favours her mother more than my Lady Fareham does."

"Have you seen Lady Fareham of late years?"

"Ay, madam, she came here in her coach-and-six the summer before the pestilence, with her two beautiful children, and a party of ladies and gentlemen. They rode here from his Grace of Buckingham's new mansion by the Thames--Clefden, I think they call it; and they do say his Grace do so lavish and squander money in the building of it, that belike he will be ruined and dead before his palace be finished. There were three coaches full, with servants and what not. And they brought wine, and capons ready dressed, and confectionery, and I helped to serve a collation for them in the garden. And after they had feasted merrily, with a vast quantity of sparkling French wine, they all rushed through the house like madcaps, laughing and chattering, regular French magpies, for there was more of 'em French than English, her ladyship leading them, till she comes to the door of this room, and finds it locked, and she begins to thump upon the panels like a spoilt child, and calls, 'Reuben, Reuben, what is your mystery? Sure this must be the ghost-chamber! Open, open, instantly.' And I answered her quietly, ''Tis the chamber where that sweet angel, your ladyship's mother, lay in state, and it has never been opened to strangers since she died.' And all in the midst of her mirth, the dear young lady burst out weeping, and cried, 'My sweet, sweet mother! I remember the last smile she gave me as if it was yesterday.' And then she dropped on her knees and crossed herself, and whispered a prayer, with her face close against the door; and I knew that she was praying for her lady-mother, as the way of your religion is, madam, to pray for the dead; and sure, though it is a simple thing, it can do no harm; and to my thinking, when all the foolishness is taken out of religion the warmth and the comfort seem to go too; for I know I never used to feel a bit more comfortable after a two hours' sermon, when I was an Anabaptist."

"Are you not an Anabaptist now, Reuben?"

"Lord forbid, madam! I have been a member of the Church of England ever since his Majesty's restoration brought the Vicar to his own again, and gave us back Christmas Day, and the organ, and the singing-boys."

Angela's life at the Manor was so colourless that the first blossoming of a familiar flower was an event to note and to remember. Life within convent walls would have been scarcely more tranquil or more monotonous. Sir John rode with his hounds three or four times a week, or was about the fields superintending the farming operations, walking beside the ploughman as he drove his furrow, or watching the scattering of the seed. Or he was in the narrow woodlands which still belonged to him, and Angela, taking her solitary walk at the close of day, heard his axe ringing through the wintry air.

It was a peaceful, and should have been a pleasant, life, for father and for daughter. Angela told herself that God had been very good to her in providing this safe haven from tempestuous seas, this quiet little world, where the pulses of passion beat not; where existence was like a sleep, a gradual drifting away of days and weeks, marked only by the changing note of birds, the deepening umber on the birch, the purpling of beech buds, and the starry celandine shining out of grassy banks that had so lately been obliterated under the drifted snow.

"I ought to be happy," she said to herself of a morning, when she rose from her knees, and stood looking across the garden to the grassy hills beyond, while the beads of her rosary slipped through her languid fingers--"I ought to be happy."

And then she turned from the sunny window with a sigh, and went down the dark, echoing staircase to the breakfast parlour, where her own little silver chocolate-pot looked ridiculously small beside Sir John's quart tankard, and where the crisp, golden rolls, baked in the French fashion by the maid from Chilton, who had been taught by Lord Fareham's *chef*, contrasted with the chine of beef and huge farmhouse loaf that accompanied the knight's old October.

After all his Continental wanderings Sir John had come back to substantial English fare with an unabated relish; and Angela had to sit down, day after day, to a huge joint and an overloaded dish of poultry, and to reassure her father when he expressed uneasiness because she ate so little.

"Women do not want much food, sir. Martha's rolls, and our honey, and the conserves old Marjory makes so well, are better for me than the meat which suits your heartier appetite."

"Faith, child, if I played no stouter a part at table than you do, I should soon be fit to play living skeleton at Aylesbury Fair. And I dubitate as to your diet-loaves and confectionery suiting you better than a slice of chine or sirloin, for you have a pale cheek and a pensive eye that smite me to the heart. Indeed, I begin to question if I was kind to take you from all the pleasures of the town to be mewed up here with a rusty old soldier."

"Indeed, sir, I could be happier nowhere than here. I have had enough of London pleasures; and I was meditating upon returning to the convent, when you came to put an end to all my perplexities; and, sir, I think God sent you to me when I most needed a father's love."

She went to him and knelt by his chair, hiding her tearful eyes against the cushioned arm. But, though he could not see her face, he heard the break in her voice, and he bent down and lifted her drooping head on his breast, and kissed the soft brown hair, and embraced her very tenderly.

"Sweetheart, thou hast all a father's love, and it is happiness to me to have thee here; but old as I am, and with so little cunning to read a maiden's heart, I can read clear enough to know thou art not happy. Whisper, dearest. Is it a sweetheart who sighs for thy favours far off, and will not beard this old lion in his den? My gentle Angela would make no ill choice. Fear not to trust me, my heart. I will love whom you love, favour whom you favour. I am no tyrant, that my sweet daughter should grow pale with keeping secrets from me."

"Dear father, you are all goodness. No, there is no one--no one! I am happy with you. I have no one in the world but you, and, in a so much lesser degree of love, my sister and her children--"

"And Fareham. He should be to you as a brother. He is of a black melancholic humour, and not a man whom women love; but he has a heart of gold, and must regard you with grateful affection for your goodness to him when he was sick. Hyacinth is never weary of expatiating upon your devotion in that perilous time."

"She is foolish to talk of services I would have given as willingly to a sick beggar," Angela answered, impatiently.

Her face was still hidden against her father's breast; but she lifted her head presently, and the pale calmness of her countenance reassured him.

"Well, it is uncommon strange," he said, "if one so fair has no sweetheart among all the sparks of Whitehall."

"Lord Fareham hates Whitehall. We have only attended there at great festivals, when my sister's absence would have been a slight upon her Majesty and the Duchess."

"But my star, though seldom shining there, should have drawn some satellites to her orbit. You see, dearest, I can catch the note of Court flattery. Nay, I will press no questions. My girl shall choose her own partner; provided the man is honest and a loyal servant of the King. Her old father shall set no stumbling-block in the highroad to her happiness. What right has one who is almost a pauper to stipulate for a wealthy son-in-law?"

CHAPTER XXIII.
PATIENT, NOT PASSIONATE.

The quiet days went on, and the old Cavalier settled down into a tranquil happiness, which comforted his daughter with the feeling of duty prosperously fulfilled. To make this dear old man happy, to be his companion and friend, to share in his rides and rambles, and of an evening to play the games he loved on the old shovel-board in the hall, or an old-fashioned game at cards, or backgammon beside the fire in the panelled parlour, reconciled her to the melancholy of an existence from which hope had vanished like a light extinguished. It seemed to her as if she had dropped back into the old life with her great-aunt. The Manor House was just a little gayer than the Flemish Convent--for the voices and footsteps of the few inhabitants had a freer sound, which made the few seem more populous than the many. And then there were the dogs. What a powerful factor in home life those four-footed friends were! Out-of-doors a stone barn had been turned into a kennel for five couple of foxhounds; indoors a couple of setters, sent by a friend over sea from Waterford, had insinuated themselves into the parlour, where they established themselves as household favourites, to the damage of those higher hereditary qualities which fitted them for distinction with the guns. Indeed, the old Knight was too fond of his fireside companions to care very much if he missed a bird now and then because Cataline was over-fed or Caesar disobedient. They stood sentinel on each side of his chair at dinner, like supporters to a coat-of-arms. Angela had her own particular favourite in a King Charles's spaniel. It was the very dog which had first greeted her in the silence of the plague-stricken house. She had chosen this one from the canine troop when her sister offered her the gift of a dog at parting, though Hyacinth had urged her to take something younger than this, which was over five years old.

"He will die just when you love him best," she said.

"Nay; but such partings must come. I love this one because he was with me in fear and sadness. He used to cling to me, and look up and lick my face, as if he were telling me to hope, when my brother seemed marked for death."

"Poor Fareham! Did you desire every dog in the house--and my spaniels are of the same breed as the King's, and worth fifty pound apiece--you have a right to take them. But, indeed, I would rather you chose a younger dog--and with a shorter nose; but, of course, if you like this one best----"

Angela held by her first choice, and Ganymede was the companion of all her hours, walked and lived with her, and slept on a satin cushion at the foot of her spacious four-post bed, and fretted and whined if she left him shut in an empty room for half an hour; yet with all his refinements, and his air of being as dainty a gentleman as any spark of quality, he had a gross passion for the kitchen, and after nibbling sweet cakes delicately out of his mistress's taper fingers, he would waddle through a labyrinth of passages, and find his way to the hog-tub, there to wallow in slush and broken victuals, till he all but drowned himself in a flood of pot-liquor. It was hard to reconcile so much beauty and grace, such eloquent eyes and satin coat, with tastes and desires so vulgar; and Angela sighed over him when a scullion brought him to her, greasy and penitent, to crouch at her feet, and deprecate her disgust with an abject tail.

Oh, tranquil, duteous life, how fair it might have seemed, as spring advanced, and the garden smiled with the promise of summer, were it not for that aching sense of loss, the some one missing, whose absence made all things grey and cold!

Yes, she knew now, fully realising as she had never done before, how long and how utterly her life had been influenced by an affection which even to contemplate was mortal sin. Yet to extinguish memory was not within her power. She looked back and remembered how Fareham's protecting love had enfolded her with its gentle warmth, in those happy days at Chilton; how all she knew of poetry and the drama, of ethics and philosophy, had been learnt from him. She recalled his evident delight in opening the rich treasures of a mind which he had never ceased to culti- vate, even amidst the vicissitudes of a soldier's life, in making her familiar with the writers he loved, and teaching her to estimate, and to discuss them. And in all their talk together he had been for the most part careful to avoid disparagement of the religion in which she believed--so that it was only some chance revelation of the infidel's narrow outlook that reminded her of his unbelief.

Yes, his love had been round her like an atmosphere; and she had been exqui- sitely happy while that unquestioning affection was hers. On her part there had been neither doubt nor fear. It seemed the most natural thing in the world that he should be fond of her and she of him. Affinity had made them brother and sister; and then they had been together in sickness and in peril of death. It might be true, as he himself had affirmed, that her so happy arrival had saved his life; since just those hours between the departure of his attendants and the physician's evening visit may have been the crisis of his disease.

Well, it was past--the exquisite bliss, the unconscious sin, the confidence, the danger. All had vanished into the grave of irrecoverable days.

She had heard nothing from Denzil since she left London, nor had she acknowledged his letter. Her silence had doubtless angered him, and all was at an end between them, and this was what she wished. Hyacinth and her children were at Chilton, whence came letters of complaining against the dulness of the country, where his lordship hunted four times a week, and spent all the rest of his time in his library, appearing only "at our stupid heavy meals; and that not always, since on his hunting days he is far afield when I have to sit down to the intolerable two-o'clock dinner, and make a pretence of eating--as if anybody with more intellectuals than a sheep could dine; or as if appetite came by staring at green fields! You remember how in London supper was the only meal I ever cared for. There is some grace in a repast that comes after conversation and music, or the theatre, or a round of visits--a table dazzling with lights, and men and women ready to amuse, and be amused. But to sit down in broad daylight, when one has scarce swallowed one's morning chocolate, and face a sweltering sirloin, or open a smoking veal pie! Indeed, dearest, our whole method of feeding smacks of a vulgar brutishness, more appropriate to a company of Topinambous than to persons of quality. Why, oh, why must these reeking hecatombs load our tables, when they might as easily be kept out of sight upon a buffet? The spectacle of huge mountains of meat, the steam and odour of rank boiled and roast under one's very nostrils, change appetite to nausea, and would induce a delicate person to rise in disgust and fly from the dining-room. Mais, je ne fais que divaguer; and almost forget what it was I was so earnest to tell thee when I began my letter.

"Sir Denzil Warner has been over here, his ostensible motive a civil inquiry after my health; but I could see that his actual purpose was to hear of you. I told him how happily your simple soul has accommodated itself to an almost conventual seclusion, and a very inferior style of living--whereupon he smiled his rapture, and praised you to the skies. 'Would that she could accommodate herself to my house as easily,' he said; 'she should have every indulgence that an adoring husband could yield her.' And then he said much more, but as lovers always sing the same repetitive song, and have no more strings to their lyre than the ancients had before Mercury expanded it, I confess to not listening over carefully, and will leave you to imagine the eloquence of a manly and honourable love. Ah, sweetheart! you do wrong to reject him. Thou hast a quiet soothing prettiness of thine own, but art no blazing star of beauty, like the Stewart, to bring a King to thy feet--he would have married her if poor Catherine had not disappointed him by her recovery--and to take a Duke as *pis aller*. Believe me, love, it were wise of you to become Lady Warner, with an unmortgaged estate, and a husband who, in these Republican times, may rise to distinction. He is your only earnest admirer; and a love so steadfast, backed by a fortune so respectable, should not be discarded lightly."

Over all these latter passages in her sister's letter Angela's eye ran with a scornful carelessness. Her womanly pride revolted at such petty schooling--that she should be bidden to accept this young man gratefully, because he was her only suitor. No one else had ever cared for her pale insignificance. She looked at her clouded image in the oblong glass that hung on the panel above her secretaire, and whose reflection made any idea of her own looks rather speculative than precise. It showed her a thoughtful face, too pale for beauty; yet she could but note the harmony of lines which recalled that Venetian type familiar to her eye in the Titians and Tintorets at Fareham House.

"I doubt I am good-looking enough for any one to be satisfied with the outward semblance who valued the soul within," she thought, as she turned from the glass with a mournful sigh.

It was not of Denzil she was thinking, but of that other who in slow contemplative days in the library where he had taught her what books she ought to love, and where she might never more enter, must naturally sometimes remember her, and cast some backward thoughts to the hours they had spent together.

Hyacinth's letter of matronly counsel was but a week old when Sir John surprised his daughter one morning, as they sat at table, by the announcement of a visitor to stay in the house.

"You will order the west room to be got ready, Angela, and bid Marjory Cook serve us some of her savourest dishes while Sir Denzil stays here."

"Sir Denzil!"

"Yes, ma mie, Sir Denzil! Ventregris, the girl stares as if I had said Sir Bevis of Southampton, or Sir Guy of Warwick! I knew this young gentleman's father before the troubles--an honest man, though he took the wrong side He paid for his perversity with his life; so we'll say requiescat. The young man is a fine young man, whom I would fain have something nearer to me than he is. So at a hint from your sister I have asked him to bring his fishing tackle and whip our streams for a May trout or two. He may catch a finer fish than trout, perhaps, while he is a-fishing; if you will be his guide through the meadows."

"Father, how could you----"

"Ah! thou art a sly one, fair mistress. Who was it told me there was no one? 'No one, dear father, and indeed, sir, I was thinking of the convent when you came to London,' while here was as handsome a spark as one would meet in a day's march, sighing and dying for you."

"Father, I do protest to you----" she began, with a pale distressed look that vouched for her earnestness; but the Knight had his face in the tankard, and set it down only to pursue his own train of thought.

"If it had not have been for that little bird at Chilton you might have hood-winked me as blind as ever gerfalcon was hooded. Well, the young man will be here before evening. I would not force your inclinations, but it is the dearest desire of my heart to see you happily married before I blow out the candle, and bid my last good night. And a man of honour, handsome and of handsomest fortune, is not to be slighted."

Angela's spirit rose against this recurrence of her sister's sermon.

"If Sir Denzil is coming to this house as my suitor, I will go to Louvain without an hour's delay that I can help," she said resolutely.

"Why, what a vixen! Nay, dearest, there is no need for that angry flush. The young man is too courteous to plague you with unwelcome civilities. I saw him in London at the tennis court, and was friendly to him for his father's memory, knowing nothing of his desire to be my son-in-law. He is a fine player at that royal game, and a fine man. He comes here this evening as my friend; and if you please to treat him disdainfully, I cannot help it. But, indeed, I wonder as much as your sister why you should not reciprocate this gentleman's love."

"When you were young, father, did you love the first comer; only because she was handsome and civil?"

"No, child; I had seen many handsome women before I met your mother. She came over in '35 with the Marquise, who had been lady of honour to Queen Marie before the Princess Henriette married our King, and Queen Henriette was fond of her, and invited her to come to London, and she divided her life between the two countries till the troubles, when she was one of the first to scamper off, as you know. My wife was little more than a child when I saw her at Court, hiding behind her mother's large sleeves. I had seen handsomer women; but she was the first whose face went straight to my heart. And it has dwelt there ever since," he concluded, with a sudden break in his voice.

"Then you can comprehend, dear sir, that a man may be honourable, and courteous, and handsome, and yet not win a woman's love."

"Ah, it is not the man; it is love that should win, sweetheart. Love is worthy of love. When that is the true coin it should buy its reward. Indeed I have rarely seen it otherwise. Love begets love. Louise de la Valliere is not the handsomest woman at the French Court. Her complexion has suffered from small-pox, and she has a defective gait; but the King discovered a so fond and romantic attachment to his person, a love ashamed of loving, the very poetry of affection; and that discovery made him her slave. The Court beauties--sultanas splendid as Vashti--look on in angry wonder. Louise is adored because she began by adoring. Mind, I do not praise or excuse her, for 'tis a mortal sin to love a married man, and steal him from his wife. Foolish child, how your cheek crimsons! I do wrong to shock your innocence with my babble of a King's mistress."

Denzil arrived at sunset, on horseback, with a mounted servant in attendance, carrying his saddle-bags and fishing tackle. It was but a short day's ride from Oxford. Fareham's rides with the hounds must have brought him sometimes within a few miles of the Manor Moat Hyacinth and her children might have ridden over in their coach; and indeed she had promised her sister a visit in more than one of her letters. But there had been always something to postpone the expedition--company at home, or bad weather, or a fit of the vapours--so that the sisters had been as much asunder as if the elder had been in Yorkshire or Northumberland.

Denzil brought news of the household at Chilton. Lady Fareham was as charming as ever, and though she had complained very often of bad health, she had been so lively and active whenever the whim took her, riding with hawk and hound, visiting about the neighbourhood, driving into Oxford, that Denzil was of opinion her ailments were of the spirits only, a kind of rustic malady to which most fine ladies were subject, the nostalgia of paving-stones and oil lamps. Henriette--she now insisted upon discarding her nick-name--was less volatile than in London, and missed her aunt sorely, and quarrelled with mademoiselle, who was painfully strict upon all points of speech and manners. George's days of unalloyed idleness were also ended, for the Roman Catholic priest was now a resident in the house as the little boy's tutor, besides teaching 'Henriette the rudiments, and instructing her in her mother's religion.

Denzil told them even of the guests he had met at the Abbey; but of the master of the house his lips spoke not, till Sir John questioned him.

"And Fareham? Has he that same air of not belonging to the family which I remarked of him in London?"

"His lordship has ever an air of being aloof from everybody," Denzil answered gravely. "He is solitary even in his sports, and his indoor life is mostly buried in a book."

"Ah, those books, they will be the ruin of nations! As books multiply, great actions will grow less. Life's golden hours will be wasted in dreaming over the fancies of dead men; and the world will be over-full of brooding philosophers like Descartes, or pamphleteers like your friend Mr. Milton."

"Nay, sir, the world is richer for such a man as John Milton, who has composed the grandest poem in our language--an epic on a scale and subject as sublime as the Divine Comedy of Dante."

"I never saw Mr. Dante's comedy acted, and confess myself ignorant of its merits."

"Comedy, sir, with Dante, is but a name. The Italian poem is an epic, and not a play. Mr. Milton's poem will be given to the world shortly, though, alas! he will reap little substantial reward for the intellectual labour of years. Poetry is not a marketable commodity in England, save when it flatters a royal patron, or takes the vulgarer form of a stage-play. But this poem of Mr. Milton's has been the solace of his darkened life. You have heard, perhaps, of his blindness?"

"Yes, he had to forego his office as Latin Secretary to that villain. To my mind the decay of sight was a judgment upon him for having written against his murdered King, even to the denial of his Majesty's own account of his sufferings. But I confess that even if the man had been a loyal subject, I have little admiration for that class; scribblers and pamphleteers, brooders over books, crouchers in the chimney-corner, who have never trailed a pike or slept under the open sky. And seeing this vast increase of book-learning, and the arising of such men as Hobbes, to question our religion--and Milton to assail monarchy--I can but believe those who say that this old England has taken the downward bent; that, as we are dwindling in stature, so we are decaying in courage and capacity for action."

Denzil listened respectfully to the old man's disquisitions over his morning drink; while Reuben stood at the sideboard carving a ham or a round of powdered beef; and while Angela sipped her chocolate out of the porcelain cup which Hyacinth had bought for her at the Middle Exchange, where curiosities from China and the last inventions from Paris were always to be had before they were seen anywhere else. Nothing could be more reverential than the young man's bearing to his host, while his quiet friendliness set Angela at her ease, and made her think that he had abandoned his suit, and henceforward aspired only to such a tranquil friendship as they had enjoyed at Chilton before any word of love had been spoken.

Apart from the question of love and marriage, his presence was in no manner displeasing to her; indeed, the long days in that sequestered valley lost something of their grey monotony now that she had a companion in all her intellectual occupations. Fondly as she loved her father, she had not been able to hide from herself the narrowness of his education and the blind prejudice which governed his ideas upon almost every subject, from politics to natural history. Of the books which make the greater part of a solitary life she could never talk to him; and it was here that she had so sorely missed the counsellor and friend, who had taught her to love and to comprehend the great poets of the past--Homer and Virgil, Dante and Tasso, and the deep melancholy humour of Cervantes, and, most of all, the inexhaustible riches of the Elizabethans.

Denzil was of a temper as thoughtful, but his studies had taken a different direction. He was not even by taste or apprehension a poet. Had he been called upon to criticise his tutor's compositions, he might, like Johnson, have objected to the metaphoric turns of Lycidas, and have missed the melody of lines as musical as the nightingale. In that great poem of which he had been privileged to transcribe many of the finest passages from the lips of the poet, he admired rather the heroic patience of the blind author than the splendour of the verse. He was more impressed by the schoolmaster's learning than by that God-given genius which lifted that one Englishman above every other of his age and country. No, he was eminently prosaic, had sucked prose and plain-thinking from his mother's breast; but he was not the less an agreeable companion for a girl upon whose youth an unnatural solitude had begun to weigh heavily.

All that one mind can impart to another of a widely different fibre, Denzil had learnt from Milton in that most impressionable period of boyhood which he had spent in the small house in Holborn, whose back rooms looked out over the verdant spaces of Lincoln's Inn Fields, where Lord Newcastle's palace had not yet begun to rise from its foundations, and where the singing birds had not been scared away by the growth of the town. A theatre now stood where the boy and a fellow-scholar had played trap and ball, and the stately houses of Queen Street hard by were alive with rank and fashion.

In addition to the classical curriculum which Milton had taught with the solemn earnestness of one in whom learning is a religion, Denzil had acquired a store of miscellaneous knowledge from the great Republican; and most interesting among these casual instructions had been the close acquaintance with nature gained in the course of many a rustic ramble in the country lanes beyond Gray's Inn, or sauntering eastward along the banks of the limpid Lee, or in the undulating meadows beside Sir Hugh Middleton's river. Mixed with plain facts about plant or flower, animal or insect, Milton's memory was stored with the quaint absurdities of the Hermetic philosophy, that curious mixture of deep-reaching theories and old women's superstitions, the experience of the peasant transmuted by the imagination of the adept. Sound and practical as the poet had ever shown himself--save where passion got the upper hand of common sense, as in his advocacy of divorce--he was yet not entirely free from a leaning to Baconian superstitions, and may, with Gesner, have believed that the pickerel weed could engender pike, and that frogs could turn to slime in winter, and become frogs again in spring. Whatever rags of old-world fatuity may have lingered in that strong brain, he had been not the less a delightful teacher, and had imparted an ardent love of nature to his little family of pupils in that peripatetic school between hawthorn hedges or in the open fields by the Lee.

And now, in quiet rambles with Angela, in the midst of a landscape trans-figured by that vernal beauty which begins with the waning of April, and is past and vanished before the end of May, Denzil loved to expound the wonders of the infinitesimal; the insect life that sparkled and hummed in the balmy air, or flashed like living light among the dewy grasses; the life of plant and flower, which seemed almost as personal and conscious a form of existence; since it was difficult to believe there was no sense of struggle or of joy in those rapid growths which shot out from a tangle of dark undergrowth upward to the sunlight, no fondness in the wild vines that clung so close to some patriarchal trunk, covering decay with the beautiful exuberance of youth. Denzil taught her to realise the wonders of creation--most wonderful when most minute--for beyond the picturesque and lovely in nature, he showed her those marvels of order, and law, and adaptation, which speak to the naturalist with a stronger language than beauty.

There was a tranquil pleasure in these rustic walks, which beguiled her into forgetfulness that this man had ever sought to be more to her than he was now--a respectful, unobtrusive friend. Of London, and the tumultuous life going on there, he had scarcely spoken, save to tell her that he meant to stand for Henley at the next Parliament; nor had he alluded to the past at Chilton; nor ever of his own ac-cord had he spoken Lord Fareham's name; indeed, that name was studiously avoid-ed by them both; and if Denzil had never before suspected Angela of an unhappy preference for one whom she could not love without sin, he might have had some cause for such suspicion in the eagerness with which she changed the drift of the conversation whenever it approached that forbidden subject.

From his Puritanical bringing up, the theory of self-surrender and deprivation ever kept before him, Denzil had assuredly learnt to possess his soul in patience; and throughout all that smiling month of May, while he whipped the capricious streams that wound about the valley, with Angela for the willing companion of his saunterings from pool to pool, he never once alarmed her by any hint of a warmer feeling than friendship; indeed, he thought of himself sometimes as one who lived in an enchanted world, where to utter a certain fatal word would be to break the spell; and whatever momentary impulse or passionate longing, engendered by a look, a smile, the light touch of a hand, the mere sense of proximity, might move him to speak of his love, he had sufficient self-command to keep the fatal words unspoken. He meant to wait till the last hour of his visit. Only when separation was imminent would he plead his cause again. Thus at the worst he would have lost no happy hours of her company. And, in the mean time, since she was always kind, and seemed to grow daily more familiar and at ease in his society, he dared hope that affection for him and forgetfulness of that other were growing side by side in her mind.

In this companionship Angela learnt many of the secrets and subtleties of the angler's craft, as acquired by her teacher's personal experience, or expounded in that delightful book, then less than twenty years old, which has ever been the angler's gospel. Often after following the meandering water till a gentle weariness invited them to rest, Angela and Denzil seated themselves on a sheltered bank and read their Izaak Walton together, both out of the same volume, he pleased to point out his favourite passages and to watch her smile as she read.

Before May was ended, she knew old Izaak almost as well as Denzil, and had learnt to throw a fly, and to choose the likeliest spot and the happiest hour of the day for a good trout; had learnt to watch the clouds and cloud-shadows with an angler's keen interest; and had amused herself with the manufacture of an artificial minnow, upon Walton's recipe, devoting careful labour and all the resources of her embroidery basket--silks and silver thread--to perfecting the delicate model, which, when completed, she presented smilingly to Denzil, who was strangely moved by so childish a toy, and had some difficulty in suppressing his emotion as he held the glistening silken fish in his hands, and thought how her tapering fingers had caressed it, and how much of her very self seemed, as he watched her, to have been enwrought with the fabric. So poor, so trivial a thing; but her first gift! If she had tossed him a flower, plucked that moment, he would have treasured it all his life; but this, which had cost her so much careful work, was far more than any casual blossom. Something of the magnetism of her mind had passed into the silver thread drawn so daintily through her rosy fingers--something of the soft light in her eyes had mixed with the blended colours of the silk. Foolish fancies these, but in the gravest man's love there is a vein of folly.

Sometimes they rode with Sir John, and in this way explored the neighbour-hood, which was rich in historical associations--some of the remote past, as when King John kept Christmas at Brill; but chiefly of those troubled times through which Sir John Kirkland had lived, an active participator in that deadly drama. He showed them the site of the garrison at Brill, and trod every foot of the earthworks to demonstrate how the hill had been fortified. He had commanded in the defence against Hampden and his greencoats--that regiment of foot raised in his pastoral shire, whose standard bore on one side the watchword of the Parliament, "God with us," and on the other Hampden's own device, "*Vestigia nulla retrorsum.*"

"'Twas a legend to frighten some of us, who had no Latin," said Sir John; "but we put his bumpkin greencoats to the rout, and trampled that insolent flag in the mire."

All was peaceful now in the hamlet on the hill. Women and children were sitting upon sunny doorsteps, with their pillows on their knees and their bobbins moving quickly in dexterous fingers, busy at the lace-making which had been established in Buckinghamshire more than a century before by Catherine of Aragon, whose dowry was derived from the revenues of Steeple Claydon. The Curate had returned to the grey old church, and rural life pursued its slumbrous course, scarce ruffled by rumours of maritime war, or plague, or fire. They rode to Thame--a stage on the journey to Oxford, Angela thought, as she noted the figures on a milestone, and at a flash her memory recalled that scene in the gardens by the river, when Fareham had spoken for the first time of his inner life, and she had seen the man behind the mask. She thought of her sister, so fair, so sweet, charming in her capriciousness even, yet not the woman to fill that unquiet heart, or satisfy that sombre and earnest nature. It was not by many words that Fareham had revealed himself. Her knowledge of his character and feelings went deeper than the knowledge that words can impart. It came from that constant unconscious study which a romantic girl devotes to the character of the man who first awakens her interest.

Angela was grave and silent throughout the drive to Thame and the return home, riding for the most part in the rear of the two men, leaving Denzil to devote all his attention to Sir John, who was somewhat loquacious that afternoon, stimulated by the many memories of the troubled time which the road awakened. Denzil listened respectfully, and went never astray in his answers, but he looked back very often to the solitary rider who kept at some distance to avoid the dust.

Sometimes in the early morning they all went with the otter hounds, the Knight on horseback, Denzil and Angela on foot, and spent two or three very active hours before breakfast in rousing the otter from his holt, and following every flash of his head upon the stream, with that briskness and active enjoyment which seem a part of the clear morning atmosphere, the inspiring breath of dewy fields and flowers unfaded by the sun. All that there was of girlishness in Angela's spirits was awakened by those merry morning scampers by the margin of the stream, which had often to be forded by the runners, with but' little heed of wet feet or splashed petticoat. The Parson and his daughters from the village of St Nicholas joined in the sport, and were invited to the morning drink and substantial breakfast afterwards, where the young ladies were lost in admiration of Angela's silver chocolate-pot and porcelain cups, while their clerical father owned to a distaste for all morning drinks except such as owed their flavour and strength to malt and hops.

"If you had lived among green fields and damp marshes as long as I have, miss, you would know what poor stuff your chocolate is to fortify a man's bones against ague and rheumatism. I am told the Spaniards brought it from Mexico, where the natives eat nothing else, from which comes the copper colour of their skins."

*   *   *   *   *

Denzi's visit lasted over a month, during which time he rode into Oxfordshire twice, to see Lady Warner, stopping a night each time, lest that worthy person should fancy herself neglected.

Sir John derived the utmost pleasure from the young man's company, who bore himself towards his host with a respectful courtesy that had gone out of fashion after the murder of the King, and was rarely met with in an age when elderly men were generally spoken of as "old puts," and considered proper subjects for "bubbling."

To Denzil the old campaigner opened his heart more freely than he had ever done to any one except a brother in arms; and although he was resolute in uphold ing the cause of Monarchy against Republicanism, he owned to the natural disappointment which he had felt at the King's neglect of old friends, and reluctantly admitted that Charles, sauntering along Pall Mall with ruin at his heels, and the wickedest men and women in England for his chosen companions, was not a monarch to maintain and strengthen the public idea of the divinity that doth hedge a King.

"Of all the lessons danger and adversity can teach he has learnt but one," said Sir John, with a regretful sigh. "He has learnt the Horatian philosophy--to snatch the pleasures of the day, and care nothing what may happen on the morrow. I do not wonder that predictions of a sudden end to this globe of ours should have been bruited about of late; for if lust and profaneness could draw down fire from heaven, London would be in as perilous a case as Gomorrah. But I doubt such particular judgments belonged but to the infancy of this world, when men believed in a Personal God, interested in all their concerns, watchful to bless or to punish. We have now but the God of Spinoza--a God who is in all things and everywhere about us, of whom this Creation in which we move is but the garment--a Universal Essence which should govern and inform all we are and all we do; but not the Judge and Father of His people, to be reached by prayer and touched by pity."

"Ah, sir, our life here and hereafter is encompassed with mystery. To think is to be lost on the trackless ocean of doubt. The Papists have the easiest creed, for they believe that which they are taught, and take the mysteries of the unseen world at second hand from their Priests. A year ago, had I been happy enough to win your daughter, I should have tried my hardest to wean her from Rome; but I have lived and thought since then, and I have come to see that Calvinism is a religion of despair, and that the doctrine of Predestination involves contradictions as difficult to swallow as any fable of the Roman Church."

"It is well that you should be prepared to let her keep her religion; for I doubt she has a stubborn affection for the creed she learnt in her childhood. Indeed, it was but the other day she talked of the cloister; and I fear she has all the disposition to that religious prison in which her great aunt lived contentedly for the space of a long lifetime. But it is for you, Denzil, to cure her of that fancy, and to spare me the pain of seeing my best-beloved child under the black veil."

"Indeed, sir, if a love as earnest as man ever experienced--"

"Yes, Denzil, I know you love her; and I love you almost as if you were my very son. In the years that went by after Hyacinth was born, before the beginning of trouble, I used to long for a son, and I am afraid I did sometimes distress my dear wife by dwelling too persistently upon disappointed hopes. And then came chaos--England in arms, a rebellious people, a King put upon his defence--and I had leisure to think of none but my royal master. And in the thick of the strife my poor lamb was born to me--the bringer of my life's great sorrow--and there was no more thought of sons. So, you see, friend, the place in my heart and home has waited empty for you. Win but yonder shy dove to consent, and we shall be of one family and of one mind, and I as happy as any broken-down campaigner in England can be--content to creep to the grave in obscurity, forgotten by the Prince whose father it is my dear memory to have served."

"You loved your King, sir, I take it, with a personal affection."

"Ah, Denzil, we all loved him. Even the common people--led as they were by hectoring preachers of sedition, of no more truth or honesty than the mountebanks that ply their knavish trade round Henry's statue on the Pont Neuf--even they, the very rabble, had their hours of loyalty. I rode with his Majesty from Royston to Hatfield, in '47, when the people filled the midsummer air with his name, from hearts melting with love and pity. They strewed the ways with boughs, and strewed the boughs with roses. So great honour has been seldom shown to a royal captive."

"I take it that the lower class are no politicians, and loved their King for his private virtues."

"Never was monarch worthier to be so esteemed. He was a man of deep affections, and it was perhaps his most fatal quality where he loved to love too much. I have no grudge against that beautiful and most accomplished woman he so worshipped, and who was ever gracious to me; but I cannot doubt that Henrietta Maria was his evil star. She had the fire and daring of her father, but none of his care and affection for the people. The daughter of the most beloved of kings had the instincts of a tyrant, and was ever urging her too pliant husband to unpopular measures. She wanted to set that little jewelled shoe of hers on the neck of rebellion, when she should have held out her soft white hand to make friends of her foes. Her beauty and her grace might have done much, had she inherited with the pride of the Medici something of their finesse and suavity. But he loved her, Denzil, forgave all her follies, her lavish spending and wasteful splendour. 'My wife is a bad housekeeper,'

I heard him say once, when she was hanging upon his chair as he sat at the end of the Council table. The palace accounts were on the table--three thousand pounds for a masque--extravagance only surpassed by Nicholas Fouquet twenty years afterwards, when he was squandering the public money. 'My wife is a bad housekeeper,' his Majesty said gently, and then he drew down the little French museau with a caressing hand, and kissed her in the presence of those greybeards."

"His son is strangely unlike him in domestic matters."

"His son has the manners of a Frenchman and the morals of a Turk. He is a despot to his wife and a slave to his mistress. There never was greater cruelty to a woman than his Majesty's treatment of Catherine while she was still but a stranger in the land, and when he forced his notorious paramour upon her as her lady of honour. Of honour, quotha! There was sorry store of honour in his conduct. He had need feel the sting of remorse t'other day when the poor lady was thought to be on her death-bed--so gentle, so affectionate, so broken to the long-suffering of consort-queens, apologising for having lived to trouble him. Ned Hyde has given me the whole story of that poor lady's subjugation, for he was behind the scenes, and in their secrets. Poor soul! Blood rushed from her ears and nostrils when that shameless woman was brought to her, and she was carried swooning to her chamber. And then she was sullen, and the King threatened her, and sent away all her Portuguese, save one ancient waiting woman. I grant you they were ugly devils, fit to set in a field to frighten crows; but Catherine loved them. Royal treatment for a Christian Queen from a Christian King! Could the Sophy do worse? And presently the poor lady yielded (as most women will, for at heart they are slavish and love to be beaten), and after holding herself aloof for a long time--a sad, silent, neglected figure where all the rest were loud and merry--she made friends with the lady, and even seemed to fawn upon her."

"And now I dare swear the two women mingle their tears when Charles is unfaithful to both; or Catherine weeps while Barbara curses. That would be more in character. Fire and not water is her ladyship's element."

"Ah, Denzil, 'tis a curious change; and to have lived to see Buckingham murdered, and Stafford sacrificed, and the Rebellion, and the Commonwealth, and the Restoration, and the Plague, and the Fire, and to have skirmished in the battles of Parliaments and Princes, t'other side the Channel, and seen the tail of the Thirty

Years' War, towns ruined, villages laid waste, where Tilly passed in blood and fire, is to have lived through as wild a variety of fortunes as ever madman invented in a dream."

*   *   *   *   *

Denzil lingered at the Manor, urged again and again by his host to stay over the day fixed for departure, and so lengthening his visit with a most willing submission till late in June, when the silence of the nightingales made sleep more possible, and the sunset was so late and the sunrise so early that there seemed to be no such thing as night. He had made up his mind to plead for a hearing in the hour of farewell; and it may have been as much from apprehension of that fateful hour as even from the delight of being in his mistress's company that he acceded with alacrity when Sir John desired him to stay. But an end must come at last to all hesitations, and a familiar verse repeated itself in his brain with the persistent iteration of cathedral chimes--

> "He either fears his fate too much,
> Or his desert is small,
> Who fears to put it to the touch,
> And win or lose it all."

Sir John pushed him towards his fate with affectionate urgency.

"Never be dastardised by a girl's refusal, man," said the Knight, warm with his morning draught, on that last day, when the guest's horses had been fed for a journey, and the saddle-bags packed. "Don't let a simpleton's coldness cow your spirits. The wench likes you; else she would scarce have endured your long sermons upon weeds and insects, or been smiling and contented in your company all these weeks. Take heart of grace, man; and remember that though I am no tyrannical father to drag an unwilling bride to the altar, I have all a father's authority, and will not have my dearest wishes baulked by the capricious humours of a coquette."

"Not for worlds, sir, would I owe to authority what love cannot freely grant--"

"Don't chop logic, Denzil. You want my daughter; and by God you shall have her! Win her with pretty speeches if you can. If she turn stubborn she shall have plain English from me. I have promised not to force her inclination; but if I am driven to harsh measures 'twill be for her own good I am severe. Ventregris! What can fortune give her better than a handsome and virtuous husband?"

Angela was in the garden when Denzil went to take leave of her. She was walking up and down beside a long border of June flowers, screened from rough winds by those thick walls of yew which gave such a comfortable sheltered feeling to the Manor gardens, while in front of flowers and turf there sparkled the waters of a long pond or stew, stocked with tench and carp, some among them as ancient and as greedy as the scaly monsters of Fontainebleau.

The sun was shining on the dark green water and the gaudy flower-bed, and Angela's favourite spaniel was running about the grass, barking his loudest, chasing bird or butterfly with impotent fury, since he never caught anything. At sight of Denzil he tore across the greensward, his silky ears flying, and barked at him as if the young man's appearance in that garden were an insufferable impertinence; but, on being taken up in one strong hand, changed his opinion, and slobbered the face of the foe in an ecstasy of affection.

"Soho, Ganymede, thou knowest I bear thee a good heart, plaything and mere pretence of a dog as thou art," said Denzil, depositing their little bundle of black-and-tan flossiness at Angela's feet.

He might have carried and nursed his mistress's favourite with pleasure during any casual sauntering and random talk; but a man could hardly ask to have his fate decided for good or ill with a toy spaniel in his arms.

"My horse is at the door, Angela, and I am come to bid you good-bye," he said in a grave voice.

The words were of the simplest; but there was something in his tone that told her all was not said. She paled at the thought of an approaching conflict; for she knew her father was against her, and that there must be hard fighting.

They walked the length of flower border and lawn in silence; and then, when they were furthest from the house, and from the hazard of eyes looking out of windows, he stopped suddenly, and took her unresisting hand, which lay cold in his.

"Dearest, I have kept silence through all those blessed days in which you and I have been together; but I have not left off loving you or hoping for you. Things have changed since I spoke to you in London last winter. I have a powerful advocate now whose pleading ought to prevail with you--a father whose anxious affection urges what my passionate love so ardently desires. Indeed, dear heart, if you will be kind, you can make a father and lover happy with one breath. You have but to say 'Yes' to the prayer you know of----"

"Alas! Denzil, I cannot. I am your true and faithful friend. If you were sick and alone--as his lordship was--I would go to you and nurse you, as your friend and sister. If you were poor and I were rich, I would divide my fortune with you. I shall always think of you with affection--always take pleasure in your society, if you will let me; but it must be as your sister. You have no sister, Denzil--I no brother. Why cannot we be to each other as brother and sister?"

"Only because from the hour when your beauty and sweetness began to grow into my mind I have been your lover, and nothing else--your adoring lover. I cannot change my fervent hope for the poor name of friend. I can never again dare be to you what I have been in this happy season last past, unless you will let me be more than I have been."

"Alas!"

Only that one word, with a sorrowful shake of the graceful head, covered with feathery ringlets in the dainty fashion of that day, so becoming in youth, so inappropriate to advancing years, when the rich profusion of curls came straight from Chedreux, or some of his imitators, and baldness was hidden by the spoils of the dead.

"Alas!"

No need for more than that sad dissyllable.

"Then I am no nearer winning this dear hand than I was at Fareham House?" he said heartbrokenly, for he had built high hopes upon her kindness and willing companionship in that Arcadian valley.

"I told you then that I should never marry. I have not changed my mind. I never can change. I am to be Henriette's spinster aunt."

"And Fareham's spinster sister?" said Denzil. "I understand. We are neither of us cured of our malady. It is my disease to love you in spite of your disdain. It is your disease to love where you should not. Farewell!"

He was gone before she could reply. The livid anger of his face, the deep resentment in his voice, haunted her memory, and made life almost intolerable.

"My sin has found me out!" she said to herself, as she paced the garden with the rapid steps that indicate a distempered spirit. "What right has he to pry into the depths of my mind, and ferret out all that there is of evil in my nature? Well, he goes the surest way to make me hate him. If ever he comes here again, I will run away and hide from all who know me. I would rather be a farm-servant, and rise at daybreak to work in the fields, than endure his insolence."

She had to bear worse pain before Denzil had ridden far upon his journey; for her father came to the garden to seek her, eager to know the result of his *protege's* wooing.

"Well, sweetheart," he began, taking her to his bosom and kissing her. "Do I salute the future Lady Warner?"

"No, sir; I am too well content with the name I inherit to desire any other."

"That is gracefully said, cherie; but I want to see my ewe lamb happily wedded. Has thy sweetheart stolen away without finding courage to ask the question that has been on the tip of his tongue for the last six weeks?"

"He has been both importunate and impertinent, sir, and he has had his answer. I hope I may never see him again."

"What! you have refused him? You must be mad!"

"No, sir; sober and sane enough to know when I am happy. I told you before this gentleman came here that I did not mean to marry. Surely I am not so unloving a daughter that I must be driven to take a husband, because my father will not have me."

"Angela, it is for your own safety and welfare I would see you married. What have you to succeed to when I am gone? An impoverished estate, in a country that has seen such rough changes within a score of years that one dare scarcely calculate upon a prolonged time of safety, even in this sequestered valley. God only knows when cannon-balls may tear up our fields, and bullets whistle through the copses. This Monarchy, restored with such a clamorous approval, may endure no longer than the Commonwealth, which was thought to be lasting. His Majesty's trivial life and gross extravagance have disgusted and alarmed some who loved him dearly, and have set the common people questioning whether the rough rule of the Protector were not better than the ascendency of shameless women and dissolute men. The pageantry of Whitehall may vanish like a parchment scroll in a furnace, and Charles, who has tasted the sours of exile, may be again a wanderer, dependent on the casual munificence of foreign states; and in such an evil hour," continued the Knight, his mind straying from the contemplation of his daughter's future to the memory of his own wrongs, "Charles Stuart may remember the old puts who fought and suffered for his father, and how scurvy a recompense they had for their services."

He reverted to Denzil's offer after a brief silence, Angela walking dutifully by his side, prepared to suffer any harshness upon his part without complaining.

"I love the young man, and he would be to me as a son," he said; "the comrade and support of my old age. I am poor, as the world goes now; have but just enough to live modestly in this retreat, where life costs but little. He is rich, and can give you a handsome seat near your sister's mansion; and a house in London if you desire one; less splendid, doubtless, than Fareham's palace on the Thames, but more befitting the habits and manners of an English gentleman's wife. He can give you hounds and hawks, your riding-horses, and your coach-and-six. What more, in God's name, can any reasonable woman desire?"

"Only one thing, sir. To live my own life in peace, as my conscience and my reason bid me. I cannot love Denzil Warner, though of late I have grown to like and respect him as a friend and most intelligent companion. Your persistence is fast changing friendship into dislike; and the very name of the man would speedily become hateful to me."

"Oh, I have done!" retorted Sir John. "I am no tyrant. You must take your own way, mistress. I can but lament that Providence gave me only two daughters, and one of them an arrant fool."

He left her in a huff, and had it not been for an astonishing event, which convulsed town and country, and suspended private interests and private quarrels in the excitement of public affairs, she would have heard much more of his discontent.

The Dutch ships were at Chatham. English men-of-war were blazing at the very mouth of the Thames, and there was panic lest the triumphant foe should sail their fire-ships up the river to London, besiege the Tower, relight the fire whose ashes were scarce grown cold, pillage, slaughter, destroy--as Tilly had destroyed the wretched Provinces in the religious war.

Here, in this sheltered haven, amidst green fields, under the lee of the Brill, the panic and consternation were as intense as if the village of St. Nicholas were the one spot the Dutch would make for after landing; and, indeed, there were rustics who went to the placid scene where the infant Thame rises in its cradle of reed and lily, half expectant of seeing Netherlandish vessels stranded among the rushes.

The Dutch fleet was at Chatham. Ships were being sunk across the Medway, to stop the invader.

Sheerness was to be fortified. London was in arms; and Brill remembered its repulse of Hampden's regiment with a proud consciousness of being invincible.

The Dutch fleet saved Angela many a paternal lecture; for Sir John rode post-haste towards London, and did not return until the end of the month.

In London he found Hyacinth, much disturbed about her husband, who had gone as volunteer with General Middleton, and was in command of a cavalry regiment at Chatham.

"I never saw him in such spirits as when he left me," Lady Fareham told her father. "I believe he is ever happiest when he breathes gunpowder."

*   *   *   *   *

Sir John's leave-taking had been curt and moody, for Angela's offence rankled deep in his mind; and it was as much as he could do to command his anger, even in bidding her good-bye.

"Did I not tell you that we live in troubled times, and that no man can foresee the coming evil, or how great our woes and distractions may be?" he asked, with a gloomy triumph. "Whoever thought to hear De Ruyter's guns at Sheerness, or to see the Royal Charles led captive? Absit omen! Who knows what destruction may come upon that other Royal Charles, for whose safety we pray morning and night, and who lolls across a basset-table, perhaps, with his wantons around him, while we are on our knees supplicating the Creator for him? Who knows? We may have

London in flames again, and a conflagration more fatal than the last, thou obstinate wench, before thou art a week older, and every able-bodied man called away from plough and pasture to serve the King, and desolation and famine where plenty now smiles at us. And is this a time in which to refuse a valiant and wealthy protector, a lover as honest as ever God made; a pious, conforming Christian, of unsullied name; a young man after my own pattern; a fine horseman and a good farmer; one who loves a pack of hounds and a well-bred horse, a flight of hawks and a match at bowls, better than to give chase to a she-rake in the Mall, or to drink himself stark mad at a tavern in Covent Garden with debauchees from Whitehall?"

Sir John prosed and grumbled to the last moment, but could not refuse to bend down from his saddle and kiss the fair, pale face that looked at him in piteous deprecation at the moment of parting.

"Well, keep a brave heart, Mistress Wilful. Thou art safe here yet awhile from Dutch marauders. I go but to find out how much truth there is in these panic rumours."

She begged him not to fatigue himself with too long stages, and went back to the silent house, thankful to be alone in her despondency. She felt as if the last page in her worldly life had been written. She had to turn her thoughts backward to that quiet retreat where there would at least be peace. She had promised her father that she would not return to the Convent while he wanted her at home. But was that promise to hold good if he were to embitter her life by urging her to a marriage that would only bring her unhappiness?

She had ample leisure for thought in one summer day of a solitude so absolute that she began to shiver in the sultry stillness of afternoon, and scarce ventured to raise her eyes from her embroidery frame, lest some shadowy presence, some ghost out of the dead past, should hover near, watching her as she sat alone in scenes where that pale spirit had been living flesh. The thought of all who had lived and died in that house--men and women of her own race, whose qualities of mind and person she had inherited--oppressed her in the long hours of silent reverie. Before her first day of loneliness had ended, her spirits had sunk to deepest melancholy; and in that weaker condition of mind she had begun to ask herself whether she had any right to oppose her father's wishes by denying herself to a suitor whom she esteemed and respected, and whose filial affection would bring new sunshine into that dear father's declining years. She had noted their manner to each other during Denzil's protracted visit, and had seen all the evidences of a warm regard on both sides. She had too complete a faith in Denzil's sterling worth to question the reality of any feeling which his words and manner indicated. He was above all things a man of truth and honesty. She was roaming about the gardens with her dog towards noon in the second day of her solitude, when across the yew hedges she saw white clouds of dust rising from the high-road, and heard the clatter of hoofs and roll of wheels--a noise as of a troop of cavalry--whereat Ganymede barked himself almost into an apoplexy, and rushed across the grass like a mad thing.

A great cracking of whips and sound of voices, horses galloping, horses trotting, dust enough to whiten all the hedges and greensward! Angela stood at gaze, wondering if the Dutch were coming to storm the old house, or the county militia coming to garrison it.

The Manor Moat was the destination of that clamorous troop, whoever they were. Wheels and horses stopped sharply at the great iron gate in front of the house, and the bell began to ring furiously, while other dogs, with voices that resembled Ganymede's, answered his shrill bark with even shriller yelpings.

Angela ran towards the gate, and was near enough to see it opened to admit three black-and-tan spaniels, and one slim personage in a long flame-coloured brocatelle gown and a large beaver hat, who approached with stately movements, a small, pert nose held high, and rosy upper lip curled in patrician disdain of common things, while a fan of peacock's plumage, that flashed sapphire and emerald in the fierce noonday sun, was waved slowly before the dainty face, scattering the tremulous life of summer that buzzed and fluttered in the sultry air.

In the rear of this brilliant figure appeared a middle-aged person in a grey silk gown and hood, and a negro page in the Fareham livery, a waiting-woman, and a tall lackey, so many being the necessary adjuncts to the Honourable Henrietta Maria Revel's state when she went abroad.

Angela ran to receive her niece with a cry of rapture, and the tall slip of a girl in the flame-coloured frock was clasped to her aunt's heart with a ruthless disregard of the beaver hat and cataract of ostrich plumage.

"Prends garde d'abimer mon chapeau, p'tite tante," cried Henriette, "'tis one of Lewin's Nell Gwyn hats, and cost twenty guineas, without the buckle, which I stole out of father's shoe t'other day. His lordship is so careless about his clothes that he wore the shoes two days and never knew there was a buckle missing, and those lazy devils his servants never told him. I believe they meant to rook him of t'other buckle."

"Chatterer, chatterer, how happy I am to see thee! But is not your mother with you?"

"Her ladyship is in London. Everybody of importance is scampering off to London; and no doubt will be rushing back to the country again if the Dutch take the Tower; but I don't think they will while my father is able to raise a regiment."

"And mademoiselle"--with a curtsy to the lady in grey--"has brought you all this long way through the heat to see me?"

"I have brought mademoiselle," Henrietta answered contemptuously, before the Frenchwoman had finished the moue and the shrug which with her always preceded speech; "and a fine plague I had to make her come."

"Madame will conceive that, in miladi's absence, it was a prodigious inconvenience to order two coaches, and travel so far. His lordship's groom of the chambers is my witness that I protested against such an outrageous proceeding."

"Two coaches!" exclaimed Angela.

"A coach-and-six for me and my dogs and my gouvernante, and a coach-and-four for my people," explained Henriette, who had modelled her equipage and suite upon a reminiscence of the train which attended Lady Castlemaine's visit to Chilton, as beheld from a nursery window.

"Come, child, and rest, out of the sun; and you, mademoiselle, must need refreshment after so long a drive."

"Our progress through a perpetual cloud of dust and a succession of narrow lanes did indeed suggest the torments of purgatory; but the happiness of madame's gracious welcome is an all-sufficient compensation for our fatigue," mademoiselle replied, with a deep curtsey.

"I was not tired in the least," asserted Henriette. "We stopped at the Crown at Thame and had strawberries and milk."

"*You* had strawberries and milk, mon enfant. I have a digestion which will not allow such liberties."

"And our horses were baited, and our people had their morning drink," said

Henriette, with her grown-up air. "One ought always to remember cattle and servants. May we put up our horses with you, auntie? We must leave you soon after dinner, so as to be at Chilton by sunset, or mademoiselle will be afraid of highwaymen, though I told Samuel and Peter to bring their blunderbusses in case of an attack. Ma'amselle has no valuables, and at the worst I should but have to give them my diamond buckle, and my locket with his lordship's portrait."

Angela's cheeks flushed at that chance allusion to Fareham's picture. It brought back a vision of the Convent parlour, and she standing there with Fareham's miniature in her hand, wonderingly contemplative of the dark, strong face. At that stage of her life she had seen so few men's faces; and this one had a power in it that startled her. Did she divine, by some supernatural foreknowledge, that this face held the secret of her destiny?

She went to the house, with Henriette's lissom form hanging upon her, and the grey governess tripping mincingly beside them, tottering a little upon her high heels.

Old Reuben had crept out into the sunshine, with a rustic footman following him, and the cook was looking out at a window in the wing where kitchen and servants' hall occupied as important a position as the dining-parlour and saloon on the opposite side. A hall with open roof, wide double staircase, and music gallery, filled the central space between the two projecting wings, and at the back there was a banqueting-chamber or ball-room, where in more prosperous days, the family had been accustomed to dine on all stately occasions--a room now shabby and grey with disuse.

While the footman showed the way to the stables, Angela drew Reuben aside for a brief consultation as to ways and means for a dinner that must be the best the house could provide, and which might be served at two o'clock, the later hour giving time for extra preparation. A capon, larded after the French fashion, a pair of trouts, the finest the stream could furnish, or a carp stewed in clary wine, and as many sweet kickshaws as cook's ingenuity could furnish at so brief a notice. Nor were waiting-woman, lackey, and postillions to be neglected. Chine and sirloin, pudding and beer must be provided for all.

"There are six men besides the black boy," sighed Reuben; they will devour us a week's provision of butcher's meat."

"If you have done your housekeeping, tante, let me go to your favourite summer-house with you, and tell you my secrets. I am perishing for a ***tete-a-tete!*** Ma'amselle"--with a wave of the peacock fan--"can take a siesta, and forget the dust of the road, while we converse."

Angela ushered mademoiselle to the pretty summer-parlour, looking out upon a geometrical arrangement of flower-beds in the Dutch manner. Chocolate and other light refreshments were being prepared for the travellers; but Henrietta's impatience would wait for nothing.

"I have not driven along these detestable roads to taste your chocolate," she protested. "I have a world to say to you: en attendant, mademoiselle, you will consider everything at your disposal in the house of my grandfather, jusqu'a deux heures."

She sank almost to the ground in a Whitehall curtsy, rose swift as an arrow, tucked her arm through Angela's, and pulled her out of the room, paying no attention to the governess's voluble injunctions not to expose her complexion to the sun, or to sit in a cold wind, or to spoil her gown.

"What a shabby old place it is!" she said, looking critically round her as they went through the gardens. "I'm afraid you must perish with ***ennui*** here, with so few servants and no company to speak of. Yes"--contemplating her shrewdly, as they seated themselves in a stone temple at the end of the bowling-green--"you are looking moped and ill. This valley air does not agree with you. Well, you can have a much finer place whenever you choose. A better house and garden, ever so much nearer Chilton. And you will choose, won't you, dearest?" nestling close to her, after throwing off the big hat which made such loving contact impossible.

"I don't understand you, Henriette."

"If you call me Henriette I shall be sure you are angry with me."

"No, love, not angry, but surprised."

"You think I have no right to talk of your sweetheart, because I am only thirteen--and have scarce left off playing with babies--I have hated them for ages, only people persist in giving me the foolish puppets. I know more of the world than you do, auntie, after being shut in a Convent the best part of your life. Why are you so obstinate, ma cherie, in refusing a gentleman we all like?"

"Do you mean Sir Denzil?"

"Sans doute. Have you a crowd of servants?"

"No, child, only this one. But don't you see that other people's liking has less to do with the question than mine? And if I do not like him well enough to be his wife----"

"But you ought to like him. You know how long her ladyship's heart has been set on the match; you must have seen what pains she took in London to have Sir Denzil always about you. And now, after a most exemplary patience, after being your faithful servant for over a year, he asks you to be his wife, and you refuse, obstinately refuse. And you would rather mope here with my poor old grandfather--in abject poverty--mother says 'abject poverty'--than be the honoured mistress of one of the finest seats in Oxfordshire."

"I would rather do what is right and honest, my dearest It is dishonest to marry without love."

"Then half mother's fine friends must be dishonest, for I dare swear that very few of them love their husbands."

"Henriette, you talk of things you don't know."

"Don't know! Why, there is no one in London knows more. I am always listening, and I always remember. De Malfort used to say I had a plaguey long memory, when I told him of things he had said a year ago."

"My dear, I love you fondly, but I cannot have you talk to me of what you don't understand; and I am sorry Sir Denzil Warner had no more courtesy than to go and complain of me to my sister."

"He did not come to Chilton to complain. Her ladyship met him on the way from Oxford in her coach. He was riding, and she called to him to come to the coach door. It was the day after he left you, and he was looking miserable; and she questioned him, and he owned that his suit had been rejected, and he had no further hope. My mother came home in a rage. But why was she angry with his lordship? Indeed, she rated him as if it were his fault you refused Sir Denzil."

Angela sat silent, and the hand Henriette was clasping grew cold as ice.

"Did my father bid you refuse him, aunt?" asked the girl, scrutinising her aunt's countenance, with those dark grey eyes, so like Fareham's in their falcon brightness.

"No, child. Why should he interfere? It is no business of his."

"Then why was mother so angry? She walked up and down the room in a towering passion. 'This is your doing,' she cried. 'If she were not your adoring slave, she would have jumped at so handsome a sweetheart. This is your witchcraft. It is you she loves--you--you--you!' His lordship stood dumb, and pointed to me. 'Do you forget your child is present?' he said. 'I forget everything except that everybody uses me shamefully,' she cried. 'I was only made to be slighted and trampled upon.' His lordship made no answer, but walked to the door in that way he ever has when he is angered--pale, frowning, silent. I was standing in his way, and he gripped me by the arm, and dragged me out of the room. I dare venture there is a bruise on my arm where he held me. I know his fingers hurt me with their grip; and I could hear my lady screaming and sobbing as he took me away. But he would not let me go back to her. He would only send her women. 'Your mother has an interval of madness,' he said; 'you are best out of her presence.' The news of the Dutch ships came the same evening, and my father rode off towards London, and my mother ordered her coach, and followed an hour after. They seemed both distracted; and only because you refused Sir Denzil."

"I cannot help her ladyship's foolishness, Papillon. She has no occasion for any of this trouble. I am her dutiful, affectionate sister; but my heart is not hers to give or to refuse."

"But was it indeed my father's fault? Is it because you adore him that you refused Sir Denzil?"

"No--no--no. My affection for my brother--he has been to me as a brother--can make no difference in my regard for any one else. One cannot fall in love at another's ordering, or be happy with a husband of another's choice. You will discover that for yourself, Papillon, perhaps, when you are a woman."

"Oh, I mean to marry for wealth and station, as all the clever women do," said Papillon, with an upward jerk of her delicate chin. "Mrs. Lewin always says I ought to be a duchess. I should like to have married the Duke of Monmouth, and then, who knows, I might have been a Queen. The King's other sons are too young for me, and they will never have Monmouth's chance. But, indeed, sweetheart, you ought to marry Sir Denzil, and come and live near us at Chilton. You would make us all happy."

"Ma tres chere, it is so easy to talk--but when thou thyself art a woman----"

"I shall never care for such trumpery as love. I mean to have a grand house--ever so much grander than Fareham House. Perhaps I may marry a Frenchman, and have a salon, and all the wits about me on my day. I would make it gayer than Mademoiselle de Scudery's Saturdays, which my governess so loves to talk of. There should be less talk and more dancing. But listen, p'tite tante," clasping her arms suddenly round Angela's neck, "I won't leave this spot till you have promised to change your mind about Denzil. I like him vastly; and I'm sure there's no reason why you should not love him--unless you really are his lordship's adoring slave," emphasising those last words, "and he has forbidden you."

Angela sat dumb, her eyes fixed on vacancy.

"Why, you are like the lady in those lines you made me learn, who 'sat like patience on a monument, smiling at grief.' Dearest, why so sad? Remember that fine house--and the dairy that was once a chapel. You could turn it into a chapel again if you liked, and have your own chaplain. His Majesty takes no heed of what we Papists do--being a Papist himself at heart, they say--though poor wretches are dragged off to gaol for worshipping in a conventicle. What is a conventicle? Will you not change your mind, dearest? Answer, answer, answer!"

The slender arms tightened their caress, the pretty little brown face pressed itself against Angela's pale, cold cheek.

"For my sake, sweetheart, say thou wilt have him. I will go to see thee every day."

"I have been here for months and you have not come, though I begged you in a dozen letters."

"I have been kept at my book and my dancing lessons. Mademoiselle told her ladyship that I was a monster of ignorance. I have been treated shamefully. I could not have come to-day had my lady been at home; but I would not brook a hireling's dictation. Voyons, p'tite tante, tu seras miladi Warner. Dis, dis, que je te fasse mourir de baisers."

She was almost stifling her aunt with kisses in the intervals of her eager speech.

"The last word has been spoken, Papillon. I have sent him away--and it was not the first time. I had refused him before. I cannot call him back."

"But he shall come without calling. He is your adoring slave," cried Henriette, leaping up from the stone bench, and clapping her hands in an ecstasy. "He will need no calling. Dearest, dearest, most exquisite, delectable auntie! I am so happy! And my mother will be content. And no one shall ever say you are my father's slave."

"Henriette, if you repeat that odious phrase I shall hate you!"

"Now you are angry. God, what a frown! I will repeat no word that angers you. My Lady Warner--sweet Lady Warner. I vow 'tis a prettier name than Revel or Fareham."

"You are mad, Henriette! I have promised nothing."

"Yes, you have, little aunt. You have promised to drop a curtsy, and say 'Yes' when Sir Denzil rides this way. You sent him away in a huff. He will come back smiling like yonder sunshine on the water. Oh, I am so happy! My doing, all my doing!"

"It is useless to argue with you."

"Quite useless. Il n'y a pas de quoi. Nous sommes d'accord. I shall be your chief bridesmaid. You must be married in her Majesty's chapel at St. James's. The Pope will give his dispensation--if you cannot persuade Denzil to change his religion. Were he my suitor I would twist him round my fingers," with an airy gesture of the small brown hand.

There is nothing more difficult than to convince a child that she pleads in vain for any ardently desired object. Nothing that Angela could say would reconcile her niece to the idea of failure; so there was no help but to let her fancy her arguments conclusive, and to change the bent of her thoughts if possible.

It wanted nearly an hour of dinner-time, so Angela suggested an inspection of the home farm, which was close by, trusting that Henriette's love of animals would afford an all-sufficient diversion; nor was she disappointed, for the little fine lady was quite as much at home in stable and cowshed as in a London drawing-room, and spent a happy hour in making friends with the live stock, from the favourite Hereford cow, queen of the herd, to the smallest bantam in the poultry-yard.

To this rustic entertainment followed dinner, in the preparation of which banquet Marjory Cook had surpassed herself; and Papillon, being by this time seriously hungry, sat and feasted to her heart's content, discussing the marrow pudding and the stewed carp with the acumen and authority of a professed gourmet.

"I like this old-fashioned rustic diet," she said condescendingly.

She reproached her governess with not doing justice to a syllabub; but showed herself a fine lady by her complaint at the lack of ice for her wine.

"My grandfather should make haste and build an icehouse before next winter," she drawled. "One can scarce live through this weather without ice," fanning herself, with excessive languor.

"I hope, dear, thou wilt not expire on the journey home."

The coaches were at the gate before Papillon had finished dinner, and Mademoiselle was in great haste to be gone, reminding her pupil that she had travelled so far against her will and at the hazard of angering Madame la Baronne.

"Madame la Baronne will be enraptured when she knows what I have done to please her," answered Papillon, and then, with a last parting embrace, hugging her aunt's fair neck more energetically than ever, she whispered, "I shall tell Denzil. You will make us all happy."

A cloud of dust, a clatter of hoofs, Ma'amselle's screams as the carriage rocked while she was mounting the steps, and with much cracking of whips and swearing at horses from the postillions who had taken their fill of home-brewed ale, hog's harslet, and cold chine, and, lo, the brilliant vision of the Honourable Henrietta Maria and her train vanished in the dust of the summer highway, and Angela went slowly back to the long green walk beside the fish-pond, where she was in as silent a solitude, but for a lingering nightingale or two, as if she had been in the palace of the sleeping beauty. If all things slumbered not, there was at least as marked a pause in life. The Dutch might be burning more ships, and the noise of war might be coming nearer London with every hour of the summer day. Here there was a repose as of the after-life, when all hopes and dreams and loves and hates are done and ended, and the soul waits in darkness and silence for the next unfolding of its wings.

Those hateful words, "your adoring slave," and all that speech of Hyacinth's which the child had repeated, haunted Angela with an agonising iteration. She had not an instant's doubt as to the scene being faithfully reported. She knew how preternaturally acute Henriette's intellect had become in the rarified atmosphere of her mother's drawing-room, how accurate her memory, how sharp her ears, and how observant her eyes. Whatever Henriette reported was likely to be to the very letter and spirit of the scene she had witnessed. And Hyacinth, her sister, had put this shame upon her, had spoken of her in the cruelest phrase as loving one whom it was mortal sin to love. Hyacinth, so light, so airy a creature, whom her younger sister had ever considered as a grown-up child, had yet been shrewd enough to fathom her mystery, and to discover that secret attachment which had made Denzil's suit hateful to her. "And if I do not consent to marry him she will always think ill of me. She will think of me as a wretch who tried to steal her husband's love--a worse woman than Lady Castlemaine--for she had the King's affection before he ever saw the Queen's poor plain face. His adoring slave!"

Evening shadows were around her. She had wandered into the woods, was slowly threading the slender cattle tracks in the cool darkness; while that passionate song of the nightingales rose in a louder ecstasy as the quiet of the night deepened, and the young moon hung high above the edge of a wooded hill.

"His adoring slave," she repeated, with her hands clasped above her uncovered head.

Hateful, humiliating words! Yet there was a keen rapture in repeating them. They were true words. His slave--his slave to wait upon him in sickness and pain; to lie and watch at his door like a faithful dog; to follow him to the wars, and clean his armour, and hold his horse, and wait in his tent to receive him wounded, and heal his wounds where surgeons failed to cure, wanting that intensity of attention and understanding which love alone can give; to be his Bellario, asking nothing of him, hoping for nothing, hardly for kind words or common courtesy, foregoing woman's claim upon man's chivalry, content to be nothing--only to be near him.

If such a life could have been--the life that poets have imagined for despairing love! It was less than a hundred years since handsome Mrs. Southwell followed Sir Robert Dudley to Italy, disguised as a page. But the age of romance was past. The modern world had only laughter for such dreams.

That revelation of Hyacinth's jealousy had brought matters to a crisis. Something must be done, Angela told herself, and quickly, to set her right with her sister, and in her own esteem. She had to choose between a loveless marriage and the Convent. By accepting one or the other she must prove that she was not the slave of a dishonourable love.

Marriage or the Convent? It had been easy, contemplating the step from a distance, to choose the Convent. But when she thought of it, to-night, amid the exquisite beauty of these woods, with the moonlit valley lying at her feet, the winding streams reflecting that silvery light, or veiled in a pale haze--to-night, in the liberty and loveliness of the earth, the vision of Convent walls filled her with a shuddering horror. To be shut in that Flemish garden for ever; her life enclosed within the straight lines of that long green alley leading to a dead wall, darkened over by flowerless ivy. How witheringly dull the old life showed, looking back at it after years of freedom and enjoyment, action and variety. No, no, no! She could not bury herself alive, could not forego the liberty to wander in a wood like this, to gaze upon scenes as beautiful as yonder valley, to read the poets she loved, to see, perhaps, some day those romantic scenes which she knew but as dreams--Florence, Vallombrosa--to follow the footsteps of Milton, to see the Venice she had read of in Howell's Letters, to kneel at the feet of the Holy Father, in the City of Cities. All these things would be for ever forbidden to her if she chose the common escape from earthly sorrow.

She thought of her whose example had furnished the theme of many a discourse at the Convent, Mazarin's lovely niece, the Princess de Conti, who, in the bloom of early womanhood, was awakened from the dream of this life to the reality of Heaven, and had renounced the pleasures of the most brilliant Court in the world for the severities of Port Royal. She thought of that sublime heretic Ferrar, whose later existence was one long prayer. Of how much baser a clay must she be fashioned when her too earthly heart clung so fondly to the loveliness of earth, and shrank with aversion from the prospect of a long life within those walls where her childhood had been so peaceful and happy.

"How changed, how changed and corrupted this heart has become!" she murmured, in her dejection, "when that life which was once my most ardent desire now seems to me worse than the grave. Anything--any life of duty in the world, rather than that living death."

She was in the garden next morning at six, after a sleepless night, and she occupied herself till noon in going about among the cottagers carrying those small comforts which she had been in the habit of taking them, and listening patiently to those various distresses which they were very glad to relate to her. She taught the children, and read to the sick, and was able in this round of duties to keep her thoughts from dwelling too persistently upon her own trouble. After the one o'clock dinner, at which she offended old Reuben by eating hardly anything, she went for a woodland ramble with her dogs, and it was near sunset when she re-turned to the house, just in time to see two road-stained horses being led away from the hall door.

Sir John had come home. She found him in the dining parlour, sitting gloomy and weary looking before the table where Reuben was arranging a hasty meal.

"I have eaten nothing upon the road, yet I have but a poor stomach for your bacon-ham," he said, and then looked up at his daughter with a moody glance, as she went towards him.

"Dear sir, we must try to coax your appetite when you have rested a little. Let me unbuckle your spurs and pull off your boots, while Reuben fetches your easiest shoes."

"Nay, child, that is man's work, not for such fingers as yours. The boots are nowise irksome--'tis another kind of shoe that pinches, Angela."

She knelt down to unbuckle the spur-straps, and while on her knees she said--

"You look sad, sir. I fear you found ill news at London."

"I found such shame as never came before upon England, such confusion as only traitors and profligates can know; men who have cheated and lied and wasted the public money, left our fortresses undefended, our ships unarmed, our sailors unpaid, half-fed, and mutinous; clamorous wives crying aloud in the streets that their husbands should not fight and bleed for a King who starved them. They have clapped the scoundrel who had charge of the Yard at Chatham in the Tower--but will that mend matters? A scapegoat, belike, to suffer for higher scoundrels. The mob is loudest against the Chancellor, who I doubt is not to blame for our unreadi-ness, having little power of late over the King. Oh, there has been iniquity upon iniquity, and men know not whom most to blame--the venal idle servants, or the master of all."

"You mean that men blame his Majesty?"

"No, Angela. But when our ships were blazing at Chatham, and the Dutch tri-umphing, the cry was 'Oh, for an hour of old Noll!' Charles has played his cards so that he has made the loyalest hearts in England wish the Brewer back again. They called him the Tiger of the Seas. We have no tigers now, only asses and monkeys. Why, there was scarce a grain of sense left in London. The beat of the drums calling out the train-bands seemed to have stupefied the people. Everywhere madness and confusion. They have sunk their richest argosies at Barking Creek to block the river; but the Dutch break chains, ride over sunken ships, laugh our petty defences to scorn."

"Dear sir, this confusion cannot last."

"It will last as long as the world's history lasts. Our humiliation will never be forgotten."

"But Englishmen will not look on idle. There must be brave men up in arms."

"Oh, there are brave men enough--Fairfax, Ingoldsby, Bethell, Norton. The Presbyterians come to the front in our troubles. Your brother-in-law is with Lord Middleton. There is no lack of officers; and regiments are being raised. But our merchant-ships, which should be quick to help us, hang back. Our Treasury is empty, and half the goldsmiths in London are bankrupt. And our ships that are burnt, and our ships that are taken, will not be conjured back again. The **Royal Charles** carried off with insulting triumph! Oh, child, it is not the loss that galls; it is the dishonour!"

He took a draught of claret out of the tankard which Angela placed at his elbow, and she carved the ham for him, and persuaded him to eat.

"Is it the public misfortune that troubles you so sadly, sir?" she asked, presently, when her father flung himself back in his chair with a heavy sigh.

"Nay, Angela, I have my peck of trouble without reckoning the ruin of my country. But my back is broad. It can bear a burden as well as any."

"Do you count a disobedient daughter among your cares, sir?"

"Disobedient is too harsh a word. I told you I would never force your inclinations. But I have an obstinate daughter, who has disappointed me, and well-nigh broken my spirit."

"Your spirit shall not rest broken if my obedience can mend it, sir," she said gently, dropping on her knees beside his chair.

"What! has that stony heart relented! Wilt thou marry him, sweetheart? Wilt give me a son as well as a daughter, and the security that thou wilt be safe and happy when I'm gone?"

"No one can be sure of happiness, father; it comes strangely, and goes we know not why. But if it will make your heart easier, sir, and Denzil be still of the same mind----"

"His mind his rock, dearest. He swore to me that he could never change. Ah, love, you have made me happy! Let the fleet burn, the ***Royal Charles*** fly Dutch colours. Here, in this quiet valley, there shall be a peaceful household and united hearts. Angela, I love that youth! Fareham, with all his rank and wealth, has never been so dear to me. That black visage repels love. But Denzil's countenance is open as the day. I can say 'Nunc Dimittis' with a light heart. I can trust Denzil Warner with my daughter's happiness."

CHAPTER XXIV.
"QUITE OUT OF FASHION."

Denzil received the good news by the hands of a mounted messenger in the following forenoon.

The Knight had written, "Ride--ride--ride!" in the Elizabethan style, on the cover of his letter, which contained but two brief sentences--

"Womanlike, she has changed her mind. Come when thou wilt, dear son."

And the son-in-law-to-be lost not an hour. He was at the Manor before night-fall. He was a member of the quiet household again, subservient to his mistress in everything.

"There are some words that must needs be spoken before we are agreed," Angela said, when they found themselves alone for the first time, in the garden, on the morning after his return, and when Denzil would fain have taken her to his breast and ratified their betrothal with a kiss. "I think you know as well as I do that it is my father's wish that has made me change."

"So long as you change not again, dear, I am of all men the happiest. Yes, I know 'tis Sir John's wooing that won you, not mine. And that I have still to conquer your heart, though your hand is promised me. Yet I do not despair of being loved in as full measure as I love. My faith is strong in the power of an honest affection."

"You may at least be sure of my honesty. I profess nothing but the desire to be your true and obedient wife----"

"Obedient! You shall be my empress."

"No, no. I have no wish to rule. I desire only to make my father happy, and you too, sir, if I can."

"Ah, my soul, that is so easy for you. You have but to let me live in your dear company. I doubt I would rather be miserable with you than happy with any other woman. Ill-use me if you will; play Zantippe, and I will be more submissive than Socrates. But you are all mildness--perfect Christian, perfect woman. You cannot miss being perfect as wife--and----"

Another word trembled on his lips; but he checked himself lest he should offend, and the speech ended in a sob.

"My Angela, my angel!"

He took her to his heart, and kissed the fair brow, cold under his passionate kisses. That word "angel" turned her to ice. It conjured back the sound of a voice that it was sin to remember. Fareham had called her so; not once, but many times, in their placid days of friendship, before the fiery breath of passion had withered all the flowers in her earthly paradise--before the knowledge of evil had clouded the brightness of the world.

A gentle peace reigned at the Manor after Angela's betrothal. Sir John was happier than he had been since the days of his youth, before the coming of that cloud no bigger than a man's hand, when John Hampden's stubborn resistance of a thirty-shilling rate had brought Crown and People face to face upon the burning question of Ship-money, and kindled the fire that was to devour England. From the hour he left his young wife to follow the King to Yorkshire Sir John's existence had known little of rest or of comfort, or even of glory. He had fought on the losing side, and had missed the fame of those who fell and took the rank of heroes by an untimely death. Hardship and danger, wounds and sickness, straitened means and scanty fare, had been his portion for three bitter years; and then had come a period of patient service, of schemes and intrigues foredoomed to failure; of going to and fro, from Jersey to Paris, from Paris to Ireland, from Ireland to Cornwall, journeying hither and thither at the behest of a shifty, irresolute man, or a passionate, imprudent woman, as the case might be; now from the King to the Queen, now from the Queen to this or that ally; futile errands, unskilful combinations, failure on every hand, till the last fatal journey, on which he was an unwilling attendant, the flight from Hampton Court to Titchfield, when the fated King broke faith with his enemies in an unfinished negotiation.

Foreign adventure had followed English hardships, and the soldier had been tossed on the stormy sea of European warfare. He had been graciously received at the French Court, but only to feel himself a stranger there, and to have his English clothes and English accent laughed at by Gramont and Bussy, and the accomplished St. Evremond, and the frivolous herd of their imitators; to see even the Queen, for whom he had spent his last jacobus, smile behind her fan at his bevues, and whisper to her sister-in-law while he knelt to kiss the little white hand that had led a King to ruin. Everywhere the stern Malignant had found himself outside the circle of the elect. At the Hotel de Rambouillet, in the splendid houses of the newly built Place Royale, in the salons of Duchesses, and the taverns of courtly roysterers and drunken poets, at Cormier's, or at the Pine Apple, in the Rue de la Juiverie, where it was all the better for a Christian gentleman not to understand the talk of the wits that flashed and drank there. Everywhere he had been a stranger and aloof. It was only under canvas, in danger and privation, that he lost the sense of being one too many in the world. There John Kirkland found his level, shoulder to shoulder with Conde and Turenne. The stout Cavalier was second to no soldier in Louis' splendid army; was of the stamp of an earlier race even, better inured to hardship than any save that heroic Prince, the Achilles of his day, who to the graces of a modern courtier joined the temper of an ancient Greek.

His daughter Hyacinth had given him the utmost affection which such a nature could give; but it was the affection of a trained singing-bird, or a pug-nosed spaniel; and the father, though he admired her beauty, and was pleased with her caresses, was shrewd enough to perceive the lightness of her disposition and the shallowness of her mind. He rejoiced in her marriage with a man of Fareham's strong character.

"I have married thee to a husband who will know how to rule a wife," he told her on the night of her wedding. "You have but to obey and to be happy; for he is rich enough to indulge all your fancies, and will not complain if you waste the gold that would pay a company of foot on the decoration of your poor little person."

"The tone in which you speak of my poor little person, sir, can but remind me how much I need the tailor and the milliner," answered Hyacinth, dropping her favourite curtsy, which she was ever ready to practise at the slightest provocation.

"Nay, petite chatte, you know I think you the loveliest creature at Saint Germain or the Louvre, far surpassing in beauty the Cardinal's niece, who has managed to set young Louis' heart throbbing with a boyish passion. But I doubt you bestow too much care on the cherishing of a gift so fleeting."

"You have said the word, sir. 'Tis because it is so fleeting I must needs take care of my beauty. We poor women are like the butterflies and the roses. We have as brief a summer. You men, who value us only for our outward show, should pardon some vanity in creatures so ephemeral."

"Ephemeral scarce applies to a sex which owns such an example as your grandmother, who has lived to reckon her servants among the grandsons of her earliest lovers."

"Not lived, sir! No woman lives after thirty. She can but exist, and dream that she is still admired. La Marquise has been dead for the last twenty years, but she won't own it. Ah, sir, c'est un triste supplice to ***have been***! I wonder how those poor ghosts can bear that earthly purgatory which they call old age? Look at Madame de Sable, par exemple, once a beauty, now only a tradition. And Queen Anne! Old people say she was beautiful, and that Buckingham risked being torn by wild horses--like Ravaillac--only to kiss her hand by stealth in a moonlit garden; and would have plunged England in war but for an excuse to come back to Paris. Who would go to war for Anne's haggard countenance nowadays?"

Even in Lady Fareham's household the Cavalier soon began to fancy himself an inhabitant too much; a dull, grey ghost from a tragical past. He could not keep himself from talking of the martyred King, and those bitter years through which he had followed his master's sinking fortunes. He told stories of York and of Beverley; of the scarcity of cash which reduced his Majesty's Court to but one table; of that bitter affront at Coventry; of the evil omens that had marked the raising of the Standard on the hill at Nottingham, and filled superstitious minds with dark forebodings, reminding old men of that sad shower of rain that fell when Charles was proclaimed at Whitehall, on the day of his accession, and of the shock of earthquake on his coronation day; of Edgehill and Lindsey's death; of the profligate conduct of the Cavalier regiments, and the steady, dogged force of their psalm-singing adversaries; of Queen Henrietta's courage, and beauty, and wilfulness, and her fatal influence upon an adoring husband.

"She wanted to be all that Buckingham had been," said Sir John, "forgetting that Buckingham was the King's evil genius."

That lively and eminently artificial society of the Rue de Touraine soon wearied of Sir John's reminiscences. King Charles's execution had receded into the dim grey of history. He might as well have told them anecdotes of Cinq Mars, or of the great Henri, or of Moses or Abraham. Life went on rapid wheels in patrician Paris. They had Conde to talk about, and Mazarin's numerous nieces, and the opera, that new importation from Italy, which the Cardinal was bringing into fashion; while in the remote past of half a dozen years back the Fronde was the only interesting subject, and even that was worn threadbare; the adventures of the Duchess, the conduct of the Prince in prison, the intrigues of Cardinal and Queen, Mademoiselle, yellow-haired Beaufort, duels of five against five--all--all these were ancient history as compared with young Louis and his passion for Marie de Mancini, and the scheming of her wily uncle to marry all his nieces to reigning princes or embryo kings.

And then the affectations and conceits of that elegant circle, the sonnets and madrigals, the "bouts-rimes," the practical jokes, the logic-chopping and straw-splitting of those ultra-fine intellects, the romances where the personages of the day masqueraded under Greek or Roman or Oriental aliases, books written in a flowery language which the Cavalier did not understand, and full of allusions that were dark to him; while not to know and appreciate those master-works placed him outside the pale.

He rejoiced in escaping from that overcharged atmosphere to the tavern, to the camp, anywhere. He followed the exiled Stuarts in their wanderings, paid his homage to the Princess of Orange, roamed from scene to scene, a stranger and one too many wherever he went.

Then came the hardest blow of all--the chilling disillusion that awaited many of Charles's faithful friends, who were not of such political importance as to command their recompense. Neglect and forgetfulness were Sir John Kirkland's portion; and for him and for such as he that caustic definition of the Act of Indemnity was a hard and cruel truth. It was an Act of Indemnity for the King's enemies and of oblivion for his friends. Sir John's spirits had hardly recovered from the bitterness of disappointed affection when he came back to the old home, though his chagrin was seven years old. But now, in his delight at the alliance with Denzil Warner, he seemed to have renewed his lease of cheerfulness and bodily vigour. He rode and walked about the lanes and woods with erect head and elastic limbs. He played bowls with Denzil in the summer evenings. He went fishing with his daughter and her sweetheart. He revelled in the simple rustic life, and told them stories of his boyhood, when James was King, and many a queer story of that eccentric monarch and of the rising star, George Villiers.

"Ah, what a history that was!" he exclaimed. "His mother trained him as if with a foreknowledge of that star-like ascendency. He was schooled to shine and dazzle, to excel all compeers in the graces men and women admire. I doubt she never thought of the mind inside him, or cared whether he had a heart or a lump of marble behind his waist-band. He was taught neither to think nor to pity--only to shine; to be quick with his tongue in half a dozen languages, with his sword after half a dozen modes of fence. He could kill his man in the French, or the Italian, or the Spanish manner. He was cosmopolitan in the knowledge of evil. He had every device that can make a man brilliant and dangerous. He mounted every rung of the ladder, leaping from step to step. He ascended, swift as a shooting star, from plain country gentleman to the level of princes. And he expired with an ejaculation, astonished to find himself mortal, slain in a moment by the thrust of a ten-penny knife. I remember as if it were yesterday how men looked and spoke when the news came to London, and how some said this murder would be the saving of King Charles. I know of one man at least who was glad."

"Who was he, sir?" asked Denzil.

"He who had the greatest mind among Englishmen--Thomas Wentworth. Buckingham had held him at a distance from the King, and his strong passionate temper was seething with indignation at being kept aloof by that silken sybarite--an impotent General, a fatal counsellor. After the Favourite's death there came a time of peace and plenty. The pestilence had passed, the war was over. Charles was happy with his Henriette and their lovely children. Wentworth was in Ireland. The Parliament House stood still and empty, doors shut, swallows building under the eaves. I look back, and those placid years melt into each other like one long summer. And then, again, as 'twere yesterday, I hear Hampden's drums and fifes in the lanes, and see the rebels' flag with that hateful legend, 'Vestigia nulla retrorsum,' and Buckinghamshire peasants are under arms, and the King and his people have begun to hate and fear each other."

"None foresaw that the war would last so long or end in murder, I doubt, sir," said Angela.

"Nay, child; we who were loyal thought to see that rabble withered by the breath of kingly nostrils. A word should have brought them to the dust."

"There might be so easy a victory, perhaps, sir, from a King who knew how to speak the right word at the right moment, how to comply graciously with a just demand, and how to be firm in a righteous denial," replied Denzil; "but with Charles a stammering speech was but the outward expression of a wavering mind. He was a man who never listened to an appeal, but always yielded to a threat, were it only loud enough."

The wedding was to be soon. Marriages were patched up quickly in the light-hearted sixties. And here there was nothing to wait for. Sir John had found Denzil compliant on every minor question, and willing to make his home at the Manor during his mother's lifetime.

"The old lady would never stomach a Papist daughter-in-law," said Sir John; and Denzil was fain to confess that Lady Warner would not easily reconcile herself with Angela's creed, though she could not fail of loving Angela herself.

"My daughter would have neither peace nor liberty under a Puritan's roof," Sir John said; "and I should have neither son nor daughter, and should be a loser by my girl's marriage. You shall be as much master here, Denzil, as if this were your own house--which it will be when I have moved to my last billet. Give me a couple of stalls for my roadsters, and kennel room for my dogs, and I want no more. You and Angela may introduce as many new fashions as you like; dine at two o'clock, and sip your unwholesome Indian drink of an evening. The fine ladies in Paris were beginning to take tea when I was last there, though by the faces they made over the stuff it might have been poison. I can smoke my pipe in the chimney-corner, and look on and admire at the new generation. I shall not feel myself one too many at your fireside, as I used sometimes in the Rue de Touraine, when those strutting Gallic cocks were quizzing me."

* * * * *

There were clouds of dust and a clatter of hoofs again in front of the floriated iron gate; but this time it was not the Honourable Henriette who came tripping along the gravel path on two-inch heels, but my Lady Fareham, who walked languidly, with the assistance of a gold-headed cane, and who looked pale and thin in her apple-green satin gown and silver-braided petticoat.

She, too, came attended by a second coach, which was filled by her ladyship's French waiting-woman, Mrs. Lewin, and a pile of boxes and parcels.

"I'll wager that in the rapture and romance of your sweethearting you have not given a thought to petticoats and mantuas," she said, after she had embraced her sister, who was horrified at the sight of that painted harridan from London.

Angela blushed at those words, "rapture and romance," knowing how little there had been of either in her thoughts, or in Denzil's sober courtship. Romance! Alas! there had been but one romance in her life, and that a guilty one, which she must ever remember with remorse.

"Come now, confess you have not a gown ordered."

"I have gowns enough and to spare. Oh, sister! have you come so far to talk of gowns? And that odious woman too! What brought her here?" Angela asked, with more temper than she was wont to show.

"My sisterly kindness brought her. You are an ungrateful hussy for looking vexed when I have come a score of miles through the dust to do you a service."

"Ah, dearest, I am grateful to you for coming. But, alas! you are looking pale and thin. Heaven forbid that you have been indisposed, and we in ignorance of your suffering."

"No, I am well enough, though every one assures me I look ill; which is but a civil mode of telling me I am growing old and ugly."

"Nay, Hyacinth, the former we must all become, with time; the latter you will never be."

"Your servant, Sir Denzil, has taught you to pay antique compliments. Well, now we will talk business. I had occasion to send for Lewin--my toilet was in a horrid state of decay; and then it seemed to me, knowing your foolish indifference, that even your wedding gown would not be chosen unless I saw to it. So here is Lewin with Lyons and Genoa silks of the very latest patterns. She has but just come from Paris, and is full of Parisian modes and Court scandals. The King posted off to Versailles directly after his mother's death, and has not returned to the Louvre since. He amuses himself by spending millions on building, and making passionate love to Mademoiselle la Valliere, who encourages him by pretending an excessive modesty, and exaggerates every favour by penitential tears. I doubt his attachment to so melancholy a mistress will hardly last a lifetime. She is not beautiful; she has a halting gait; and she is no more virtuous than any other young woman who makes a show of resistance to enhance the merit of her surrender."

Hyacinth prattled all the way to the parlour, Mrs. Lewin and the waiting-woman following, laden with parcels.

"Queer, dear old hovel!" she exclaimed, sinking languidly upon a tabouret, and fanning herself exhaustedly, while the mantua-maker opened her boxes, and laid out her sample breadths of richly decorated brocade, or silver and gold enwrought satin. "How well I remember being whipped over my horn-book in this very room! And there is the bowling green where I used to race with the Italian greyhound my grandmother brought me from Paris. I look back, and it seems a dream of some other child running about in the sunshine. It is so hard to believe that joyous little being--who knew not the meaning of heart-ache--was I."

"Why that sigh, sister? Surely none ever had less cause for heart-ache than you?"

"Have I not cause? Not when my glass tells me youth is gone, and beauty is waning? Not when there is no one in this wide world who cares a straw whether I am handsome or hideous? I would as lief be dead as despised and neglected."

"Sorella mia, questa donna ti ascolta," murmured Angela; "come and look at the old gardens, sister, while Mrs. Lewin spreads out her wares. And pray consider, madam," turning to the mantua-maker, "that those peacock purples and gold embroideries have no temptations for me. I am marrying a country gentleman, and am to lead a country life. My gowns must be such as will not be spoilt by a walk in dusty lanes, or a visit to a farm-labourer's cottage."

"Eh, gud, your ladyship, do not tell me that you would bury so much beauty among sheep and cows, and odious ploughmen's wives and dairy-women. A month or so of rustic life in summer between Epsom and Tunbridge Wells may be well enough, to rest your beauty--without patches or a French head--out of sight of your admirers. But to live in the country! Only a jealous husband could ever propose more than an annual six weeks of rustic seclusion to a wife under sixty. Lord Chesterfield was considered as cruel for taking his Countess to the rocks and ravines of Derbyshire as Sir John Denham for poisoning his poor lady."

"Chut! tu vas un peu trop loin, Lewin!" remonstrated Lady Fareham.

"But, in truly, your ladyship, when I hear Mrs. Kirkland talk of a husband who would have her waste her beauty upon clod-polls and dairy-maids, and never wear a mantua worth looking at----"

"I doubt my husband will be guided by his own likings rather than by Mrs. Lewin's tastes and opinions," said Angela, with a stately curtsy, which was designed to put the forward tradeswoman in her place, and which took that personage's breath away.

"There never was anything like the insolence of a handsome young woman before she has been educated by a lover," she said to her ladyship's Frenchwoman, with a vindictive smile and scornful shrug of bloated shoulders, when the sisters had left the parlour. "But wait till her first intrigue, and then it is 'My dearest Lewin, wilt thou make me everlastingly beholden to thee by taking this letter--thou knowest to whom?' Or, in a flood of tears, 'Lewin, you are my only friend--and if you cannot find me some good and serviceable woman who would give me a home where I can hide from the cruel eye of the world, I must take poison.' No insolence then, mark you, Madame Hortense!"

"This demoiselle is none of your sort," Hortense said. "You must not judge English ladies by your maids of honour. Celles la sont des drolesses, sans foi ni loi."

"Well, if she thinks I am going to make up linsey woolsey, or Norwich drugget, she will find her mistake. I never courted the custom of little gentlemen's wives, with a hundred a year for pin-money. If I am to do anything for this stuck-up peacock, Lady Fareham must give me the order. I am no servant of Madame Kirkland."

*   *   *   *   *

Alone in the garden, the sisters embraced again, Lady Fareham with a fretful tearfulness, as of one whose over strung nerves were on the verge of hysteria.

"There is something that preys upon your spirits, dearest," Angela said interrogatively.

"Something! A hundred things. I am at cross purposes with life. But I should have been worse had you been obstinate and still refused this gentleman."

"Why should that affect you, Hyacinth?" asked her sister, with a sudden coldness.

"Chi lo sa? One has fancies! But my dearest sister has been wise in good time, and you will be the happiest wife in England; for I believe your Puritan is a saintly person, the very opposite of our Court sparks, who are the most incorrigible villains. Ah, sweet, if you heard the stories Lewin tells me--even of that young Rochester--scarce out of his teens. And the Duke--not a jot better than the King--and with so much less grace in his iniquity. Well, you will be married at the Chapel Royal, and spend your wedding night at Fareham House. We will have a great supper. His Majesty will come, of course. He owes us that much civility."

"Hyacinth, if you would make me happy, let me be married in our dear mother's oratory, by your chaplain. Sure, dearest, you know I have never taken kindly to Court splendours."

"Have you not? Why, you shone and sparkled like a star, that last night you were ever at Whitehall, Henri sitting close beside you. 'Twas the night he took ill of a fever. Was it a fever? I have wondered sometimes whether there was not a mystery of attempted murder behind that long sickness."

"Murder!"

"A deadly duel with a man who hated him. Is not that an attempt at murder on the part of him who deliberately provokes the quarrel? Well, it is past, and he is gone. For all the colour of the world I live in, there might never have been any such person as Henri de Malfort."

Her airy laugh ended in a sob, which she tried to stifle, but could not.

"Hyacinth, Hyacinth, why will you persist in being miserable when you have so little cause for sadness?"

"Have I not cause? Am I not growing old, and robbed of the only friend who brought gaiety into my life; who understood my thoughts and valued me? A traitor, I know--like the rest of them. They are all traitors. But he would have been true had I been kinder, and trusted him."

"Hyacinth, you are mad! Would you have had him more your friend? He was too near as it was. Every thought you gave him was an offence against your husband. Would you have sunk as low as those shameless women the King admires?"

"Sunk--low? Why, those women are on a pinnacle of fame--courted--flattered--poetised--painted. They will be famous for centuries after you and I are forgotten. There is no such thing as shame nowadays, except that it is shameful to have done nothing to be ashamed of. I have wasted my life, Angela. There was not a woman at the Louvre who had my complexion, nor one who could walk a coranto with more grace. Yet I have consented to be a nobody at two Courts. And now I am growing old, and my poor painted face shocks me when I chance on my reflection by daylight; and there is nothing left for me--nothing."

"Your husband, sister!"

"Sister, do not mock me! You know how much Fareham is to me. We were chosen for each other, and fancied we were in love for the first few years, while he was so often called away from me, that his coming back made a festival, and renewed affection. He came crimson from battles and sieges; and I was proud of him, and called him my hero. But after the treaty of the Pyrenees our passion cooled, and he grew too much the school-master. And when he recovered of the contagion, he had recovered of any love-sickness he ever had for me!"

"Ah, sister, you say these things without thinking them. His lordship needs but some sign of affection on your part to be as fond a husband as ever he was."

"You can answer for him, I'll warrant"

"And there are other claims upon your love--your children."

"Henriette, who is nearly as tall as I am, and thinks herself handsomer and cleverer than ever I was. George, who is a lump of selfishness, and cares more for his ponies and peregrines than for father and mother. I tell you there is nothing left for me, except fine houses and carriages; and to show my fading beauty dressed in the latest mode at twilight in the Ring, and to startle people from the observation of my wrinkles by the boldness of my patches. I was the first to wear a coach and horses across my forehead--in London, at least. They had these follies in Paris three years ago."

"Indeed, dearest?"

"And thou wilt let me arrange thy wedding after my own fancy, wilt thou not, ma tres chere?"

"You forget Denzil's hatred of finery."

"But the wedding is the bride's festival. The bridegroom hardly counts. Nay, love, you need fear no immodest fooling when you bid good night to the company; nor shall there be any scuffling for garters at the door of your chamber. There was none of that antique nonsense when Lady Sandwich married her daughter. All vulgar fashions of coarse old Oliver's day have gone to the ragbag of worn-out English customs. We were so coarse a nation, till we learnt manners in exile. Let me have my own way, dearest. It will amuse me, and wean me from melancholic fancies."

"Then, indeed, love, thou shalt have thy way in all particulars."

After this Lady Fareham was in haste to return to the house in order to choose the wedding gown; and here in the panelled parlour they found the two gentlemen, with the dust of the road and the warmth of the noonday sun upon them, newly returned from Aylesbury, where they had ridden in the freshness of the early morning to choose a team of plough-horses at the fair; and who were more disconcerted than gratified at finding the dinner-parlour usurped by Mrs. Lewin, Madame Hortense, and an array of finery that made the room look like a stall in the Exchange.

It was on the stroke of one, yet there were no signs of dinner. Sir John and Sir Denzil were both sharp set after their ride, and were looking by no means kindly on Mrs. Lewin and her wares when Hyacinth and Angela appeared upon the scene.

"Nothing could happen luckier," said Lady Fareham, when she had saluted Denzil, and embraced her father with "Pish, sir! how you smell of clover and new-mown grass! I vow you have smothered my mantua with dust."

Father and sweetheart were called upon to assist in choosing the wedding gown--a somewhat empty compliment on the part of Lady Fareham, since she would not hear of the simple canary brocade which Denzil selected, and which Mrs. Lewin protested was only good enough to make his lady a bed-gown; or of the pale grey atlas which her father considered suitable--since, indeed, she would have nothing but a white satin, powdered with silver fleurs de luces, which she remarked, *en passant*, would have become the Grande Mademoiselle, had she but obtained her cousin's permission to cast herself away on Lauzun.

"Dear sister, can you consider a fabric fit for a Bourbon Princess a becoming gown for me?" remonstrated Angela.

"Yes, child; white and silver will better become thee than poor Louise, who has no more complexion left than I have. She was in her heyday when she held the Bastille, and when she and Beaufort were two of the most popular people in Paris. She has made herself a laughing-stock since then. That is settled, Lewin"--with a nod to the milliner--"the silver fleurs de luces for the wedding mantua. And now be quick with your samples."

All Angela's remonstrances were as vain to-day as they had been on the occasion of her first acquaintance with Mrs. Lewin. The excitement of discussing and selecting the finery she loved affected Lady Fareham's spirits like a draught of saumur. She was generous by nature, extravagant by long habit.

"Sure it would be a hard thing if I could not give you your wedding clothes, when you are marrying the man I chose for you," she protested. "The cherry-coloured farradine, by all means, Lewin; 'tis the very shade for my sister's fair skin. Indeed, Denzil"--nodding at him, as he stood watching them, with that hopelessly bewildered air of a man in a milliner's shop--"I have been your best friend from the beginning, and, but for me, you might never have won your sweetheart to listen to you. Mazarine hoods are as ancient as the pyramids, Lewin. Pr'ythee show us something newer."

It was late in the evening when the two coaches left the Manor gate. Hyacinth had been in no haste to return to the Abbey. There was nobody there who wanted her, she protested, and there would be a moon after nine o'clock, and she had servants enough to take care of her on the road; so Mrs. Lewin and her ladyship's woman were entertained in the steward's room, where Reuben held forth upon the splendour that had prevailed in his master's house before the troubles--and where the mantua-maker ate and drank all she could get, and dozed and yawned through the old man's reminiscences.

The afternoon was spent more pleasantly by the quality, who sat about in the sunny garden, or sauntered by the fish pond and fed the carp--and took a dish of the

Indian drink which the sisters loved, in the pergola at the end of the grass walk.

Hyacinth now affected a passion for the country, and quoted the late Mr. Cowley in praise of rusticity.

"Oh, how delicious is this woodland valley," she cried.

"'Here let me, careless and unthoughtful lying,   Hear the soft winds, above me plying,   With all their wanton boughs dispute.'

Poor Cowley, he might well love the country, for he was shamefully treated in town--a devoted servant to bankrupt royalty for all the best years of his life, and fobbed off with a compliment when the King came into power. Ah me, 'tis an ill world we live in, and London is the most hateful spot in it," she concluded, with a sigh.

"And yet you will have me married nowhere else, sister?"

"Oh, for a wedding or a christening one must have a crowd of fine people. It would go about that Lady Fareham was quite out of fashion if I were content to see only ploughmen and dairy-maids, and a petty gentleman or two with their ill-dressed wives, at my sister's marriage. London is the only decent place--after Paris--to live in; but the country is a peacefuller place in which to die."

A heart-breaking sigh emphasised the sentence, and Angela scrutinised her sister's face with increased concern.

"Dear love, I fear you are hiding something from me; and that you are seriously indisposed," she said earnestly.

"If I am I do not know it. But when one is weary of living there is only one sensible thing left to do--if Providence will but be kind and help one to do it. I am not for dagger or poison, or for a plunge in deep water. But to fade away in a gentle disease--a quiet ebbing of the vital stream--is the luckiest thing that can befall one who is tired of life."

Alarmed at hearing her sister talk in this melancholy strain, and still more alarmed by the change in her looks, sunken cheeks, hectic flush, fever-bright eyes, Angela entreated Lady Fareham to stay at the Manor, and be nursed and cared for.

"Oh, I know your skill in nursing, and your power over a sick person," Hyacinth interjected scornfully, and then in the next moment apologised for the little spurt of retrospective jealousy.

"Stay with us, love, and let us make you happier than you are at Chilton," pleaded Angela; but Hyacinth, who had been protesting that nobody wanted her, now declared that she could not leave home, and recited a list of duties, social and domestic.

"I shall not have half an hour to spare until I go to London next week to prepare for the wedding," she said. The date had been fixed while they sat at dinner; Sir John and his elder daughter settling the day, while Denzil assented with radiant smiles, and Angela sat by in pale silence, submissive to the will of others. They were to be married on a Thursday, July 19, and it was now the end of June--little more than a fortnight's interval in which to meditate upon the beginning of a new life.

Mrs. Lewin promised the white and silver mantua, and as many of the new clothes as a supernatural address, industry, and obligingness, could produce within the time. Hyacinth grew more lively after supper, and parted from her father and sister in excellent spirits; but her haggard face haunted Angela in troubled dreams all that night, and she thought of her with anxiety during the next few days, and most of all upon one long sultry day, the 4th of July, which was the third day she had spent in unbroken solitude since her father and Denzil had ridden away in the dim early morning, while the pastures were veiled in summer haze, on the first stage of a journey to London, hoping, with a long rest between noon and evening, to ride thirty-seven miles before night.

They were to consult with a learned London lawyer, and to execute the marriage settlement, Sir John vastly anxious about this business, in his ignorance of law and distrust of lawyers. They were to stay in London only long enough to transact their business, and would then return post-haste to the Manor; but as they were to ride their own horses all the way, and as lawyers are notoriously slow, Angela had been told not to expect them till the fourth evening after their departure. In her lonely rambles that long summer day, with her spaniel Ganymede, and her father's favourite pointer, for her only companions, Angela's thoughts dwelt ever on the past. Of the future--even that so near future of her marriage--she thought hardly at all. That future had been disposed of by others. Her fate had been settled for her; and she was told that by her submission she would make those she loved happy. Her father would have the son he longed for, and would be sure of her faithful devotion till the end of his days--or of hers, should untimely death intervene. Hyacinth's foolish jealousy would be dispelled by the act which gave her sister's honour into a husband's custody. And for him, that presumptuous lover who had taken so little pains to hide his wicked passion, if in any audacious hour he had dared to believe her guilty of reciprocating his love, that insolent suspicion would be answered at once and for ever by her marriage with Denzil--Denzil who was Fareham's junior by fifteen years, his superior in every advantage of person, as she told herself with a bitter smile; for even while she thought of that superiority--the statuesque regularity of feature, the clear colouring of a complexion warmed with the glow of health, the deep blue of large well-opened eyes, the light free carriage of one who had led an active country life--even while she thought of Denzil, another face and figure flashed upon her memory--rugged and dark, the forehead deeper lined than years justified, the proud eye made sombre by the shadow of the projecting brow, the cheek sunken, the shoulders bent as if under the burden of melancholy thoughts.

O God! this was the face she loved. The only face that had ever touched the springs of joy and pain. It was nearly half a year since she had seen him. Their meetings in the future need be of the rarest. She knew that Denzil regarded him with a distrust which made friendship out of the question; and it would be her duty to keep as far aloof from that old time as possible. Family meetings there must be, considering the short distance between Chilton and the Manor, feastings and junketings in company once or twice in the summer, lest it should be thought Sir John and his lordship were ill friends. But Angela knew that in any such social gathering, sitting at the overloaded board, amid the steam of rich viands, and the noise of many voices, she and Fareham would be as far apart as if the Indian Ocean rolled between them.

Once, and very soon, they must meet face to face; and he would take her hand in greeting, and would kiss her on the lips as she stood before him in her wedding finery, that splendour of white and silver which would provoke him to scornful wonder at her trivial pleasure in sumptuous clothes. Thus once they must meet. Her heart thrilled at the thought. He had so often shunned her, taking such obvious trouble to keep his distance; but he could hardly absent himself from her wedding. The scandal would be too great.

Well, she had accepted her fate, and this dull aching misery must be lived through somehow; and neither her father nor Denzil must ever have occasion to suspect her unhappiness.

"Oh, gracious Mary, Mother of God, help and sustain me in my sorrow! Guard and deliver me from sinful thoughts. What are my fanciful griefs to thy great sorrows, which thou didst endure with holy patience? Subdue and bend me to obedience and humility. Let me be an affectionate daughter, a dutiful wife, a friend and comforter to my poor neighbours."

So, and with many such prayers she struggled against the dominion of evil, kneeling meekly in the leafy stillness of that deep beechwood, where no human eye beheld her devotions. So in the long solitude of the summer day she held commune with heaven, and fought against that ever-recurring memory of past happiness, that looking back to the joys and emotions of those placid hours at Chilton Abbey, before the faintest apprehension of evil had shadowed her friendship with Fareham. Not to look back; not to remember and regret. That was the struggle in which the intense abstraction of the believer, lifting the mind to heaven, alone could help her. Long and fervent were her prayers in that woodland sanctuary where she made her pious retreat; nor was her sister forgotten in those prayers, which included much earnest supplication for the welfare here and hereafter of that lighter soul for whom she had ever felt a protecting and almost maternal love. Years counted for very little in the relations between these sisters.

The day wore to its close--the most solemn day in Angela's life since that which she had spent in the Reverend Mother's death-chamber, kneeling in the faint yellow glow of the tall wax-candles, in a room from which daylight was excluded. She remembered the detachment of her mind from all earthly interests as she knelt beside that death-bed, and how easily her thoughts had mounted heavenward; while now her love clung to this sinful earth. How had she changed for the worse, how was she sunk from the holy aspirations of that time!

CHAPTER XXV.
HIGH STAKES.

Angela had eaten her lonely supper, and was sitting at her embroidery frame between nine and ten, while the sounds of bolts and bars in the hall and corridors, and old Reuben's voice hectoring the maids, told her that the servants were closing the house before going to bed. Reuben would be coming to her presently, no doubt, to remind her of the lateness of the hour, wanting to carry her candle to her chamber, and as it were to see her safely disposed of before he went to his garret. She meant, on this occasion, to resist his friendly tyranny, having so little inclination for sleep, and hoping to find peace of mind and distraction in this elaborate embroidery of gold thread and many-coloured silks, which was destined to adorn her father's person, on the facings of a new-fashioned doublet.

Suddenly, as she bent over the candle to scrutinize the shading of her silks, the hollow sound of hoofs broke upon the silence, and in a minute afterwards a bell rang loudly.

Who could it be at such an hour? Her father, no doubt; no one else. He had hurried his business through, and returned a day earlier than he had hoped. Or could it be that he had fallen sick in London, and Denzil had come to tell her ill news? Or was it a messenger from her sister? She had time to contemplate several evil contingencies while she stood in the hall watching Reuben withdraw various bolts and bars.

The door swung back at last, and she saw a man in high-riding boots and slouched hat standing on the threshold, while in the moonlight behind him she could distinguish a mounted groom holding the bridle of a led horse, as well as the horse from which the visitor had just dismounted.

The face that looked at her from the doorway was the face which had haunted her with cruel persistency through that long day, chaining her thoughts to earth.

Fareham stood looking at her for a few moments, deadly pale, while she was collecting her senses, trying to understand this most unlooked-for presence. Why was he here? Ah, no doubt, a messenger of evil.

"Oh, sir, my sister is ill!" she cried; "I read sorrow in your face--seriously ill--dangerously? Speak, my lord, for pity's sake!"

"Yes, she is ill."

"Not dead?"

"No, no."

"But very ill? Oh, I feared, I feared when I saw her that there was something amiss. Has she sent you to fetch me?"

"Yes; you are wanted."

"Reuben, I must set out this instant. Order the coach to be got ready. And Betty must go with me."

"You will need no coach, Angela. Nor is there time to spare for any such creeping conveyance. I have brought Zephyr. You remember how you loved him. He is swift, and gentle as the wind after which we named him; sure of foot, easy to ride. The roads are good after yesterday's rain, and the moon will last us most of our way. We shall be at Chilton in two hours. Put on your coat and hat. Indeed, there is no time to be lost."

"Do you mean that she may die before I can reach her?"

"I know not," stamping his foot impatiently. "Fate holds the keys. But you had best waste no time on questions."

His manner was one of command, and he seemed to apprehend no possibility of hesitation on her part. Reuben ran to his pantry, and came back with a tankard of wine, which he offered to the visitor with tremulous respect, almost ready to kneel.

"Our best Burgundy, my lord. Your lordship must be dry after your long ride; and if your lordship would care to sup, there is good picking on last Monday's chine, and a capon from madam's supper scarce touched with the carving-knife."

"Nothing, I thank you, friend. There is no time for gluttony."

Reuben, pressing the tankard upon him, he drank some wine with an automatic air, and still stood with his eyes fixed on Angela's pallid countenance, waiting her decision.

"Are you coming?" he asked.

"Does she want me? Has she asked for me? Oh, for God's sake, my lord, tell me more! Is she dangerously ill? Have the doctors given her over?"

"No. But she is in a bad way. And you--you--you--are wanted. Will you come? Ay or no?"

"Yes. It is my duty to go to her. But when my father and Denzil come back to-morrow, Reuben must be able to tell them why I went; and the nature of my sister's illness. Were it not so serious that there is no time for hesitation, it would ill become me to leave this house in my father's absence."

He gave his head a curious jerk at Denzil's name, as if he had been stung.

"Yes, I will explain; I can make all clear to this gentleman here while you put on your cloak. Bring the black to the door," he called to his man.

"Will not your lordship bait your horses before you start?" Reuben asked deferentially.

"No time, fellow. There is no time. How often must I tell you so?" retorted Fareham.

Reuben's village breeding had given him an exaggerated respect for aristocracy. He had grown up in the midst of small country gentlemen, rural squires, among whom the man with three thousand a year in land was a magnate, and there had never been more than one nobleman resident within a day's ride of the Manor Moat. To Reuben, therefore, a peer was like a god; and he would have no more questioned Lord Fareham's will than a disciple of Hobbes would have imputed injustice to Kings.

Angela returned in a few minutes, having changed her silken gown for a neat cloth riding-skirt and close-fitting hood. She carried nothing with her, being assured that her sister's wardrobe would be at her disposal, and having no mind to spend a minute more in preparation than was absolutely necessary. Brief as her toilet was, she had time to consider Lord Fareham's countenance and manner, the cold distance of his address, and to scorn herself for having thought of him in her reveries that day as loving her always and till death. It was far better so. The abyss that parted them could not yawn too wide. She put a stern restraint upon herself, so that there should be nothing hysterical in her manner, lest her fears about her sister's health should be mistaken for agitation at his presence. She stood beside the horse, straight and firm, with her hand on the pommel, and sprang lightly into the saddle as Fareham's strong arm lifted her. Yet she could but notice that his hand shook as he gave her the bridle, and arranged the cloth petticoat over her foot.

Not a word was spoken on either side as they rode out at the gate and through the village of St. Nicholas, beautiful in the moonlight. Such low crumbling walls and deeply sloping roofs of cottages squatting in a tangle of garden and orchard; such curious outlines of old brick gables in the better class houses of miller, butcher, and general dealer; orchards and gardens and farm buildings, with every variety of thatch and eaves, huddled together in picturesque confusion; large spaces everywhere--pond, and village green, and common, and copse beyond; a peaceful, prosperous settlement, which had passed unharmed through the ordeal of the civil war, safe in its rural seclusion. Not a word was spoken even when the village was left behind, and they were riding on a lonely road, in so brilliant a moonlight that Angela could see every line in her companion's brooding face.

Why was he so gloomy and so unkind, in an hour when his sympathy should naturally have been given to her? Was he consumed with sorrow for his wife's in-disposition, and did anxiety make him silent; or was he angry with himself for not being as deeply distressed as a husband ought to be at a wife's peril? She knew too well how he and Hyacinth had been growing further apart day by day, till the only link between husband and wife seemed to be a decent courtesy and subservience to the world's opinion.

She recalled that other occasion when they two had made a solitary journey together, and in as gloomy a silence--that night of the great fire, when he had flung off his doublet and taken the sculls out of her hands, and rowed steadily and fast, with his eyes downcast, leaving her to steer the boat as she would, or trusting to the lateness of the hour for a clear course. He had seemed to hate her that night just as he seemed to hate her now, as they rode mile after mile side by side, the groom following near, now at a fast trot, now galloping along a stretch of waste grass that bordered the highway, now breathing their horses in a walk.

In one of those intervals he asked her if she were tired.

"No, no. I have no power to feel anything but anxiety. If you would only be kinder and tell me more about my sister! I fear you consider her in danger."

"Yes, she is in danger. There is no doubt of that."

"O God! she looked so ill when I saw her last, and she talked so wildly. I feared she was in a bad way. How soon shall we be at Chilton, my lord?"

"My lord! Why do you 'my lord' me?"

"I can find no other name. We seem to be strangers to-night; but, indeed, names and ceremonies matter nothing when the mind is in trouble. How soon shall we reach the Abbey, Fareham?"

"In an hour, at latest, Angela."

His voice trembled as he spoke her name, and all of force and passion that could be breathed into a single word was in his utterance. She flushed at the sound, and looked at him with a sudden fear; but his countenance might have been wrought-iron, so cold and passionless and cruelly resolute looked that rough-hewn face in the moonlight.

"I have a fresh horse waiting for you at Thame," he said. "I will not have you wearied by riding a tired horse. We are within five minutes of the inn. Will you rest there for half an hour, and take some refreshment?"

"Rest, when my sister may be dying! Not a moment more than is needed to change horses."

"I have brought Queen Bess, another of your favourites. 'Twas she who taught you to ride. She will know your voice, and your light hand upon her bridle."

They found the Inn wrapped in slumber, like every house or cottage they had passed; but a lantern shone within an open door in the quadrangle round which house and stables were built. One of the Fareham grooms was there, with an ostler to wait upon him, and three horses were brought out of their stable, ready saddled, as the travellers rode under the archway into the yard.

The mare was excited at finding herself on the road in the clear cool night, with the moonlight in her eyes, and was gayer than Fareham liked to see her under so precious a load; but Angela was no longer the novice by whose side he had ridden nearly two years before. She handled Queen Bess firmly, and soon settled her into a sharp trot, and kept her at it for nearly three miles. The hour Fareham had spoken of was not exceeded by many minutes when Chilton Abbey came in sight, the grey stone walls pale in the moonlight. All things--the long park wall, the pillared gates, the open spaces of the park, the depth of shadow where the old oaks and beeches spread wide and dark, had a look of unreality which contrasted curiously with the scene as she had last beheld it in all its daylight verdure and homeliness.

She dropped lightly from her horse, so soon as they drew rein at an angle of the long irregular house, where there was a door, half hidden under ivy, by which Lord Fareham went in and out much oftener than by the principal entrance. It opened into a passage that led straight to the library, where there was a lamp burning to-night. Angela saw the light in the window as they rode past.

He opened the door, which had been left on the latch, and nodded a dismissal to the groom, who went off to the stables, leading their horses. All was dark in the passage--dark and strangely silent; but this wing was remote from the chief apartments and from the servants' offices.

"Will you take me to my sister at once?" Angela asked, stopping on the threshold of the library, when Fareham had opened the door.

A lamp upon the tall mantelpiece feebly lighted the long low room, gloomy with the darkness of old oak wainscot and a heavily timbered ceiling. There were two flasks of wine upon a silver salver, and provisions for a supper, and a fire was burning on the hearth.

"You had better warm yourself after your night ride, and eat and drink something before you see her."

"No, no. What, after riding as fast as our horses could carry us! I must go to her this moment. Can you find me a candle?"--looking about her hurriedly as she spoke. "But, indeed, it is no matter; I know my way to her room in the dark, and there will be light enough from the great window."

"Stop!" he cried, seizing her arm as she was leaving the room; "stop!" dragging her back and shutting the door violently. "Your sister is not there."

"Great God! what do you mean? You told me your wife was here--ill--dying perhaps."

"I told you a lie, sweetheart; but desperate men will do desperate things."

"Where is my sister? Is she dead?"

"Not unless the Nemesis that waits on woman's folly has been swifter of foot than common. I have no wife, Angela; and you have no sister that you will ever care to own. My Lady Fareham has crossed the narrow sea with her lover, Henri de Malfort--her paramour always--though I once thought him yours, and tried to kill him for your sake."

"A runaway wife! Hyacinth! Great God!" She clasped her hands before her face in an agony of shame and despair, falling upon her knees in sudden self-abasement, her head drooping until her brow almost touched the ground. And then, after but a few minutes of this deep humiliation, she started to her feet with a cry of anger. "Liar! villain! despicable, devilish villain! This is a lie, like the other--a wicked lie! Your wife--your wife a wanton? My sister? My life upon it, she is in London--in your house, busy preparing for my marriage. Unlock that door, my lord; let me go this instant--back to my father. Oh, that I could be so mad as to leave his protection at your bidding! Open the door, sir, I command you!"

She seemed to gain in height, and to be taller than he had thought her--he who had so watched her, and whose memory held every line of that slender, graceful figure. She stood straight as an arrow, looking at him with set lips and flaming eyes, too angry to be afraid, trembling, but with indignation, not fear of him.

"Nay, child," he said gravely, "I have got you, and I mean to keep you. But you have trusted yourself to my hospitality, and you are safe in my house as in a sanctuary. I may be a villain, but I am not a ruffian. If I have brought you here by a trick, you are as much mistress of your life and fate under this roof as you ever were in your father's house."

"I have but one thing to say, sir. Let me out of this hateful house."

"What then? Would you walk back to the Manor Moat, through the night--alone?"

"I would crawl there on my hands and knees if I could not walk; anything to get away from you. Oh, the baseness of it! To vilify my sister--for your own base purposes. Intolerable villain!"

"Mistress, we will soon put an end to that charge. Lies there have been, but that is none. 'Tis you are the slanderer there."

He took a letter from the pocket of his doublet, and handed it to her. Then he took the lamp from the mantelshelf and held it while she read.

Alas, it was her sister's hand. She knew those hurried characters too well. The letter was blotted with ink and smeared as with tears. Angela's tears began to rain upon the page as she read:--

"I have tried to be a good woman and a true wife to you, tried hard for these many years, knowing all the time that you had left off loving me, and but for the shame of it would have cared little, though I had as many lovers as a maid of honour. You made life harder for me in this year last past by your passion for my sister, which mystery of yours, silent and secret as you were, these eyes must have been blind not to discover.

"And while you were cold in manner and cruel of speech--slighting me ever--there was one who loved and praised me, one whose value I knew not till he left this country, and I found myself desolate without him.

"He has come back. He, too, has found that I was the other half of his mind; and that he could taste no pleasure in life unshared by me. He has come to claim one who ever loved him, and denied him only for virtue's sake. Virtue! Poor fool that I was to count that a woman's noblest quality! Why, of all attributes, it is that the world least values. Virtue! when the starched Due de Montausier fawns upon Louise de la Valliere, when Barbara Palmer is de facto Queen of England. Virtue!

"Farewell! Forget me, Fareham, as I shall try to forget you. I shall be in Paris perhaps before you receive this letter. My house in the Rue de Touraine is ready for me. I shall dishonour you by no open scandal. The man I love will but rank as the friend I most value, and my other friends will ask no questions so long as you are silent, and do not seek to disgrace me. Indeed, it were an ill thing to pursue me with your anger; the more so as I am weak and ailing, and may not live long to enjoy my happiness. You have given me so little that you should in common justice spare me your hate.

"I leave you your children, whom you have affected to love better than I; and who have shown so little consideration for me that I shall not miss them."

*　　*　　*　　*　　*

"What think you of that, Angela, for the letter of a she-cynic?"

"It is blotted with her tears. She wrote in sorrow, despairing of your love."

"She managed to exist for a round dozen years without my love--or doubting it--so long as she had her *cavaliere servante*. It was only when he deserted her that she found life a burden. And now she has crossed the Rubicon. She belongs to her age--the age of Kings' mistresses and light women. And she will be happy, I dare swear, as they are. It is not an age of tears. And when the fair Louise ran away to her Convent the other day, in a passion of penitence, be sure she only went on purpose to be brought back again. But now, sweet, say have I lied to you about the lady who was once my wife?" he asked, pointing to the letter in her hand.

"And who is my sister to the end of time; my sister in Eternity: in Purgatory or in Paradise. I cannot cast her off, though you may. I will set out for Paris to-morrow, and bring her home, if I can, to the Manor. She need trouble you no more. My husband and I can shelter and pity her."

"Your husband!"

"He will be my husband a fortnight hence."

"Never! Never, while I live to fling my body between you at the altar. His blood or mine should choke your marriage vows. Angela, Angela, be reasonable. I have brought you out of that trap. I have cut the net in which they had caught you. My love, you are free, and I am free, and you belong to me. You never loved Denzil Warner, never would love him, were you to live with him a quarter of a century. He is ice, and you are fire. Dearest, you belong to me. He who made us both created us to be happy together. There are strings in our hearts that harmonize as concords in music do. We are miserable apart, both of us. We waste, and fade, and torture ourselves in absence; but only to breathe the same air, to sit, silent, in the same room, is to be happy."

"Let me go!" she cried, looking at him with wild eyes, leaning against the locked door, her hands clutching at the latch, seeming neither to hear nor heed his impassioned address, though every word had sunk deep enough to remain in her memory for ever. "Let me go! You are a dishonourable villain! I came to London alone to your deserted house. I was not afraid of death or the plague then. I am not afraid of you now. Open this door, and let me go, never to see your wicked face again!"

"Angela, canst thou so play fast and loose with happiness? Look at me," kneeling at her feet, trying to take her hands from their hold on the latch. "Our fate is in our power to-night. The day is near dawning, and at the stroke of five my coach will be at the door to take us to Bristol, where the ship lies that shall carry us to New England--to a new world, and liberty; and to the sweet simple life that will please my dear love better than all the garish pleasures of a licentious court. Ah, dearest, I know thy mind and heart as well as I know my own. I know I can make thee happy in that fair new world, where we shall begin life again, free from all old burdens; and where, if thou wilt, my motherless children can join us, and make one loving household. My Henriette adores you; and it were Christian charity to rescue her and her brother from Charles Stuart's England, and to bring them up to an honest life in a country where men are free to worship God as He moves them. Love, you cannot deny me. So sweet a life waits for us; and you have but to lay that dear hand in mine and give consent."

"Oh, God!" she murmured. "I thought this man held me in honour and esteem."

"Do I not honour you? Ah, love, what can a man do more than offer his life to her he loves----"

"And if he is another woman's husband?"

"That tie is broken."

"I deny it. But if it were, you have been my sister's husband, and you could be nothing to me but my brother. You have made sisterly affection impossible, and so, my lord, we must be strangers; and, as you are a gentleman, I bid you open this door, and let me make my way to some more peaceful shelter than your house."

"Angela!"

He tried to draw her to his breast; but she held him off with outstretched arm, and even in the tumult of his passion the knowledge of her helplessness and his natural shame at his own treachery kept him in check.

"Angela, call me villain if you will, but give me a fair hearing. Dearest, the joy or sorrow of two lives lies in your choice to-night. If you will trust me, and go with me, I swear I will make you happy. If you are stubborn to refuse--well, sweetheart, you will but send a man to the devil who is not wholly bad, and who, with you for his guardian angel, might find the way to heaven."

"And begin the journey by a sin these lips dare not name. Oh, Fareham," she said, growing suddenly calm and grave, and with something of that tender maternal manner with which she had soothed and controlled him while he had but half his wits, and when she feared he might be lying on his death-bed, "I would rather believe you a madman than a villain; and, indeed, all that you have done to-night is the work of a madman, who follows his own wild fancy without power to reason on what he does. Surely, sir, you know me too well to believe that I would let love--were it the blindest, most absorbing passion woman ever felt--lead me into sin so base as that you would urge. The vilest wanton at Whitehall would shrink from stealing a sister's husband."

"There would be no theft. Your sister flings me to you as a dog drops the bone he has picked dry. She had me when I was young, and a soldier--with some reflected glory about me from the hero I followed--and rich and happy. She leaves me old and haggard, without aim or hope, save to win her I worship. Shall I tell you when I began to love you, my angel?"

"No, no; I will listen to no more raving. Thank God, there is the daylight!" as the cold wan dawn flickered across the room. "Will you let me beat my hands against this door till they bleed?"

"Thou shalt not harm the loveliest hands on earth," seizing them both in his own. "Ah, sweet, I began to love thee before ever I rose from that bed of horror where I had been left to perish. I loved thee in my unreason, and my love strengthened with each hour of returning sense. Our journey, I so weak, and sick, and helpless--was a ride through Paradise. I would have had it last a year; would have suffered sickness and pain, aching limbs and parched lips, only to feel the light touch of this dear hand upon my brow 'twixt sleep and waking; only to look up as I awoke, and see those sweet eyes looking down at me. Ah, dearest, my heart arose from among the dead, and came out of the tomb of all human affections to greet thee. Till I knew you I knew not the meaning of love. And if you are stubborn, and will not come with me to that new world, where we may be so happy, why, then I must go down to my grave a despairing wretch that never knew a woman's love."

"My sister--your wife?"

"Never loved me. Her heart--that which she calls heart--was ever Malfort's and not mine. She gave me to know as much by a hundred signs and tokens which read plain enough now, looking back, but which I scarce heeded at the time. I believed her chaste, and she was civil, and I was satisfied. I tell you, Angela, this heart never beat for woman till I knew you. Ah, love, be not stone! Make not our affinity an obstacle. The Roman Church will ever grant dispensation for a union of affinities where there is cause for indulgence. The Church would have had Philip married to his wife's sister Elizabeth."

"The Church holds the bond of marriage indissoluble," Angela answered. "You are married to my sister; and while she lives you can have no other wife."

Her brow was stern, her courage unfaltering; but physical force was failing her. She leant against the door for support, and she no longer struggled to withdraw her hands from that strong grasp which held them. She fought against the faintness that was stealing over her senses; but her heavy eyelids were beginning to droop, and there was a sound like rushing water in her ears.

"Angela--Angela," pleaded the tender voice, "do you forget that afternoon at the play, and how you wept over Bellario's fidelity--the fond girl-page who followed him she loved; risked name and virtue; counted not the cost, in that large simplicity of love which gives all it has to give, unquestioning? Remember Bellario."

"Bellario had no thought that was not virtue's," she answered faintly; and he took that fainter tone for a yielding will.

"She would not have left Philaster if he had been alone in the wilderness, miserable for want of her love."

Her white lips moved dumbly, her eyelids sank, and her head fell back upon his shoulder, as he started up from his knees to support her sinking figure. She was in his arms, unconscious--the image of death.

He kissed her on the brow.

"My soul, I will owe nothing to thy helplessness," he whispered. "Thy free will shall decide whether I live or die."

Another sound had mingled with the rushing waters as her senses left her--the sound of knocking at a distant door. It grew louder and louder momently, indicating a passionate impatience in those who knocked. The sound came from the principal door, and there was a long corridor between that door and Fareham's room.

He stood listening, undecided; and then he laid the unconscious form gently on the thick Persian carpet--knowing that for recovery the fainting girl could not lie too low. He cast one agitated glance at the white face looking up at the ceiling, and then went quickly to the hall.

As he came near, the knocking began again, with greater vehemence, and a voice, which he knew for Sir John's, called--

"Open the door, in the King's name, or we will break it open!"

There was a pause; those without evidently waiting for the result of that last and loudest summons.

Fareham heard the hoofs of restless horses trampling the gravel drive, the jingle of bit and chain, and the click of steel scabbards.

Sir John had not come alone.

"So soon; so devilish soon!" muttered Fareham. And then, as the knocking was renewed, he turned and left the hall without a word of answer to those outside, and hastened back to the room where he had left Angela. His brow was fixed in a resolute frown, every nerve was braced. He had made up his mind what to do. He had the house to himself, and was thus master of the situation, so long as he could keep his pursuers on the outside. The upper servants--half a dozen coach-loads--had been packed off to London, under convoy of Manningtree and Mrs. Hubbock. The under servants--rank and file--from housemaids to turnspits, slept in a huge barrack adjoining the stables, built in Elizabeth's reign to accommodate the lower grade of a nobleman's household. These would not come into the house to light fires and sweep rooms till six o'clock at the earliest; and it was not yet four. Lord Fareham, therefore, had to fear no interruption from his own people.

There was broad daylight in the house now; yet he looked about for a candle; found one on a side-table, in a tall silver candlestick, and stopped to light it, before he raised the lifeless figure from the floor and lifted it into the easiest position for carrying, the head lying on his shoulder. Then, holding the slender waist firmly, circled by his left arm, he took the candlestick in his right hand, and went out of the room with his burden, along a passage leading to a seldom-used staircase, which he ascended, carrying that tall, slim form as if it had been a feather-weight, up flight after flight, to the muniment room in the roof. From that point his journey, and the management of that unconscious form, and to dispose safely of the lighted candle, became more difficult, and occupied a considerable time; during which interval the impatience of an enraged father and a betrothed husband, outside the hall door, increased with every minute of delay, and one of their mounted followers, of whom they had several, was despatched to ride at a hand-gallop to the village of Chilton, and rouse the Constable, while another was sent to Oxford for a Magistrate's warrant to arrest Lord Fareham on the charge of abduction. And meanwhile the battering upon thick oaken panels with stout riding-whips, and heavy sword-hilts, and the calling upon those within, were repeated with unabated vehemence, while a couple of horsemen rode round the house to examine other inlets, and do picket duty.

The Constable and his underling were on the ground before that stubborn citadel answered the reiterated summons; but at last there came the sound of bolts withdrawn. An iron bar dropped from its socket with a clang that echoed long and loud in the empty hall, the door opened, and Fareham appeared on the threshold, corpse-like in the cold raw daylight, facing his besiegers with a determined insolence.

"Thou most infernal villain!" cried Sir John, rushing into the hall, followed closely by Denzil and one of the men, "what have you done with my daughter?"

"Which daughter does your honour seek? If it be she whom you gave me for a wife, she has broken the bond, and is across the sea with her paramour?"

"You lie--reprobate! Your wife had doubtless business relating to her French estate, which called her to Paris. My daughters are honest women, unless by your villainy, one, who should have been sacred, as your sister by affinity, should bear a blighted name. Give me back my daughter, villain--the girl you lured from her home by the foulest deceit!"

"You cannot see the lady to-day, gentlemen; even though you threaten me with your weapons," pointing with a sardonic smile to their drawn swords, "and out-number me with your followers. The lady is gone. I am alone in the house to submit to any affront your superior force may put upon me."

"Our superiority can at least search your house," said Denzil. "Sir John, you had best take one way and I another. I doubt I know every room and passage in the Abbey."

"And your yeoman's manners offer a handsome return for the hospitality which made you acquainted with my house," said Fareham, with a contemptuous laugh.

He followed Denzil, leaving Sir John to grope alone. The house had been deserted but for a few days, yet the corridors and rooms had the heavy atmosphere of places long shut from sunshine and summer breezes; while the chilling hour, the grey ghostly light, added something phantasmal and unnatural to the scene.

Denzil entered room after room--below stairs and above--explored the picture-gallery, the bed-chambers, the long low ball-room in the roof, built in Elizabeth's reign, when a wing had been added to the Abbey, and of late used only for lumber. Fareham followed him close, stalking behind him in sullen silence, with an unalterable gloom upon his face which betrayed no sudden apprehensions, no triumph or defeat. He followed like doom, stood quietly on one side as Denzil opened a door; waited on the threshold while the searcher made his inspection, always with the same iron visage, offering no opposition to the entrance of this or that chamber; only following and watching, silent, intent, sphinx-like; till at last, fairly worn out by blank disappointment, Denzil turned upon him in a sudden fury.

"What have you done with her?" he cried, desperately. "I will stake my life she has not left this house, and by Him who made us you shall not leave it living unless I find her."

He glanced downward at the naked sword he had carried throughout his search. Fareham's was in the scabbard, and he answered that glance with an insulting smile.

"You think I have murdered her, perhaps," he said. "Well, I would rather see her dead than yours. So far I am in capacity a murderer."

They met Sir John in Lady Fareham's drawing-room, when Denzil had gone over the whole house, trusting nothing to the father's scrutiny.

"He has stabbed her and dropped her murdered body down a well," cried the Knight, half distraught. "He cannot have spirited her away otherwise. Look at him, Denzil; look at that haggard wretch I have called my son. He has the assassin's aspect."

Something--it might be the room in which they were standing--brought back to Angela's betrothed the memory of that Christmas night when aunt and niece had been missing, and when he, Denzil, had burst into this room, where Fareham was seated at chess; who, at the first mention of Angela's name, started up, white with horror, to join in the search. It was he who found her then; it was he who had hidden her now; and in the same remote and secret spot.

"Fool that I was not to remember sooner!" cried Denzil. "I know where to find her. Follow me, Sir John. Andrew"--calling to the servant who waited in the hall--"follow us close."

He rushed along a passage, ran upstairs faster than old age, were it ever so eager, could follow. But Fareham was nearly as fast--nearly, but not quite, able to overtake him; for he was older, heavier, and more broken by the fever of that night's work than his colder-tempered rival.

Denzil was some paces in advance when he reached the muniment room. He found the opening in the wainscot, and the steep stair built into the chimney. Half way to the bottom there was a gap--an integral part of the plan--and a drop of six feet; so that a stranger in hurried pursuit would be likely to come to grief at this point, and make time for his quarry to escape by the door that opened on the garden. Memory, or wits sharpened by anxiety, enabled Denzil to avoid this trap; and he was at the door of the Priest's Hole before Fareham began the descent.

Yes, she was there, kneeling in a corner, a candle burning dimly on a stone shelf above her head. She was in the attitude of prayer, her head bent, her face hidden, when the door opened, and she looked up and saw her betrothed husband.

"Denzil! How did you find me here?"

"I should be a poor slave if I had not found you, remembering the past. Great God, how pale you are! Come, love, you are safe. Your father is here. Angela, thou that art so soon to be my wife--face to face--here--before we leave this accursed pit--tell me that you did not go with that villain, except for the sake of your sick sister--that you were the victim of a heartless lie--not a party to a trick invented to blind your father and me!"

"I doubt I have not all my senses yet," she said, putting her hand to her head. "I was told my sister wanted me, and I came. Where is Lord Fareham?"

The terror in her countenance as she asked that question froze Denzil. Ah, he had known it all along! That was the man she loved. Was she his victim--and a willing victim? He felt as if a great gulf had opened between him and his betrothed, and that all his hopes had withered.

Fareham was at his elbow in the next moment. "Well, you have found her," he said; "but you shall not have her, save by force of arms. She is in my custody, and I will keep her; or die for her if I am outnumbered!"

"Execrable wretch! would you attempt to detain her by violence? Come, madam," said Denzil, turning coldly to Angela, "there is a door on those stairs which will let you out into the air.

"The door will not open at your bidding!" Fareham said fiercely.

He snatched Angela up in his arms before the other could prevent him, and carried her triumphantly to the first landing-place, which was considerably below that treacherous gap between stair and stair. He had the key of the garden door in his pocket, unlocked it, and was in the open air with his burden before Denzil could overtake him.

He found himself caught in a trap. He had his coach-and-six and armed postillions waiting close by, and thought he had but to leap into it with his prey and spirit her off towards Bristol; but between the coach and the door one of Sir John's pickets was standing, who the moment the door opened whistled his loudest, and brought Constable and man and another armed servant running helter-skelter round an angle of the house, and so crossing the very path to the coach.

"Fire upon him if he tries to pass you!" cried Denzil.

"What! And shoot the lady you have professed to love!" exclaimed Fareham, drawing himself up, and standing firm as a rock, with Angela motionless in his arms.

He dropped her to her feet, but held her against his left shoulder with an iron hold, while he drew his sword and made a rush for the coach. Denzil sprang into his path, sword in hand, and their blades crossed with a shrill clash and rattle of steel. They fought like demons, Fareham holding Angela behind him, sheltering her with his body, and swaying from side to side in his sword-play with a demoniac swiftness and suppleness, his thick dark brows knitted over eyes that flamed with a fiercer fire than flashed from steel meeting steel. A shriek of horror from Angela marked the climax, as Denzil fell with Fareham's sword between his ribs. There had been little of dilettante science, or graceful play of wrist in this encounter. The men had rushed at each other savagely, like beasts in a circus, and whatever of science had guided Fareham's more practised hand had been employed automatically. The spirit of the combatants was wild and fierce as the rage that moves rival stags fighting for a mate, with bent heads and tramping hoofs, and clash of locked antlers reverberating through the forest stillness.

Fareham had no time to exult over his prostrate foe; Sir John and his servants, Constable and underlings, surrounded him, and he was handcuffed and hauled off to the coach that was to have carried him to a sinner's paradise, before any one had looked to Denzil's wound, or discovered whether that violent thrust below the right lung had been fatal. Angela sank swooning in her father's arms.

CHAPTER XXVI.
IN THE COURT OF KING'S BENCH.

The summer and autumn had gone by--an eventful season, for with it had vanished from the stage of politics one who had played so dignified and serious a part there. Southampton was dead, Clarendon disgraced and in exile. The Nestor and the Ulysses of the Stuart epic had melted from the scene. Down those stairs by which he had descended on his way to so many a splendid festival, himself a statelier figure than Kings or Princes, the Chancellor had gone to banishment and oblivion. "The lady" had looked for the last time, a laughing Jezebel, from a palace window, exultant at her enemy's fall; and along the river that had carried such tragic destinies eastward to be sealed in blood, Edward Hyde, Earl of Clarendon, had drifted quietly out of the history he had helped to make. The ballast of that grave intellect was flung overboard so that the ship of fools might drift the faster.

But in Westminster Hall, upon this windy November morning, nobody thought of Clarendon. The business of the day was interesting enough to obliterate all considerations of yesterday. The young barristers, who were learning their trade by listening to their betters, had been shivering on their benches in the Common Pleas since nine o'clock, in that chilly corner where every blast from the north or northeast swept over the low wooden partition that enclosed the court, or cut through the chinks in the panelling. The students and juniors were in their usual places, sitting at the feet of their favourite Common-law Judge; but the idlers who came for amusement, to saunter about the hall, haggle for books with the second-hand dealers along the south wall, or flirt with the milliners who kept stalls for bands and other legal finery on the opposite side, or to listen on tiptoe, with an ear above the panelled enclosure, to the quips and cranks or fierce rhetoric of a famous advocate- -these to-day gravitated with one accord towards the south-west corner of the Hall, where, in the Court of King's Bench, Richard Revel, Baron Fareham, of Fareham, Hants, was to be tried by a Buckinghamshire jury for abduction, with fraud, malice, and violence, and for assault, with intent to murder.

The rank of the offender being high, and the indictment known to involve tragic details of family history, there had been much talk of the cause which was on the paper for to-day; and, as a natural consequence, besides the habitual loungers and saunterers, gossips, and book-buyers, there was a considerable sprinkling of persons of quality, who perfumed the not too agreeable atmosphere with pulvilio and Florentine iris powder, and the rustle of whose silks and brocades was audible all over the Hall. Not often did such gowns sweep the dust brought in by plebeian feet, nor such Venetian point collars rub shoulders with the frowsy Norwich drugget worn by hireling perjurers or starveling clerks. The modish world had come down upon the great Norman Hall like a flock of pigeons, sleek, iridescent, all fuss and flutter; and among these unaccustomed visitors there was prodigious impatience for the trial to begin, and a struggle for good places that brought into full play the primitive brutality which underlies the politeness of the civillest people.

Lady Sarah Tewkesbury had risen betimes, and, in her anxiety to secure a good place, had come out in her last night's "head," which somewhat damaged edifice of ginger-coloured ringlets and Roman pearls was now visible above the wooden partition of the King's Bench to the eyes of the commonalty in the hall below, her ladyship being accommodated with a seat among the lawyers.

One of these was a young man in a shabby gown and rumpled wig, but with a fair complexion and tolerable features--a stranger to that court, and better known at Hicks's Hall, and among city litigators, with whom he had already a certain re-pute for keen wits and a plausible tongue--about the youngest advocate at the Eng-lish Bar, and by some people said to be no barrister at all, but to have put on wig and gown two years ago at Kingston Assizes and called himself to the Bar, and stayed there by sheer audacity. This young gentleman, Jeffreys by name, having deserted the city and possible briefs in order to hear the Fareham trial, was inclined to resent being ousted by an obsequious official to make room for Lady Sarah.

"Faith, one would suppose I was her ladyship's footman and had been keep-ing her seat for her," he grumbled, as he reluctantly rose at the Usher's whispered request, and edged himself sulkily off to a corner where he found just standing-room.

It was a very hard seat which Mr. Jeffreys had vacated, and her ladyship, after sitting there over two hours, nodding asleep a good part of the time, began to feel internal sinkings and flutterings which presaged what she called a "swound," and necessitated recourse to a crystal flask of strong waters which she had prudently brought in her muff. Other of Lady Fareham's particular friends were expected--Sir Ralph Masaroon, Lady Lucretia Topham, and more of the same kidney; and even the volatile Rochester had deigned to express an interest in the case.

"The man was mistaken in his metier," he had told Lady Sarah, when the scan-dal was discussed in her drawing-room. "The *role* of seducer was not within his means. Any one could see he was in love with the pale sister-in-law by the manner in which he scowled at her; but it is not every woman who can be subjugated by gloom and sullenness, though some of 'em like us tragical. My method has been to laugh away resistance, as my wife will acknowledge, who was the cruellest she I ever tackled, and had baffled all her other servants. Indeed she must have been in Butler's eye when he wrote--

'That old Pyg--what d'ye call him--malion   That cut his mistress out of stone,   Had not so hard a hearted one.'

Even Lady Rochester will admit I conquered without heroics," upon which her ladyship, late mistress Mallett, a beauty and a fortune, smiled assent with all the complacency of a six-months' bride. "To see a man tried for an attempted abduction is a sight worth a year's income," pursued Rochester. "I would travel a hundred miles to behold that rare monster who has failed in his pursuit of one of your obliging sex!"

"Do you think us all so easily won?" asked Lady Sarah, piqued.

"Dear lady, I can but judge by experience. If obdurate to others you have still been kind to me."

*   *   *   *   *

Lady Sarah had nearly emptied her flask of Muscadine before Masaroon elbowed his way to a seat beside her, from which he audaciously dislodged a coffee-house acquaintance, an elderly lawyer upon whom fortune had not smiled, with a condescending civility that was more uncivil than absolute rudeness.

"We'll share a bottle in Hell after the trial, mon ami," he said; and on seeing Lady Sarah's look of horror, he hastened to explain that Heaven, Hell, and Purgatory, were the cant names of three taverns which drove a roaring trade in strong drinks under the very roof of the Hall.

"The King's Attorney-general is prosecuting," answered Sir Ralph, replying to a question from Lady Sarah, whose inquiries betrayed that dense ignorance of legal technicalities common even to accomplished women. "It is thought the lady's father would have been glad for the matter to be quashed, his fugitive daughter being restored to his custody--albeit with a damaged character--and her elder sister having run away from her husband."

"I will not hear you slander my dearest friend," protested Lady Sarah. "Lady Fareham left her husband, and with good cause, as his after-conduct showed. She did not run away from him."

"Nay, she had doubtless the assistance of a carriage-and-six. She would scarce foot it from London to Dover. And now she is leading grand train in Paris, and has taken almost as commanding a place as her friend Madame de Longueville, penitent and retired from service."

"Hyacinth, under all her appearance of silliness, is a remarkably clever woman," said Lady Sarah, sententiously; "but, pray, Sir Ralph, if Mistress Angela's father has good reason for not prosecuting his daughter's lover--indeed I ever thought her an underhand hussy--why does not Sir Denzil Warner--who I hear has been at death's door--pursue him for assault and battery?"

"Nay, is so still, madam. I question if he be yet out of danger. The gentleman is a kind of puritanical Quixote, and has persistently refused to swear an information against Fareham, whereby I doubt the case will fall through, or his lordship get off with a fine of a thousand or two. We have no longer the blessing of a Star Chamber, to supply state needs out of sinners' pockets, and mitigate general taxation; but his Majesty's Judges have a capacious stomach for fines, and his Majesty has no objection to see his subjects' misdemeanours transmuted into coin."

And now the business of the day began, the panelled enclosure being by this time crowded almost to suffocation; and Lord Fareham was brought into court.

He was plainly dressed in a dark grey suit, and looked ten years older than when Lady Sarah had last seen him on his wife's visiting day, an uninterested member of that modish assembly. His eyes were deeper sunken under the strongly marked brows. The threads of iron-grey in his thick black hair were more conspicuous. He carried his head higher than he had been accustomed to carry it, and the broad shoulders were no longer bent in the Stafford stoop. The spectators could see that he had braced himself for the ordeal, and would go through the day's work like a man of iron.

Proclamation was made for silence, and for information, if any person could give any, concerning the misdemeanour and offence whereof the defendant stood impeached; and the defendant was bid to look to his challenges, and the Jury, being gentlemen of the county of Bucks, were called, challenged, and sworn.

The demand for silence was so far obeyed that there followed a hush within the enclosure of the court; but there was no cessation of the buzz of voices and the tramp of footsteps in the hall, which mingled sounds seemed like the rise and fall of a human ocean, as heard within that panelled sanctuary.

The lawyers took snuff, shuffled on their seats, nudged each other and whispered now and then, during the reading of the indictment; but among Lady Fareham's friends, and the quality in general, there was a breathless silence and expectancy; and Lady Sarah would gladly have run her hat-pin into a snuffy old Serjeant close beside her, who must needs talk behind his hand to his pert junior.

To her ladyship's unaccustomed ears that indictment, translated literally from the Latin original, sounded terrible as an impeachment in the subterranean halls of the Vehm Gericht, or in the most select and secret council in the Venetian Doge's Palace.

The indictment set forth "that the defendant, Richard Revel, Baron Fareham, on the 4th day of July, in the 18th year of our sovereign lord the King that now is, at the parish of St. Nicholas in the Vale, in the county of Bucks, falsely, unlawfully, unjustly, and wickedly, by unlawful and impure ways and means, contriving, practising, and intending the final ruin and destruction of Mrs. Angela Kirkland, unmarried, and one of the daughters of Sir John Kirkland, Knight--the said lady then and there being under the custody, government, and education of the said Sir John Kirkland, her father--he, the said Richard Revel, Baron Fareham, then and there falsely, unlawfully, devilishly, to fulfil, perfect, and bring to effect, his most wicked, impious, and devilish intentions aforesaid--the said Richard Revel, Lord Fareham (then and long before, and yet, being the husband of Mrs. Hyacinth, another daughter of the said Sir John Kirkland, Knight, and sister of the said Mrs. Angela), against all laws as well divine as human, impiously, wickedly, impurely, and scandalously, did tempt, invite, and solicit, and by false and lying pretences, oaths, and affirmations, unlawfully, unjustly, and without the leave, and against the will of the aforesaid Sir John Kirkland, Knight, in prosecution of his most wicked intent aforesaid, did carry off the aforesaid Mrs. Angela, she consenting in ignorance of his real purpose, about the hour of twelve in the night-time of the said 4th day of July, in the year aforesaid, and at the aforesaid, parish of St. Nicholas in the Vale, in the county of Bucks aforesaid, out of the dwelling-house of the said Sir John Kirkland, Knight, did take and convey to his own house in the county of Oxford, and did then and there detain her by fraud, and did there keep her hidden in a secret chamber known as the Priest's Hole in his own house aforesaid, at the hazard of her life, and did oppose her rescue by force of arms, and with his sword, unlawfully, murderously, and devilishly, and in the prosecution of his wicked purpose did stab and wound

Sir Denzil Warner, Baronet, the lady's betrothed husband, from which murderous assault the said Sir Denzil Warner, Baronet, still lies in great sickness and danger of death, to the great displeasure of Almighty God, to the ruin and destruction of the said Mrs. Angela Kirkland, to the grief and sorrow of all her friends, and to the evil and most pernicious example of all others in the like case offending; and against the peace of our said sovereign lord the King, his crown and dignity."

The defendant having pleaded "Not guilty," the Jury were charged in the usual manner and with all solemnity.

"If you find him 'guilty' you are to say so; if you find him 'not guilty' you are to say so, and no more, and hear your evidence."

The Attorney-General confined himself to a brief out-line of the tragic story, leaving all details to be developed by the witnesses, who were allowed to give their evidence with colloquial freedom and expansiveness.

The first witness was old Reuben, the steward from the Manor Moat, who had not yet emerged from that mental maze in which he had found himself upon beholding the change that had come to pass in the great city, since the well-remembered winter of the King's execution, and the long frost, when he, Reuben, was last in London. His evidence was confused and confusing; and he drew upon himself much good-natured ridicule from the junior who opened the case. Out of various muddle-headed answers and contradictory statements the facts of Lord Fareham's unexpected appearance at the Manor Moat, his account of his lady's illness, and his hurried departure, carrying the young madam with him on horseback, were elicited, and the story of the ruse by which Mrs. Angela Kirkland had been beguiled from her home was made clear to the comprehension of a superior but rustic jury, more skilled in discriminating the points of a horse, the qualities of an ox, or the capacity of a hound, than in differentiating truth and falsehood in a story of wrong-doing.

Sir John Kirkland was the next witness, and the aspect of the man, the noble grey head, fine features, and soldierly carriage, the old-fashioned habit, the fashion of an age not long past, but almost forgotten, enlisted the regard and compassion of Jury and audience.

"Let me perish if it is not a ghost from the civil wars!" whispered Sir Ralph to Lady Sarah. "Mrs. Angela might well be romanesque and unlike the rest of us, with such a father."

A spasm of pain convulsed Fareham's face for a moment, as the old Cavalier stood up in the witness-box, towering above the Court in that elevated position, and, after being sworn, took one swift survey of the Bench and Jury, and then fixed his angry gaze upon the defendant, and scarcely shifted it in the whole course of his examination.

"Now, Gentlemen of the Jury," said the Attorney-General, "we shall tell you what happened at Chilton Abbey, to which place the defendant, under such fraudulent and lying pretences as you have heard of from the last witness, conveyed the young lady. Sir John, I will ask you to acquaint the Jury as fully and straightforwardly as you can with the circumstances of your pursuit, and the defendant's reception of you and your intended son-in-law, Sir Denzil Warner, whose deposition we have failed to obtain, but who could relate no facts which are not equally within your own knowledge."

"My words shall be straight and plain, sir, to denounce that unchristian wretch whom, until this miserable business, I trusted as if he had been my son. I came to my house, accompanied by my daughter's plighted husband, within an hour after that villain conveyed her away; and on hearing my old servant's story was quick to suspect treachery. Nor was Sir Denzil backward in his fears, which were more instantaneous than mine; and we waited only for the saddling of fresh horses, and rousing a couple of grooms from their beds, fellows that I could trust for prudence and courage, before we mounted again, following in that wretch's track. We heard of him and his victim at the Inn where they changed horses, she going consentingly, believing she was being taken in this haste to attend a dying sister."

"And on arriving at the defendant's house what was your reception?"

"He opposed our entrance, until he saw that we should batter down his door if he shut us out longer. We were not admitted until after I had sent one of my servants for the nearest Constable; and before we had gained an entrance into his house he had contrived to put away my daughter in a wretched hiding-place, planned for the concealment of Romish Priests or other recusants and malefactors, and would have kept her there, I believe, till she had perished in that foul cavern, rather than restore her to her father and natural guardian."

"That is false, and you know it!" cried Fareham. "My life is of less account to me than a hair of her head. I hid her from you, to save her from your tyranny, and the hateful marriage to which you would have compelled her."

"Liar! Impudent, barbarous liar!" roared the old Knight, with his right arm raised, and his body half out of the box, as if he would have assaulted the defendant. "Sir John," said the Judge, "I would be very loath to deal otherwise than becomes me with a person of your quality; but, indeed, this is not so handsome, and we must desire you to be calm."

"When I remember his infamy, and that vile assumption of my daughter's passion for him, which he showed in every word and act of that miserable scene."

He went on to relate the searching of the house, and Warner's happy inspiration, by which Angela's hiding-place was discovered, and she rescued in a fainting condition. He described the defendant's audacious attempt to convey her to the coach which stood ready for her abduction, and his violence in opposing her rescue, and the fight which had well-nigh resulted in Warner's death.

When Sir John's story was finished the defendant's advocate, who had declined to question the old butler, rose to cross-examine this more important witness.

"In your tracing of the defendant's journey between your house and Chilton you heard of no outcries of resistance upon your daughter's side?"

"No, sir. She went willingly, under a delusion."

"And do you think now, sir, as a man of the world, and with some knowledge of women, that your daughter was so easily hoodwinked; she having seen her sister, Lady Fareham, so shortly before, in good health and spirits?"

"Lady Fareham did not appear in good health when she was last at the Manor, and her sister was already uneasy about her."

"But not so uneasy as to believe her dying, and that it was needful to ride to her helter-skelter in the night-time. Do you not think, sir, that the young lady, who was so quick to comply with his lordship's summons, and bustled up and was in the saddle ten minutes after he entered the house, and was willing to got without her own woman, or any preparation for travel, had a strong inclination for the journey, and a great kindness for the gentleman who solicited her company?"

"Has that barbarous wretch set you on to slander the lady whose ruin he sought, sir?" asked the Knight, pallid with the white heat of indignation.

"Nay, Sir John, I am no slanderer; but I want the Jury to understand the sentiments and passions which are the springs of action here, and to bear in mind that the case they are hearing is a love story, and they can only come at the truth by remembering their own experience as lovers--"

The deep and angry tones of his client interrupted the silvery-tongued Counsellor.

"If you think to help me, sir, by traducing the lady, I repudiate your advocacy."

"My lord, you are not allowed to give evidence or to interrupt the Court. You have pleaded not guilty, and it is my duty to demonstrate your innocence. Come, Sir John, do you not know that his lordship's unhappy passion for his sister-in-law was shared by the subject of it; and that she for a long time opposed all your efforts to bring about a proper alliance for her, solely guided and influenced by this secret passion?"

"I know no such thing."

"Do I understand, then, that from the time of your first proposals she was willing to marry Sir Denzil Warner?"

"She was not willing."

"I would have wagered as much. Did you fathom her reason for declining so proper an alliance?"

"I did not trouble myself about her reasons. I knew that time would wear them away."

"And I doubt you trusted to a father's authority?"

"No, sir. I promised my daughter that I would not force her inclinations."

"But you used all methods of persuasion. How long was it before July the 4th that Mrs. Angela consented to marry Sir Denzil?"

"I cannot be over precise upon that point. I have no record of the date."

"But you have the faculty of memory, sir; and this is a point which a father would not easily forget."

"It may have been a fortnight before."

"And until that time the lady was unwilling?"

"Yes."

"She refused positively to accept the match you urged upon her?"

"She refused."

"And finally consented, I will wager, with marked reluctance?"

"No, sir, there was no reluctance. She came to me of her own accord, and surprised me by her submission."

"That will do, Sir John. You can stand down. I shall now proceed to call a witness who will convince the Jury of my client's innocence upon the first and chief count in the indictment, abduction with fraud and violence. I shall tell you by the lips of my witness, that if he took the lady away from her home, she being of full age, she went freely consenting, and with knowledge of his purpose."

"Lies--foul lies!" cried the old Cavalier, almost strangled with passion.

He plucked at the knot of his cravat, trying to loosen it, feeling himself threatened with apoplexy.

"Call Mistress Angela Kirkland," said the Serjeant, in strong steady tones that contrasted with the indignant father's hoarse and gasping utterance.

"S'life! the business becomes every moment more interesting," whispered Lady Sarah. "Will he make that sly slut own her misconduct in open court?"

"If she blush at her slip from virtue, it will be a new sensation in a London law-court to see the colour of shame," replied Sir Ralph, behind his perfumed glove; "but I warrant she'll carry matters with a high hand, and feel herself every inch a heroine."

Angela came into the court attended by her waiting-woman, who remained near the entrance, amid the close-packed crowd of lawyers and onlookers, while her mistress quietly followed the official who conducted her to the witness-box.

She was dressed in black, and her countenance under her neat black hood looked scarcely less white than her lawn neckerchief; but she stood erect and unfaltering in that conspicuous station, and met the eyes of her interrogator with an untroubled gaze. When her lips had touched the dirty little book, greasy with the kisses of innumerable perjurers, the Serjeant began to question her in a tone of odious familiarity.

"Now, my dear young lady, here is a gentleman's liberty, and perhaps his life, hanging on the breath of those pretty lips; so I want you to answer a few plain questions with as plain speech as you can command, remembering that you are to tell us the truth, and the whole truth, and nothing but the truth. Come, now, dear miss, when you left your father's house on the night of July 4, in this present year, in Lord Fareham's company, did you go with him of your own free will, and with a knowledge of his purpose?"

"I knew that he loved me."

A heart-breaking groan from Sir John Kirkland was hushed down by an usher of the court.

"You knew that he loved you, and that he designed to carry you beyond seas?"

"Yes."

"And you were willing to leave your father's custody and go with the defendant as his paramour?"

There was a pause, and the white cheek crimsoned, and the heavy eyelids fell over agonised eyes.

"I went willingly--because I loved him;" and then with a sudden burst of passion, "I would have died for him, or lived for him. It mattered not which."

"And she has lied for him--has sworn to a lie--and that to her own dishonour!" cried Sir John, beside himself; whereupon he was sternly bidden to keep silence.

There was no intention that this little Buckinghamshire gentleman should be indulged, to the injury of a person of Lord Fareham's wealth and consequence. The favour of the Bench obviously leant towards the defendant.

Fareham's deep tones startled the audience.

"In truth, your Honour, the young lady has belied herself in order to help me," he said. "I cannot accept acquittal at the cost of her good name."

"Your lordship has pleaded not guilty."

"And his lordship's chivalry would revoke that plea," cried the Counsel; "this is most irregular. I must beg that the Bench do order the defendant to keep silence. The witness can stand down."

Angela descended from the witness-box falteringly, and would perhaps have fallen but for her father's strong grasp, which clutched her arm as she reached the last step.

He dragged her out of the close-packed court, and into the open Hall.

"Wanton!" he hissed in her ear, "shameless wanton!"

She answered nothing; but stood where he held her, with wild eyes looking out of a white, rigid countenance. She had done what she had come there to do. Persuaded by Fareham's attorney, who had waited upon her at her lodgings when Sir John was out of the way, she had made her ill-considered attempt to save the man she loved, ignorant of the extent of his danger, exaggerating the potential severity of his punishment, in the illimitable fear of a woman for the safety of the being she loves. And now she cared nothing what became of her, cared little even for her father's anger or distress. There was always the Convent, last refuge of sin or sorrow, which meant the annihilation of the individual, and where the world's praise or blame had no influence.

Her woman fussed about her with a bottle of strong essence, and Sir John dragged rather than led her along the Hall, to the great door where the coach that had carried her from his London lodgings was in waiting. He saw her seated, with her woman beside her, supporting her, gave the coachman his orders, and then went hastily back to the Court of King's Bench.

The Court was rising; the Jury, without leaving their seats, had pronounced the defendant guilty of a misdemeanour, not in conveying Sir John Kirkland's daughter away from her home, to which act she had avowed herself a consenting party; but in detaining her in his house with violence, and in opposition to her father and proper guardian. The Lord Chief Justice expressed his satisfaction at this verdict, and after expatiating with pious horror upon the evil consequences of an ungovernable passion, a guilty, soul-destroying love, a direct inspiration of Satan, sentenced the defendant to pay a fine of ten thousand pounds, upon the payment of which sum he would be set at liberty.

The old Cavalier heard the brief sermon and the sentence, which seemed to him of all punishments the most futile. He had hoped to see his son-in-law sent to the Plantations for life; had been angry at the thought that he would escape the gallows; and for sole penalty the seducer was sentenced to forfeit less than a year's income. How corrupt and venal was a bench that made the law of the land a nullity when a great personage was the law-breaker!

He flung himself in the defendant's way as he left the court, and struck him across the breast with the flat of his sword.

"An unarmed man, Sir John! Is that your old-world chivalry?" Fareham asked, quietly.

A crowd was round them and swords were drawn before the officer could interfere. There were friends of Fareham's in the court, and two of his gentlemen; and Sir John, who was alone, might have been seriously hurt before the authorities could put down the tumult, had not his son-in-law protected him.

"Sheath your swords, if you love me!" he exclaimed, flinging himself in front of Sir John. "I would not have the slightest violence offered to this gentleman."

"And I would kill you if I had the chance!" cried Sir John; "that is the difference between us. I keep no measures with the man who ruined my daughter."

"Your daughter is as spotless a saint as the day she left her Convent, and you are a blatant old fool to traduce her," said Fareham, exasperated, as the Usher led him away.

His detention was no more than a formality; and as he had been previously allowed his liberty upon bail, he was now permitted to return to his own house, where by an order upon his banker he paid the fine, and was henceforward a free man.

The first use he made of his freedom was to rush to Sir John's lodgings, only to hear that the Cavalier, with his daughter and two servants, had left half an hour earlier in a coach-and-four for Buckinghamshire. The people at the lodgings did not know which road they had taken, or at what Inn they were to lie on the way.

"Well, there will be a better chance of seeing her at the Manor than in London," Fareham thought; "he cannot keep so close a watch upon her there as in the narrow space of town lodgings."

CHAPTER XXVII.
BRINGERS OF SUNSHINE.

It was December, and the fields and pastures were white in the tardy dawn with the frosty mists of early winter, and Sir John Kirkland was busy making his preparations for leaving Buckinghamshire and England with his daughter. He had come from Spain at the beginning of the year, hoping to spend the remnant of his days in the home of his forefathers, and to lay his old bones in the family vault; but the place was poisoned to him for evermore, he told Angela. He could not stay where he and his had been held in highest honour, to have his daughter pointed at

by every grinning lout in hob-nailed shoes, and scorned by the neighbouring quality. He only waited till Denzil Warner should be pronounced out of danger and on
the high-road to recovery, before he crossed the Channel.

"There is no occasion you should leave Buckinghamshire, sir," Angela argued.
"It is the dearest wish of my heart to return to the Convent at Louvain, and finish
my life there, sheltered from the world's contempt."

"What, having failed to get your fancy, you would dedicate yourself to God?"
he cried. "No, madam. I am still your father, though you have disgraced me; and I
require a daughter's duty from you. Oh, child, I so loved you, was so proud of you!
It is a bitter physic you have given me to drink."

She knelt at his feet, and kissed his sunburnt hands shrunken with age.

"I will do whatever you desire, sir. I wish no higher privilege than to wait upon
you; but when you weary of me there is ever the Convent."

"Leave that for your libertine sister. Be sure she will finish a loose life by a conspicuous piety. She will turn saint like Madame de Longueville. Sinners are the stuff
of which modern saints are made. And women love extremes--to pass from silk and
luxury to four-o'clock matins, and the Carmelite's woollen habit. No, Angela, there
must be no Convent for you, while I live. Your penance must be to suffer the company of a petulant, disappointed old man."

"No penance, sir, but peace and contentment; so I am but forgiven."

"Oh, you are forgiven. There is that about you with which one cannot long be
angry--a creature so gentle and submissive, a reed that bends under a blow. Let us
not think of the past. You were a fool--but not a wanton. No, I will never believe
that! A generous, headstrong fool, ready with thine own perjured lips to blacken
thy character in order to save the villain who did his best to ruin thee. But thou art
pure," looking down at her with a severe scrutiny. "There is no memory of guilt in
those eyes. We will go away together, and live peacefully together, and you shall
still be the staff of my failing steps, the light of my fading eyes, the comfort of my
ebbing life. Were I but easy in my mind about those poor forsaken grandchildren,
I could leave England cheerfully enough; but to know them motherless--with such
a father!"

"Indeed, sir, I believe, however greatly Lord Fareham may have erred, he will
not prove a neglectful father," Angela said, her voice growing low and tremulous as

she pronounced that fatal name.

"You will vouch for him, no doubt. A licentious villain, but an admirable father! No, child, Nature does not deal in such anomalies. The children are alone at Chilton with their English gouvernante, and the prim Frenchwoman, who takes infinite pains to perfect Henriette's unlikeness to a human child. They are alone, and their father is hanging about the Court."

"At Court! Lord Fareham! Indeed, sir, I think you must be mistaken."

"Indeed, madam, I have the fact on good authority."

"Oh, sir, if you have reason to think those dear children neglected, is it not your duty to protect and care for them? Their poor, mistaken mother has abandoned them."

"Yes, to play the great lady in Paris, where, when I went in quest of her last July--while thou wert lying sick here--hoping to bring back a penitent, I was received with a triumphant insolence, finding her the centre of a circle of flatterers, a Princess in little, with all the airs and graces and ceremonies and hauteur of the French Blood-royal. When I charged her with being Malfort's mistress, and bade her pack her traps and come home with me, she deafened me with her angry volubility. I to slander her--I, her father, when there was no one in Paris, from the Place Royale to the Louvre, more looked up to! But when I questioned my old friends they answered with enigmatical smiles, and assured me that they knew nothing against my daughter's character worse than all the world was saying about some of the highest ladies in France--Madame, to wit; and with this cold comfort I must needs be content, and leave her in her splendid infamy."

"Father, be sure she will come back to us. She has been led into wrong-doing by the artfullest of villains. She will discover the emptiness of her life, and come back to seek the solace of her children's love. Let us care for them meanwhile. They have no other kindred. Think of our sweet Henriette--so rich, so beautiful, so over-intelligent--growing from child to woman in the care of servants, who may spoil and pervert her even by their very fondness."

"It is a bad case, I grant; but I can stir no finger where that man is concerned. I can hold no communication with that scoundrel."

"But your lawyer could claim custody of the children for you, perhaps."

"I think not, Angela, unless there was a criminal neglect of their bodies. The law takes no account of souls."

Angela's greatest anxiety--now that Denzil's recovery was assured--was for the welfare of these children whom she fondly loved, and for whom she would have gladly played a mother's part. She wrote in secret to her sister, entreating her to return to England for her children's sake, and to devote herself to them in retirement at Chilton, leaving the scandal of her elopement to be forgotten in the course of blameless years; so that by the time Henriette was old enough to enter the world her mother would have recovered the esteem of worthy people, as well as the respect of the mob.

Lady Fareham's tardy answer was not encouraging. She had no design of returning to a house in which she had never been properly valued, and she admired that her sister should talk of scandal, considering that the scandal of her own intrigue with her brother-in-law had set all England talking, and had been openly mentioned in the London and Oxford Gazettes. Silence about other people's affairs would best become a young miss who had made herself so notorious.

As for the children, Lady Fareham had no doubt that their father, who had ever lavished more affection upon them than he bestowed upon his wife, might be trusted with the care of them, however abominable his conduct might be in other matters. But in any case her ladyship would not exchange Paris for London, where she had been slighted and neglected at Court as well as at home.

The letter was a tissue of injustice and egotism; and Angela gave up all hope of influencing her sister for good; but not the hope of being useful to her sister's children.

Now, as the short winter days went by, and the preparations for departure were making, she grew more and more urgent with her father to obtain the custody of his grandchildren, and carry them to France with him, where they might be reared and educated under his own eye. Montpelier was the place of exile he had chosen, a place renowned alike for its admirable climate and educational establishments; and where Sir John had spent the previous winter, and had made friends.

It was to Montpelier the great Chancellor had retired from the splendours of a princely mansion but just completed--far exceeding his own original intentions in splendour, as the palaces of new-made men are apt to do--and from a power and authority second only to that of kings. There the grandfather of future queens was now residing in modest state, devoting the evening of his life to the composition of an authentic record of the late rebellion, and of those few years during which he had been at the head of affairs in England. Sir John Kirkland, who had never forgotten his own disappointments in the beginning of his master's restored fortunes, had a fellow-feeling for "Ned Hyde" in his fall.

"As a statesman he was next in capacity to Wentworth," said Sir John, "and yet a painted favourite and a rabble of shallow wits were strong enough to undermine him."

The old Knight confessed that he had ridden out of his way on several occasions when he was visiting Warner's sick-bed, in the hope of meeting Henrietta and George on their ponies, and had more than once been so lucky as to see them.

"The girl grows handsomer, and is as insolent as ever; but she has a sorrowful look which assures me she misses her mother; though it was indeed of that wretch, her father, she talked most. She said he had told her he was likely to go on a foreign embassy. If it is to France he goes, there is an end of Montpelier. The same country shall not hold him and my daughter while I live to protect you."

Angela began to understand that it was his fear, or his hatred of Fareham, which was taking him out of his native country. No word had been said of her betrothal since that fatal night. It seemed tacitly understood that all was at an end between her and Denzil Warner. She herself had been prostrate with a low, nervous fever during a considerable part of that long period of apprehension and distress in which Denzil lay almost at the point of death, nursed by his grief-stricken mother, to whom the very name of his so lately betrothed wife was hateful. Verily the papistical bride had brought a greater trouble to that house than even Lady Warner's prejudiced mind had anticipated. Kneeling by her son's bed, exhausted with the passion of long prayers for his recovery, the mother's thoughts went back to the day when Angela crossed the threshold of that house for the first time, so fair, so modest, with a countenance so innocent in its pensive beauty.

"And yet she was guilty at heart even then," Lady Warner told herself, in the long night-watches, after the trial at Westminster Hall, when Angela's public confession of an unlawful love had been reported to her by her favourite Nonconformist Divine, who had been in court throughout the trial, with Lady Warner's lawyer, watching the proceedings in the interest of Sit Denzil. Lady Warner received the news of the verdict and sentence with unspeakable indignation.

"And my murdered son!" she gasped, "for I know not yet that God will hear my prayers and raise him up to me again. Is his blood to count for nothing--or his sufferings--his patient sufferings on that bed? A fine--a paltry fine--a trifle for a rich man. I would pay thrice as much, though it beggared me, to see him sent to the Plantations. O Judge and Avenger of Israel! Thou hast scourged us with pestilence, and punished us with fire; but Thou hast not convinced us of sin. The world is so sunk in wickedness that murder scarce counts for crime."

The day of terror was past. Denzil's convalescence was proceeding slowly, but without retrograde stages. His youth and temperate habits had helped his recovery from a wound which in the earlier stages looked fatal. He was now able to sit up in an armchair, and talk to his visitor, when Sir John rode twenty miles to see him; but only once did his lips shape the name that had been so dear, and that occasion was at the end of a visit which Sir John announced as the last.

"Our goods are packed and ready for shipping," he said. "My daughter and I will begin our journey to Montpelier early next week."

It was the first time Sir John had spoken of his daughter in that sick-room.

"If she should ever talk of me, in the time to come," Denzil said--speaking very slowly, in a low voice, as if the effort, mental and physical, were almost beyond his strength, and holding the hand which Sir John had given him in saying good-bye--"tell her that I shall ever remember her with a compassionate affection--ever hold her the dearest and loveliest of women--yes, even if I should marry, and see the children of some fair and chaste wife growing up around me. She will ever be the first. And tell her that I know she forswore herself in the court; and that she was the innocent dupe of that villain--never his consenting companion. And tell her that I pity her even for that so misplaced affection which tempted her to swear to a lie. I knew, sir, always, that she loved him and not me. Yes, from the first. Indeed, sir, it was but too easy to read that unconscious beginning of unholy love, which grew and strengthened like some fatal disease. I knew, but nursed the fond hope that I could win her heart--in spite of him. I fancied that right must prevail over wrong; but it does not, you see, sir, not always--not----" A faintness came over him; whereupon his mother, re-entering the room at this moment, ran to him and restored him with the strong essence that stood handy among the medicine bottles on the table by his chair.

"You have suffered him to talk too much," she said, glancing angrily at Sir John. "And I'll warrant he has been talking of your daughter--whose name must be poison to him. God knows 'tis worse than poison to me!"

"Madam, I did not come to this house to hear my daughter abused----"

"It would have better become you, Sir John Kirkland, to keep away from this house."

"Mother, silence! You distress me worse than my illness----"

"This, madam, is my farewell visit. You will not be plagued any more with me," said Sir John, lifting his hat, and bowing low to Lady Warner.

He was gone before she could reply.

*   *   *   *   *

The baggage was ready--clothes, books, guns, plate, and linen--all necessaries for an exile that might last for years, had been packed for the sea voyage; but the trunks and bales had not yet been placed in the waggon that was to convey them to the Tower Wharf, where they were to be shipped in one of the orange-boats that came at this season from Valencia, laden with that choice and costly fruit, and returned with a heterogeneous cargo. At Valencia the goods would be put on board a Mediterranean coasting vessel, and landed at Cette.

Sir John began to waver about his destination after having heard from Henriette of her father's possible embassy. Certainly if Fareham were to be employed in foreign diplomacy, Paris seemed a likely post for a man who was so well known there, and had spent so much of his life in France. And if Fareham were to be at Paris, Sir John considered Montpelier, remote as it was from the capital, too near his enemy.

"He has proved himself an indomitable villain," thought the Knight. "And I could not always keep as close a watch upon my daughter as I have done in the last six weeks. No. If Fareham be for France, I am for some other country. I might take her to Florence, and put the Apennines between her and that daring wretch."

It may be, too, that Sir John had another reason for lingering, after all was ready for the journey. He may have been much influenced by Angela's concern about his grandchildren, and may have hesitated at leaving them alone in England with only salaried guardians.

"Their father concerns himself very little about them, you see," he told Angela, "since he can entertain the project of a foreign embassy, while those little wretches are pining in a lonely barrack in Oxfordshire."

"Indeed, sir, he is a fond father. I would wager my life that he is deeply concerned about them."

"Oh, he is an angel, on your showing! You would blacken your sister's character to make him a saint."

The next day was fine and sunny, a temperature as of April, after the morning frost had melted. There was a late rose or two still lingering in the sheltered Buckinghamshire valley, though it wanted but a fortnight of Christmas. Angela and her father were sitting in a parlour that faced the iron gates. Since their return from London Sir John had seemed uneasy when his daughter was out of his sight; and she, perceiving his watchfulness and trouble, had been content to abandon her favourite walks in the lanes and woods and to the "fair hill of Brill," whence the view was so lovely and so vast, on one side reaching to the Welsh mountains, and on another commanding the nearer prospect of "the great fat common of Ottmoor," as Aubrey calls it, "which in some winters is like a sea of waters." For her father's comfort, noting the sad wistful eyes that watched her coming in and going out, she had resigned herself to spend long melancholy hours within doors, reading aloud till Sir John fell asleep, playing backgammon--a game she detested worse even than shove-halfpenny, which latter primitive game they played sometimes on the shovel-board in the hall. Life could scarcely be sadder than Angela's life in those grey winter days; and had it not been for an occasional ride across country with her father, health and spirits must alike have succumbed to this monotony of sadness.

This morning, as on many mornings of late, the subject of the boy and girl at Chilton had been discussed with the Knight's tankard of home-brewed and his daughter's chocolate.

"Indeed, sir, it would be a cruel thing for us to abandon them. At Montpelier we shall be a fortnight's journey from England; and if either of those dear creatures should fall ill, dangerously ill, perhaps, their father beyond the seas, and we, too, absent--oh, sir, figure to yourself Henriette or George dying among strangers! A cold or a fever might carry them off in a few days; and we should know nothing till all was over."

Sir John groaned and paced the room, agitated by the funereal image.

"Why, what a raven thou art, ever to croak dismal prophecies. The children are strong and well, and have careful custodians. I can have no dealings with their father. Must I tell you that a hundred times, Angela? He is a consummate villain: and were it not that I fear to make a bigger scandal, he or I should not have survived many hours after that iniquitous sentence."

A happy solution of this difficulty, which distressed the Knight much more than his stubbornness allowed him to admit, was close at hand that morning, while Angela bent over her embroidery frame, and her father spelt through the last *London Gazette* that the post had brought him.

The clatter of hoofs and roll of wheels announced a visit; and while they were looking at the gate, full of wonder, since their visitors were of so small a number, a footman in the Fareham livery pulled the iron ring that hung by a chain from the stone pillar, and the bell rang loud and long in the frosty air. The Fareham livery! Twice before the Fareham coaches and liveries had taken that quiet household by surprise; but to-day terror rather than surprise was in Angela's mind as she stood in front of the window looking at the gate.

Could Fareham be so rash as to face her father, so daring as to seek a farewell interview on the eve of departure? No, she told herself; such folly was impossible. The visitor could be but one person--Henriette. Even assured of this in her own mind, she did not rush to welcome her niece, but stood as if turned to stone, waiting for the opening of the gate.

Old Reuben, having seen the footman, went himself to admit the visitors, with his grandson and slave in attendance.

"It must be her little ladyship," he said, taking his young mistress's view of the case. "Lord Fareham would never dare to show his deceiving face here."

A shrill voice greeted him from the coach window before he reached the gate.

"You are the slowest old wretch I ever saw!" cried the voice. "Don't you know that when visitors of importance come to a house they expect to be let in? I vow a convent gate would be opened quicker."

"Indeed, your ladyship, when your legs are as old as mine----"

"Which I hope they never will be," muttered Henriette, as she descended with a languid slowness from the coach, assisted on either side by a footman; while George, who could not wait for her airs and graces, let himself out at the door on the off side just as Reuben succeeded in turning the key.

"So you are old Reuben!" he said, patting the butler on the shoulder with the gold hilt of his riding-whip. "And you were here, like a vegetable, all through the Civil Wars and the Commonwealth?"

"Yes, your lordship, from the raising of Hampden's regiment."

"Ah, you shall tell me all about it over a pipe and a bottle. You must be vastly good company. I am come to live here."

"To live here, your honour?"

"Yes; sister and I are to live here while my father represents his Majesty beyond seas. I hope you have good stabling and plenty of room. My ponies and Mistress Henriette's Arab horse will be here to-morrow. I doubt I shall have to build a place for my hawks; but I suppose Sir John will find me a cottage for my Dutch falconer."

"Lord, how the young master do talk!" exclaimed Reuben, with an admiring grin.

The boy was so rapid in his speech, had such vivacity and courage in his face, such a spring in every movement, as if he had quicksilver in his veins, Reuben thought; but it was only the quicksilver of youth, that Divine ichor which lasts for so brief a season.

"It made me feel twenty years younger only to hear him prattle," Reuben said afterwards.

Sir John and his daughter had come to meet the children by this time, and there were fond embracings, in the midst of which Henriette withdrew herself from her grandfather's arms, and retired a couple of paces, in order to drop him the Jennings curtsy, sinking almost to the ground, and then rising from billows of silk, like Venus from the sea, and handing him a letter, with a circular sweep of her arm, learnt in London from her Parisian dancing mistress, an apprentice of St. Andre's, not from the shabby little French cut-caper from Oxford.

"My father sends you this letter, sir."

"Is your father at Chilton?"

"No, sir. He was with us the day before yesterday, to bid us good-bye before he started upon his foreign embassy," replied Henriette, struggling with her tears, lest she should seem a child, and not the woman of fashion she aspired to be. "He left us early in the afternoon to ride back to London, and he takes barge this afternoon to Gravesend, to embark for Archangel, on his way to Moscow. I doubt you know he is to be his Majesty's Ambassador at Muscovy?"

"I know nothing but what you told me t'other day, Henriette," the Knight answered, as they went to the house, where George began to run about on an exploration of corridors, and then escaped to the stables, while Henriette stood in front of the great wood fire, and warmed her hands in a stately manner.

Angela had found no words of welcome for her niece yet. She only hugged and kissed her, and now occupied herself unfastening the child's hood and cloak. "How your hands shake, auntie. You must be colder than I am; though that leathern coach lets in the wind like a sieve. I suppose my people will know where to dispose themselves?" she added, resuming her grand air.

"Reuben will take care of them, dearest."

"Why, your voice shakes like your hands; and oh, how white you are. But you are glad to see us, I hope?"

"Gladder than I can say, Henriette."

"I am glad you don't call me Papillon. I have left off that ridiculous name, which I ought never to have permitted."

"I doubt, mistress, you who know so much know what is in this letter," said Sir John, staring at Fareham's superscription as if he had come suddenly upon an adder.

"Nay, sir, I only know that my father was shut in his library for a long time writing, and was as white as my aunt is now when he brought it to me. 'You and George, and your gouvernante and servants, are to go to the Manor Moat the day after to-morrow,' he said, 'and you are to give this letter into your grandfather's hand.' I have done my duty, and await your Honour's pleasure. Our gouvernante is not the Frenchwoman. Father dismissed her for neglecting my education, and walking out after dark with Daniel Lettsome. 'Tis only Priscilla, who is something between a servant and a friend, and who does everything I tell her."

"A pretty gouvernante!"

"Nay, sir, she is as plain as a pikestaff; that is one of her merits. Mademoiselle thought herself pretty, and angled for a rich husband. Please be so good as to read your letter, grandfather, for I believe it is about us."

Sir John broke the seal, and began to read the letter with a frowning brow, which lightened as he read. Angela stood with her niece clasped in her arms, and watched her father's countenance across the silky brown head that nestled against her bosom.

"SIR,--Were it not in the interests of others, who must needs hold a place in your affection second only to that they have in my heart, I should scarce presume to address you; but it is to the grandfather of my children I write, rather than to the gentleman whom I have so deeply offended. I look back, sir, and repent the violence of that unhappy night; but know no change in the melancholy passion that impelled me to crime. It would have been better for me had I been the worst rake-hell at Whitehall, than to have held myself aloof from the modish vices of my day, only to concentrate all my desires and affections there, where it was most sinful to place them.

"Enough, sir. Did I stand alone I should have found an easy solution of all difficulties, and you, and the lady my madness has so insulted, would have been rid for ever of the despicable wretch who now addresses you.

"I had to remember the dear innocents who bring you this letter, and it was of them I thought when I humbled myself to turn courtier in order to obtain the post of Ambassador to Muscovy--in which savage place I shall be so remote from all who ever knew me in this country, that I shall be as good as dead; and you would have as much compunction in withholding your love and protection from my boy and girl as if they were de facto orphans. I send them to you, sir, unheralded. I fling them into the bosom of your love. They are rich, and the allowance that will be paid you for them will cover, I apprehend, all outlays on their behalf, or can be increased at your pleasure. My lawyers, whom you know, will be at your service for all communications; and they will spare you the pain of correspondence with me.

"I leave the nurture, education, and happiness of these, my only son and daughter, solely in your care and authority. They have been reared in over-much luxury, and have been spoiled by injudicious indulgence. But their faults are trivial faults, and are all on the surface. They are truthful, and have warm and generous hearts. I shall deem it a further favour if you will allow their nurse, or nurse-gouvernante, Mrs. Priscilla Baker, to remain with them, as your servant, and subject to your authority. Their horses, ponies, hawks, and hounds, carriages, etc., must be accommodated, or not, at your pleasure. My girl is greatly taken up with the Arab horse I gave her on her last birthday, and I should be glad if your stable could shelter him. I subscribe myself, perhaps for the last time, sir,

"Your obedient servant, and a penitent sinner,

"FAREHAM."

When he had come to the end of the letter, reading slowly and thoughtfully, Sir John handed it to his daughter, in a dead silence.

She tried to read; but at sight of the beloved writing a rush of tears blinded her, and she gave the letter back to her father.

"I cannot read it, sir," she sobbed; "tell me only, are we to keep the children?"

"Yes. Henceforward they are our children; and it will be the business of our lives to make them happy."

"If you cry, tante, I shall think you are vexed that we have come to plague you," said Henriette, with a pretty, womanly air. "I am very sorry for his poor lordship, for he also cried when he kissed us; but he will have skating and sledging in Muscovy, and he will shoot bears; so he will be very happy."

CHAPTER XXVIII.
IN A DEAD CALM.

The great bales and chests, and leather trunks, on the filling whereof Sir John's household had bestowed a week's labour, were all unpacked and cleared out of the hall, to make room for a waggon load of packages from Chilton Abbey, which preliminary waggon was followed day after day by other conveyances laden with other possessions of the Honourable Henriette, or the Honourable George. The young lady's virginals, her guitar, her embroidery frames, her books, her "babies," which the maids had packed, although it was long since she had played with them; the young gentleman's guns and whips, tennis rackets, bows and arrows, and a mass of heterogeneous goods; there seemed no end to the two children's personal property, and it was well that the old house was sufficiently spacious to afford a wing for their occupation. They brought their gouvernante, and a valet and maid, the falconer, and three grooms, for whom lodgings had to be found out-of-doors. The valet and waiting-woman spent some days in distributing and arranging all that mass of belongings; but at the end of their labour the children's rooms looked more cheerful than their luxurious quarters at Chilton, and the children themselves were delighted with their new home.

"We are lodged ever so much better here than at the Abbey," George told his grandfather. "We were ever so far away from father and mother, and the house was under a curse, being stolen from the Church in King Henry's reign. Once, when I had a fever, an old grey monk came and sat at the foot of the bed, between the curtains, and wouldn't go away. He sat there always, till I began to get well again. Father said there was nothing there, and it was only the fever made me see him; but I know it was the ghost of one of the monks who were flung out to starve when the Abbey was seized by Cromwell's men. Not Oliver Cromwell, grandfather; but another bad man of the name, who had his head cut off afterwards; though I doubt he deserved the axe less than the Brewer did."

There was no more talk of Montpelier or exile. A new life began in the old house in the valley, with new pleasures, new motives, new duties--a life in which the children were paramount. These two eager young minds ruled at the Manor Moat. For them the fish-pond teemed with carp and tench, for them hawks flew, and hounds ran, and horses and ponies were moving from morning till twilight; for them Sir John grew young again, and hunted fox and hare, and rode with the hawks with all the pertinacity of youth, for whom there is no such word as enough. For them the happy grandfather lived in his boots from October to March, and the adoring aunt spent industrious hours in the fabrication of flies for trout, after the recipes in Mr. Walton's agreeable book. The whole establishment was ordered for their comfort and pleasure; but their education and improvement were also considered in everything. A Roman Catholic gentleman, from St. Omer, was engaged as George's tutor, and to teach Angela and Henriette Latin and Italian, studies in which the niece was stimulated to industry by her desire to surpass her aunt, an ambition which her volatile spirits never allowed her to realise. For all other learning and accomplishments Angela was her only teacher, and as the girl grew to woman-hood aunt and niece read and studied together, like sisters, rather than like pupil and mistress; and Angela taught Henriette to love those books which Fareham had given her, and so in a manner the intellect of the banished father influenced the growing mind of the child. Together, and of one opinion in all things, aunt and niece visited and ministered to the neighbouring poor, or entertained their genteel neighbours in a style at once friendly and elegant. No existence could have been calmer or happier, to one who was content to renounce all passionate hopes and desires, all the romantic aspirations of youth; and Angela had resigned herself to such renunciation when she rose from her sick-bed, after the tragedy at Chilton. Here was the calm of the Convent without its restrictions and limitations, the peace which is not of this world, and yet liberty to enjoy all that is fairest and noblest in this world; for had not Sir John pledged himself to take his daughter and niece and nephew for the grand tour through France and Italy, soon after George's seven-teenth birthday? Father Andrea, who was of Florentine birth, would go with them; and with such a cicisbeo, they would see and understand all the treasures of the past and the present, antique and modern art.

Lord Fareham was still in the north of Europe; but, after three years in Russia, had been transferred from Moscow to Copenhagen, where he was in high favour with the King of Denmark.

Denzil Warner had lately married a young lady of fortune, the only child and heiress of a Wiltshire gentleman, who had made a considerable figure in Parliament under the Protector, but was now retired from public affairs.

And all that remained to Angela of her story of impassioned love, sole evidence of the homage that had been offered to her beauty or her youth, was a letter, now long grown dim with tears, which Henriette had given to her on the first night the children spent under their grandfather's roof.

"I was to hand you this when no one was by," the girl said simply, and left her aunt standing mute and pale with a sealed letter in her hand.

*   *   *   *   *

"How shall I thank or praise you for the sacrifice your love made for one so unworthy--a sacrifice that cut me to the heart? Alas, my beloved, it would have been better for both of us hadst thou given me thyself rather than so empty a gift as thy good name. I hoped to tell you, lip to lip, in one last meeting, all my gratitude and all my hopeless love; but though I have watched and hung about your gardens and meadows day after day, you have been too jealously guarded, or have kept too close, and only with my pen can I bid you an eternal farewell.

"I go out of your life for ever, since I am leaving for a distant country with the fixed intention never to return to England. I bequeath you my children, as if I left you a rag of my own lacerated heart. "If you ever think of me, I pray you to consider the story of my life as that of an invincible passion, wicked and desperate if you will, but constant as life and death. You were, and are, and will be to my latest breath, my only love. "Perhaps you will think sometimes, as I shall think always, that we might have lived innocently and happily in New England, forgetting and forgotten by the rabble we left behind us, having shaken off the slough of an unhappy life, beginning the world again, under new names, in a new climate and country. It was a guilty dream to entertain, perhaps; but I shall dream it often enough in a strange land, among strange faces and strange manners--shall dream of you on my death-bed, and open dying eyes to see you standing by my bedside, looking down at me with that sweetly sorrowful look I remember best of all the varying expressions in the face I worship.--Farewell for ever.

"F."

While her son and daughter were growing up at the Manor Moat, Lady Fareham sparkled at the French Court, one of the most brilliant figures in that brilliant world, a frequent guest at the Louvre and Palais Royal, and the brand-new palace of Versailles, where the largest Court that had ever collected round a throne was accommodated in a building of Palladian richness in ornament and detail, a Palace whose offices were spacious enough for two thousand servants. No foreigner at the great King's court was more admired than the lovely Lady Fareham, whose separation from her black-browed husband occasioned no scandal in a society where the husbands of beautiful women were for the most part gentlemen who pursued their own vulgar amours abroad, and allowed a wide liberty to the Venus at home; nor was Henri de Malfort's constant attendance upon her ladyship a cause of evil-speaking, since there was scarce a woman of consequence who had not her *cavaliere servante*. Madame de Sevigne, in one of those budgets of Parisian scandal with which she cheered a kinsman's banishment, assured Bussy de Rabutin that Lady Fareham had paid her friend's debts more than once since her return to France; but constancy such as De Malfort's could hardly be expected were not the golden fetters of love riveted by the harder metal of self-interest. Their alliance was looked on with favour by all that brilliant world, and even tolerated by that severe moralist, the Due du Montausier, who had been lately rewarded for his wife's civility to Mademoiselle de la Valliere, now Duchess and reigning favourite, by being made guardian of the infant Dauphin.

Every one approved, every one admired; and Hyacinth's life in the land she loved was like a long summer day. But darkness came upon that day as suddenly as the night of the tropics. She rose one morning, light-hearted and happy, to pursue the careless round of pleasure. She lay down in a darkened chamber, never again to mix in that splendid crowd.

Betwixt noon and twilight Henri de Malfort had fallen in a combat of eight, a combat so savage as to recall that fatal fight of five against five during the Fronde, in which Nemours had fallen, shot through the heart by Beaufort.

The light words of a fool in a tavern, backed by three other fools, had led to this encounter, in which De Malfort had been the challenger. He and one of his friends died on the ground, while three on the other side were mortally wounded. It would henceforth be fully understood that Lady Fareham's name was not for ribald jesters; but the man Lady Fareham loved was dead, and her life of pleasure had ended with a pistol-ball from an unerring hand. To her it seemed the hand of Fate. She scarcely thought of the man who had killed him.

As her life had been brilliant and conspicuous, so her retirement from the world was not without *eclat*. Royalty witnessed the solemn office of the Church which transformed Hyacinth, Lady Fareham, into Mere Agnes, of the Seven Wounds; while, seated in the royal tribune, a King's mistress, beautiful and adored, thought of a day when she, too, might bring to yonder altar the sacrifice of a broken spirit and a life that had outlived earthly happiness.

THE END.

The Codes Of Hammurabi And Moses
W. W. Davies

QTY

The discovery of the Hammurabi Code is one of the greatest achievements of archaeology, and is of paramount interest, not only to the student of the Bible, but also to all those interested in ancient history...

Religion   **ISBN:** *1-59462-338-4*

Pages:132
MSRP $12.95

The Theory of Moral Sentiments
Adam Smith

QTY

This work from 1749. contains original theories of conscience amd moral judgment and it is the foundation for systemof morals.

Philosophy   **ISBN:** *1-59462-777-0*

Pages:536
MSRP $19.95

Jessica's First Prayer
Hesba Stretton

QTY

In a screened and secluded corner of one of the many railway-bridges which span the streets of London there could be seen a few years ago, from five o'clock every morning until half past eight, a tidily set-out coffee-stall, consisting of a trestle and board, upon which stood two large tin cans, with a small fire of charcoal burning under each so as to keep the coffee boiling during the early hours of the morning when the work-people were thronging into the city on their way to their daily toil...

Childrens   **ISBN:** *1-59462-373-2*

Pages:84
MSRP $9.95

My Life and Work
Henry Ford

QTY

Henry Ford revolutionized the world with his implementation of mass production for the Model T automobile. Gain valuable business insight into his life and work with his own auto-biography... "We have only started on our development of our country we have not as yet, with all our talk of wonderful progress, done more than scratch the surface. The progress has been wonderful enough but..."

Biographies/   **ISBN:** *1-59462-198-5*

Pages:300
MSRP $21.95

The Art of Cross-Examination
Francis Wellman

QTY

I presume it is the experience of every author, after his first book is published upon an important subject, to be almost overwhelmed with a wealth of ideas and illustrations which could readily have been included in his book, and which to his own mind, at least, seem to make a second edition inevitable. Such certainly was the case with me; and when the first edition had reached its sixth impression in five months, I rejoiced to learn that it seemed to my publishers that the book had met with a sufficiently favorable reception to justify a second and considerably enlarged edition. ..

Reference   ISBN: *1-59462-647-2*

Pages:412

MSRP $19.95

On the Duty of Civil Disobedience
Henry David Thoreau

QTY

Thoreau wrote his famous essay, On the Duty of Civil Disobedience, as a protest against an unjust but popular war and the immoral but popular institution of slave-owning. He did more than write—he declined to pay his taxes, and was hauled off to gaol in consequence. Who can say how much this refusal of his hastened the end of the war and of slavery ?

Law   ISBN: *1-59462-747-9*

Pages:48

MSRP $7.45

Dream Psychology Psychoanalysis for Beginners
Sigmund Freud

QTY

Sigmund Freud, born Sigismund Schlomo Freud (May 6, 1856 - September 23, 1939), was a Jewish-Austrian neurologist and psychiatrist who co-founded the psychoanalytic school of psychology. Freud is best known for his theories of the unconscious mind, especially involving the mechanism of repression; his redefinition of sexual desire as mobile and directed towards a wide variety of objects; and his therapeutic techniques, especially his understanding of transference in the therapeutic relationship and the presumed value of dreams as sources of insight into unconscious desires.

Psychology   ISBN: *1-59462-905-6*

Pages:196

MSRP $15.45

The Miracle of Right Thought
Orison Swett Marden

QTY

Believe with all of your heart that you will do what you were made to do. When the mind has once formed the habit of holding cheerful, happy, prosperous pictures, it will not be easy to form the opposite habit. It does not matter how improbable or how far away this realization may see, or how dark the prospects may be, if we visualize them as best we can, as vividly as possible, hold tenaciously to them and vigorously struggle to attain them, they will gradually become actualized, realized in the life. But a desire, a longing without endeavor, a yearning abandoned or held indifferently will vanish without realization.

Self Help   ISBN: *1-59462-644-8*

Pages:360

MSRP $25.45

The Rosicrucian Cosmo-Conception Mystic Christianity *by Max Heindel*   ISBN: *1-59462-188-8*   **$38.95**
The Rosicrucian Cosmo-conception is not dogmatic, neither does it appeal to any other authority than the reason of the student. It is: not controversial, but is: sent forth in the, hope that it may help to clear...   New Age/Religion Pages 646

Abandonment To Divine Providence *by Jean-Pierre de Caussade*   ISBN: *1-59462-228-0*   **$25.95**
"The Rev. Jean Pierre de Caussade was one of the most remarkable spiritual writers of the Society of Jesus in France in the 18th Century. His death took place at Toulouse in 1751. His works have gone through many editions and have been republished...   Inspirational/Religion Pages 400

Mental Chemistry *by Charles Haanel*   ISBN: *1-59462-192-6*   **$23.95**
Mental Chemistry allows the change of material conditions by combining and appropriately utilizing the power of the mind. Much like applied chemistry creates something new and unique out of careful combinations of chemicals the mastery of mental chemistry...   New Age Pages 354

The Letters of Robert Browning and Elizabeth Barret Barrett 1845-1846 vol II   ISBN: *1-59462-193-4*   **$35.95**
by Robert Browning and Elizabeth Barrett   Biographies Pages 596

Gleanings In Genesis (volume I) *by Arthur W. Pink*   ISBN: *1-59462-130-6*   **$27.45**
Appropriately has Genesis been termed "the seed plot of the Bible" for in it we have, in germ form, almost all of the great doctrines which are afterwards fully developed in the books of Scripture which follow...   Religion/Inspirational Pages 420

The Master Key *by L. W. de Laurence*   ISBN: *1-59462-001-6*   **$30.95**
In no branch of human knowledge has there been a more lively increase of the spirit of research during the past few years than in the study of Psychology, Concentration and Mental Discipline. The requests for authentic lessons in Thought Control, Mental Discipline and...   New Age/Business Pages 422

The Lesser Key Of Solomon Goetia *by L. W. de Laurence*   ISBN: *1-59462-092-X*   **$9.95**
This translation of the first book of the "Lernegton" which is now for the first time made accessible to students of Talismanic Magic was done, after careful collation and edition, from numerous Ancient Manuscripts in Hebrew, Latin, and French...   New Age/Occult Pages 92

Rubaiyat Of Omar Khayyam *by Edward Fitzgerald*   ISBN:*1-59462-332-5*   **$13.95**
Edward Fitzgerald, whom the world has already learned, in spite of his own efforts to remain within the shadow of anonymity, to look upon as one of the rarest poets of the century, was born at Bredfield, in Suffolk, on the 31st of March, 1809. He was the third son of John Purcell...   Music Pages 172

Ancient Law *by Henry Maine*   ISBN: *1-59462-128-4*   **$29.95**
The chief object of the following pages is to indicate some of the earliest ideas of mankind, as they are reflected in Ancient Law, and to point out the relation of those ideas to modern thought.   Religiom/History Pages 452

Far-Away Stories *by William J. Locke*   ISBN: *1-59462-129-2*   **$19.45**
"Good wine needs no bush, but a collection of mixed vintages does. And this book is just such a collection. Some of the stories I do not want to remain buried for ever in the museum files of dead magazine-numbers an author's not unpardonable vanity..."   Fiction Pages 272

Life of David Crockett *by David Crockett*   ISBN: *1-59462-250-7*   **$27.45**
"Colonel David Crockett was one of the most remarkable men of the times in which he lived. Born in humble life, but gifted with a strong will, an indomitable courage, and unremitting perseverance...   Biographies/New Age Pages 424

Lip-Reading *by Edward Nitchie*   ISBN: *1-59462-206-X*   **$25.95**
Edward B. Nitchie, founder of the New York School for the Hard of Hearing, now the Nitchie School of Lip-Reading, Inc, wrote "LIP-READING Principles and Practice". The development and perfecting of this meritorious work on lip-reading was an undertaking...   How-to Pages 400

A Handbook of Suggestive Therapeutics, Applied Hypnotism, Psychic Science   ISBN: *1-59462-214-0*   **$24.95**
by Henry Munro   Health/New Age/Health/Self-help Pages 376

A Doll's House: and Two Other Plays *by Henrik Ibsen*   ISBN: *1-59462-112-8*   **$19.95**
Henrik Ibsen created this classic when in revolutionary 1848 Rome. Introducing some striking concepts in playwriting for the realist genre, this play has been studied the world over.   Fiction/Classics/Plays 308

The Light of Asia *by sir Edwin Arnold*   ISBN: *1-59462-204-3*   **$13.95**
In this poetic masterpiece, Edwin Arnold describes the life and teachings of Buddha. The man who was to become known as Buddha to the world was born as Prince Gautama of India but he rejected the worldly riches and abandoned the reigns of power when...   Religion/History/Biographies Pages 170

The Complete Works of Guy de Maupassant *by Guy de Maupassant*   ISBN: *1-59462-157-8*   **$16.95**
"For days and days, nights and nights, I had dreamed of that first kiss which was to consecrate our engagement, and I knew not on what spot I should put my lips..."   Fiction/Classics Pages 240

The Art of Cross-Examination *by Francis L. Wellman*   ISBN: *1-59462-309-0*   **$26.95**
Written by a renowned trial lawyer, Wellman imparts his experience and uses case studies to explain how to use psychology to extract desired information through questioning.   How-to/Science/Reference Pages 408

Answered or Unanswered? *by Louisa Vaughan*   ISBN: *1-59462-248-5*   **$10.95**
Miracles of Faith in China   Religion Pages 112

The Edinburgh Lectures on Mental Science (1909) *by Thomas*   ISBN: *1-59462-008-3*   **$11.95**
This book contains the substance of a course of lectures recently given by the writer in the Queen Street Hail, Edinburgh. Its purpose is to indicate the Natural Principles governing the relation between Mental Action and Material Conditions...   New Age/Psychology Pages 148

Ayesha *by H. Rider Haggard*   ISBN: *1-59462-301-5*   **$24.95**
Verily and indeed it is the unexpected that happens! Probably if there was one person upon the earth from whom the Editor of this, and of a certain previous history, did not expect to hear again...   Classics Pages 380

Ayala's Angel *by Anthony Trollope*   ISBN: *1-59462-352-X*   **$29.95**
The two girls were both pretty, but Lucy who was twenty-one who supposed to be simple and comparatively unattractive, whereas Ayala was credited, as her Bombwhat romantic name might show, with poetic charm and a taste for romance Ayala when her father died was nineteen...   Fiction Pages 484

The American Commonwealth *by James Bryce*   ISBN: *1-59462-286-8*   **$34.95**
An interpretation of American democratic political theory. It examines political mechanics and society from the perspective of Scotsman James Bryce   Politics Pages 572

Stories of the Pilgrims *by Margaret P. Pumphrey*   ISBN: *1-59462-116-0*   **$17.95**
This book explores pilgrims religious oppression in England as well as their escape to Holland and eventual crossing to America on the Mayflower, and their early days in New England...   History Pages 268

QTY

The Fasting Cure *by Sinclair Upton*   ISBN: *1-59462-222-1* **$13.95**
In the Cosmopolitan Magazine for May, 1910, and in the Contemporary Review (London) for April, 1910, I published an article dealing with my experi-
ences in fasting. I have written a great many magazine articles, but never one which attracted so much attention... New Age/Self Help/Health Pages 164

Hebrew Astrology *by Sepharial*   ISBN: *1-59462-308-2* **$13.45**
In these days of advanced thinking it is a matter of common observation that we have left many of the old landmarks behind and that we are now pressing
forward to greater heights and to a wider horizon than that which represented the mind-content of our progenitors... Astrology Pages 144

Thought Vibration or The Law of Attraction in the Thought World   ISBN: *1-59462-127-6* **$12.95**

by William Walker Atkinson   *Psychology/Religion Pages 144*

Optimism *by Helen Keller*   ISBN: *1-59462-108-X* **$15.95**
Helen Keller was blind, deaf, and mute since 19 months old, yet famously learned how to overcome these handicaps, communicate with the world, and
spread her lectures promoting optimism. An inspiring read for everyone... Biographies/Inspirational Pages 84

Sara Crewe *by Frances Burnett*   ISBN: *1-59462-360-0* **$9.45**
In the first place, Miss Minchin lived in London. Her home was a large, dull, tall one, in a large, dull square, where all the houses were alike, and all the
sparrows were alike, and where all the door-knockers made the same heavy sound... Childrens/Classic Pages 88

The Autobiography of Benjamin Franklin *by Benjamin Franklin*   ISBN: *1-59462-135-7* **$24.95**
The Autobiography of Benjamin Franklin has probably been more extensively read than any other American historical work, and no other book of its kind
has had such ups and downs of fortune. Franklin lived for many years in England, where he was agent... Biographies/History Pages 332

Name	
Email	
Telephone	
Address	
City, State ZIP	

☐ **Credit Card**   ☐ **Check / Money Order**

Credit Card Number	
Expiration Date	
Signature	

Please Mail to: Book Jungle
                      PO Box 2226
                      Champaign, IL 61825
or Fax to: 630-214-0564

ORDERING INFORMATION

web: *www.bookjungle.com*
email: *sales@bookjungle.com*
fax: *630-214-0564*
mail: *Book Jungle PO Box 2226 Champaign, IL 61825*
or PayPal *to sales@bookjungle.com*

Please contact us for bulk discounts

DIRECT-ORDER TERMS

**20% Discount if You Order
Two or More Books**
Free Domestic Shipping!
Accepted: Master Card, Visa,
Discover, American Express